Secrets
of the
TUDOR COURT
→ *By Royal Decree* ←

KATE
EMERSON

GALLERY BOOKS
New York London Toronto Sydney

G

Gallery Books
A Division of Simon & Schuster, Inc.
1230 Avenue of the Americas
New York, NY 10020

First Gallery Books trade paperback edition December 2010

GALLERY BOOKS and colophon are trademarks of Simon & Schuster, Inc.

For information about special discounts for bulk purchases, please contact Simon & Schuster Special Sales at 1-866-506-1949 or business@simonandschuster.com.

The Simon & Schuster Speakers Bureau can bring authors to your live event. For more information or to book an event contact the Simon & Schuster Speakers Bureau at 1-866-248-3049 or visit our website at www.simonspeakers.com.

Manufactured in the United States of America

1   3   5   7   9   10   8   6   4   2

Library of Congress Cataloging-in-Publication Data

Emerson, Kate
Secrets of the Tudor court. By royal decree / Kate Emerson.—1st Gallery Books trade pbk ed.
p. cm.
1. Northampton, Elizabeth Parr, Marchioness of, 1526–1565—Fiction.
2. Northampton, William Parr, Marquis of, 1513–1571—Fiction. 3. Ladies-in-waiting—Great Britain—Fiction. 4. Great Britain—Court and courtiers—Fiction.
5. Henry VIII, King of England, 1491–1547—Fiction. 6. Great Britain—History—Henry VIII, 1509–1547—Fiction. I. Title. II. Title: By royal decree.
PS3555.M414S427   2010
813'.54—dc22
2010019895

ISBN 978-1-4391-7781-5
ISBN 978-1-4391-7783-9 (ebook)

Lavish praise for Kate Emerson and
the *Secrets of the Tudor Court* series

✢ Between Two Queens ✢

"Emerson skillfully crafts a strong heroine who maintains careful command
of her sexuality and independence. Nan's behavior is as brave as it is scandalous for the time, and Emerson makes readers appreciate the consequences of
Nan's choices."

—*Publishers Weekly*

"Emerson's sharp eye for court nuances, intrigues, and passions thrusts
readers straight into Nan's life, and the swift pace will sweep you along."

—*Romantic Times*

✢ The Pleasure Palace ✢

"Emerson creates a riveting historical novel of the perils of the Tudor court,
vividly _____ their
perso _____

_____klist

"Jane _____ layer
in th _____ vants
with _____ that
sepa _____

_____ekly

"No _____ dor
cou _____ fully
rese _____ love,
lust _____

_____ness

"Ri _____ ovel
in w _____

_____imes

To Elaine Emerson Smith

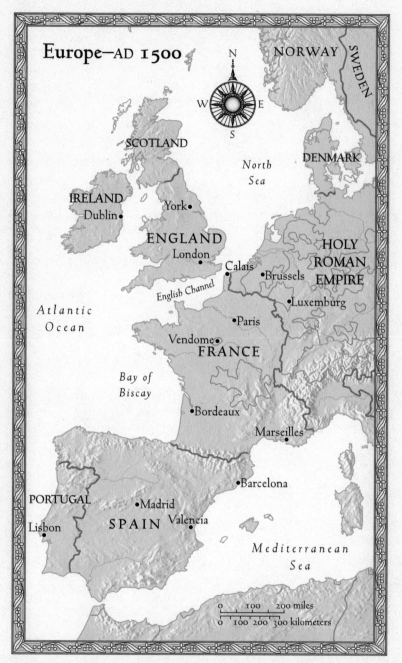

Europe—AD 1500

NORWAY

SWEDEN

SCOTLAND

DENMARK

North
Sea

IRELAND

York

Dublin

ENGLAND

London

Calais

Brussels

HOLY
ROMAN
EMPIRE

English Channel

Luxemburg

Atlantic
Ocean

Paris

Vendome

FRANCE

Bay of
Biscay

Bordeaux

Marseilles

Barcelona

PORTUGAL

Madrid

SPAIN

Valencia

Lisbon

Mediterranean
Sea

0   100   200 miles
0   100   200   300 kilometers

Map by Paul J. Pugliese.

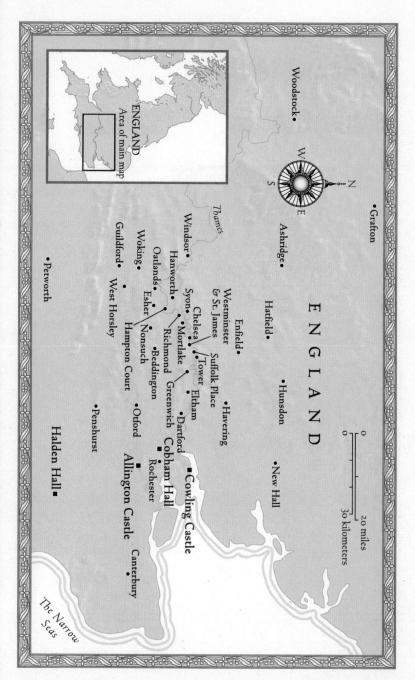

Map by Paul J. Pugliese.

FAMILY CONNECTIONS OF ELIZABETH BROOKE

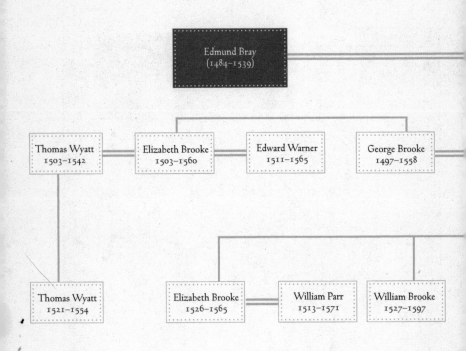

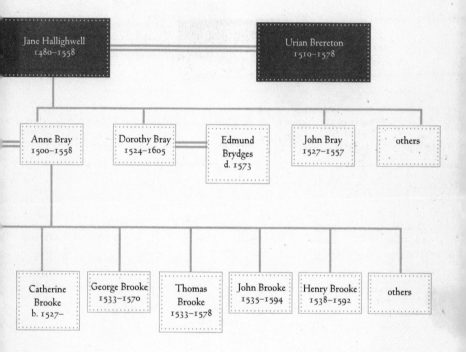

Jane Hallighwell
1480–1558

Urian Brereton
1510–1578

Anne Bray
1500–1558

Dorothy Bray
1524–1605

Edmund
Brydges
d. 1573

John Bray
1527–1557

others

Catherine
Brooke
b. 1527–

George Brooke
1533–1570

Thomas
Brooke
1533–1578

John Brooke
1535–1594

Henry Brooke
1538–1592

others

DESCENDANTS OF HENRY VII

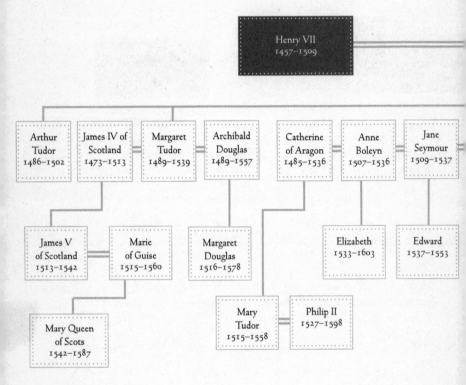

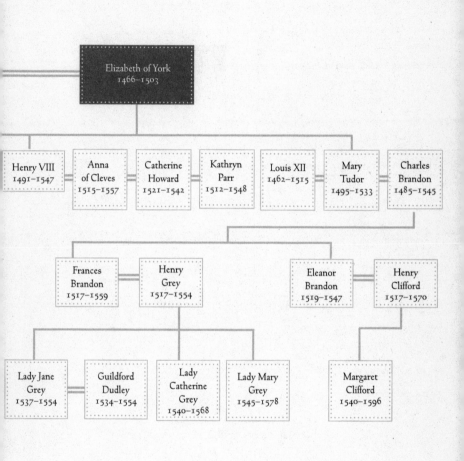

SECRETS OF THE TUDOR COURT
→ *By Royal Decree* ←

1

On the twenty-ninth day of January in 1542, twenty-six eligible young women sat at table in Whitehall Palace with King Henry. An additional thirty-five occupied a second table close by. We were arranged by precedence, with the highest-born maidens closest to the king. As the daughter of a baron, I was assigned a seat at the first table, but there were others of nobler birth between me and His Grace.

From that little distance, King Henry the Eighth of England was a glorious sight. At first I could scarcely take my eyes off him. He glittered in the candlelight. Not only did he wear a great many jewels on his person, everything from a diamond cross to a great emerald with a pearl pendant, but the cloth itself was embroidered with gold thread.

I pinched myself to make certain I was not dreaming. Everything at court seemed to sparkle, from the rich tapestries to the painted ceilings to the glass in the windows. I had arrived from Kent the previous day and was still in awe of my surroundings. I had lived in comfort for all of my fifteen and a half years, but this opulent level of luxury stunned me.

Wondrous dishes appeared before me, one after another. When I tasted the next offering, I closed my eyes in delight. The sweet taste of sugar, combined with ginger and the tart flavor of an unknown fruit, exploded on my tongue. I sighed with pleasure and took another spoonful of this marvelous concoction.

"Have you tried the syllabub?" I asked the woman seated beside me. "It is most delicious."

She did not appear to have eaten anything. Although she'd taken a piece of bread and a bit of meat from the platters the king's gentlemen had brought around, she'd done no more than toy with the food. At my urging, she spooned a small portion of the syllabub into her mouth.

"Indeed," she said. "Most delicious." But instead of eating more, she fixed her bright, dark blue eyes on me, examining me so intently that I began to feel uncomfortable under her steady stare.

I reminded myself that I looked my best. My copper-colored gown was richly embroidered. My pale yellow hair had been washed only that morning. Barely two inches of it showed at the front of my new French hood, but it was a very pretty color and it would have reached nearly to my waist if it had not been caught up in a net at the back.

"Mistress Brooke?" my neighbor asked. "Lord Cobham's daughter?"

I gave her my most brilliant smile. "Yes, I am Bess Brooke."

Thawing in the face of my friendliness, she introduced herself as Nan Bassett. She was only a few years older than I was. The tiny bit of hair that showed at the front of her headdress was light brown and she had the pink-and-white complexion I'd heard was favored at court. I had such a complexion myself, and eyes of the same color, too, although mine were a less intense shade of blue.

We chatted amiably for the rest of the meal. I learned that she had been a maid of honor to each of King Henry's last three wives. She'd been with Queen Jane Seymour when Queen Jane gave birth to the king's heir, Prince Edward, who was now five years old. She'd been with Queen Anna of Cleves, until the king annulled that marriage in order to wed another of Queen Anna's maids of honor, Catherine Howard. And she had served Queen Catherine Howard, too, until Catherine betrayed her husband with another man and was arrested for treason.

Queen no more, Catherine Howard was locked in the Tower of London awaiting execution. The king needed a new bride to replace her. If the rumors I'd heard were true, that was why there were no gentlemen among our fellow guests. His Grace had gathered together prospective wives from among the nobility and gentry of England.

I had been summoned to court by royal decree. My parents had accompanied me to Whitehall Palace and impressed upon me that this was a great opportunity. They did not expect the king to choose me, but whatever lady did become the next queen would need maids of honor and waiting gentlewomen.

Conversation stopped when King Henry stood. Everyone else rose from their seats as well and remained on their feet while His Grace moved slowly from guest to guest, using a sturdy wooden staff to steady his steps. As he made his ponderous way down the length of the table, shuffling along through the rushes that covered the tiled floor, I saw to my dismay that, beneath the glitter, he was not just a large man. He was fat. He wore a corset in a futile attempt to contain his enormous bulk. I could hear it creak with every step he took.

The king spoke to each woman at table. When he spent a little longer with one particular pretty, dark-haired girl, a buzz of speculation stirred the air. Whispers and covert nudges and winks followed in the king's wake. As His Grace approached, I grew more and more anxious, although I was not sure why. By the time he stopped in front of Mistress Bassett, I was vibrating with tension.

She sank into a deep curtsy, her eyes fixed on the floor.

"My dear Nan." The king took her hand and drew her upright. "You appear to thrive in my daughter's household."

"The Lady Mary is a most kind mistress, Your Grace," Nan Bassett said.

He chuckled and shifted his meaty, bejeweled fingers from her hand to her shoulder. "She is fortunate to have you, sweeting."

Nan's smile never wavered, although his grip must have pinched. I admired her self-control.

I had no warning before His Grace shifted his attention to me. "And who is this beautiful blossom?" he demanded in a loud, deep voice that caught the interest of everyone else in the great hall.

I hastily made my obeisance. As I sank lower, I caught a whiff of the stench wafting up from the king's game leg. In spite of layers of gaudy clothing, I could see the bulge of bandages wrapped thickly around His Grace's left thigh.

King Henry stuck a sausage-shaped index finger under my chin and lifted my face until I was forced to meet his gimlet-eyed stare. It was fortunate that he did not expect me to do much more than give him my name. That I'd attracted the predatory interest of the most powerful man in England very nearly struck me dumb.

"I am Lord Cobham's daughter, Your Grace," I managed in a shaky whisper. "I am Elizabeth Brooke," I added, lest he confuse me with one of my sisters.

I lowered my eyes, hoping he'd think me demure. The truth of the matter was that I was appalled by the ugliness of Henry Tudor's bloated face and body. Any awe I'd felt earlier had been displaced by a nearly paralyzing sense of dread.

"Hah!" said the king, recognizing Father's title. "Imagine George Brooke producing a pretty little thing like you!"

Next to King Henry, who was the tallest man in England, any woman would be dwarfed. As for Father, I'd always thought him exceptionally well favored. But I had the good sense not to contradict His Grace.

"What do you think of our court?" King Henry asked.

"It is very grand, Sire. I am amazed by all I have seen."

The king took that as a compliment to himself and beamed down at me. I repressed a shudder. We had a copy of one of His Grace's portraits at Cowling Castle. Once upon a time, he'd been a good-looking man. But now, at fifty, the bold warrior prince of yesteryear had disappeared into a potentate of mammoth proportions and chronic ill health.

Still, I knew my duty. I must pretend that the king was the most fascinating person I had ever met. That way lay advancement at court for my father and brothers as well as myself. I arranged my lips into a tremulous smile and tried to focus on His Grace's pretty compliments. He praised my graceful carriage, my pink cheeks, and the color of my hair. All the while, his gaze kept straying from my face to my bosom. I have no idea what I said in reply to his effusive praise, but when he chucked me under the chin and moved on, I felt weak with relief.

King Henry stopped to speak a few brief words to the woman who was seated on the other side of me, my kinswoman Dorothy Bray, then abandoned her for a redhead with a noble nose and a nervous smile. Dorothy, her dark eyes alive with dislike, glared at me. "Brazen flirt," she whispered.

I was not certain if she meant me or the redhead.

Although she was only two years my senior, Dorothy was my aunt, my mother's much younger sister. Like Nan Bassett, Dorothy had been a maid of honor to Queen Catherine Howard. In common with most young women who held that post, she was attractive. She looked very fine dressed in dark blue. Her best feature was a turned-up nose, but her lips were too thin for true beauty and just now they were pursed in a way that made her almost ugly.

I was sorry that the king had not spent more time with Dorothy, since she was clearly envious of the attention he'd paid to me, but there was nothing I could do to remedy the situation. That being so, I ignored her and turned back to Nan Bassett. Nan was as friendly as before, but now she seemed distracted. I wondered if she, too, felt alarm at having caught the king's interest.

Until the moment the king had called me a "beautiful blossom," I had never regretted being pretty. I had taken it for granted that I was attractive, accepted without demur the compliments from the scattering of courtiers who'd visited my father at Cowling Castle, the Cobham family seat. Now, for the first time, I realized that it could be dangerous to be pretty.

What if His Grace chose me to be his next queen?

It was a terrifying thought, but so absurd that I was soon able to dismiss it. After all, the king had paid far more attention to Nan and to that dark-haired young woman, too.

When everyone adjourned to the king's great watching chamber, where an assortment of sweets was served, we were free to move about as we sampled the offerings—pastries, comfits, suckets, marchpane, Florentines, candied fruits, and nuts dipped in sugar. Musicians played softly in the background, as they had during the meal, but the sound was nearly drowned out by talk and laughter.

I turned to ask Nan Bassett another question and discovered that she was no longer by my side. She'd reached the far side of the chamber before I located her. I watched her look all around, as if she wanted to be sure she was unobserved, and then slip past the yeoman of the guard and out of the room.

Considering, I bit into a piece of marchpane, a confection of blanched almonds and sugar. I found the sweetness cloying. The scent of cinnamon rose from another proffered treat, teasing me into inhaling deeply. I regretted giving in to the impulse. Along with a mixture of exotic aromas and the more mundane smell of melting candle wax, I once again caught a whiff of the horrible odor that emanated from the king's ulcerous leg. Without my noticing his approach, he'd moved to within a foot of the place where I stood.

All at once the hundreds of tapers illuminating the chamber seemed far too bright. They revealed not only the ostentatious display, but also the less appealing underpinnings of the court. Beneath the jewels and expensive fabrics, the colors and the perfumes, there was rot.

His Grace stood with his back to me, but if I stayed where I was he could turn around and see me at any moment. To escape his notice, I followed Nan Bassett's example. Palms sweating, I retreated, backing slowly away until other ladies filled the space between us. Then I turned and walked faster, toward the great doors that led to the rest of Whitehall Palace.

My steps slowed when I was faced with a yeoman of the guard clad in brilliant scarlet livery and holding a halberd. There was one problem with my escape plan. Whitehall was a maze of rooms and corridors so vast that I did not think I could find my way back to my parents' lodgings on my own. With Nan Bassett gone, I knew only one other person at the banquet—Dorothy Bray. She was family, I told myself. If I asked for her help, she'd be obliged to give it.

As I searched for my young aunt, the musicians struck up a lively tune and the dancing began. Ladies partnered each other for the king's entertainment, but Dorothy was not among them. The chamber was crowded, making it difficult to find anyone, and I was beginning to despair of ever making my escape when I passed a shadowy alcove. A bit of dark blue brocade protruded from it, the same color and fabric as Dorothy's gown. Without stopping to think that she might not be alone, I stepped closer.

A man was kissing Dorothy with enthusiastic abandon. By his dress—a green velvet doublet with slashed and puffed sleeves and a jewel the size of a fist pinned to his bonnet—he was a member of the king's household. One hand rested on Dorothy's waist. The other was hidden from sight in the vicinity of her breast.

At the sound of my startled gasp, they sprang apart, exposing a good deal of Dorothy's bosom. Abashed, I started to back away.

"Stay," the man ordered in a low-pitched growl, and stepped out of the shadows.

I obeyed. Then I simply stared at him.

He was one of the most toothsome gentlemen I had ever seen. Tall and well built, his superb physical condition suggested that he participated in tournaments. I had never attended one, but I had heard that such events were a fixture of court life. Gentlemen vied with each other to show off their prowess with lance and sword. A man who looked this athletic was certain to be a champion jouster. His face, too, was perfection, with regular features, close-cropped auburn hair, and a neatly trimmed beard and mustache.

His eyes were light brown and full of annoyance as his gaze swept over me, from the top of my French hood to the toes of my new embroidered slippers and back up again. By the time they met mine for the second time, approval had replaced irritation.

Sheltered by her companion's much larger body, Dorothy put her bodice to rights. Still tucking loose strands of dark brown hair into place beneath her headdress, she shoved him aside. Temper contorted her features into an ugly mask. "Begone, Bess!" she hissed. "Have you nothing better to do than spy on me?"

"I did not invade your privacy out of malice. I only wish to retire to my lodgings before His Grace notices me again and I do not know the way."

The man chuckled. His mouth crinkled at the corners when he smiled at me, making him even more attractive. He doffed his bejeweled bonnet and bowed. "Will Parr at your service, mistress."

Dorothy slammed the back of her hand into his velvet-clad chest the moment he straightened, preventing him from stepping closer to me. It was no gentle love tap, and if the look she turned my way could have set a fire, I'd have burst into flames on the spot. "That is Baron Parr of Kendal to you, niece."

I was unimpressed by his title. My father was a baron, too, and so was my uncle, Dorothy's younger brother. "Lord Parr," I said, bobbing a brief curtsy in acknowledgment of his courtesy bow, as if we were about to be partners in a dance.

Our eyes met for the third time. I recognized a spark of male interest in his gaze, along with a twinkle of wry amusement. Without warning, butterflies took wing in my stomach. It was the most peculiar sensation, and one I had never experienced before. For a moment my mind went blank. I continued to stare at him, transfixed, my heart racing much too fast.

"If you truly wish to return to your mother," Dorothy said with some asperity, "then do so. No one here will stop you."

Her cold voice and harsh words broke the spell. I forced myself to look away from Lord Parr. Although I could not help but be pleased that such a handsome man found me attractive, I knew I should be annoyed with him on Dorothy's behalf. "How am I to find my way there on my own?" I asked in a small, plaintive voice.

Dorothy's fingers curled, as if she would like to claw me, but Lord Parr at once offered me his arm. "Allow me to escort you, Mistress Brooke. Brigands haunt the palace at night, you know, men who might be tempted to pluck a pretty flower like you if they found her alone in a dark passageway."

I looked up at him and smiled. He was just a head taller than I.

"We will *both* accompany you." Dorothy clamped a possessive hand on Lord Parr's other arm with enough force to make him wince. We left the king's great watching chamber with Lord Parr between us and walked the first little way in silence.

Dorothy's anger disturbed me. She'd resented the few minutes His Grace had spent talking to me. And now she wanted to keep Lord Parr all to herself. But I was not her rival. And even if I was, I would be gone from court in another day or two.

My steps faltered as comprehension dawned. Dorothy would not be staying much longer either. There was no place at court for maids of honor or ladies of the privy chamber or even chamberers when the king lacked a queen. Dorothy would have to return to her mother—my grandmother Jane at Eaton Bray in Bedfordshire—until the king remarried. What I had interrupted must have been her farewell to her lover.

I glanced her way. Poor Dorothy. It might be many months before she saw Lord Parr again, and I had deprived her of an opportunity, rare at court, for a few moments of privacy.

Worse, although I had not intended it, I had caught Will Parr's interest. I rushed into speech, uncomfortable with my memory of the profound effect he'd had on me. "Do you think the king has someone in mind to marry?"

"He paid particular attention to you." Dorothy's voice dripped venom. She walked a little faster along the torch-lit corridor, forcing us to match her pace.

A wicked thought came into my head. If the king made me his queen and Dorothy were *my* maid of honor, she'd be obliged to obey my slightest whim. I felt my lips twitch, but I sobered quickly when I remembered that in order to be queen, I'd first have to marry old King Henry. Nothing could make that sacrifice worthwhile!

"I wager Mistress Bassett has the lead," Lord Parr said in a conversational tone, ignoring Dorothy's simmering temper.

"Do you think so? Nan has caught His Grace's eye in the past and nothing came of it." Dorothy had reined in her emotions with the skill of a trained courtier.

They bandied about a few more names, but none that I recognized. I practiced prudence and held my tongue as we made our way through the maze of corridors and finally stopped before a door identical to dozens of others we'd passed.

"We have arrived," Dorothy announced with an unmistakable note of relief in her voice. "Here are your lodgings, Bess. We'll leave you to—"

The door abruptly opened to reveal my father, a big, barrel-chested man with a square face set off by a short, forked beard. His eyebrows lifted when he recognized Dorothy and Lord Parr. "Come in," he said. "Have a cup of wine." He fixed Dorothy with a stern look when she tried to excuse herself. "Your sister has been expecting a visit from you ever since we arrived at court."

Father, Mother, and I had been assigned a double lodging—two large rooms with a fireplace in each and our own lavatory. The outer room was warm and smelled of spiced wine heating on a brazier. Somehow, in only a day, Mother had made the place her own. She'd brought tapestries from Cowling Castle to hang on the walls, including my favorite, showing the story of Paris and Helen of Troy. Our own servants had come with us to make sure we received food and drink in good time and that there was an adequate supply of wood for the fireplaces and coal for the braziers.

Unexpected company never perturbed my mother. She produced bread and cheese and gave the spiced wine a stir with a heated poker before filling goblets for everyone. The drink was a particular favorite of Father's, claret mixed with clarified honey, pepper, and ginger.

Lord Parr made a face after he took his first sip. "Clary, George? What's wrong with a good Rhenish wine, perhaps a Brabant?"

"Nothing . . . if you add honey and cloves," Father said with a laugh. "You are too plain in your tastes, Will."

"Only in wines."

I was not surprised that the two men knew each other. They both sat in the House of Lords when Parliament was in session. Standing by the hearth, they broadened their discussion of wines to include Canary and Xeres sack.

I joined Mother and Dorothy, who sat side by side on a long, low-backed bench, exchanging family news in quiet voices. I settled onto a cushion on the floor, leaning against Mother's knees. At once she reached out to rest one hand on my shoulder.

The sisters did not look much alike. Mother's hair was light brown and her eyes were blue like mine. She was shorter than Dorothy, too, and heavier, and markedly older, since she'd been married with at least one child of her own by the time Dorothy was born. She might never have been as pretty as her younger sister, but she had always been far kinder.

"Speaking of imports," Lord Parr said, "I have just brought a troupe of musicians to England from Venice, five talented brothers who were delighted to have found a patron."

The mention of music caught Mother's attention. "How fortunate for you," she said.

"My wife dearly loves music," Father said. "She insists that all our children learn to play the lute and the virginals and the viol, too."

"I play the virginals," Lord Parr confessed, after which he and my mother discussed the merits of that instrument for nearly a quarter of an hour, until Dorothy, with a series of wide but unconvincing yawns, prevailed upon him to escort her to the chamber she shared with several other former maids of honor.

"As you told Bess," she reminded him, "it is not safe for a woman to walk unescorted through Whitehall Palace at night." She all but pushed him out the door.

A moment later, she stuck her head back in. "You should take Bess home and keep her there, Anne," she said to my mother. "The king singled her out and admired her beauty. You know what that means."

Dorothy's second departure left behind a startled silence.

"Did His Grace pay uncommon attention to you?" Mother exchanged a worried glance with Father. The concern in her voice made me long to reassure her, but there was no way to hide the truth. Too many people had noted the king's interest in me and would remember exactly how long we had spoken together.

"He . . . he called me a pretty little thing." I squirmed under their scrutiny, feeling like a fly caught in a spider's web.

"And what did you think of him?" Father asked.

"That he is old and fat and diseased and that I want no part of him!"

"Oh, George," Mother said. "What shall we do? What if His Grace wants Bess to remain at court?"

"He's not yet said he does, and as I've no desire to dangle our daughter in front of him like a carrot before a mule, we will leave for home first thing in the morning."

"But if he is looking for a wife, as everyone says he is—"

"Then he will have to look elsewhere. It is not as if there are not plenty of willing wenches available."

"Sixty of them, by my count," I said. Relief made me giddy. "Although I suppose a few of them, even though they are still unmarried, may already be betrothed." I had been myself, to a boy I'd met only once, but he'd died. So far, no other arrangement had been made for me.

Mother exchanged another speaking glance with Father but said only, "Are you certain, Bess, that you wish to cut short your first visit to court?"

"I would gladly stay on if I could avoid the king," I admitted. "But for the nonce, I much prefer to be gone. Perhaps I can return after King Henry makes his selection. Surely, with so many ladies to choose from, it will not take His Grace long to find a new queen."

2

owling Castle, in Kent, had been built by an ancestor of mine for the defense of the realm. Or at least for the defense of our particular section of the north coast of Kent. Way back in the reign of King Richard the Second, a force of Frenchmen and Spaniards had sailed into the Thames Estuary and pillaged villages as far upriver as Gravesend. Vowing they'd never do so again, the third Lord Cobham constructed a mighty fortress to guard the port of Cliffe and the rest of the Hoo Peninsula from invaders.

Nearly two hundred years later, we had little need for walls six feet thick or two moats. Neither of our drawbridges had been raised more than a handful of times that I could remember and never because we were under attack.

After my return to Cowling Castle, I waited expectantly for news of a royal wedding, but weeks stretched into months and still King Henry did not remarry. In the summer, Father began to cast about for a suitable husband for me, but he was in no great hurry. He said he intended to find me a man of strong moral character who was also possessed of sufficient worldly goods to keep me in comfort. In Mother's opinion, that combination was as scarce as hens' teeth, but she had no objection to keeping me at home awhile longer. I was content, too. For the most part.

On a fine mid-October afternoon, freed from their lessons in Latin so that they might practice archery, three of my brothers raced across the drawbridge that connected the inner and outer wards. My sister Kate and I followed more slowly. We brought our sewing with us and planned to sit on a wooden bench near the butts to cheer on the competitors.

"Shall we wager on the outcome?" Kate asked as we made our way to the targets set up near the top of the upward-sloping ground. She was a younger version of our mother with the same light brown hair, sparkling blue eyes, and even temperament.

"Which of the boys do you favor?" I asked as we climbed. The outer ward was twice as big as the inner ward. To make the castle defensible, the curtain walls crowned the high ground around it. The east wall towered over the moat, even though it had been built lower than the other three.

Kate was only fourteen, but she'd already picked up the habit of gambling from our parents. She wagered on the outcome of everything, from card games to wrestling matches. I, on the other hand, saw no sense in committing myself unless I thought I had a good chance of winning.

Five of our brothers were still at home, all younger than we were. Our oldest brother, William, was also junior to me, but he was older than Kate. The year before he had been sent abroad to study in Padua. He'd taken with him two servants, three horses, and Father's instructions on proper behavior while living in a foreign land. William would have won any archery contest with ease. He was an excellent shot, and a good teacher, too.

Competing at the butts in William's absence were George and Thomas, both of them nine years old—ten months separated them—and John, who was seven. Henry, at four, and Edmund, who was only two years old, were not yet old enough to manage a longbow, not even one of the smaller models purpose-made for boys just learning archery.

We had an older sister, too, eight years my senior, but she had married and gone away four years earlier. I rarely thought of her anymore. Neither did I think much about the babies Mother had lost, although I knew that there had been five of them, three boys and two girls.

"George will win the day." Kate sounded confident.

It was true that George was steady and deliberate and usually hit what he aimed at, but Thomas, although he could be unpredictable, excelled at the things he enjoyed. Since he liked to pretend he was Robin Hood, he practiced shooting with a bow and arrow more often than George did.

"An embroidered handkerchief and a cloak pin on Thomas," I said, naming two items we both had upon our persons. Kate nodded her agreement and we settled ourselves on the bench, our needlework in our laps.

Kate industriously stitched at a shirt, but I left my needle stuck in the smock I was hemming. Both garments would be given to the poor when they were finished. It was a good cause, but on such a splendid day I was not inclined to keep my head bent over my stitches.

An oak tree just beginning to shed its leaves shaded our bench. I caught one of the bright bits of foliage as it drifted down, admiring its perfection, and breathed deeply of the salty air. Cowling Castle had been built at the edge of a marsh.

The raucous cry of a gull was clearly audible, even over the shouts and laughter of my siblings. Instead of watching my brothers, I contemplated the sky and was rewarded not only by the sight of several gulls, but also by a glimpse of a redwing. Redwings migrated to Kent every autumn but only stayed until the holly berries were gone, just like fieldfares.

A shout of "Well shot!" from John pulled my attention back to the butts. I'd been bird-watching longer than I'd realized. Thomas had already won the first match.

"Wretched boy," Kate grumbled as she handed over my winnings. "George is older. He should have won."

"Does that mean you think I will always surpass you?"

Kate laughed. "I'll wager it does." Before I knew what she intended, she had left the bench to advance on the butts and seize George's bow. "Bess will show you how it should be done," she said, "and a three-penny piece says she can hit the center of the target with her first arrow."

"Done!" George sneered a little. "I say she'll go wide of the mark."

Never one to run from a challenge and confident of my ability to hit what I aimed at, I set aside my sewing and joined them. Archery is a skill that, once learned, is never forgotten. I took the bow, nocked the arrow, aimed with care, and took my best shot. I hit the target dead center. William would have been pleased. He'd taught me well.

"Oh, excellent!" Kate cried, clapping her hands.

In the spirit of the moment, I bent at the waist, sweeping the hand with the bow out to one side like a courtier's bonnet.

"Girls curtsy," John piped up. "Only boys bow."

"That is because boys are too clumsy to manage a curtsy," Kate shot back. "Girls are graceful."

George, embarrassed to have been shown up by a female, jerked the bow out of my hand. "Girls are—"

He never finished what he was about to say. That was just as well, considering that I was prepared to throttle him myself if he heaped any more insults on womankind. Instead he paused, head cocked. He'd always had excellent hearing.

"Horseman," he announced. "Coming fast."

Our differences immediately forgotten, united by curiosity about the approaching arrival, we hurried back down the slope toward the other drawbridge, the one in the southwest corner of the outer ward. We did not have long to wait before a man rode in. He passed us without a single glance, intent upon reaching the inner ward.

"A messenger," George said, and raced after him.

The arrival of a letter was not an unusual event, but this fellow's lathered horse combined with his grim countenance suggested that his message was something out of the ordinary. Kate and I gathered up our skirts, running as fast as our feet could carry us to keep pace with the boys. The messenger had already dismounted by the time we reached him.

"Take me to Lady Wyatt," he barked at one of my father's gentlemen.

"My aunt will be in her solar at this time of day," I said, panting a little from the unaccustomed exertion. "I will show you the way."

"I am much obliged, mistress."

The messenger's eyes were bloodshot and his deeply lined face looked haggard, as if he'd been riding for days. Indeed, the marks of a long journey were plain upon his clothing. Mud streaked his boots and hose and his cloak stank of sweat and horse.

Kate started to accompany us, but as the eldest daughter still at home I was entitled to take ruthless advantage of my status. "Fetch Father," I ordered. "Plainly, something is amiss."

"Clever lass," the messenger muttered.

The boys, although still curious, hung back. They had learned to be wary of their aunt Elizabeth. I, on the other hand, was at ease with my father's sister. That she was my godmother probably helped. She'd always been fond of me.

When I was eleven, Aunt Elizabeth had come to live with us. She now resided at Cowling Castle most of every year, spending the remainder at Cobham Hall with her stepmother. Aunt Elizabeth's lodgings were located in the southeast tower of the inner ward, above the vaulted corner chamber we used as a bathing room. As I'd predicted, she was in her solar.

My mother was there, too, together with their gentlewomen. They were playing cent, a popular card game. From the size of the pile of pennies, halfpennies, and shillings in front of her, my aunt was winning. Everyone turned to look at me when I appeared without warning in the doorway. They gaped when they caught sight of the man behind me.

Mother was the first to find her voice. "Whatever is the matter, Bess?"

Before I could answer, the messenger pushed past me into the room to stand glowering down at Aunt Elizabeth.

"What do you want, Rudstone?" She stood, putting her eye to eye with him. She was a tall woman, lean and angular. The fulminating glare she gave the messenger would have turned most men to stone.

"Your son sent me." Master Rudstone's tone suggested that he'd been coerced into making the journey to Cowling Castle.

Aunt Elizabeth's son was my cousin, Thomas Wyatt the Younger. Tom lived at Allington Castle, near Maidstone, a journey of less than a day on horseback. Since I was certain this travel-stained courier had ridden a much greater distance, I waited with keen anticipation to hear his news.

Aunt Elizabeth was even more impatient than I. "Well? Speak up, man, and then begone."

Rudstone's lip curled in dislike but he obeyed. "I bring word of your husband, madam. My good master, Sir Thomas Wyatt the Elder, died last week at the house of Sir John Horsey, in Dorset."

Aunt Elizabeth blinked once, slowly, as she absorbed this information. Then she smiled. "I am a widow," she whispered. "At last!"

Father barged into the chamber at that moment. He was at his autocratic best, outraged that a stranger had dared confront his womenfolk without his presence or permission. "What is going on here?" he demanded.

"Wyatt's dead." Eyes dancing, voice jubilant, Aunt Elizabeth looked as if she were about to dance a jig. "That great hypocrite, Thomas Wyatt the Elder, will never torment me again."

Father gave his sister a stern look but his tone was sardonic. "Contain your grief, Eliza. Think of the repercussions. You will have to wear mourning for at least a year and you've never looked your best in black."

"I will do no such thing. Wyatt threw me out of his house years ago. I owe him nothing." A petulant look on her narrow face, Aunt Elizabeth resumed her seat at the table and picked up her cards. She wished to continue the game, but the other players did not cooperate.

Mother, ever the good hostess, had already gone to the sideboard to pour a cup of barley water for the messenger. He looked disgusted, but not surprised, by my aunt's attitude.

"What was Sir Thomas doing in Dorset, Master Rudstone?" Mother asked when she'd handed him the goblet.

"He was on his way to Falmouth to welcome a group of foreign diplomats to England on King Henry's behalf." Rudstone drank thirstily before he continued. "He caught a chill on the way. It turned into pneumonia, and three days later he was dead. We buried him in the Horsey family vault in the church in Sherborne."

The waiting gentlewomen murmured and clucked over this, for it seemed peculiar that the body had not been brought back to Allington for burial.

Belatedly, Father realized that Kate had followed him into the solar and that she and I were hanging on every word. "Leave us, girls," he ordered.

Reluctantly, we obeyed.

"Whatever Master Rudstone has to say next," Kate observed, "must be something Father does not want us to know."

"It is pointless to send us away," I complained. "Someone will tell us sooner or later." The servants were always a reliable source of information.

"Why did Aunt Elizabeth hate her husband so?" Kate asked as we crossed the inner court toward the dwelling rooms in the northeast corner.

I was surprised she didn't already know, but willing enough to tell her the tale. "It happened before I was born," I said as soon as we reached the bedchamber we shared and had closed the door against intruders. "Shortly after Cousin Tom was born, Sir Thomas accused Aunt Elizabeth of adultery and refused to let her live with him anymore." I calculated quickly and was surprised by the result. "That must have been more than twenty years ago."

"That is a very long time to be angry with each other, but Aunt Elizabeth should not have taken a lover." Kate plucked an apple from the bowl on the table and settled herself in the middle of the bed we shared.

"She claims she was never unfaithful to her husband. She says he invented the story because they never got along and he didn't want her at Allington Castle with him and their son." I clambered up onto the bed beside her, my own apple in hand, and took a huge bite of the crisp, tart fruit.

"Why didn't he divorce her, the way King Henry does when he tires of one of his wives?"

"They separated so long ago that the king hadn't yet broken with Rome. Back then the pope was the only one who could dissolve a marriage or grant permission for a divorced man or woman to marry again, if they had a mind to. Sir Thomas must not have had any proof that Aunt Elizabeth had a lover."

Satisfied with my explanation, I went back to munching my apple.

"But King Henry has been head of the Church of England for years," Kate objected. "Why didn't Sir Thomas ask His Grace to annul their marriage?"

I pondered her question, the fruit in my hand forgotten. "I don't think the king does that sort of thing. When I was at court, I overheard two gentlewomen talking about a lord—they didn't say which one—who'd just managed to push through an Act of Parliament to dissolve his unhappy marriage. They felt sorry for him because, even though he's been granted a legal separation from his wife on the grounds of her adultery, he is forbidden to remarry as long as she still lives. Marriage is for life."

"Unless you are the king," Kate quipped. "I wonder if Aunt Elizabeth will take a second husband. She's still young enough to have more children and she has a pleasing appearance."

I suspected that my aunt's prickly temperament would keep suitors at bay, but I did not voice that thought. "I wonder if she will have the use of her jointure, now that Sir Thomas is dead. He was stingy about providing for her while he was alive. He supported her at first. She told me once that he paid her an annuity for a number of years after they separated. But then, all of a sudden, he cut her off without a penny. That's when she came to live with us. She had nowhere else to go but back to her family."

"He had a mistress," Kate said, proving once again that children hear more in a busy household than their elders realize. "Last year, when Sir Thomas was arrested and imprisoned in the Tower of London, the king made him promise to give her up and take Aunt Elizabeth back. Sir Thomas wasn't set free until he agreed."

"But he didn't reconcile with Aunt Elizabeth. She stayed right here with us." As I slowly munched the remainder of my apple, I could not help but feel a grudging respect for my late uncle's courage. A courtier would either have to be very brave . . . or very foolish . . . to deliberately ignore a royal decree.

3

My mother's mother, Lady Bray, and her only remaining unmarried daughter, Dorothy, came to us for a visit during Lent. Kent had a better supply of fish than Bedfordshire and more variety, too. We dined on sea bass, red mullet, cod, haddock, pollack, hake, halibut, turbot, plaice, flounder, sole, salmon, sturgeon, trout, herring, and eels. Father arrived home several days later, after both houses of Parliament adjourned for the Easter holy days.

Although I was very fond of Grandmother Jane, I had mixed feelings about Dorothy's presence at Cowling Castle. At our last meeting, nearly fourteen months earlier at court, she had been angry and unpleasant. She did not appear to have mellowed since.

On the day before Palm Sunday, the nineteenth of March, I came upon her in the garden where I walked daily for exercise. Dorothy sat on a stone bench, wrapped tightly against the cold in a bright red cloak. She was reading a letter and had about her the air of a cat that has just licked up an entire bowl of cream.

"You will have icicles hanging off the end of your nose if you do not get up and move around," I said.

Dorothy's glance was as sharp as a poniard. "I have memories to keep me warm and the promise of more heat to come." She folded the single page with exaggerated care, smoothing the edges flat with gloved fingers.

"Is that from Lord Parr?" It was a logical conclusion but Dorothy's reaction surprised me.

"I am going to marry him." Her voice, her bearing, even the way she clasped the letter to her bosom, shouted defiance, as if she expected me to argue the point.

I reined in an unwanted pang of envy. "I am sure he will make you an excellent husband. Have you seen him since you left court?"

"We have been reduced to writing to each other." She tucked the letter into a pocket sewn in the lining of her cloak. When she rearranged the garment's folds, she made room for me to join her on the bench.

"It seems a most suitable match," I said. "When will you be formally betrothed?"

"There are . . . reasons we must delay. And keep matters between us private for now."

"What reasons? Is it Cousin John? Must your brother approve of the contract?" Cousin John was Lord Bray, and as such, I supposed, the head of Dorothy's family.

"John is a mere boy. He cannot approve or disapprove of anything." Contempt laced Dorothy's words.

I bristled. The "mere boy" was my age. "Then it must be Grandmother Jane who objects. You'll have to elope."

"If only it were that simple."

"Are you certain Lord Parr *wants* to marry you?"

Too late, I realized how Dorothy would interpret my impulsive question. Truly, I had not meant to imply that he had no need to marry her, having already sampled her favors, but she took my words that way and sprang to her feet, incensed.

"You know nothing of matters between men and women! Will Parr is besotted with me and has been since first we met. And I *will* be Lady Parr one day, while you, you foolish country mouse, will be fortunate if some simpleminded yeoman farmer can be found to marry you!"

After that encounter, I gave Dorothy a wide berth. When we were obliged to be in the same room—often the case, since I delighted in Grandmother Jane's company—I was careful to keep Kate between us.

On the last day of March the weather was bleak. A constant drizzling rain and gray skies dampened spirits as well as objects. In the solar we lit candles, but it was still difficult to see our stitches.

Grandmother Jane complained that her swollen knuckles were even less flexible than usual. She clenched and unclenched her hands in the hope of working the stiffness out of her fingers. She had lived more than six decades and borne eleven children, but that was the only sign of age or infirmity I ever saw in her. Small and sprightly, my grandmother was the liveliest person I knew.

All the women of the castle except the laundresses and the girl who helped in the kitchen had gathered, with their needlework—Mother, Grandmother Jane, Aunt Elizabeth, their gentlewomen, Kate and I, and Dorothy. Dorothy sat hunched over a piece of embroidery, a sour expression on her face. In addition to the human inhabitants, the room was occupied by a linnet in a cage, three spaniels—Yip, Perky, and Sleepy—and Hunter, an old hound so devoted to my mother that he slept with his muzzle resting on her shoe. Two charcoal braziers gave off fitful heat and the fire in the hearth smoked and spat with every draft.

Warmly dressed, I'd chosen to curl up on the window seat, as far from Dorothy as possible, and thus I was the first to see three men ride in. I recognized one of them at once, even though he wore a long cloak and his rain-sodden hat drooped down over his ears.

"Lord Parr has just arrived," I announced.

Dorothy went perfectly still. Her needle froze halfway through a stitch. As I watched, a satisfied smile curved her thin lips upward and she resumed stitching.

Grandmother Jane's reaction was both more vocal and more volatile. "That blackguard! Anne, you must not let him into the house."

My mother stared at Grandmother in astonishment. "Why ever not? He is high in King Henry's favor and I have never heard any ill report of him."

"Immured here in the country, you would not, but take my word for it, he's a bad lot. And I hear he's an evangelical, too, all for doing away with what's left of the Mass and tearing down every church in the land to use for building stone."

"Mother," Dorothy warned, not quite under her breath.

Grandmother jabbed a misshapen finger in Dorothy's direction. "Not a word out of you, girl. I know what I know."

I wondered how, since she spent most of her time at Eaton Bray. Bedfordshire was even more remote from court and courtiers than our rural peninsula. News took a long time to reach us and sometimes people forgot entirely to send us word of events that took place elsewhere.

"Do you suppose Lord Parr will sup with us and stay the night?" Kate asked, oblivious to the daggers shooting back and forth between Dorothy and her mother. The linnet, equally unconcerned, began to sing. High, lilting notes filled the chamber, forcing Mother to raise her voice in order to be heard.

"It is too late in the day for him to travel elsewhere," she said, sending Grandmother a stern look. "It is the obligation of every household to offer hospitality to travelers. If you cannot behave civilly toward him, perhaps you should sup in your chamber."

"And miss hearing the latest scandals from court? Never think it!"

And so it was that we all went down to supper. I anticipated an entertaining evening.

The great chamber of Cowling Castle rose to a height of two stories but had few windows, making it a dark and dismal place even on sunny days. For family meals we customarily used the much smaller dining chamber and we continued that practice even though we had a guest. The younger boys ate with their tutors, but Father decided that George, who had turned ten in January, was old enough to join the rest of us. My little brother sat next to me, so excited at being treated as an adult that he could barely sit still. I knew just how he felt.

However much Grandmother might have disliked Lord Parr, she had no qualms about interrogating him. "Does Sir Anthony Browne still live?" she demanded the moment everyone was seated, "Or has that young bride of his danced him into his grave?"

Old Sir Anthony, I recalled, had married a lady more than twenty-five years his junior in late December. News of the wedding had reached us at Cowling Castle more than a month after the event but had still provided several hours of entertaining conversation. The age difference was not all that unusual, but the bride, Lady Elizabeth Fitzgerald, was the same young noblewoman who'd once been the subject of a sonnet written by Henry Howard, the Earl of Surrey. Surrey's name never failed to stir comment at Cowling Castle. My cousin, Tom Wyatt, was one of Surrey's boon companions. Because he was, and because the earl had admired the poetry written by Aunt Elizabeth's late husband, Sir Thomas the Elder, Surrey had composed several laments to commemorate Wyatt's death. My aunt despised both the poet and his poems and, by association, anyone else Surrey honored with his verses.

As I'd predicted on the day we learned my uncle was dead, Kate and I had soon learned the rest of the story, the part Father had tried to keep from us. It was not a pretty tale. Sir Thomas Wyatt had died deeply in debt, obliging Cousin Tom to sell most of his inheritance to the Crown in order to raise enough money to settle with his father's creditors. Tom had instructed Master Rudstone to obtain Aunt Elizabeth's permission to include in that sale some of the properties that comprised her widow's third of the estate. My aunt had been willing to agree . . . until she'd discovered that, in spite of Tom's desperate need for ready money, he intended to grant an entire manor in Kent to his father's longtime mistress. Mother and son had not spoken to each other since.

Lord Parr could add nothing to our knowledge of the new Lady Browne. She'd retired to the country after her marriage.

"And what of your sister, Lady Latimer?" Mother asked Lord Parr. "How does she fare? We heard of her husband's recent death."

Lord Latimer had died at the beginning of the month. Father had brought that news home with him. Since I had never met either Lady Latimer or her late husband, I was not much interested in Will Parr's reply, but Dorothy was acquainted with both of Lord Parr's siblings.

"The other sister," she whispered to Kate, "was a maid of honor until she married William Herbert, one of the King's Spears."

"Kathryn joined the Lady Mary's household some months ago," Lord Parr said, "and has resumed her duties there."

"So soon?" My grandmother, who still wore black for Grandfather Bray, dead these four years and more, looked disapproving. Widows customarily went into seclusion, at least for a while.

"The king insisted that she return," Lord Parr said, "and by His Grace's decree, Kathryn has also forgone wearing mourning dress."

The exchange of meaningful looks between my mother and grandmother assured me that they thought this as odd as I did, but no one pursued the subject.

"What else is new at court?" Dorothy asked.

"The king has acquired a new pet," Will Parr said as he sampled the stewed pike, a favorite of mine. It was seasoned with currants, sugar, cinnamon, barberries, and prunes. "An ape. The creature is half as big as a man and wears a damask collar studded with pearls. It has its own keeper, but I fear it needs more than one man to look after it. The beast escaped last week and went on a rampage in the lodgings of an unfortunate courtier. It ripped his best bonnet to shreds." Parr's light brown eyes twinkled as he paused for effect. "And then it ate the feather."

When our laughter died away, I realized that Father was frowning.

"Did they ever identify those drunken ruffians who caused so much damage in London back in January? It was one night after curfew," he explained for the benefit of those of us unfamiliar with the incident. "They broke dozens of windows, targeting prominent citizens and churches, too. Then they crossed the Thames in boats and attacked several whore-houses in Southwark."

"I am certain no one complained about *that*," Aunt Elizabeth said with some asperity.

We all looked at Lord Parr expectantly. He toyed with his food and appeared ill at ease.

"Well," Father demanded. "Have the brigands been caught?"

"It has become a matter of some delicacy," Lord Parr hedged.

He took a swallow of wine, but that only delayed the inevitable. No one changed the subject. He sighed and gave in.

"It appears that the young men were in the company of the Earl of Surrey." His glance slid to Aunt Elizabeth, then quickly away. "The last I heard, just before I left court, was that the earl had been ordered to appear before four members of the Privy Council on the first of April. Two of his boon companions have already been sent to the Tower of London. At first, they denied taking part in the rampage. Then they confessed. I regret to tell you, Lady Wyatt, that one of them is your son."

Aunt Elizabeth's lips compressed into a flat, disapproving line, but she did not look surprised by this news, nor unduly upset by it. After a moment, she gave a careless wave of one hand. "A few months in prison will do Tom good, but I feel sorry for his poor wife."

"Are you certain you were not one of them, Lord Parr?" Grandmother Jane asked. She had the look of a cat toying with a mouse when she added, "I was under the impression that you were also one of Surrey's minions."

Lord Parr opened his mouth, then closed it again. He did not seem to know how to react to my grandmother's rudeness. Had she been a man, I am sure he'd have made some arrogant denial, perhaps even let his anger at the insult show. But he was our guest and she was a baron's widow. Long years of training in courtly behavior rose to the fore. He sent her a charming if insincere smile. "Alas, dear lady, I fear your information is some decades out of date. As boys, the earl and I were both members of the late Duke of Richmond's household. We were the king's son's devoted servants until the day he died."

My mother, ever the good hostess, stepped in to smooth over the awkwardness. "As I recall, Lord Parr, you are the patron of a troupe of Italian musicians and I see that one of the servants you brought with you has the look of a foreigner. Is he, by chance, a Bassano?"

"Indeed he is, Lady Cobham. Jasper Bassano. Shall I have him perform for you? He sings and plays any number of instruments with great skill and, should you have others to provide the music, dances extraordinarily well, too."

"Your other servant is not musical?"

"Griggs?" Lord Parr chuckled. "He can gentle a horse with a whisper but his singing sets the hounds to howling and frightens small children."

When the trestle table had been removed to leave a space in the middle of the room, Master Bassano, swarthy and black haired but handsome for all that, demonstrated each of his skills, first the dancing, then the singing, and finally the playing. When he launched into a pavane and Father's musicians joined in, Lord Parr asked Dorothy to dance with him.

"There are enough of us for an alman," Grandmother said in a carrying voice. The music abruptly stopped. She rose and crooked a gnarled finger at Matthew Rowlett, one of Father's gentlemen. "You there. You'll do for my partner."

Rowlett's ruddy complexion lost some of its color, but he obediently presented himself before her and managed a respectable bow. Grandmother gave a satisfied nod, but she was not through rearranging things. A shove here and a deft tug there and by the time we were lined up with the men on the left and the women on the right, Rowlett was holding hands with Dorothy and I stood face-to-face with Lord Parr.

"Mistress Bess," he greeted me, taking my hands in his.

"Lord Parr." My voice shook a little, affected by his touch in spite of my resolve not to show any interest in him. Dorothy was already wroth with me. I had no desire to increase her ire.

The hopping steps kept me close to him for a measure, then carried us apart. When it was time to repeat the pattern from the beginning, he leaned close to whisper in my ear, "Surely you can call me Will. We are all friends here."

"I do not believe my grandmother would agree."

His laughter followed me as I danced away to clasp hands, each in their turn, with George, my father, and Master Rowlett.

Lord Parr partnered me twice more that evening. The tug of physical attraction grew stronger every time our hands touched or our bodies swayed side by side in the movements of the dance. No wonder Dorothy was so determined to have him for her husband! Although I did my best to ignore these tingles of awareness, when Will Parr was close to me a thrill of excitement penetrated straight to my vitals. When his arm brushed against my breast—an accident, I am sure—my entire body tightened deliciously in response.

That night my sleep was broken by vivid and disconcerting dreams.

The next morning, when I caught sight of Lord Parr, at a distance, I followed him. It was as if I had no control over the impulse. I had no plan, should I overtake him, but I was disappointed when he entered my father's closet, the small room Father used when he wished to be private to write letters or read his Bible.

I turned back the way I'd come and stopped short. Dorothy blocked my path.

"Is he in there?"

When I nodded, she brushed past me and applied her ear to a panel of the door.

"You will not be able to hear what they are saying that way. The wood is too thick."

Her eyes narrowed as she considered my words. "Where, then?"

I hesitated. I had no reason to help Dorothy, but I was curious, too. "Follow me."

Around the corner and along a narrow passage we came to a wall hanging painted with a pastoral scene of sheep and shepherdesses. It hid a peephole I'd discovered years before. I did not know if someone had deliberately bored it or if it were a knothole left by nature, but just on the other side was Father's closet.

There was room for only one person at a time. I let Dorothy take the first peek. After a moment, she backed away. "They are talking of *Parliament*," she complained.

I stepped up to take my turn at the peephole. With my eye close to the opening, I had an excellent view of both Will Parr and my father. Will's words were clearly audible.

"As you know, George," he said, "I have already secured a legal separation from my estranged wife on the grounds of her adultery, and a bill has been introduced to prevent her children from inheriting my estates. I would appreciate your support in this matter."

I barely contained my gasp of surprise. Will Parr already had a wife? No wonder Grandmother Jane objected to his attentions to Dorothy. And no wonder he had not asked Dorothy to marry him. He was not free to wed.

Deceitful brute! I thought, and leaned closer. Lord Parr's case was the one I had heard discussed during my brief sojourn at court. He was the unnamed lord all the ladies had pitied because, even with his unhappy marriage dissolved, he could not remarry until after the death of his cast-off wife.

"I wed Anne Bourchier," Will said, "when she was ten years old and I was fifteen. I had no say in the matter, nor did she."

Reluctant sympathy stabbed at me. The circumstances made his plight more pitiable, but they carried no weight under English law. He was still married and would be as long as this Anne Bourchier lived— just as Aunt Elizabeth had been tied to Sir Thomas Wyatt until she'd finally been set free by his death. As for the children his wife had borne, they were innocent victims, but they gave me even more reason to feel sorry for Will Parr. Under the law, they were his heirs, no matter who their father had been.

Dorothy tugged at my sleeve, demanding her turn at the peephole, but I refused to budge.

"It seems certain," Will said, "that the king will marry my sister."

This news was just as startling as the revelation of his marital status. Kathryn, Lady Latimer, the recent widow, was *old*, at least compared to King Henry's last wife. Catherine Howard had not lived to see her twentieth year. I tried to wrap my mind around the idea of a matronly queen, all the while straining to hear more.

"His Grace visits Kathryn daily in his daughter's household," Will said as Dorothy seized me bodily and hauled me away from the peephole. "Sometimes three or four times a day."

"What are they saying?" she demanded.

"That Lady Latimer is to be our next queen."

"Truly?"

"Lord Parr just said so."

"Oh, excellent! That means I will soon return to court. The king himself promised me that I would be one of his next queen's maids of honor. And with Will's sister as queen, His Grace will surely agree to unmake Will's marriage to that wicked woman in Essex."

"So you knew he already had a wife."

"Everyone knows, and everyone knows he would gladly be rid of her." She stepped up to the listening post, but Father and Lord Parr had finished their conversation and were already on their way out of Father's closet.

Dorothy, ever the bold one, intercepted them. I crept quietly away and did not see Will Parr again before he left Cowling Castle.

4

More than three months passed before word reached our remote peninsula that King Henry had wed for the sixth time. By then it was late July. It had been an unusually wet summer. There were outbreaks of the plague all over England. In an attempt to avoid both the worst of the inclement weather and the deadly path of the disease, the court went on progress in Surrey and Buckinghamshire, far away from Kent. Using the excuse of limited accommodations at some of the king's smaller manors, large numbers of courtiers fled to their own estates.

No one knows what causes a visitation of the plague, but fewer people seemed to contract the dread disease in the country. At Cowling Castle with my family, I remained safe from infection.

Mother, well aware that I had hoped to return to court once there was a new queen in residence, spent most of August and the first part of September sending letters to influential acquaintances. To distract me, she kept Kate and me busy in the stillroom, teaching us how to make herbal remedies and preventives. Most of the latter were intended to keep the plague at bay.

It is the duty of every wife, whether she be married to a cobbler or a great lord, to look after the health of her household. To that end, Mother taught us to identify dozens of healing herbs and how to prepare them for use. Ceramic pots covered with thin goatskin, glass and horn containers plugged with stopples, and even a few imported stoneware jugs with parchment tied over their mouths to keep the contents dry filled the stillroom shelves. They contained powders, extracts, oils, ointments, and pills. Drying roots hung in bunches from the ceiling. The long table where we worked held equipment, everything from a small still to a handpress used to squeeze the juice out of fruit.

"But why must preventives always smell so vile?" I asked, wrinkling my nose in distaste as I labored with mortar and pestle. The stench of burning leather permeated the entire castle because the purifying fumes created by setting fire to old shoes warded off disease.

"The onions are not so bad," Kate said. Peeled onions left in a house for ten days absorbed infection from the air, but not even the sweet herbs we used for strewing could mask their pungent odor.

"If remedies do not smell awful, then they taste terrible." I bore down harder on a handful of briar leaves.

Mother stopped beside me to inspect my handiwork. "*Stamp* the herbs, Bess. Do not grind them into powder. Bruise them *gently*."

I sighed and started over. When I'd *bruised* the leaves properly, I added them to handfuls of sage, rue, and elder leaves and strained them with a quart of white wine sprinkled with ginger. Everyone in the family had been drinking a little of this concoction, morning and night, for two months. It was not the worst thing I had ever tasted, but I was heartily sick of it.

Just as I finished the straining, Matthew Rowlett came into the stillroom with a letter that had just arrived for Mother. Her face lit up when she recognized the seal. She wasted no time in breaking the wax to read the contents. She was still smiling when she finished.

"Well, Bess," she said, "it seems you will be going to court after all."

"But I thought there was no hope of a post as a maid of honor to the queen." There were only six such positions and all had been filled. My aunt, Dorothy Bray, held one. She'd written to Mother to boast of it. The other five were Mistress Anne Bassett, the young woman who had been so friendly to me at the king's supper, and four ladies I did not know—a Carew, a Windsor, a Guildford, and one of Sir Anthony Browne's daughters by his first marriage.

"Before she accepted the post as a maid of honor," Mother explained, "the Guildford girl was in service to her kinswoman, Lady Lisle. That position is now vacant."

I frowned in puzzlement. "Do you mean Nan Bassett's mother?"

Mother shook her head. "Honor Lisle has lived in retirement in the West Country since her second husband's death. Lord Lisle had no son to succeed him, so King Henry gave the title to his stepson. The new Viscount Lisle is Sir John Dudley. He is also lord admiral of England. His wife, Jane, was a Guildford of Halden Hall before her marriage. She is one of Queen Kathryn's great ladies of the household. That means she holds an unpaid post at court but is entitled to lodgings there. As a viscountess, she is permitted to keep waiting gentlewomen of her own. This letter invites you to become one of them. It is an excellent opportunity, Bess. You might well advance into the queen's service, if there is an opening. Even if you do not, you will be at court. And Lady Lisle vows in her letter that she will treat you with as much affection as if you were her own daughter."

"Does she *have* a daughter?" All I knew about Jane Lisle, other than what Mother had just told me, was that she was a close friend of my father's stepmother.

"She lost one of her girls earlier this year, but the eldest, Mary Dudley, is thriving. Mary must be about twelve years old. Since Jane holds an honorary post at court, she could keep her children with her, but she'd not be given any additional space in which to house them. For all the enormous size of the king's palaces and great houses, lodgings are always hard to come by. Accommodations are even more crowded when the court is on progress."

"Are most ladies in service to the queen obliged to leave young children behind?" I busied myself scouring the mortar and pestle with sand and putting them away. Mother insisted the stillroom be kept clean and neat.

"Mothers regularly turn even newborn infants over to nurses and governesses so that they can rush back to their duties. But, in truth, most well-born ladies have little to do with their children, even when they stay at home."

"Not you, Mother," Kate said. "And we are glad of it."

"Is that why you never accepted a post at court?" I asked. "Because you'd have had to leave us behind?"

"I was never offered a permanent place, but I was pleased to have it so. But you, Bess—you enjoy meeting new people and seeing new things. You will thrive in that environment."

It was true that I was eager to see more of the world, but I loved my family and life at Cowling Castle. "I will miss you terribly, Mother." I glanced at my sister. "I will even miss Kate and the boys."

"If you do not go," Kate said, ever practical, "Father will feel obliged to find you a husband and you will leave us anyway. And at court you might meet someone you'd *like* to marry. I wish I could go, too."

"Your turn will come," Mother promised her. "Now, we must make preparations for Bess's departure. Jane Lisle is already here in Kent. She writes that the king and queen are still on progress and that their next stop is Woodstock, a royal manor in Oxfordshire. They plan to stay for a month. Since Woodstock is one of the king's great houses, with room for as many as fifteen hundred people at a time, Jane will rejoin the court there. She'll travel from Halden Hall accompanied by a large band of retainers. They will stop at Cowling Castle on their way north."

Four days later, Lady Lisle was carried through the outer gate in her litter, a large box fixed to poles that rested on the backs of two horses harnessed in tandem. I was more nervous than I'd anticipated as I watched the entourage pour into the inner court. Liveried men and gaily caparisoned horses filled the area to capacity. The air smelled of leather and sweat, and the clatter of hooves on cobblestones drowned out every other sound.

Kate stood beside me, already shedding tears. My youngest brother, Edmund, was just as reluctant to let me leave and clung to my skirts with the tenacity of a terrier gripping a rat in its teeth.

A liveried servant attached a small stepladder to the door frame of the litter and folded back the sturdy flap of leather that covered it to keep out the elements during travel. Some kind of coarse canvas cloth, treated to make it waterproof, had been used to form the roof, but the sides were open. Striped curtains suspended from rings could be kept open or closed as suited the occupant. At the moment, they were wide open, giving me a clear view of the interior.

Lady Lisle traveled in luxury. She had cushions and pillows both, all covered with silk and so plump that they were likely filled with the softest down. And when she stepped out onto the stepladder, I saw that carpet padded the floor of the litter.

Jane Lisle was a little younger than my mother, a tall, pale woman whose body had been thickened by frequent childbearing. She was an island of calm in the roiling sea of her retainers. When she saw Kate and Edmund and me standing a little apart from Father, Mother, and Aunt Elizabeth, she seemed to know instinctively that I was beset by second thoughts. As soon as she had exchanged greetings with the three of them, she approached us. Her reassuring manner alone calmed my nervousness.

Unperturbed by Edmund's grimy fingers, Lady Lisle detached him from my skirts and lifted him into her arms. When they were face-to-face, she made him a promise: "I will take good care of your sister. You need have no fear for her."

Edmund at first responded with a steady, three-year-old stare. Then he flashed an engaging grin. "I like you," he said. "You smell like roses."

Kate also took to Lady Lisle. "I should like to go to court, too," she announced.

"You are young yet, but perhaps when you are seventeen, as your sister is, something can be arranged."

Lady Lisle's diplomatic refusal left my sister disappointed but resigned. I vowed in that moment to try to emulate my new mistress. Clearly, she had mastered the art of dealing tactfully with other people's feelings.

"Allow me to present my two oldest sons," Lady Lisle said, turning once again to my parents and my aunt. She signaled for a young man of about my own age to step forward. "This is Henry."

When he doffed his cap, I saw that Henry Dudley had a shock of light brown hair. After he greeted his elders, he turned clear hazel eyes on me and winked.

"And that," Lady Lisle said, indicating another boy, this one half hidden behind his horse, apparently more interested in making sure the animal received proper care than he was in meeting strangers, "is John."

John Dudley was Kate's age. He was shorter, darker in coloring, and less polished in his manners than his brother. He came forward only after his mother called attention to him, but he showed proper manners when he was presented to the senior members of our household.

Both Henry and John Dudley seemed to appreciate the effort I'd gone to with my appearance. First thing that morning, I'd taken a bath. Then mother had filled her deepest silver basin with heated water and washed my hair with soap and ashes. After it had been combed dry, she'd brushed it until it shone. I'd left it loose, like a bride's, and worn my newest kirtle and gown, decorated with embroidered flowers and birds. The predominant color in all my clothing exactly matched the pale blue of my eyes. John Dudley, although he obviously preferred horses to people, kept staring at me. I made a wager with myself that he'd spend at least part of the journey to Woodstock riding by my side.

At supper I sat between the two brothers. It did not take long for them to start calling me Bess or for me to become comfortable addressing them as Harry and Jack. Harry told wonderful stories of life at court, where he'd spent considerable time during the last two years.

"My father will meet us at Woodstock," Harry said. "It will be good to see him again."

"Where has he been?" I asked between bites of haddock in herb sauce—it was Friday, so we had no meat at table, only varieties of fish and dishes made with cheese.

"He was in Northumberland until April as lord warden and keeper of the Western Marches toward Scotland. Then, after Lord Parr was appointed to replace him, Father had to go to Dudley Castle to supervise the rebuilding there."

I paused with my food halfway to my mouth. "Lord Parr? The new queen's brother?"

Harry nodded. "He's the new lord warden, and welcome to it, Father says. The north is a bleak, barren place and deadly dull except for chasing border reivers. Or when we are at war with the Scots. Lord Parr has been there since May."

May—well before his sister's marriage to the king. Dorothy would not yet have returned to court by the time he left. I supposed he might have stopped at Eaton Bray, but somehow I did not think so. Not with Grandmother Jane so set against him.

"There's a maze at Woodstock," Jack Dudley said, abruptly changing the subject. "I'll show you the way to the center if you like. You shouldn't go in alone. If you lose your way, you might never come out again."

"A maze? Truly?" I'd heard of such things but had never seen one.

"The second King Henry built it a long time ago," Harry chimed in. "The story goes that it was constructed to hide his mistress from his wife. She was called Fair Rosamund—the mistress, not the wife—and her house was at the center of the maze."

That struck me as an odd place to build a house, but I did not say so. The conflicting versions of the story the two Dudley brothers told in competition for my attention contained contradictions enough. No one knew the real story anymore. It had all happened too long ago. But I looked forward to exploring the maze at Woodstock and to all the other new and exciting experiences that awaited me at court.

We set out at first light the next morning. Lady Lisle again occupied the litter, together with her waiting gentlewoman, Bridget Mardlyn.

Mistress Mardlyn was a decade my senior and had been in Lady Lisle's service for many years. Thin and wiry in build, her hands were always busy. If she was not plying a needle, then she was tugging at her cuffs or kneading the folds of her overskirt.

Several armed men rode ahead of the litter. Following after came the two-wheeled baggage carts, together with the rest of the entourage on horseback. Two maidservants rode on pillions. I'd traveled that way once as a child and hadn't cared for it. Sitting sideways on a pillion attached to the back of a saddle requires a woman to clasp her arms around the waist of the man in front of her, lest she fall off. When I'd been a little older, I'd ridden using a man's saddle, but now that I was grown I had to ride like a lady.

My horse was a gentle bay named Prancer, and I had a new saddle with its own leather cover to keep it clean when I wasn't using it. It was worked in velvet with flowers of gold thread. Off the side was a velvet sling on which both of my feet rested while one of my knees nestled in a purpose-cut hollow. This position was not as comfortable on a long journey as riding astride, but it was better than being perched on a pillion and less likely to leave me with bruises than traveling by litter. In spite of all the cushions, Lady Lisle and Mistress Mardlyn would be jounced and jostled all the way to Woodstock.

We reached London late on Saturday and remained there for the Sabbath. With nearly forty people in the retinue and almost sixty horses, we moved at a snail's pace when we set out again on Monday. We did well to cover twenty miles in a day. If I had not had one Dudley brother riding on each side of me, vying for my attention and entertaining me with stories both real and cribbed from books they'd read, the four days that followed would have bored me to tears.

By the time we reached Woodstock, my back ached and my bottom was sore, even though Prancer had the gentlest of gaits. Although we'd had comfortable accommodations every night, either staying at one of Lord Lisle's manors or at the country estate of one of his friends, I'd spent all the hours in between on horseback. I felt it in every bone of my body.

The road from the nearest town approached the royal manor of Woodstock from the east, winding past the privy gardens. I am certain they were an impressive sight, but I was too travel weary to care. Still, my first glimpse of the great house, solitary in a large park, had me staring like the simplest country bumpkin.

I'd visited the palace of Whitehall, and we passed Greenwich every time we made a trip to London. Woodstock could not compare to them, and yet there was something about this majestic structure that made a deep impression on me. Perhaps it was just that I knew this was the place where I would be presented to the queen, meet the king for the second time, and come in contact with all the other important and influential denizens of the court.

If I meant to become a courtier myself, I would have to be constantly on my guard lest I displease one of them. Even if I remained only a short time before I left to marry, I still had to be careful. My every action would reflect upon my family. My ability to make a good impression on the right people affected not only my future but also the future of my father and brothers. Suddenly I was beset by insecurity.

"What if no one here likes me?" I whispered to Jack Dudley. His brother had ridden ahead, impatient with the pace of the litter and baggage carts.

"How could anyone not think you were wonderful?" Jack asked.

My spirits soared, even though I knew his opinion to be biased. Banishing both doubt and fear from my thoughts, I rode boldly onward. Whatever happened next, it would be the start of a great adventure.

5

y first two days at Woodstock were a great disappointment. I spent most of that time in the cramped quarters assigned to Lady Lisle and in the even smaller space given over to her attendants. My assigned bedfellow and nearly constant companion was Lady Lisle's other waiting gentlewoman, Bridget. She had the keeping of the viscountess's jewels and was responsible for the care of her wardrobe and for dressing her person and her hair.

"What are my duties?" I asked her the first morning, after Lady Lisle had left her lodgings to wait upon the queen.

"You fetch and carry at my lady's command. You make yourself available to do her bidding, day and night."

I sighed. "In other words, I wait upon her whim. But what do I do when she is not here? She does not need me to run errands for her when she is with the queen. Does Lady Lisle spend a great deal of her time in Queen Kathryn's company?"

Bridget rolled her eyes at my ignorance. "Lady Lisle," she informed me, "is one of the queen's inner circle of friends."

"I am delighted to hear it."

Bridget sighed. "Do not expect me to nursemaid you, Mistress Brooke."

"Have pity, Mistress Mardlyn. I know nothing of the ways of the court. I would not want to embarrass our lady mistress."

She gave me a sour look but condescended to explain the workings of the court to me. "You must keep to the schedule," she warned when she'd given me a brief and far from illuminating account of the hierarchy of the royal household. "We rise at seven, dine at ten, and sup at four."

"And in between meals? How am I expected to occupy my time as I wait for orders from Lady Lisle?"

"There is always mending." Turning her back on me, Bridget unlocked Lady Lisle's jewel box. Her task for the morning was to make certain every piece was accounted for after our journey.

"It is the job of the maids to do the mending." Curious, I stepped closer. Inside the ornately carved wooden box, a series of nested drawers contained brooches and necklaces and rings. Each piece was stored in its own soft cloth pouch.

"Do you think yourself too highborn to ply a needle, Mistress Brooke?"

Stung, I considered offering to make clothing for the poor but stopped myself in time. I was living at the royal court. If I was to have leisure to amuse myself, I would engage in courtly pleasures. And I would not let a mere waiting gentlewoman spoil my enjoyment at being out in the world.

Plucking up my lute, I began to play a sad song about lost love. Bridget ignored me and continued to count pearls and diamonds, rubies and emeralds, sapphires and garnets. The goldsmiths' work was intricate and beautiful and some of the lockets opened to reveal tiny portraits. I repressed an envious sigh. One day, I vowed, I would own jewelry just as beautiful.

In the meantime, as Lady Lisle's waiting gentlewoman, I . . . waited. I remained in her lodgings while she attended the queen, even taking meals there, as Bridget and the two maidservants did. It was not forbidden for me to visit Queen Kathryn's public rooms—the watching chamber, the presence chamber, and the privy chamber—but I had no good reason to go there, either. As I knew few people at court, I shied away from pushing myself forward. I wanted to be accepted, to have friends, but I was fearful of making a bad first impression.

By the third day, I craved the outdoors. Keeping a wary eye peeled for anyone who might object to my presence, I crossed the large, square outer court and skirted the kennels and the stables. I was tempted to stop and look for Prancer, but I was not quite brave enough to venture unescorted into such an all-male preserve as the stables. Instead, I set my course for the orchard.

Fruit trees stretched as far as I could see. A broad path followed the stone wall that surrounded them, encompassed by a low hedge of cornelian cherry trees and rose, gooseberry, and current bushes. At the outside of the orchard, damson, bullace, and tall plum trees had been planted. On the inside were low plum, cherry, apple, and pear trees, together with a few filberts and medlars. I wandered aimlessly for some time, wondering if it was treason to filch and eat one of the king's apples. I decided not to take any risks and eventually abandoned the orchard for pleasure gardens full of knot beds and statues, sundials and mounts, shaded alleys, turfed seats, and even works of topiary. In places the wide, graveled walkways had been planted with wild thyme and other sweet-smelling herbs. They released a pleasant aroma when crushed underfoot.

The most colorful flowers of summer were long gone, but some varieties of rose still bloomed. Bright green plants grew in profusion— rosemary and lavender, myrtle and germander, too. I walked for nearly an hour among these familiar friends.

Although I saw other people out taking the air, I wasn't brave enough to approach anyone. I returned to the cramped little room I shared with Bridget and the maids—they slept on the truckle bed—still starved for company. I needed friends. I craved laughter. But I lacked the courage to do so much as venture up the stairs that led to the queen's apartments.

I pondered this as I lay awake, listening to Bridget snore. I had never been timid at home. What harm would it have done to speak to someone I met in the gardens? And if I ventured into the presence chamber, surely Lady Lisle would acknowledge me, perhaps even present me to the queen.

The next morning I went walking again, but there were far fewer people about than there had been the previous day. None of them seemed approachable. Beset by self-pity, I was on the verge of retreat when a spaniel dashed across my path. A moment later, a young woman about my own age burst out of the shrubbery in hot pursuit.

"Rig!" she called, frantic and out of breath. "Rig, come back!"

"He went that way," I said, and pointed.

"Wretched beast! If I have to leave the path again, my shoes will be ruined."

"Take them off," I suggested.

Her wide-spaced, sea green eyes widened for a moment. Then she laughed. "I will if you will."

I kicked off my soft leather slippers and left them on the graveled path. In stocking feet, we raced across a terrace and down a flight of steps, past open flower beds raised above the level of the path on oak frames, and through a covert walk created by entwining the branches of two rows of willow trees overhead.

Rig led us on a merry chase. We could climb over the low-growing hedges of lavender or box or rosemary, but every time he ducked under one of the high, clipped hedges planted in privet or briar or whitethorn, we had to go around. By the time we ran him to ground, he had reached the man-high hedgerow that surrounded all of Woodstock. We would not have caught him then had he not found something interesting to sniff.

My companion pounced, scooping him up. "Bad dog," she scolded, trying to hold on to him and pluck leaves and twigs from his fur at the same time.

I studied the young woman as I untangled the spaniel's leash for her. She had a long face that narrowed toward a pointed chin and pale, flawless skin. Her cloak concealed most of her clothing, but that cloak was made of brocade and had pearls set into the trim, as did the border of her French hood. The little dog squirming in her arms wore a collar of crimson velvet. It had been embroidered in gold thread with the head of St. Katherine—the queen's emblem.

"Is Rig Her Grace's spaniel?"

"He is, and a more spoilt and pampered pup you will never meet." We began to retrace our steps toward the place where we had discarded our shoes.

"I am Elizabeth Brooke, Lady Lisle's waiting gentlewoman."

"And I am Alys Guildford, Lady Lisle's kinswoman. You replaced me in her household when I left to wait upon the queen."

We recovered our shoes and walked together toward the palace. I was uncertain of what to say next, but Alys solved that problem for me.

"Tell me," she said, eyes twinkling as she glanced my way, "how have you been sleeping? Does Bridget's snoring keep you awake? I always found it useful to stuff cotton in my ears before I went to bed."

6

Alys Guildford and I soon became fast friends. Even though she had only been a maid of honor for a short time, she seemed to know everyone at court. It was not long before I met all the maids of honor and chamberers. I found another kindred spirit in Mary Woodhull, a plump, pretty girl with sand-colored hair and mild gray eyes. She was the queen's kinswoman, the granddaughter of Kathryn Parr's uncle, but she did not push herself forward because of that. She was happy just to be at court. As a chamberer, she waited on Her Grace in the royal bedchamber but did not attend Queen Kathryn in public.

Both Alys and Mary shared my interest in exploring the maze.

"You promised you would show me the way to the center," I teased Jack Dudley when he joined us in the great hall after supper to laugh at the antics of the king's fool, a juggler, and a man who could walk on his hands. "Instead you abandoned me for nearly a week." I pretended to pout.

"I would have found you sooner if we had not been forced to lodge so far away."

Jack and Harry Dudley, and many other late arrivals at Woodstock, had of necessity been billeted at nearby manors. Even one of the king's "great houses" filled up quickly when the entire court assembled.

It was Harry who suggested that we gather together a congenial group, eat our supper while sitting on blankets on the grass near the entrance to the maze, and afterward make the trip to its center together. Besides the Dudley brothers, Mary Woodhull, and Alys Guildford, our little company included Dorothy Bray and two more young gentlemen. Ned Brydges, the oldest at twenty-one, was a gentleman pensioner and an esquire of the king's body. He was a moonfaced young man with blue-black hair and eyes so dark a brown that they appeared to be black, too. He had a little tuft of a beard that I thought looked foolish, but he was quite proud of it and stroked it continually. Davy Seymour was a member of the queen's household. Like Ned, he had a beard, a wispy little thing beneath a trailing mustache, but he'd been blessed with high cheekbones that allowed him to carry it off.

Harry Dudley was the most toothsome of the lot, with his sculpted features and his height and his muscular build. Jack might be nearly as tall as his brother, but he was beanpole thin, all angles and gangly limbs. He was also slightly bowlegged from the endless hours he spent on horseback. I supposed that the rest of him would catch up to his height in time, but for the nonce he was gawky and uncoordinated and I was shallow enough to prefer his older brother's company.

Servants delivered food packed in baskets, and one of the queen's musicians played soft music while we ate. Halfway through our meal, I realized that I knew him. He was Jasper Bassano, the same Venetian musician who had performed at Cowling Castle.

"That's Will Parr's man," I whispered to Alys.

"No longer. The Bassano brothers are the queen's musicians now."

Jasper paid no attention to me, but he watched Dorothy all the while he played, a look of disapproval on his swarthy face. She was oblivious to his scrutiny. She was too busy flirting with Ned Brydges. I was glad that

Jasper left us when we finished our meal. His glower had begun to cast a pall. He took his lute and the empty food basket with him.

"Are you ready for a great adventure?" Harry asked, helping me to my feet.

I grinned up at him. "Lead on."

Jack glared at his brother, but allowed Alys to partner him. They followed Dorothy and Ned into the maze, leaving Davy to escort Mary. Harry and I came last, chatting amiably, in no great hurry to overtake the others. But within moments of entering the hedge maze, my smile faded. I tightened my grip on Harry's arm.

Even though I had seen the maze from the outside and had a vague sense of how large it was, I had expected to be able to see over the plantings. I'd been under the impression that mazes were low, using hyssop or winter savory or germander to lay out the paths. This one rose man high, just like the hedgerow that surrounded Woodstock. It was impossible for any of us, even the tallest of the gentlemen, to peer over the top. Moreover, the royal gardeners had clipped the thick growth of evergreens to make the sides flat and as solid as stone.

Sound was eerily muted. The path was sanded, not graveled, so that we could not even hear our own footsteps. I felt cut off from everything I knew. A deep uncertainty crept over me, the fear that I would never be able to return to the world that lay outside the maze.

Why had I imagined this would be a pleasant walk? I knew the path inside would twist and turn, but I'd reckoned without the shadows and the sense of confinement. I was trapped. Imprisoned by impenetrable green walls.

"Are you sure you know the way out?" I whispered.

Harry freed his arm from the death grip I had on it and slung it around my shoulder. "Would I ever put you in harm's way? Trust me, Bess."

The others were some distance ahead, out of sight. I shivered at the sound of Dorothy's disembodied laughter. My sense of impending doom increased with each step I took.

As we continued along the path, I glanced over my shoulder. Everywhere I looked there were tangled green branches. Only overhead was there open space and, to my dismay, I realized that the day was fast fading into twilight.

"Harry, what if we are still in here when darkness falls? Won't it be impossible to find our way out?"

"Never fear," he whispered, his mouth close to my ear. "If we are obliged to stay in the maze overnight, I will keep you safe and warm."

I pulled free of his grasp, my heart racing. "I want to leave now." I started to run back the way we'd come.

"Bess, wait! Stop! You *will* be lost if you keep going."

A solid mass of evergreen loomed in front of me. I did not understand how it could be there, blocking the path. Had it been there earlier? Wherever it had come from, its presence forced me to choose. Left or right? I had no notion which way led to the entrance.

Harry came up behind me and circled my waist with his hands. "Lost?" he asked, turning me in his arms. His eyes were alight with mischief.

My voice went high and breathy. "How do I get out?" He had only been teasing me about spending the night in the maze . . . hadn't he?

"I'll tell you," Harry said, "for a kiss." His hands slid up from my waist to cup my breasts.

"I'd rather kiss a frog!" Furious with him, I brought one heel down on his foot. It did little damage. I wore soft leather slippers. He had on sturdy boots. But at the same time, I rammed my fist into his stomach.

"Oof!" he cried, and released me.

I backed up as far as I could and stood with both hands fisted. I was so angry with Harry that I momentarily forgot my fear of being trapped in the maze. I began to think more clearly. Our absence would soon be noticed, if it had not been already. Questions would be asked. Jasper Bassano must know we planned to explore the maze. Surely he'd tell Lady Lisle. Even if Harry did not show me the way out, I would soon be rescued.

I glared at Harry. He could not meet my eyes. He shifted his weight from foot to foot and looked embarrassed, as well he should!

"You and Jack told me you knew the way out," I said. "I want to leave now."

"As you wish." He placed his right palm flat against the nearest section of evergreen. "The trick to navigating a maze is to walk so that the face of the hedge is always on the same side. Left or right, it does not matter, so long as you choose one. That will lead you to the center."

"I do not want to go to the heart of the maze. I want to leave it entirely."

"You have to go to the middle first, then use the same method to take you to the exit."

"Why should I believe you?"

He looked offended. "I am not so desperate for a kiss that I'd imprison you here." Keeping his right hand on the wall, he started walking again.

I had to scurry to match his rapid pace. I caught hold of his arm to make him slow down, afraid of losing my guide. "I believe you, Harry. It was just that, for a moment, you reminded me of my brothers when they play tricks on me. George or Thomas would strand me in this maze without a second thought."

"I'd never do such a thing."

"I know that," I said in my most soothing voice, although secretly I had my doubts.

Harmony restored, we made half a dozen more turns before, without warning, we encountered the others in our party coming back. The stricken expression on Jack Dudley's face alarmed me, as did the fact that Mary Woodhull had tears in her eyes. Alys just looked mad enough to spit.

"The maze is separated into islands," she said. "It is impossible to find the center by the usual means."

Taken aback, Harry blurted out, "That cannot be!"

"What does she mean?" I asked. "What are islands?"

It was Jack who answered. "Parts of the hedge have been removed to create sections that go nowhere. When the walls of a maze are all of a piece, no matter how many branches it has, it is always possible to find the center by keeping a hand on the wall. But with this kind of hedge, that will not work."

I glared at him. "I thought you said you knew this maze."

"I've been in mazes before," he mumbled.

"But not *this* one." I did not trouble to hide my exasperation.

"It may be difficult, but surely it will not be impossible to find our way back." Davy Seymour slung a comforting arm around Mary's shoulders and looked gratified when she buried her face in the front of his doublet.

"We could cut our way out," I suggested. "You gentlemen have daggers. We all have our eating knives. Why not just hack a hole in the hedge?"

Everyone stared at me.

"It is a simple and straightforward solution," I said.

But Alys shook her head. "This is a *royal* maze."

"I am certain His Grace will understand."

"His Grace is just as likely to chop off our heads," Harry muttered.

There had to be a means of escape. I thought for a moment. "What if two of you lift a third onto your shoulders? Harry, you are the tallest. If Jack and Davy hoist you high enough, you should be able to see the way we must go to get out."

With Mary acting as spotter, the three gentlemen did a fair imitation of the king's tumblers preparing to fling one of their number into the air. Alys and I stood back to give them room. It was only then that I realized two of our number were missing.

"Where are Ned and Dorothy?"

"Perhaps they found their way to Rosamund's Bower." Alys's smirk told me she was certain they had, and that she had a good idea of what they were doing there to pass the time.

So much, I thought, for my young aunt's devotion to Will Parr.

A cheer went up as Harry, from the top of the pyramid, reported that he had a clear view of the pattern of the maze and could see the shortest way to the exit. A few minutes later, the six of us burst out into the open air, laughing in relief. Jubilant, Harry swung me around and kissed me soundly on the lips.

It was a very nice kiss, and I did not scold him for stealing it. Neither did I permit him to take his celebration any further.

7

At court there was always something to do and always someone to do it with. I flirted with Harry Dudley, and with his brother, and with Davy Seymour, too. Alys and Mary and I spent long hours together in the garden and the gallery and in the queen's presence chamber. From them I learned what persons had influence at court and why some of them were best avoided.

"Be wary of Lady Hertford," Mary warned, pointing out a slender woman in earnest conversation with the queen. "She's the wife of Edward Seymour, Earl of Hertford, elder brother of the late Queen Jane. She likes to get her own way and will trample anyone in her path."

Queen Kathryn was a slightly built woman in crimson velvet worked with gold. Lady Hertford was also small in stature, but she had an arrogant manner that the queen, who might have been expected to put on airs, did not. I studied Lady Hertford's face, what I could see of it from that distance, taking note of a broad forehead, a sharp nose, and a negligible chin. Her form was fine boned and dainty looking.

"She looks too frail to have such a dangerous reputation."

"Do not be deceived by appearances."

"Seymour," I mused, turning away from Lady Hertford so she would not think we were talking about her. "Is Davy kin to the earl?"

"Only a very distant connection. A poor relation, as I am to Her Grace." Mary hid her smile behind plump fingers. "Davy does his best to avoid the countess. He says the earl's first wife was far more pleasant, but she was put aside and her children declared illegitimate."

"A divorce?"

Mary nodded. "And then she died, so he was allowed to remarry."

"The queen is coming this way," Alys whispered, and dropped into a curtsy.

I turned too quickly and almost lost my balance. Her Grace strode toward us between two rows of male courtiers sweeping off their hats and bowing. I hastened to follow Alys's example, as did Mary, and remained in that position until a crimson velvet skirt appeared at eye level.

"Mistress Brooke, I presume?" The queen's voice was soft and melodious and instantly put me at ease.

"Yes, Your Grace." I looked up into luminous hazel eyes. She was queen of England now, but only a few months earlier she'd been just another country-bred gentlewoman like myself.

Queen Kathryn had been blessed with a clear complexion. What I could see of her hair beneath her French hood was a bright reddish gold. She was several inches shorter than I was and just slightly taller than Lady Hertford, who stood next to her, staring at me with unnerving intensity.

"My dear," the queen said, "I hope you are enjoying the pleasures of Woodstock."

"She has already discovered the maze." Lady Hertford's dry voice sent a flutter of alarm coursing through me. How had she known that? And what more did she know?

"I hope you had a guide who knew the way to the center." Queen Kathryn sounded amused. "I was most fortunate in that regard. My lord the king escorted me to Rosamund's Bower."

A sudden image came into my mind—old, infirm King Henry in the legendary lovers' trysting place, forcing his attentions on his bride. I swallowed convulsively and prayed my revulsion was not obvious. "Lady Lisle's sons kindly offered to show me the way, Your Grace. And, as it turned out, my aunt, Mistress Bray, already knew the secret of the maze."

She and Ned Brydges had emerged a full hour after the rest of us made good our escape. Grinning, Ned had assured everyone that they had not been lost. Dorothy had said nothing, but one of the points holding her bodice to her skirt had been broken.

Queen Kathryn evidently knew Dorothy well. Her laugh was a light, musical sound. "I am certain it was a grand adventure," she said before moving on to speak with one of her gentlewomen of the privy chamber. They were distinguished by their livery, gowns of black, double-jean velvet and with the queen's badge pinned to their caps.

A few days later, I encountered the king in the garden. I had seen him several times since arriving at Woodstock, but only from a distance. Most often he'd been sitting next to Queen Kathryn, his heavily bandaged leg resting in her lap.

Alys was walking Rig again, while I kept her company. His Grace entered the gardens, moving slowly, leaning on his staff. He appeared to be debating some weighty issue with one of his courtiers. A half dozen more trailed after them.

"Rig was sick last night," Alys said, pulling my attention back to the spaniel dancing at our feet. "The queen was most distressed."

I looked at the little dog, happily padding along the graveled path, head swiveling left and right at every new sound and scent. "It cannot have been anything serious."

"The greedy little pig ate the king's game pie. All of it."

I smothered a laugh. "I trust His Grace pardoned Rig, else there'd have been a beheading on the spot."

"The queen pleaded for clemency, and His Grace, being still a newly-wed, graciously granted it."

Poor queen, I thought, having to bed that fat old man. I glanced toward King Henry and his entourage and was wise enough not to say such a thing aloud, not even in a whisper. It would doubtless be accounted treason. Instead I opened my mouth to ask Alys about the masque planned for that evening. Before I could get a word out, Rig started to bark. That attracted the king's attention. He made his ponderous way over to us to glare down at the hapless spaniel.

"Take that nasty little beast away," he ordered.

Tugging on Rig's leash, Alys hastened to obey, but when I would have followed, the king laid a heavy hand on my forearm.

"Stay a moment, Mistress Brooke. It has been some time since you last graced our court. You were a beauty then, but now you have surpassed all our expectations."

"Your Grace is too kind." I felt my cheeks heat but my hands went cold as ice. The king might be safely married, but I still did not want him paying too much attention to me.

"Does your brother still study in Italy?" he asked.

I was surprised he remembered that William was in Padua, until I recalled that peers, and their sons, needed the Crown's permission to travel abroad. I recounted what little I knew of William's travels and then, to my great relief, His Grace left me where he'd found me.

8

When the progress ended in late October, the court settled in at Whitehall Palace. Distinguished by its rose-colored brick walls, Whitehall stood at Thamesside just at the curve of that great river. To the east lay London. The old palace of Westminster was a short distance to the south. It had been heavily damaged by fire early in King Henry's reign. Only the Great Hall remained intact and Westminster was no longer used as a royal residence. The two land entrances to Whitehall were towers that straddled the narrow, cobbled road that ran from Charing Cross to Westminster Abbey. Farther to the west was the Palace of St. James, King Henry's "house in the fields," built when Anne Boleyn was queen.

The interior of Whitehall was as great a rabbit warren as I remembered, but I soon learned my way around. I was particularly fond of the queen's gallery, which overlooked the Thames. There was always traffic on the river, an ever-changing panorama of wherries and tilt boats, rowing barges and sailing ships. On clear days, I could see all the way from

Lambeth Palace, just opposite Whitehall on the other side of the river, to London Bridge.

A week after our arrival, I was walking in the gallery with Mary Woodhull when I overheard one of the queen's ladies tell another that Will Parr had returned from the north.

His sudden appearance set tongues wagging. It was customary to wait to be recalled by the king.

"Will he be reprimanded?" I asked Mary.

"With his sister so newly married to the king?" Her eyes danced with merriment. "Cousin Will would have to go out and lead a rebellion before anyone would accuse *him* of putting a foot wrong."

I hoped Mary was correct. The king's temper was uncertain, especially when his leg pained him. Even the queen knew to be wary of His Grace when he was out of sorts.

By the next day, wagering favored Lord Parr remaining in royal favor. It went against the resumption of his courtship of Dorothy Bray.

I'd barely spoken to Dorothy since our sojourn in the maze. I tried to tell myself I did not care if she won Will Parr back or not, but it was a lie. She did not deserve to keep him when she'd been carrying on with another man in his absence.

Two days after Lord Parr's return, Mary and I were again in the queen's gallery. This time Alys was with us. We could not walk for exercise in the garden. Rain fell in cold torrents outside the windows.

"I believe I am going to win my bet with Jack Dudley," Alys said.

"What happened?" Mary asked. Alys had bet Jack a half angel that Dorothy Bray would not be able to entrap Will Parr again.

"I saw Lord Parr's face when Dorothy made so bold as to attempt to drag him behind an arras. He broke free, scowling, and would have naught to do with her."

"Foolish creature," Mary said. "When a man decides he's had enough of a woman, it is pointless to try to change his mind."

"Do not be so certain." I remembered Dorothy's boast that she had

Will Parr wrapped around her little finger. "He was besotted with her once."

We reached the end of the gallery and turned in unison to walk back the other way.

"That was before Ned Brydges," Alys said. "Someone will have told Lord Parr about Ned and Dorothy."

Jasper Bassano, I thought. But I did not underestimate Dorothy's wiles, nor her desire to be Lady Parr. "I wonder," I mused, "given the king's inclination to humor the queen, if His Grace will now permit her brother to remarry, even though his discarded wife still lives."

"It is difficult to guess what His Grace will do," Mary answered, "but if he does allow Lord Parr to wed again, I do not think he will take Dorothy Bray for his bride. A crown says he'll choose someone new."

I did not make any wagers and was glad of it when, later that same day, I accompanied Lady Lisle to the queen's presence chamber to carry her embroidery frame. I brought my own needlework with me to pass the time until we returned to the viscountess's lodgings. To take advantage of what little natural light there was even on this dark, dismal day, I settled myself on a cushion on the floor next to a window. The buzz of conversation and all the other usual noise around me faded away as I concentrated on a new stitch Bridget had taught me. I was unaware that the queen and her brother were nearby until I heard Her Grace speak.

"Your sojourn in the north should have been a means of advancement for you," Queen Kathryn said. "What went wrong?"

"What did not?" Will Parr's familiar voice washed over me like a balmy breeze, soothing and pleasing as it passed . . . until I abruptly realized two things. He sounded desperately unhappy. And he did not know that I could overhear what he must assume was a private conversation with his sister. A large wooden chest hid me from view.

"It began well enough," Will continued. "As you know, I was named lord warden and keeper of the Western Marches toward Scotland last April, well *before* you married the king. I was pleased to have the post.

Lord Lisle urged me to seek the office. The Earl of Hertford supported my appointment. They both said it would give me an opportunity to prove myself to the king and at long last secure the earldom of Essex for myself. I was sure they had the right of it. Was I not given wages for a personal retinue of one hundred soldiers? I arrived in Newcastle upon Tyne fully intending to make a success of myself. I meant to settle in for a long stay."

"Yes, yes," the queen interrupted. "I do know all that. You wrote to me that you chose Warkworth Castle for your chief residence and refurbished it extensively."

Trapped, I stayed still as a mouse. If either of them moved even one step closer to the window, they would stumble over me.

"Warkworth was badly decayed and in desperate need of repairs." A defensive tone came into Will's voice. "It took months just to improve the kitchens, great hall, and living quarters to the point where I could live there comfortably."

"You truly intended a long stay in the north?"

"Can you doubt it? I thought it an excellent post. As it was first explained to me, my only duties were to take musters, carry out reprisal raids, secure redress for Scottish raids during periods of truce, and keep the king and council informed of activities on the border." He made a derisive sound. "In truth, I was no more than a glorified errand boy, passing letters, news, and rumors back and forth. Every time I attempted to do more, or wrote letters to the Privy Council to give the councilors the benefit of my advice, I was reprimanded. I was told it was the lord lieutenant of the North's responsibility to report to the Privy Council, not mine."

"The Duke of Suffolk," Queen Kathryn murmured.

"Yes."

I recognized the title and knew how important that nobleman was. Charles Brandon, Duke of Suffolk, had once been married to the king's sister. His current wife, Catherine, Baroness Willoughby d'Eresby in her own right, was one of Queen Kathryn's inner circle. And Suffolk's daughter, Lady Frances Brandon, the king's niece, Marchioness of Dorset by her marriage to Henry Grey, was often at court.

"The duke is King Henry's oldest friend," the queen said.

"Old is the word for it. The man's in his dotage. It is past time for younger blood to take command."

"That is not your decision to make, Will."

"No decision is, or so it appears. When I turned my attention to local matters, I was once more reined in. I was told that I did not have the authority to judge a murder case unless the accused had also committed treason within the March."

Hearing the bewilderment in his voice, I sympathized. He truly did not understand how his actions had appeared to his superiors. He'd meant well, but his enthusiasm had annoyed men with more experience in the field. He'd needed to take the time to learn the ways of the Scottish border, just as I had needed tutoring in how to behave at court when I'd first arrived. Instead he'd rushed in and tried to impose his own ideas, without stopping to ask why things were done the way they were.

"They accused me of meddling," Will complained, "when all I sought to do was recruit spies among the Scots." He made a short, explosive sound of disgust. "The Scots are barbarians, a crafty and malicious people, always working against His Highness and this realm. Add to that the fact that the lord lieutenant of the North and the Privy Council kept me on leading strings and I never had a prayer of making my reputation north of the Trent."

"But by leaving your post," the queen pointed out in a gentle voice, "you forfeited your opportunity to impress His Grace with your military prowess."

"You know nothing about it!" Now anger laced his words. "There are no great battles left to fight with Scotland, only border skirmishes and cattle raids. There is no opportunity for glory there. I need to be at court. "

"Perhaps if you had stayed just a little longer—"

"Is His Grace displeased to have me here?"

The queen hesitated. "I do not believe so, no."

"Then I see no reason to remain in exile."

I dared shift on my cushion until I could peek around the edge of the chest. The presence chamber was crowded, but no one else was nearby. Even the maids of honor had withdrawn, out of earshot, to allow Her Grace privacy to speak with her brother. Lady Lisle and Lady Hertford stood at the far side of the room, deep in conversation with the Duchess of Suffolk.

Will Parr looked just as I remembered him, with his dark auburn hair close cropped and his beard neatly trimmed. But his bearing betrayed both disillusionment and anger. While his shoulders slumped, his hands were curled into tight fists.

Sister and brother continued their conversation, but in such low voices that I could no longer make out what they were saying. I told myself that was just as well. Will Parr's business was none of mine.

The two were clearly in charity with each other by the time Her Grace bade farewell to her brother with a kiss and a smile. Will Parr remained where he was. I continued to watch him, and saw his benign expression slowly change to a frown. When the queen rejoined her ladies and started toward the door to her privy chamber, he turned slightly, so that he could stare out the window, took a step closer to the glass, and saw me sitting on my cushion on the floor.

We both froze. Warmth flooded into my face

Will cleared his throat. "Mistress Brooke. I did not realize you were there."

"Lord Parr." A little clumsily, I rose to my feet. To my surprise, I saw that we were the only two people left in the presence chamber aside from the liveried yeomen warders on duty as guards. When the queen had collected her ladies and departed, everyone else had gone, too.

"I should go," I said.

He caught my hand. "Not yet. You overheard?"

"I did not wish to intrude," I murmured, shaken yet again by the way his touch sent a jolt of sensation straight to my core.

"That is a pitiful excuse and we both know it."

I squared my shoulders and met his eyes, relieved to find amusement there rather than censure. "I am glad the king is not wroth with you and very happy to have you back at court."

A little of his tension returned. "His Grace rarely deigns to notice me, and he had no trouble at all ignoring the letters I wrote to his Privy Council. You heard me say that, I suppose?"

"I did not intend to spy upon you, Lord Parr, and I will not repeat anything you said to Her Grace."

"Then you are a paragon indeed."

"I know most courtiers love hearing any hint of scandal and are quick to spread rumors, even when they are unfounded, but I swear I will say nothing."

"Why not?" His grip tightened until I winced.

"I would never willingly cause you distress." It was the simple truth, but my passionately spoken words seemed to take him aback. He gazed at me with a new intensity that was most disconcerting.

"I had hoped to renew our acquaintance when I heard you were at court," he murmured. "Tell me, Mistress Brooke, can you think of me as a friend?"

"You are pleasant company," I allowed.

"I strive to be, Mistress Brooke."

When he smiled it was if the sun had come out. He was a well-favored man. There was no denying it. Nor could I deny that I felt the tug of physical attraction when we stood so close.

But no good could come of encouraging a man who already possessed both an estranged wife and a spurned mistress. I tugged my hand free. "Lady Lisle will be looking for me," I blurted out . . . and fled.

9

*I*n November, the court moved to Greenwich Palace, where Bridget and I shared a tiny room off the base court. My mother and sister came for a visit, since Cowling Castle was not very far away. They took rooms for three nights in the nearby Greyhound Inn. While my mother paid her respects to Lady Lisle, Kate and I set off to explore the grounds.

The orchard at Greenwich ran parallel to the tiltyard with the great garden beyond, flanking the road that ran between Rochester and London. There were more apple and cherry trees at Greenwich than there had been at Woodstock. Kent was famous for cherries and for the two varieties of apples known as Kentish codlings and the Flower of Kent.

"That building is a banqueting house," I said, pointing to a structure to the southeast.

Kate paid no attention. "What is that sound?"

Now that she'd called my attention to it, I realized that the rhythmic thump had been audible from the moment we entered the orchard. "It is coming from the tiltyard."

"Is there a tournament?" Eyes bright with anticipation, Kate lifted her skirts and set off in that direction at a pace just short of a run.

"Kate! Wait! We have no business there."

In the manner of younger sisters, she ignored me. I scurried after her, exasperated and amused at the same time. Tournaments were a special event, but contests at arms went on all the time. According to Jack Dudley, only throwing snowballs was a more popular outdoor sport during the winter months.

The stands erected to seat spectators were deserted. Kate appropriated the place where the king and queen usually sat. Since there was no royal canopy overhead, I settled in beside her to watch the action on the field. For a real tournament, this platform would be richly draped with expensive fabric. The wooden benches would be padded with cushions. We made do with hard, unadorned surfaces, but we had an excellent view of a dozen mounted gentlemen.

For practice, some tilted at the quintain, a stuffed figure on a revolving bar. Others took turns charging at a detachable ring affixed to a post, attempting to dislodge it with their lances. A great deal of whooping and hollering accompanied each effort, no matter whether it succeeded or failed.

It was not long before one of the participants noticed us. He nudged his companion and soon all the gentlemen were aware that they were performing for a female audience. They rode faster and took more risks, showing off their skills. I hoped no one would be hurt. They were not wearing full suits of armor, only helmets, breastplates, and cuisses on their legs.

"Do you know any of the competitors?" Kate asked.

"A few. So do you." I pointed out Harry and Jack Dudley. And Will Parr.

When my gaze fell upon Will, he happened to be turned my way. Even at that distance, I could see his lips curve into a smile. A moment later, he abandoned the field to ride over. He reined in his horse, a massive chestnut-colored charger with a white blaze between his eyes, and dipped his lance in my direction.

"Will you honor me with your favor, my lady, to carry into battle?"

I felt as if every eye was fixed upon me, but I looked only at Will as I peeled off one of my gloves and gave it to him. "See that you return it to me undamaged," I admonished him, "else my hand will grow cold." Although the sun shone brightly down on the field, a brisk breeze made the pennants flutter and eddied under cloak and cuff.

"I have heard it said that a cold hand is the sign of a warm heart," Will replied.

"More than a hand will be chilled if you are unseated by the quintain." The revolving arm swung back around after it was struck with a lance. In the short time Kate and I had been watching, it had already knocked one rider clean off his horse.

"I will take especial care, both of my person and your token," Will promised, and rode not to the quintain but into the lists to run at the ring.

When two men competed in a joust, they charged straight at each other without swerving aside. In a practice session, there was no oncoming horse and rider to avoid. Will ran no risk of being hit with violent impact by an opponent's lance, but he still had to manage his own weapon with strength and skill. It took superb eye-arm coordination to run a lance that stood as high as a man through a small metal ring. More than one gentleman missed his target. Most rode past unscathed, but a few rammed their lances into the post instead, with painful consequences.

In common with most other young women, I had been entertained since nursery days with tales of chivalry—stories of bold knights who rescued fair maidens from dragons and other dangers. As I watched Sir William Parr repeatedly pluck the ring from the post and outshine every other competitor at the quintain, too, I could not help but imagine him in that role. He was the embodiment of the ideal hero, destined to vanquish all obstacles in his path.

I knew full well the folly of such daydreams. If the king had meant to free Will from his wife, he'd have done so already. But no matter how sensible my thoughts, I found it impossible to tear my admiring gaze away from the handsome knight who wore my favor.

"Oh, look!" Kate's squeal of delight made me jump.

She was pointing at the Dudley brothers. As I watched, Harry leapt onto his horse after the gray was already running. Then he dismounted and repeated the trick from the other side and from the back. Not to be outdone, Jack mounted and dismounted without using the stirrups, grabbing his big bay by the mane to jump into the saddle. Unable to compete with an older and more experienced jouster in the traditional contests, the two Dudleys sought to attract our attention another way.

Will did not find their antics amusing. I hid a smile when I caught him scowling at them. How could I not feel flattered by his show of jealousy? Nor was I displeased that the Dudley boys were vying for my attention. I was fond of them both and had once or twice allowed Harry more kisses. Truth be told, Harry Dudley was very good at kissing.

When I caught myself wondering how Will Parr's skills in that area would compare, I told Kate it was too cold to remain in the gallery any longer and hustled her back to the safety of Lady Lisle's lodgings.

Neither Lady Lisle nor Mother was there, having gone to visit Queen Kathryn, but a good fire burned in the hearth. I was glad of the opportunity to warm myself. My gloveless hand was chilled to the bone.

Kate was chattering excitedly to Bridget about the "tournament" when Dorothy Bray burst into the room. She came straight at me, eyes flashing with hatred, and gave me a violent shove. I tumbled to the floor on my backside, tangled in a welter of skirts. One flailing hand struck the edge of a chest as I fell. I cried out at the sudden, shocking pain. Cradling my bruised fingers, I glared up at her.

"What was that for?"

She stood over me, fists upraised, looking for all the world as if she'd like to fall on me and beat me senseless. No one else in the chamber moved.

When Dorothy didn't answer, I pushed myself to my feet. "What is the matter with you?"

She called me a vile name.

My eyes widened in shock. "Dorothy, I do not understand why—"

"He doesn't want me anymore," she said in a harsh whisper. "He wants you."

Although there was no question in my mind as to who "he" was, my first impulse was to tell her she was imagining things. Then I remembered the way Will had smiled at me, and the tender way he'd been teasing me only a short time before in the tiltyard.

"You set out to steal him from me. Do not trouble to deny it. I know it's true."

"When did I have an opportunity to set traps for your lover? He's been in the north, far away from both of us."

"You danced with him at Cowling Castle."

"Oh, a great sin, that one! I am sorry if he lost interest in you, Dorothy, but it had nothing to do with me."

"It had everything to do with you. He admitted as much to me before we left Whitehall, when I confronted him and demanded an explanation for his lack of warmth. He said he'll never marry me, that when he is able to wed, he will take an innocent as his bride. Someone *malleable*. No doubt he thinks you will suit him very well!"

Before I could point out that Will Parr's words did not prove he had anyone in mind, let alone me, Dorothy advanced on me again. This time she seized me by the shoulders, using both hands. Her nails bit into my skin, even through the thickness of gown and kirtle. She brought her face so close to mine that I could feel every word as a separate puff of air.

"Whore. Trollop!" She added a few other names I'd never heard before, although I had no doubt about their meaning. "You're a fool, too, if you fall prey to his sweet promises. The king will never grant his petition. Never! There will be no second marriage by royal decree."

Belatedly, Bridget decided it was time to intervene. The older woman cleared her throat. "If a man strikes another in a royal palace when the king is in residence, he can be sentenced to have his hand cut off. Do you suppose the punishment is the same for a woman?"

As abruptly as Dorothy had grabbed hold of me, she let go.

"It is true," Bridget said. "And why should His Grace show you mercy, Mistress Bray, when he does not quail at executing his own wives?"

Face pale, eyes wide, Dorothy turned and fled. I stared after her, my mind awhirl. I'd have pitied her if I'd believed for a moment that she was suffering from a broken heart, but her behavior with Ned Brydges at Woodstock argued against that conclusion. It was thwarted ambition that made her so furious with me, not unrequited love. Ned had yet to attain a knighthood, while Will Parr was already Baron Parr of Kendal.

"What was all that about?" Kate demanded.

"Dorothy has taken leave of her senses."

"She was talking about Lord Parr. And she is right. He does fancy you."

"He may be attracted to my person," I said, smoothing my hands over skirts that did not need any adjustment, "but if he thinks me *malleable*, he does not know me very well." Did he think he could fashion me into the perfect, biddable mate? I was not a lump of clay to be molded. I looked up to find Bridget watching me. "You are not to say a word about this to Lady Lisle or to my mother," I told her. "There is no truth to Dorothy Bray's accusations. And even if there were, I would never be cozened by empty promises." I would never, I told myself, make the same mistakes Dorothy had.

Bridget sent me a skeptical look, but agreed to keep silent. Soon after, she went out to run an errand for Lady Lisle, leaving me alone with my little sister.

"Will Parr wants you, Bess," Kate said, "and I saw the way you watched him at the tiltyard." She giggled.

"I was admiring his athletic prowess. I admired Jack and Harry, too. And . . . and I've *kissed* Harry."

"Do you want to marry Harry Dudley?"

"I do not want to marry anyone. At least, not yet."

"Harry is young and virile." Kate lifted one hand, then the other, as if to imitate weighing relative merits on a scale. "But Lord Parr is wealthy. And pleasing to look at, even if he is old."

"He is hardly ancient! And any woman with sense much prefers a man to a boy." A wave of heat climbed into my face. Annoyed by my lack of control—it seemed to me that I blushed much too easily of late—I reminded both Kate and myself of the one thing that must stop me from encouraging Will Parr's suit, even if I wanted to accept him. "He is married, Kate. So long as he already has a wife, he has nothing honorable to offer me."

10

The good weather held after Mother and Kate left for home. The following day the entire royal household—or so it seemed—rode out into the open country between Greenwich and the smaller royal palace of Eltham to go hawking. This was one of the king's favorite pastimes. The mews at Greenwich were located in the inner court, separated from His Grace's bedchamber by only one room. He kept his falcons closer to him than he did the queen.

I rode my own horse, Prancer, and attended Lady Lisle, but I did not have a hunting bird on my glove. I was happy not to. Their beaks were sharp and their talons sharper.

Will Parr dropped back to ride beside me. He doffed his bonnet, a marvelous creation of dark green velvet with a white plume. "Mistress Brooke. You look especially fine this morning."

"As do we all. My mother always says there is nothing like a brisk ride on a chilly day to put roses in one's cheeks."

"You far outshine every other damsel present."

"If you grow too flowery in your speech, sir, I will not believe a word you say."

"So practical for one so young." Amusement shone in his expressive light brown eyes.

"You do well to note that quality in me. I am quite set in my ways. I have not a *malleable* bone in my body."

Prancer shied away from Will's mount at that moment, preventing me from seeing his reaction. I couldn't tell if he remembered what he'd said to Dorothy. Had he made the remark at all? It would be just like my dear aunt to lie to me. If she couldn't have Will for herself, she wouldn't want anyone else to have him, either.

Will turned the subject to the newest fashion in sport—shooting ducks with a handgun in the marshes near Greenwich. He had accompanied the king on such an expedition a few days earlier. This topic sufficed until we began to follow a trail through a wooded copse.

When Will abruptly fell silent, I realized we had entered a small clearing and that, by chance or design, we'd become separated from the rest of the hunting party. Will put his hand on the pommel of Prancer's saddle and brought both horses to a stop.

"I do not think I knew what love was until I met you, Bess." He spoke in a quiet voice and his words were all the more potent for being so simple.

"You scarcely know me."

"I know enough."

Although my heart swelled with pleasure, I forced myself to answer in a cold and haughty tone. "More likely you are the sort of man who falls in and out of love at the drop of a hat."

"Never!"

"It was not so long ago that you were eager as a lapdog for my aunt's smallest favor."

His lips tightened. I reminded myself that it would be best if he took me in dislike. He invaded my dreams far too often as it was, and I had begun to have difficulty putting thoughts of him out of my mind during waking hours.

"I was under a spell," Will said after a long, tense moment. "Dorothy used her woman's wiles on me until I could no longer remember my own name."

I looked at him askance. "When you first met her, she was a girl younger than I am now, and you had long since attained your majority. You were no green lad to—"

"She was never as innocent as you are, Bess."

I bit my lip to keep from blurting out that I was no innocent. He would misunderstand. I *was* innocent in the way he meant. I had never lain with a man, never been the recipient of any greater attention from one than a few enthusiastic kisses. But I knew what men and women did in private when they yielded to lust. Both Mother and Aunt Elizabeth had described the act of coupling to me in frank terms, warning me that I must not give myself to any man before marriage, no matter how much I might want to.

"You wrote love letters to Dorothy," I said.

"One or two," he admitted.

"She said—"

"What? That I promised her marriage? How could I?"

"But you came to Cowling Castle to see her."

"I came to solicit your father's support in Parliament. I did not even know she was there until after I arrived."

My hand clenched so hard on Prancer's reins that the horse shied. Will turned his mount so that we were facing each other. Everything he felt was there for me to see in his face. When he spoke again, I could no longer doubt his sincerity.

"I want to marry you, Bess. Why does that so surprise you?"

"We can count on one hand the number of occasions we have spoken together." I tried to urge Prancer forward, out of the clearing, but she was skittish, sensing the conflicted emotions of her rider. "And how can you marry me? You are not free to marry anyone."

Once again he caught hold of the pommel. "Is the idea so repulsive to you?" His teasing smile told me that he knew it was not.

"Have you forgotten that you already have a wife?" This time my attempt at coldness failed utterly. My voice shook.

"That marriage was declared invalid by a special act of Parliament."

"But your wife is still alive. You cannot wed again as long as she lives. I hope you do not plan to murder the poor woman." I made the suggestion without thinking, but in the next instant I realized how simple a matter it would be to do away with an unwanted spouse. "You must not even consider such a thing! If any harm came to her because of me, I should never forgive myself."

His smile turned into a scowl. "She betrayed me with another man!"

"And you betrayed your marriage vows with Dorothy. And no doubt with others, too." A man as well favored as Will Parr had never lived celibate at court.

"I will not lie to you, Bess. I wish Anne were dead." At last he released the pommel. "But I will do nothing to hasten her end. I swear it."

Now it was my turn to reach out to him. An overwhelming need to know more had me touching his forearm with my fingers. "Will you tell me about her?"

"You . . . you want to know about Anne Bourchier?"

I nodded. How else could I understand Will?

His reluctance was palpable, but so was my determination. Resigned, he dismounted and lifted me from my saddle. The clearing contained a large, flat-topped boulder, just the right height to serve as a bench. In the distance I heard the occasional shout, but the hawking party had moved on.

Will spread his cloak over the boulder to protect us from the chill of the stone. Just his nearness was enough to warm me. And his willingness to share his past did more to convince me of his sincerity than any of his pretty words of love.

"My mother was ambitious for her children," he began when we were settled side by side on the hard surface of the rock. "She was widowed young, but she was one of Queen Catherine of Aragon's ladies. Thus she was able to arrange a match for me with the only child of the old Earl of Essex. The expectation was that I would be granted his title when he died. I married Anne Bourchier when we were both children. She was barely ten years old. I was fifteen."

I nodded. I'd learned that much from listening at the peephole in Cowling Castle.

"After the wedding, I did not see her again for twelve years. In the interim I served in the household of the king's bastard, Henry Fitzroy, Duke of Richmond, God rest his soul. There I was surrounded by great music, and the art of the finest painters and sculptors, and books of every kind. Anne knew nothing of such pleasures. She had been given little education of any sort. We had nothing to say to each other when I finally went to live with her in her father's house."

"Many couples lack common interests," I murmured.

Will's voice, normally so deep and melodious, lapsed into a mono-tone. "We lived together as man and wife, but even in bed we found no joy in each other. There was no spark between us. Anne is pretty enough, in a whey-faced, bone-thin fashion, but she is delicate. She did not care for what she called my rough ways." He gave a self-deprecating laugh. "No one else has ever complained. I must assume the fault lies with her."

And yet, I thought, she took a lover. I might be physically attracted to Will Parr, but I had not entirely lost my common sense. "Men never take the blame in such matters."

Where another man would have taken offense, my comment made Will laugh. "Do you reproach me for my lack of sympathy? I assure you, Bess, I did my best. I was tender with her. After all, a man needs an heir."

He shifted on the rock until we were pressed together at hip and thigh. I eased away. I was certain he was a talented lover, but I was not fool enough to allow him to demonstrate his skills. Should he get a child on me, the babe would not be his heir, but only his bastard.

Resuming his story, Will stared into the surrounding woods. "She did not conceive, and by the time I was called away to court, I was glad to go. We've lived apart ever since, and when the old earl died, to add insult to injury, the king bestowed the Essex title upon Lord Cromwell."

"And you remained at court and took my aunt as your mistress. Dorothy thought you intended to marry her."

"I *want* to remarry." Will caught both my hands in his. A wave of heat flowed up my arms. "I want to marry *you*, Bess. It is not impossible. I have taken steps to repudiate my wife. Parliament granted me a legal separation on the grounds of her adultery. The children Anne has borne have been barred from succeeding to her inheritance."

"*Her* inheritance?" For a moment, I thought I'd misunderstood. It made sense that children who were not Will's be prevented from inheriting *his* estates. But a wife, even an unfaithful one, was supposed to be protected from penury by the grant of her dower rights. I could not help but remember the way Sir Thomas Wyatt the Elder had treated Aunt Elizabeth. "Do you mean to leave her impoverished?"

Will did not seem to understand my objection. "Anne ran off with another man. The prior of St. James in Tandridge, in Surrey. She had *children* by him."

"Have you left your wife destitute?" I asked again.

"She has enough to live on. She will not starve."

"An earl's daughter? She must have been accustomed to luxury."

"You cannot think I did wrong to disown her bastards!"

The anguish in Will's voice made my heart stutter in my breast. My feelings for him were so intense, so overwhelming, so complex that I found myself unable to condemn him. "I wonder if she is happy with her choice," I said instead, "for she cannot remarry any more than you can."

"A royal decree will free me to wed again. My sister has promised her help. And the Essex earldom, in abeyance since Cromwell's execution, will also be mine. The investiture ceremony is set for the twenty-third day of this month."

"You will have the title," I agreed, "but the right to acquire a countess is by no means certain. Without the assurance of marriage, how can I permit you to court me?"

"Will you banish me from your company?"

"I cannot," I admitted. "I . . . care for you, too, Will." And we were both at court. Meetings were inevitable. "But—"

He stopped further protest with a kiss. His lips were soft but firm and oh so talented. Lost in sensation, I kissed him back. If he had been a less honorable man, he could have taken me there on that rocky surface. I'd not have resisted. Instead, he let me go.

"We had best rejoin the others." His husky voice and the light caress of his gloved knuckles along my cheek made me shiver with desire.

I managed to nod and I stood on legs that did not want to hold my weight.

"We will speak of this again," he promised as he lifted me into my saddle.

11

In mid-December, with Yuletide fast approaching, the king and queen moved to Hampton Court. There the queen's apartments were located on the east side of the inner court. The queen's privy kitchen and her wardrobe were on the ground floor, linked by a small spiral stairway to the chambers above. Heat from the kitchen helped warm the upper rooms. Unfortunately, cooking odors also made their way in. The sweet-smelling herbs Queen Kathryn ordered strewn on the floors did not quite mask the smells of roasting meat and, on occasion, burnt sauces.

Alys, Mary, and I sat and wrought in the presence chamber. I had nearly finished embroidering the collar of a linen shirt with silver thread, my New Year's gift for the king. For the queen I had used my modest winnings at cards to purchase a pair of white stockings embossed in gold. "I wonder what Queen Kathryn intends to give His Grace," I said.

"I've no idea," Alys said. "Do you know what Lord Parr plans as a gift for the queen's grace?"

"A crossbow case and a dozen crossbow strings," I replied without thinking. The queen was an excellent shot with a crossbow. Will had mentioned it the previous day. I looked up to find both Mary and Alys grinning at me. "What?"

"It is no secret that he pursues you, Bess."

"Catching me is another matter entirely! He has a wife, Alys. He cannot offer me an honorable marriage."

I told myself so daily. We had seen each other often since the hunt, but always in company, and I'd taken pains since our arrival at Hampton Court to spend as much time with Harry Dudley as I did with Will. Harry had been happy to oblige me. We'd danced together, been partners at cards, and gone for long walks in the gardens . . . during which I'd spent far too much time comparing Harry to Will, to Harry's detriment.

Alys lowered her voice. "Why not enjoy him for your pleasure, then? Is there any man more charming or better to look at in all of the court?"

"A dozen at least," I lied. "Your cousins the Dudleys, and Ned Brydges, not to mention Davy Seymour. And if you prefer older gentlemen, there are many to choose from, too." I rattled off a half dozen names at random.

Alys laughed and launched into a wickedly accurate, slightly ribald analysis of each of those gentlemen's attractions. Mary and I laughed so hard that Lady Hertford temporarily banished us from the presence chamber for making too much noise.

That same evening, as Lord Lisle was leaving his wife's lodgings, he paused to send a piercing stare my way. I had little to do with the viscount, although he often visited Lady Lisle in the evening. Harry took after his father for looks, although Lord Lisle had a more prominent nose and wore a forked beard that called attention to his heavy underlip. I shifted uncomfortably under his scrutiny and was glad when he continued on his way without speaking to me.

A short time later, Lady Lisle bade me sit beside her by the fire. "My lord tells me that Lord Parr has spoken to him about you, Bess. He hopes to make you his wife."

I sighed. "He says he is in love with me."

"Has he spoken to your father?"

"I doubt it."

"No, I do not suppose he has. I feel sorry for the man, Bess, but he's not for you."

I bristled at her tone but I nodded. "I know. He is already married."

"And you have more suitable prospects near at hand. My own son, for example."

"I . . . I enjoy Harry's company. And Jack's, too."

"But Harry is his father's heir." Lady Lisle pursed her lips. I was certain she was about to say that he could look higher than a baron's daughter for a wife. She surprised me. "I would be pleased to have you as my daughter, should matters fall out that way. I hope you already count me as a second mother."

"I do, my lady. And if I am not too bold, I would like to count you as my friend as well."

My parents, I knew, would be delighted if I made a match with either of the Dudley sons, but how could I agree to marry either one when I had such strong feelings for Will Parr?

"I have four more boys at home," Lady Lisle continued, "Ambrose, Robert, Guildford, and our second Henry. They are all younger than you are, but that is of little importance when it comes to making alliances."

"I do not believe I would care to be married to a child."

"And I am certain you are in no hurry to wed. There are many unmarried girls your age and older here at court."

The transition was so smooth it slid past me without causing a ripple of disquiet. Only later did I realize that she'd warned me against rushing into *any* alliance.

12

The king kept his word. He made Will Parr Earl of Essex. He also put him in charge of the gentlemen pensioners, the fifty gently born men assigned to guard His Grace's person at court. Will's new duties kept him busy throughout January and into February. I spent far more time with Harry Dudley, but it was Will who was most often in my thoughts.

Life at court continued to offer a wide variety of activities. Women did not play at tennis or bowls, but we were welcome as spectators. And everyone turned out to witness spectacles. On a Sunday in mid-February, Queen Kathryn entertained her first important foreign guest, Don Juan Estaban Manriquez de Lara, third Duke of Najera. I joined the other courtiers crowded into the queen's watching chamber, eager to see what amusements Her Grace would provide.

Soft music played in the background, provided by the Bassano brothers. When I glanced his way, Jasper Bassano winked at me. I hid a smile. If I were to choose a suitor purely by his appearance, I decided, I'd have to add Jasper to my list of candidates. His exotic looks had an undeniable allure.

The Spanish duke was escorted by two English earls. One was Will, looking very fine in black velvet embroidered in silver and sparkling with jewels. The other was Henry Howard, the poetry-writing Earl of Surrey. I had heard that he had regained the king's favor, but this was the first time I had seen him at court.

I studied him with interest, remembering that Will had told me they had been educated together in the late Duke of Richmond's household. I remembered something else, too—that Surrey had led my cousin, Tom Wyatt, into a drunken rampage that had led to a lengthy imprisonment for poor Tom.

Surrey had a pleasing appearance. His hair and beard were auburn, his eyes hazel. His face, a perfect oval, was dominated by full, sensuous lips, but there was an arrogance about him, a certain air of self-importance, that I could not like. I wondered that others were not put off by that su-perior manner, but perhaps they had grown accustomed to his attitude. Or else they accepted without question his innate superiority. Surrey's father was the Duke of Norfolk, one of the most powerful noblemen in the land. No doubt he had been raised from the cradle to think that the Howards were second only to the Tudors.

The queen advanced, smile radiant, to greet her noble guests. She wore heavily brocaded crimson. Two crosses and a brooch, all studded with diamonds, caught the light. Her robe was cloth-of-gold and had a train more than two yards long. She was flanked by the two highest-ranking ladies in the land, her stepdaughter, Princess Mary, and King Henry's niece, Lady Margaret Douglas, the daughter of his older sister.

I had glimpsed both royal ladies before but had paid little attention to either. Now I noticed only that both bore a strong resemblance to the king in his younger days—the king of the portrait at Cowling Castle. Their Graces were much smaller physically, but the Tudor features, from reddish hair to piercing stare, bred true. Like the queen, they glittered with jewels.

Looking dazzled, the Duke of Najera kissed Queen Kathryn's hand.

After the initial greetings were over, the queen led the company into her presence chamber. She seated herself in a brocade-covered chair beneath a canopy of brocade and bade the duke sit, too, that they might enjoy an evening of music and dancing. Although Queen Kathryn did not speak Spanish and the duke's command of English was poor, they managed to converse in French and Latin, with the occasional assistance of the Earl of Surrey, who was, it appeared, fluent in Spanish.

I shifted my attention to the Earl of Essex—to Will. His gaze swept over the gathered courtiers, stopping when he found me. At his first opportunity, he slipped away from queen, duke, and earl and made his way to my side.

"It has been too long," he said. "I have missed you, Bess."

"You knew where to find me," I reminded him, painfully aware that every word we spoke could be overheard.

"The king has kept me too busy to do anything but follow his commands. And for the last five days, I have been almost constantly in the Duke of Najera's company. Surrey and I met him upon his arrival and have been providing diversions for him ever since."

"What entertainments did you produce?" I asked, once again recalling that Surrey had a penchant for breaking merchants' windows and rioting through the streets.

"We visited the menagerie in the Tower of London."

"I did not know there was such a place."

"It is scarce worth the time to see four lions and two leopards. The poor beasts are confined behind wooden railings, but they do not look very fierce. We also took the duke to Paris Garden for the bear baiting."

I wondered if they had made any other stops in Southwark, an area notorious for its whorehouses.

"Then today," Will continued, "we dined with Najera and brought him to court. He had a brief interview with the king before we came here."

Applause interrupted us. The queen had called upon Jasper Bassano to dance. As always, he was a marvel of agility, executing the steps in what the Spaniards called the *gallarda* so lightly that he seemed to have wings on his feet.

I sighed in appreciation. "What a beautiful man."

"He is a *musician*."

"Jealous?" I sent him a teasing look. "I think you are beautiful, too."

Before he could respond, Queen Kathryn called to him to lead her out for the first pavane.

I did not lack for partners when the general dancing began. Harry Dudley was the first of many. Midway through the evening, I even danced with that august personage, the Earl of Surrey, but he seemed less interested in me than in watching Lady Hertford. I had to admit that she was an attractive woman, and an excellent dancer, but she was somewhat older than Surrey and she did have that reputation as a shrew. I could not imagine what it was about her that so fascinated him. When she noticed him staring, she shot back a look of pure loathing.

"Does Lady Hertford's husband disapprove of Surrey's antics?" I asked Davy Seymour when he requested the next dance, "Or is it the lady herself who dislikes him?"

Davy was kin to Edward Seymour, Earl of Hertford. He gave a bark of laughter. "She despises both the man and his poetry. On another evening such as this, she refused his invitation to dance. He retaliated in verse, a poem wherein a wolf acts 'with spite and disdain' to a lion, although she is an interloper of the most common sort and the lion's antecedents are far superior."

"An allegory, I presume?" The music began and I curtsied.

Davy bowed deeply in response. "And not a very subtle one. The Seymour family seat is called Wulf Hall, while a white lion is one of the Howard family's emblems."

I stole another glance at the Earl of Surrey as I danced. He chatted with the Duke of Najera and Queen Kathryn. Although he stood a step below them, as was proper, everything about him shouted that he considered himself their equal, perhaps even their better. I thought him very foolish to be so bold.

The evening ended when the queen ordered that gifts be brought forth to present to the duke. After accepting them, Najera kissed Queen

Kathryn's hand in parting and asked if he might be permitted to also kiss Princess Mary's hand. The king's daughter laughed and offered him her lips instead.

Mary Tudor was no beauty, but she had a pleasing appearance, with a clear complexion, regular features, dark red-gold hair, and a slender build. Najera was happy to comply. Then he declared that he must bid farewell in the same manner to every other lady present. Amid much laughter and goodwill he made his way around the presence chamber.

I was awaiting my turn when Will suddenly reappeared at my side. Without a by-your-leave, he hauled me into a nearby alcove. "You'll kiss no man but me," he whispered, and caught my lips with his.

This was no gentle wooing but rather a full-scale assault on my senses. His hands swept down my back to caress my bottom and pull me tight against his hardness. His tongue teased the seam of my mouth until I let him in. Thrilled, I reveled in his masterful lovemaking. The feel and smell of him surrounded me, wrapping me in a cocoon that blocked out everything else. I wanted that wickedly wonderful moment to last forever, but it was not to be.

Will released me. "I must go," he whispered.

Leaving me dazed and shaken, he rejoined the Spaniard's party. I touched trembling fingers to my lips. With that display of possessiveness and need, Will had stolen much more than a kiss. I'd lost my heart to him . . . and perhaps my soul.

13

For months after that evening, I was never alone with Will for more than a few moments at a time. Frequent moves from one royal palace to another—fifteen of them between January and May—put some of the barriers in our path. But my greatest rival was war with France. King Henry was determined upon invasion and Will was deeply involved in the preparations.

On the twentieth day of March, Lord Lisle visited his wife's lodgings to bid her farewell. "I leave in the morning for Harwich," he announced. He was King Henry's lord admiral, and his flagship, together with most of the fleet, waited there to embark. The first expedition would be against Scotland, since the Scots always attacked England when England invaded France. Lord Lisle's orders were to take the ships north to join the Earl of Hertford's land forces. They intended to make a preemptive strike.

Lady Lisle received the news in her usual placid manner. "Is all in readiness, my dear? Have you everything you need?"

His full lips twitched. "This is not my first campaign, Jane."

"Nor will it be the last. What of Harry? War is new to him."

My hand stilled in the middle of embroidering a rose and I glanced up in time to see Lord Lisle frown. Lady Lisle's gaze had returned to her stitches but, like mine, her fingers were no longer moving. Lord Lisle placed a comforting hand on her shoulder.

"Harry has been trained for war. He is eager for the opportunity to prove his mettle."

"To risk his life, you mean." Abruptly, Lady Lisle's calm shattered. "I am surprised you do not take Jack, as well."

"Next time," Lisle said in all seriousness.

His wife burst into tears.

"Jane?" Lisle backed up a step. "What is the matter?"

Jane Lisle bolted for the inner room, closely followed by her bewildered spouse. I started to go after them, but Bridget caught my arm.

"Let them be," she said. "My lady has something of importance to tell her lord."

I sat down again, braced for an emotional scene. No wife who cared for her husband and son could fail to be upset when they went off to war. I was worried myself about Will, and for that matter about Harry and Davy and my father. Men died in battle, but they never seemed to be concerned about that possibility beforehand. They actually looked forward to risking their lives in combat.

I took up my needle again, but Bridget and I could hear every word Lady Lisle said to her husband.

"I am going to have another child," she announced. "It is due in September."

"Excellent news!"

To judge by the soft rustling sounds that followed, Lord Lisle took his wife in his arms and she nestled against him. I felt heat creep into my cheeks as I continued to stitch. It should not surprise me that they shared intimacies. Lady Lisle had conceived eleven children in the last eighteen years. But the thought of them going to their naked bed made me uncomfortable. They were so old! Was it truly possible they could derive as much excitement and pleasure from kissing and coupling as did people my own age?

When low moans and hushed whispers issued from the inner chamber, I had my answer. I sighed, longing for Will, dreaming of the day when he could carry me off to bed and show me the delights of wedded bliss.

14

In a battle at Leith in May, the Scots were soundly defeated. Right after that, all the English troops were ordered to Calais for the invasion of France. Even the Earl of Surrey went, at the head of his own company. And my father, who had been in Scotland, attached to the Earl of Hertford, was appointed lord deputy of Calais.

In late June, Lord Lisle and his son returned to court, which was then at Greenwich Palace, so that they could travel to France in the king's retinue. Harry Dudley sought me out soon after they arrived.

"Walk with me," he invited, and we set off on the path along the riverfront. The Thames was crowded with large ships. A few were headed upstream to London with the usual cargoes, but most were part of the Royal Navy on their way out to sea to join the fleet.

Harry regaled me with stories of his time in Scotland and I could tell he was looking forward to the coming campaign against France. He expected to return home with a knighthood.

"I am to leave soon, too," I said. "Your lady mother intends to retire to Halden Hall to await the birth of her child." She was not the only one of the queen's inner circle who was breeding. Lady Hertford had gone to her new house near Richmond, called Sheen after the religious house that had once stood there, and Lady Herbert—sister to both Will Parr and Queen Kathryn—was at Hanworth Manor, one of the queen's dower properties, for her lying-in.

Harry made a face. "One more addition to the brood. I'd have thought there were enough of us already. Will you miss life at court?"

"I like being at the center of things, but with all you gentlemen off fighting the war, the court will be a very dull place."

"Not even Jack is staying." Harry scooped up a flat rock and sent it skimming across the water.

"Is he bound for France, too?" Jack would be pleased if that were so. He'd chafed at being left behind when his father and brother set off for Scotland.

"Have you not heard?" Harry asked with a slightly superior air that annoyed me. "Prince Edward is to have his own establishment at Hampton Court. Jack has been assigned to His Grace's new household."

"That is a great honor," I said, although I suspected that Jack would have preferred to go and fight. The prince was only six years old, the same age the Duke of Richmond had been when Will Parr joined his household.

We reached the dock, turned, and started back the way we had come.

"Will you miss me, Bess?" Harry asked, suddenly serious.

"I am sure I will think of you as often as you think of me," I quipped.

"Give me something before I go, then, to keep you daily in my thoughts."

"A token? What would you have? I suppose I could cut off a lock of my hair, or—"

Harry caught my hand to pull me to a halt. When he took me in his arms and lowered his head, I went up on my toes to kiss him. He'd been practicing, I thought, enjoying the feel of his lips moving expertly on mine.

"Lie with me, Bess," he whispered.

I jerked back.

"Just one time before I leave. What if I die in battle without our ever knowing the joy of coupling?"

That he was risking his life in a war frightened me, but I sent him off to France with no more than another kiss or two and a few stolen caresses to remember me by.

15

The king's retinue left for Calais on the ninth day of July. It included Lord Lisle, Harry Dudley, and Will Parr. I found no opportunity to say farewell to Will in private. Indeed, I did my best to avoid being alone with him. The temptation I could resist with Harry would have been impossible to overcome with Will.

For months, I had told myself repeatedly that it was foolish to waste my life pining for a man I could not marry. It was not as if I could not live happily with another. Harry Dudley and I would suit very well. When he returned from France, I might even tell him so. But at the public parting of the king and queen, it was not Harry I looked for, but Will.

He stood well back in the crowd of courtiers, while I was at the rear of the queen's contingent. And yet he must have felt me staring at him. When he turned his head my way, our eyes locked. Tears blinded me before I finally forced myself to look away.

Once the king was gone, Queen Kathryn, who would serve as His Grace's regent in his absence, moved from Greenwich to Whitehall. The Earl of Hertford and other councilors left behind to advise her went along. Lady Lisle and I set off in the opposite direction, journeying into Kent, where Lady Lisle's younger children awaited us at Halden Hall.

Ambrose was the oldest of those still at home. At fourteen, he was about three years junior to Jack. Mary, nearly thirteen, came next, then Robert, who had just passed his twelfth birthday. Guildford—called Gil by the family—was a year younger than Robert. The second child to be christened in honor of the king, called Henry to distinguish him from Harry, was eight. Lady Lisle had given birth to four other children, too, but they had died.

The Dudleys were a lively lot, barely kept in check by their tutors. To my surprise, young Mary shared her brothers' lessons. I confess that I envied her. When I'd told Father that I wanted to learn everything my brother William did, he'd declared that it was unnecessary for a girl to master more than simple ciphering and the ability to read and write. Even the latter skill was considered extravagant by some noblemen, since there were always clerks available to pen letters for ladies.

Messages from France arrived almost daily at Halden Hall. We rejoiced at the news of the fall of Boulogne to our English troops. I was relieved to learn that no one I knew had been killed in the fighting.

A week later a royal messenger brought a letter to Lady Lisle. She read it in her bedchamber, where she had already been sequestered in anticipation of the birth of her child. All the curtains were pulled tight across shuttered windows, not to keep out the unseasonably cold weather but because tradition dictated that a noblewoman in childbed should be protected from the harmful outside air. Such dark, oppressive surroundings disturbed me, as did seeing Lady Lisle so pale and bloated, but I was careful to hide my uneasiness.

"The queen has asked for you, Bess," Lady Lisle informed me. "She has an opening in her household and wishes you to fill it. Dorothy Bray has married Edmund Brydges and can no longer serve as a maid of honor."

"Ned *married* her?"

"So it seems." Lady Lisle absently massaged her bulging belly, making me wonder if Dorothy had caught a child. "The queen is currently on progress in Surrey and Kent with the royal children. You are to join her at Eltham Palace at the end of the month. In the meantime, if you wish, you may spend a few days with your family. At present they are at Cobham Hall with my dear friend, the senior Lady Cobham."

Although my parents and siblings lived for most of the year at Cowling Castle, they left it periodically to allow for a thorough cleaning. At those times, they often visited my father's stepmother at Cobham Hall, which had been left to her for life by my grandfather. The house had originally been built as a hunting lodge and was located in the center of a park well stocked with deer.

"My father is still in Calais," I said.

"And likely to remain there for some time," Lady Lisle said. "The lord deputy usually resides there. If we were not at war, your mother would no doubt have joined him."

It was difficult to imagine Mother living anywhere but Kent, but I did not contradict Lady Lisle. Nor did I refuse the opportunity to visit my family. The entire household gathered to welcome me to Cobham Hall. They already knew that I was to become a maid of honor and everyone was pleased for me, especially Kate. I could tell she was only waiting until we were alone to pepper me with questions.

I had brought gifts and greetings from Lady Lisle, including a fan made of black ostrich feathers set in gold for the senior Lady Cobham, as Lady Lisle had called her. I had never been able to think of her as my grandmother. She was much too young. But she was certainly family. She'd married my grandfather, one of her brothers had married my mother's sister, and her mother had been married, as her second husband, to one of my father's brothers.

There were less spectacular presents for Mother and my brothers and Kate, and then everyone had questions about life at court. It was late before Kate and I finally retired to the bedchamber we shared.

"Do you think Lady Lisle will have me in your place, Bess?" Kate asked the moment the door closed behind us. "I am more than old enough to leave home."

"Mother can ask her, but are you sure you want to join her household now? Not only is she away from court, but she is awaiting the birth of a baby."

Kate made a face. She no more liked the idea of being trapped in a dark room than I did.

Together we flung open the window.

"If there are evil vapors in the night breezes," I said, "I am prepared to ignore them."

Kate laughed.

All the moonlight revealed were acres of parkland and a massive oak tree that grew close to the house. It had the greatest girth I'd ever seen. I'd been told it was more than a century old.

"Did anyone tell you about the wedding?" Kate asked as we rested our elbows on the casement and breathed deeply of the cool September air. "Mother is still reeling from the shock."

"Lady Lisle told me Dorothy married Ned Brydges."

"Not Dorothy's wedding. Grandmother Jane's."

"Grandmother Jane's what?"

"Grandmother Jane's *wedding*. She married right after Dorothy did. She said she'd only been waiting until the last of her children was provided for to choose a husband for herself."

"But she's *old*!" Grandmother Jane had lived for more than six decades. I did not know anyone older than she was.

"That's what makes her choice all the more astonishing. She picked Sir Urian Brereton. He's a younger son with no particular fortune or prospects. And, Bess—he's at least twenty years younger than she is!"

Shock kept me silent, but inside my head were thoughts I'd never had before, half-formed ideas about love and companionship and the many long years that stretched out before a couple after they married. "I think I envy Grandmother Jane," I murmured.

"Because she *could* choose?"

I nodded.

"She has to pay a fine," Kate said, "for marrying without the king's permission. And her son is furious with her."

"He's probably envious, too. He had to wed where he was told to."

Two days later, news arrived from Halden Hall that Lady Lisle had been delivered of her twelfth child, a girl she had named Temperance. Both mother and daughter were in excellent health.

The remainder of my week at Cobham Hall sped by, enlivened by games with my youngest brothers and visits from neighbors and friends. We all traveled back to Cowling Castle together but I spent only one night there before setting out for Eltham Palace and my new post as a maid of honor.

The queen welcomed me warmly, as did the young women with whom I would now be sharing the maid's dormitory. I already knew them all, Alys Guildford and Nan Bassett better than the rest. It was Nan, the oldest of the group, who took me aside for a word of warning.

"You owe your appointment to the queen's brother," she said. "He heard of Dorothy Bray's plans to marry and asked this boon of Her Grace before he left for France. But that does not mean you should follow Dorothy's example and creep out of your bed at night to meet a lover."

"I am not Dorothy, and I do not believe that Her Grace would honor me with this post if she believed I was."

Nan fixed me with a steady stare. "Remember that your first loyalty is to Queen Kathryn. You took an oath to serve her faithfully and to abide by her wishes, whatever they might be."

I frowned after her as she walked away. Had Nan been telling me that it was the queen's wish that I discourage her brother's interest? Or was that just a friendly bit of advice, given to any new-made maid of honor? I supposed it did not matter. After all, Will was still in France.

16

King Henry returned from his French war in the first week in October to a grand and glorious reunion at one of his lesser houses, a place called Otford. Will was with him, but His Grace had left Lord Lisle and Harry behind in Boulogne, along with most of the army. They were to hold that captured city for England.

Davy Seymour also returned with the king. He brought with him a letter for me from Harry.

"His handwriting is as poor as mine is," I observed.

Alys sat beside me on a window seat in the queen's privy chamber. "What does he say?"

"That he was knighted by the king just before His Grace left for home."

"That must have pleased his father."

"It pleased Harry, as well." I could tell by the bold pen strokes he'd used when writing the news.

"Was he wounded?" Belatedly, Alys looked concerned. "Knighthoods are often a reward for bravery in battle."

I hurriedly skimmed the next lines then breathed a sigh of relief. "He says he came through the campaign without a scratch."

"What else?"

I read on, summarizing as I went until I came to the last sentence. Then my breathing hitched and for a moment I lost the ability to speak. I must have had an addlepated look on my face because Alys seized me by the shoulders and gave me a hard shake.

"Bess! What is it?" I held out the letter, my hand atremble. Alys snatched it away from me and read the rest for herself. When she glanced up from the page, a wide grin split her face. "He says his father has agreed to a match between you and that he hopes the betrothal can be arranged as soon as he gets back to England. This is wonderful, Bess. He wants to marry you."

"Wonderful," I echoed.

Why, then, did I suddenly feel trapped?

I did not speak of my impending betrothal to anyone else during the next two weeks. The celebrations surrounding the king's return continued, as did the royal progress. The court traveled to Leeds Castle, then back to Otford, and finally set off in the direction of London. Will Parr was not with us. He'd gone to visit his estates in Essex and Surrey.

He was still absent when I received a second letter sent from Boulogne. This one came from Lord Lisle. I broke the seal with mild trepidation, assuming that he had met with my father to discuss the terms of my marriage to his son.

The first words made my heart stutter. As I read on, my limbs grew cold. The letter dropped from nerveless fingers and fluttered to the floor. I was not to marry Harry Dudley, after all. No one would ever marry Harry because Harry was dead.

Dazed, grief-stricken, I was scarcely aware of it when Alys plucked the letter from the rushes and read the terrible news for herself. "After King Henry left France," she relayed to Mary Woodhull in a choked whisper, "there was sickness among the troops. Camp fever. It was so widespread that even those in the command tents were infected. Harry—" She broke off, unable to say the words aloud.

"Harry died of it." I grabbed the letter back and tore it into tiny bits and threw them into the fire.

Tears streamed down my face. "It would have been a good match," I sobbed. "We were well suited." And there had been no impediment to our marriage.

None but death.

17

I do not remember much about the next few weeks. I performed my duties by rote, an insincere smile pasted on my face. I had to force myself to eat. It seemed unbelievable to me that someone as full of life as Harry Dudley should be so suddenly and finally gone. When Lady Lisle returned to court, we wept together for what we'd both lost.

Soon after that, the queen went on progress again, this time into Buckinghamshire and Bedfordshire. This time the king did not accompany her, nor did her brother. The days passed with great sameness until, on the return journey, Her Grace decided to stop at Ashridge to visit the king's younger daughter.

I had seen Princess Elizabeth from a distance when I first joined the court as the queen's maid of honor, but I had never spoken to the fragile-looking, red-haired, eleven-year-old. As soon as the king returned from France, she'd been sent back to her own household. In Nan Bassett's opinion, that was because His Grace was uncomfortable in her presence. She had her mother's eyes.

I was seated by a window, staring out at the bleak November

landscape, when I heard the rustle of satin behind me and smelled marjoram, the light fragrance the princess always wore. I rose, bade her good morrow, and dropped into a curtsy.

Her Grace peered into my face, her large black eyes unblinking. "Why are you so sad?" she asked.

Disconcerted by that stare and disarmed by her directness, I blurted out an honest answer. "I lost someone I loved."

The princess nodded, her expression solemn. "It is best not to love anyone," she said. "The people you love *always* leave you."

She had reason to believe that. Her mother, Anne Boleyn, had been beheaded when Elizabeth was only three and she had since lost two stepmothers and who knew how many devoted servants to the whims of her father the king.

"I am not certain it is possible to stop love," I said.

Princess Elizabeth considered this, all the while continuing her intense scrutiny. "I love my governess," she said after a few moments of thought. "Who are you?"

"My name is Elizabeth Brooke. I am Lord Cobham's daughter and a maid of honor to Queen Kathryn."

There was something about Her Grace, even as young as she was, that compelled me to answer the questions that followed. By the time she left me at the end of a quarter of an hour, she knew a good deal about me, even that I'd been planning to marry Harry Dudley.

Alone again, I pondered the princess's philosophy. Was it better not to love anyone for fear of losing them? No doubt it was, but love was not something anyone could control. I loved my parents and siblings. I'd loved Harry, after a fashion. And, God help me, I loved Will Parr.

Months of separation punctuated by fleeting contact had only made the attraction stronger. What I felt for Will defied common sense, but it was very real. As I stared blindly out at the grounds of Ashridge, I accepted a very great truth—I could no longer imagine living the rest of my life without Will in it.

18

By the time the progress was over, it was almost Yuletide. We were to spend Christmas at the king's favorite palace, Greenwich, and celebrate with masques and other pageantry. Then we would move to Hampton Court for the Twelfth Night festivities.

Will arrived at Greenwich a few days after I did. The moment I caught sight of him, I felt the powerful pull of attraction. I stared at him until he glanced my way and met my eyes. It did not take him long after that to find an opportunity to speak privately with me in a secluded corner of the queen's presence chamber.

He kissed me first, a searing bonding of lips that left me breathless.

"I have missed you, Bess," he murmured.

"And I, you. More than you can know."

He kissed me again and ran the tips of his fingers over my cheek. I shivered with pleasure.

"I . . . I love you, Will," I whispered.

"And I, you, from the first moment I saw you."

I frowned, remembering that occasion all too well. "You were kissing Dorothy the first time we met."

He chuckled. "Jealous, my sweet? There is no one else for me. Not anymore. I cleave only to you."

But when he reached for me again, I put both hands on his chest to keep him at a distance. "Does your wife still live?"

"Sadly, yes. But that does not matter. I am free of her, free to wed again. We need only obtain the king's permission."

"And my father's," I reminded him, scarcely daring to hope it would be that simple.

"George will not go against the king's wishes."

"His Grace's consent is all we need? Truly?"

"It is a trifle more complicated than that," Will admitted. "I must convince King Henry to grant a royal decree that will allow me to remarry. But I am high in His Grace's favor and my sister will support our cause."

He'd said that before. "The king is nothing if not unpredictable," I reminded him. "Especially if his leg pains him."

"If I approach him at the right moment, catch him in an expansive mood . . . you will see, Bess. His Grace will favor my suit."

I smiled up at him, struck by an idea. "What if I help you persuade the king?"

He winced. "It might be best if you keep your distance. He might find you too tasty a morsel to resist." To prevent any argument, he caught me to him and found my lips. I threw my arms around his neck and kissed him back, reveling in the passion I'd unleashed until the sound of approaching footsteps forced us apart again.

"We must be circumspect," I said in a breathless whisper. "No hint of scandal must touch us. We cannot expect the queen to help us if she thinks I am just another Dorothy Bray."

Reluctantly, Will released me, but he made no promises.

We spent a great deal of time together after that, for the most part in the queen's apartments. I resisted the temptation to visit him in his lodgings. In other circumstances conceiving a child would have led to the marriage we both desired, but so long as Will was not completely free, that was no solution for us. If the king did not sanction our union, I'd be banished from court and might never see Will again. Far better to bide our time and wait for an opportunity to broach the subject of a royal decree with the king. It had to be the perfect moment, else His Grace might forbid us to wed at all. He might even take it into his head to find a more "suitable" husband for me.

My closest friends, Alys Guildford and Mary Woodhull, knew how I felt about Will. They knew, too, that I heartily wished his faithless wife would die. But no one else was aware of our commitment to each other. Or so I thought.

On a dismal day in late February, in the queen's privy chamber, Alys and I were feeding hempseed to the queen's parrot when Jane the Fool capered across the room and stopped directly in front of me. She pressed both hands over her heart.

"I sigh, I pine," she said in her carrying, singsong voice, and rolled her protuberant eyes.

I laughed, anticipating entertaining antics. Jane's sole purpose at court was to amuse the queen and her ladies. Although she was dressed in beautiful court clothing, with a bright red pleated underskirt and a bodice and gown of brocaded damask, she wore the hose and shoes of a jester. A close-fitting cap covered her oversize head and she had bells sewn onto her sleeves. The tinkling sound attracted the attention of everyone in the privy chamber. They were all watching when Thomas, the queen's male fool, skipped over to Jane, fell to his knees at her feet, clasped his hands high in the air in front of him, and began to declaim.

"I will do whatever it takes to have you, my love!"

"You already have a wife!" she cried.

"I will remove the impediment! Oh I, Will, will!" And he began to make stabbing motions with a wooden knife. Then he tossed it aside and mimed strangling an imaginary wife.

Horrified, I could do nothing but watch as the queen's ladies tittered and Jane cheered Thomas on. When he abandoned strangulation and pretended to take out a pistol, prime and fire it, Jane mimed combing out long hair and placing a circlet on her head—like a bride.

"Stop," I whispered. "Oh, please, stop."

"Hush, Bess," Alys warned. "Do not let on that you know they are mocking you and Will."

Although I saw the sense in what she said, it was already far too late to salvage the situation. I heard laughter, hastily muffled, and saw the knowing glances directed my way. It was left to the queen herself to put an end to my torment.

"Jane. Thomas," she said in her sweet, quiet voice. "That will do."

At once the two fools fell into a tumbling routine that ended with Thomas juggling four wooden knives. Queen Kathryn ordered me into her bedchamber. She dismissed her other ladies and led me through into the secret lodgings beyond, the one area of her apartments where we could be truly private.

Five adjoining rooms made up the secret lodgings: the queen's bed-chamber—the one where she actually slept; a withdrawing chamber with a garderobe; a privy chamber; another withdrawing chamber, one that the king and queen both used; and another private bedchamber. The latter was where the king and queen slept together, an increasingly rare occurrence if the rumors were to be believed. That bedchamber, in turn, connected to yet another privy chamber, one of the king's, and to a private stair that led outside the palace. All the rooms looked out over the park and privy garden. The queen bade me sit beside her on a window seat in the middle room.

"Bess, this incident is most regrettable."

"Yes, Your Grace."

"I should send you back to your parents."

"Yes, Your Grace, but I pray you will not." My heart was hammering so hard that I feared it might leap out of my chest. I could barely hear the queen's words over the rushing sound in my ears.

She tilted her head to better study my face. Then she reached out and patted my hand. "My brother is a good man, Bess."

"Yes, Your Grace." I took a deep, calming breath and reminded myself that we both loved Will Parr.

"I sympathize with you, my dear, but there is little hope that he will be permitted to remarry while his wife lives. The king disapproves of such unions."

I bit back a rude reply. The king kept one standard for himself and another for everyone else. "Perhaps His Grace will change his mind."

"I do not believe he will, and no good can come of pining for what you cannot have."

The sudden hitch in the queen's voice told me Her Grace spoke from experience. I had heard the story. Queen Kathryn had been courted by someone else before the king decided he wanted her—Thomas Seymour, younger brother of the late Queen Jane. I wondered if she had been in love with him. How sad if that were true. She'd had to yield to the king, even though her heart belonged to another. To defy King Henry was never wise.

"I believe that Will's feelings for you are genuine," the queen continued. She sounded as if this surprised her. "But you must be sensible. Discourage him, Bess. You have admirers aplenty here at court. Choose one of them, marry, and be happy."

"I should like to be happy, Your Grace."

She frowned at my answer. "Will is not besotted enough to kill his wife for you."

"He would never kill anyone!" I sprang to my feet, for a moment forgetting that I was talking to the queen of England. "And her death is not the only way for us to wed." Will was a member of the king's Privy Council now. Surely that meant His Grace favored him.

"Stubborn fools, you and Will both, to live in hope of a royal decree." Although the words were harsh, the queen's tone of voice was tolerant, almost affectionate. Then she sighed. "I will not send you away, Bess, but I do ask that you be more discreet."

"Yes, Your Grace. I will strive to be."

I thought she would dismiss me then. Instead she added one more warning. "I have enemies at court, Bess. I am certain they were behind today's attempt to discredit you. Have a care what persons you trust."

I left the secret lodgings in a troubled frame of mind. Someone had put Jane Fool up to her antics. Jane's mind was no more complex than a small child's. She had to have been given lines to say and actions to pantomime.

I found Jane with her keeper in the poultry pen in one corner of the privy garden. The queen had given three geese and several hens to Jane to tend. The fool was industriously throwing grain at them when I called to her. She trotted over to the fence, a lopsided smile on her pale, unlined face.

"Jane," I said slowly, "who told you to pretend to be a bride?"

"Her Grace said to entertain the ladies."

I rephrased the question, but it did no good. Jane had no idea what I was talking about.

Discouraged, I returned to the privy chamber. I thought about pursuing the matter. I could talk to the other fool, Thomas. But to continue to ask questions would only call attention to the incident, and more notoriety was the last thing I wanted.

19

I did not need to tell Will about the pantomime. The story was all over court by the next morning. That afternoon, as we strolled together in the queen's gallery, surrounded by other members of her household, I relayed my conversation with his sister in a whisper and told him about my unproductive effort to question Jane.

"Kathryn may be correct," he said "There are warring factions at court. Religious matters divide them. My sister has made a powerful enemy of Stephen Gardiner, bishop of Winchester. Gardiner is always careful not to offend the king, but everyone else knows he'd return the Church of England to Rome if he could. He blames Kathryn for persuading His Grace to be lenient toward reformers. That the king and queen discuss religion in private infuriates him. He thinks he should be the only one guiding His Grace in such matters."

Her Grace favored the evangelical point of view—further reform of the Church of England and the right to study the Scriptures for ourselves. There were all manner of religious books and translations of the Bible in her apartments. I had not read them. I was more interested in music and games, dancing and masques. When I read at all, it was a let-ter from my family or a newly composed sonnet.

"Does the king need guidance?" I asked. By declaring himself head of the Church of England, King Henry had replaced the pope. I wondered if that made him equally infallible.

"At times." Will's smile appeared for a brief moment only. "But His Grace could do worse than to allow my sister to instruct him."

The queen's ladies and gentlemen had drifted toward the other end of the gallery, where the Bassano brothers were about to play a new composition. For the moment, we could speak freely, unafraid of being overheard.

"But why should Bishop Gardiner concern himself with me?" Our love was a private matter, or should have been. Especially when we de-nied ourselves the pleasures of coupling.

"Your father supports reform, just as I do. Gardiner would be de-lighted to see both of us burn for heretics."

Alarmed, I stopped walking. "Surely it will not come to that!"

He tugged at my arm to start me moving again, lest we draw atten-tion to ourselves. We had almost reached the courtiers lounging on the gallery floor on cushions to listen to the music. "Be patient, Bess. And cautious. And never doubt my love for you."

I tried to follow Will's advice, but as another spring edged toward another summer and there were no more stolen kisses in dark corners, I wanted nothing more than to find enough privacy to give myself to the man I loved. I longed to be held in Will's arms again.

Instead, long conversations in public had to suffice. The queen's warning was always on my mind—*Have a care what persons you trust.*

It was in May, when the court was at Whitehall, that I realized someone was following me every time I left the queen's apartments. I could not get a good look at him. He was just a shadow, vanishing when I turned his way.

Whitehall was an enormous place. Included in grounds that encom-passed more than twenty acres were gardens and orchards, a bowling green, a cockpit, four tennis plays, and a tiltyard. There were also three galleries and more passages and stairs than anyone could count. I could hear the man's soft footfalls on the rush-covered floor as I made my way toward the council chamber, hoping to catch Will when he left that day's meeting. I was too late. The Privy Council had already adjourned.

I considered returning to the maids' dormitory, but what if the man stalking me waylaid me in one of the narrow passageways? Instead I set out at a brisk pace along the gallery near the lord chamberlain's chamber. A winding stair took me toward the water gate, but my destination was not a boat or a barge but rather the private rooms of the sergeant porter, the gentleman in charge of palace security.

I had almost reached my goal when I glanced over my shoulder and for the first time got a good look at the man pursuing me. I stopped and turned. I knew that face—the ruddy complexion, the hair combed forward to form a short fringe over the forehead, the tuft of hair at the point of the chin.

"Matthew Rowlett!" I shouted. "Stay right where you are!"

My father's man turned and started to run. In his panic he tripped over his own feet and nearly fell. His ruddy complexion darkened further when I caught him by the coattail and dragged him to a halt.

"How dare you spy on me!" Hands clenched into fists at my hips, I glared at him, fighting an urge to strike him.

He snatched off his cap, mangling it as he tucked his head in like a turtle. He refused to meet my eyes. "I was only following orders, Mistress Bess," he mumbled.

"Well, here is another for you. Go away. You've no business at court."

Rowlett shifted uneasily from foot to foot, his scuffed leather boots stirring the rushes on the stone floor. He was dressed to blend into the background, looking like a lowly clerk in a long, fitted, rat's-color fustian doublet with close-set buttons. "Lord Cobham won't like that, Mistress Bess."

"And I don't like what *he's* done by sending you here to spy on me!"

"He heard rumors, mistress."

"I don't care what he's heard!" And I was too angry to care. "Leave Whitehall at once!"

Matthew Rowlett went, but a few days later my father made the crossing from Calais. I was not surprised that he'd come to court, and I was prepared with good arguments in favor of my eventual marriage to Will Parr.

Father did not want to hear them. "If I could do so without insulting Queen Kathryn, I would order you away from the royal court entirely."

Our confrontation took place outdoors, in the open space between the queen's gallery and Princess Mary's lodgings, a separate building along the riverfront. To any observer, we would have looked unexceptionable, a father and daughter taking the air on a fine spring day. Beneath the surface, I was as furious with him as I'd ever been with anyone. I was also determined to have my own way.

"I love Will Parr," I said. "I want to marry him."

"The Earl of Essex," Father corrected me in a low, angry voice. "I use the title deliberately to remind you that he laid claim to it through his wife. He is not free to wed you, Bess."

"There is no impediment to our union. Will's marriage to Anne Bourchier was invalidated by an act of Parliament. You yourself voted to divorce them."

"It is not the place of women to choose their own husbands. That is a father's duty."

"You were pleased enough when my choice was Harry Dudley."

His thick eyebrows lifted in surprise. "*Your* choice? His father and I made that decision and talked the boy into it. It is a great pity that he died but, as he did, it is my responsibility to arrange for a new betrothal. I have been negligent in not doing so ere now."

My temper spiked. Perhaps I had been wrong about Harry's feelings for me, but I was not mistaken about Will's. All those long, chaste conversations had allowed our understanding of each other to grow and, along with it, mutual liking had developed. Our love, our desire to wed, had not diminished, but our feelings had deepened and matured.

"You cannot force me into a marriage I do not want. I have the right to refuse, and I will refuse any betrothal that is not to Will."

I had rarely seen my father lose control, but he did so then. His face turned a terrible purplish-red and he gripped my shoulders with bruising force to shout directly into my face, "I forbid it! You are not to speak to him again, not to dance with him, and most certainly not to be alone with him! No other man will have you if he thinks you're Parr's leavings."

I slapped at his hands. "Dorothy did well enough for herself!"

He released me so abruptly that I stumbled and nearly fell. "Brydges is a fool and Dorothy another. I thought you had more sense. Stay away from Parr. You are obliged to obey your father's commands."

But the more he barked orders at me, the more determined I became to go my own way. "I will follow my heart. And I will never agree to a loveless marriage."

Father's face worked as he struggled for self-control. He turned away from me, staring at Lambeth Palace, the archbishop of Canterbury's great house on the opposite side of the Thames, until he could speak calmly again. As stone faced as a gargoyle, he asked if I was Will Parr's mistress.

"No, I am not," I said and added, pride in my voice, "we agreed to wait until we are married to couple."

"You will have a long wait!"

With that, Father stalked off. I did not see him again before he returned to his duties in Calais.

20

Soon after my confrontation with my father, rumors surfaced of an impending French invasion. By midsummer, everyone was on the lookout for strangers who might turn out to be French agents, and Lord Lisle, as lord admiral, attempted a daring plan that involved sending fireships against the French in their own port at the mouth of the Seine. It failed, but he redeemed himself in a battle with twenty-one French galleys in which the French were put to flight. In July he sailed his fleet to Portsmouth Harbor. There some sixty-three warships soon gathered for provisioning and repair. The king, leaving most of the court behind, joined Lisle there to oversee the preparations for war.

I knew all this from my old mistress, Jane Lisle. I knew, too, that Jane was once again with child. I envied her. I had begun to wonder if I was ever to know the joy of coupling with Will, let alone the fulfillment of bearing his children.

I envied Anne Bourchier. *She* had children. She might live in strained circumstances at the manor of Little Wakering in Essex, but she lived there with her own choice of a mate. As far as I knew, she had not even been made to endure the usual punishment doled out by the church for adultery—public penance while barefoot and wearing nothing but a shift.

On the nineteenth day of July, a ship called the *Hedgehog* blew up on the Thames, at Westminster. No one knew if it was an accident or a case of enemy sabotage but the event made everyone nervous. We did not learn until later that the *Hedgehog* met its fate on the very same day that the French fleet appeared off Portsmouth. Lord Lisle succeeded in driving them away, but there were many losses, not the least of which was the king's great warship the *Mary Rose*. While attempts were still under way to try to salvage her, especially her ordnance, the king returned to court. He was in remarkably high spirits for having lost so many men.

"The French ran off like whipped curs with their tails between their legs," His Grace declared.

Along with the other maids of honor, I sat on a cushion on the floor. We formed a half circle around the king and queen. I studied King Henry as he regaled us with stories of his activities with the fleet in Portsmouth Harbor. Renewed hostilities with France seemed to agree with him.

Seizing the chance to take advantage of his good mood, I took every opportunity to flatter His Grace. I asked questions that allowed him to recount more of his own exploits. I praised the decisions he'd made, even though I had no idea whether they were good ones or not. I hoped that if he looked upon me with particular favor he might be willing to grant me a boon.

The next day the entire court embarked on a hunting progress. Our first stop was Nonsuch, where we would stay for three nights. The palace was an astonishing sight, with many towers and turrets. It was situated in an enormous hunting park stocked with over a thousand head of deer. But when Will and I rode into the outer court, some of the magic disappeared.

"It is unfinished," I said.

"It is a miracle there is as much here as there is. Building began fewer than ten years ago, when the king ordered an entire village razed."

I wondered what had happened to the people who had lived there, but I did not have time to ask. Will and I were among the select few, along with the queen, Lady Lisle, Lady Hertford, and Lady Suffolk, who were to be given a guided tour by the king himself.

His Grace was like a small boy showing off a new toy, escorting us into the royal lodgings by means of an elaborate staircase that led from the inner court to the first floor. In other palaces, we'd have entered the watching chamber first. Here we went directly into the king's presence chamber.

"The guard chamber is below us, on the ground floor," King Henry explained. "And we have done away with the great hall entirely. Nonsuch is a privy palace. The entire court will not be invited here again."

Furniture and hangings sent ahead from Whitehall were already in place. The king led us through the presence chamber and into the short gallery that connected it to His Grace's privy chamber. From there doors opened onto a privy gallery, the privy lodgings—two chambers with the king's bedchamber beyond—and a small tower room. From the king's bedchamber, another small room behind a stair turret gave access to the queen's bedchamber.

"How delightful!" Queen Kathryn exclaimed, even though her apartments were much smaller than the king's and there was only one chamber in her privy lodgings.

"Do you see the roundels?" King Henry asked, indicating the linenfold paneling decorating the walls of the queen's privy chamber. I peered at one of the small round carvings and saw a maiden issuing from a Tudor rose—a variation of the queen's personal emblem.

It was all very luxurious, but I was not to enjoy it. The maids of honor were housed in a tent. A forest of them had sprung up on the grounds. Few courtiers were pleased by the prospect of living rough, but they were given no choice in the matter. To add to their discontent, it rained all night.

In the morning, I stepped out into bright sunlight and a sea of mud. My sturdy riding boots sank in it with every step and made disgusting sucking sounds each time I lifted one out of the mire. I did not care. I was to join the hunt at the king's express invitation. If His Grace had a successful day—as surely he would, with the help of his hunts-men—then I intended to keep him sweet with flattery and flirtation. When the right moment came, I could broach the subject of a royal decree. Will had not yet found an opportunity to do so, not for lack of desire on his part, but because the king was so often distracted by affairs of state.

Some years before, the king had suffered a serious fall while coursing. Since then he had, for the most part, given up hunting with dogs. In-stead, he shot at game from a platform called a standing. Timber framed and plastered, it stood two stories high.

The huntsmen flushed a hart and chased it past the standing. Using nets on poles, they forced the deer to flee directly toward the spot where the king waited. Not surprisingly, His Grace made the kill, putting him in a jovial mood. The queen made her shot just as cleanly.

Halfway through the day's hunt, we adjourned to a banqueting house atop a little hill. After the king dined, he ascended to a viewing platform on the roof. While His Grace chatted amiably with Will, I positioned myself as close as I dared and waited for the king to notice me. It did not take long.

"What do you think of our park, Mistress Brooke?" His Grace asked.

"It is the best I have ever seen, Your Grace. And the palace is magnificent."

"Have you had time to explore the gardens?"

"Not yet, Your Grace, but I look forward to doing so."

All the while we spoke together, the king edged closer to me, until he stood only inches away. I tried to ignore his mottled skin and the thick rolls of fat around his neck and the pouches beneath his eyes, but he had become grossly obese in the last year. His back was humped like an old woman's. I repressed a shudder, smiled, and flattered His Grace for all I was worth. At least the ulcers on his leg were not giving off that putrid smell I still remembered with nightmare clarity.

After the hunt, Will took me on a tour of the gardens. Nonsuch boasted a wonderland of groves, rockeries, aviaries, and trellis walks. Eventually, there was to be a maze in the privy garden, but it was still in the planning stages. We stopped in a picturesque hollow.

"This is called the Grove of Diana," Will said.

"Why?"

He pointed to one of two statues—a woman in her bath. "Diana the huntress, a goddess."

I was unfamiliar with the legend. "The other statue is grotesque."

"Actaeon being turned into a stag," Will said, and related the entire legend.

"I am glad mere mortal kings do not have such powers. Beheading is a terrible fate, but at least it is quick."

Will ran a finger beneath the edge of his collar. "Do not jest about such matters, Bess. And have a care what you say to the king." He fixed me with a stern look. "You have gone out of your way to bring yourself to his attention."

"If His Grace is well disposed toward me, then he will be inclined to grant a request."

"I feared that was your plan."

"What harm in trying? At worst, he will refuse."

"Can you still be such an innocent?" He put his hands on my shoulders, his expression full of concern. "Choose the wrong moment and you could ruin everything. Or, worse, lead him to think you are prepared to offer him more than smiles in return for his largesse."

I took a step toward him, so that our bodies were lightly touching from chest to thigh. "How much longer must we wait, Will?"

"God's teeth, Bess!" The strain in his voice reassured me. "Now more than ever we must be circumspect."

"We've waited so long," I whispered. "I am tired of being patient." I had to bite my lip to hold back tears. "Perhaps I can convince the king—"

"Bess, no." He held me tenderly. "It is not worth the risk. If you force His Grace's hand and he refuses to allow our marriage, he can no longer ignore our desire to wed. He will feel obliged to keep us apart. What if he sends you back to Cowling Castle? Or marries you off to someone else?"

The tears did come then, but even as I cried, my resolution hardened. If I could not marry Will, then I would live with him unwed. Neither father nor king would part us.

21

After Nonsuch, the court moved on to Petworth. There reports reached the king of a tempest that had caused widespread destruction in Derbyshire, Lancashire, and Cheshire. Then experts in such matters determined that the *Mary Rose* could not be salvaged.

"There is a great dearth of corn and victuals in some parts of England," Will told me, "and fears that it may lead to famine. And the bloody flux is raging among sailors on the king's ships, incapacitating entire crews." He heard these things at the daily meetings of the Privy Council and shared them with me to discourage me from approaching King Henry.

"And yet His Grace continues to be in excellent humor." Council business dispensed with, he spent the remainder of each day killing defenseless deer from a standing or mounted his horse, with the help of a purpose-built flight of steps, and set off with his favorite hawk on one gauntleted hand.

"King Henry's temper is uncertain. Do not speak to him out of turn lest his anger be unleashed on you."

I ignored Will's warnings and continued to flirt with His Grace. The queen looked on with mild amusement, knowing full well what I was about. Her Grace did not speak to me of Will, but I was certain she would give us her blessing if only the king could be persuaded to agree to our marriage.

On the eighteenth day of August, the court left Petworth for Guildford. In spite of its name, Guildford did not belong to Lady Lisle's family but to Will, a gift to him from the king. Will had received many gifts from King Henry, both large and small. His Grace had even parted with one of his own walking staffs when Will fell while playing tennis and twisted his ankle. It was an ornate creation decorated with silver and gilt and boasting a little shipman's compass set into the top.

Guildford was a moated hunting lodge in a park that contained a rabbit warren and a horse-breeding operation as well as a herd of the king's deer. Once again, tents had to be set up to house most of the court. The king continued in a jovial mood.

I decided that there would be no better place to plead our case to the king than here in Will's own house. I spent the next two days alert for an opening to speak to the king of what was in my heart. I had not yet found one by the third morning when, as had become our habit, I met with Will following the daily meeting of the Privy Council.

"Good news, Bess," he said when he'd greeted me with a brief kiss— the kind no one could take exception to. "The French fleet is no longer a threat. Their remaining ships have retreated all the way back to their own ports."

"Oh, excellent! His Grace must be delighted." This could be the moment I had been waiting for. The king would be in an excellent mood. He would be inclined to be generous.

"He is so well pleased that to celebrate he means to move on to Woking this very day."

"He cannot!" The protest burst out of me before I could stop it. I clapped both hands over my mouth.

Will sighed and shook his head. "I was afraid you had not given up.

Well, you must perforce abandon such foolishness now. The king will leave Guildford within the hour."

"I will speak to him at Woking, then." I started to return to the house. We had walked, as was our wont, toward the ruins of an old castle on the grounds. Only the Great Tower still stood, and behind it was a secluded, overgrown garden where we had stolen a few minutes of privacy.

Will caught my arm. "You will not be going with him. His Grace is taking only a small number of courtiers, all male. Everyone else is to remain here for another day or two."

"Will you go or stay?"

"The Privy Council meets tomorrow at Woking. I will be expected to attend."

"Make some excuse and remain here with me."

"Since the Duke of Suffolk has already begged leave to stay behind, I do not think it would be wise for me to do so."

My scheme to ask a favor of the king had been thwarted, at least temporarily. Frustration sparked a sudden, overwhelming need in me to exert control over something in my life. Desire, so long repressed, broke free.

I trailed my fingers up the front of Will's doublet. "Would you not prefer to spend tonight with me?"

The answering heat in his gaze made my knees weak, but his words denied me. "The duke has the excuse of illness. I am not sick."

I moved closer, slid my arms around him, nestled against him. "What good has waiting done us?" I rubbed myself against him.

"God's Blood, Bess! You would drive a saint into sin!"

"The duke's ill health will distract attention away from us."

"This is not wise, Bess. Not prudent."

"Prudence be damned!" But I released him. If lust would not convince him, then logic must. "You have always insisted that there is no real impediment to our marriage. Was that a lie?"

"How can you think such a thing?"

"Then if we were to exchange vows in private, we would be as truly wed as if we had a priest in attendance. It would not be a sin to to-gether."

My bold proposal left him speechless, but his eyes gleamed.

"We will enter into a clandestine marriage." My body hummed with desire. I wanted nothing more than to consummate our love. We had waited months. Years. I was nineteen, far older than my mother had been when she wed. It was time to take this step. A clandestine marriage might not be sanctioned by the church, but it was irrevocable.

"Woking is close enough to Guildford that I can ride there on the morrow to attend the council meeting," Will said. "I will tell His Grace that I have matters to attend to concerning the manor."

An hour later, the king rode away without Will, but we still had the rest of the day and the evening to endure. We passed the time playing primero in the queen's presence chamber. Will lost £5. Had the queen not been distracted by her concern for the ailing duke, she might have been made suspicious by that.

The long hours of waiting were agonizing, but at last Alys fell soundly asleep. I crept out of the bed we shared. Wearing a night gown to cover my nakedness, I left the tent that served as the maidens' cham-ber. Will was waiting for me. Since Guildford belonged to him, he had a room inside the house and knew the best way to spirit me there without anyone being the wiser.

Lit by candles, the bedchamber smelled of roses. He'd ordered masses of them cut and brought inside. Taking my hand, he led me to the foot of the bed, an enormous carved and gilded object hung with crimson brocade.

"Are you certain, Bess?"

I nodded. "What must we say?"

"We commit ourselves each to the other by words of consent uttered *per verba de presenti*." He held my gaze as he made his vows. "I, William Parr, Lord Parr of Kendal and Earl of Essex, do take thee, Elizabeth Brooke, to be my wedded wife. Now you."

"I, Elizabeth Brooke, do take thee, William Parr, to be my wedded husband." The smile I gave him was tremulous. My heart was full to bursting. I felt light-headed, too, but my thoughts had not yet scattered. "Do we need a witness?"

"The words are enough. We are married."

At last, I thought as he kissed me deeply. Then I did not think at all for a very long time.

Will had the patience to be gentle with me my first time, and the experience to give me so much pleasure that I barely felt it when he took my maidenhead.

"You are so beautiful," he whispered afterward. He took my hand and placed it over his heart. "I am yours, Bess. Forever. No one will ever force us to part."

"And I am yours, Will. Forever." Tears of happiness filled my eyes as I embraced him. I kissed his chin, his cheek, even his eyelids, and all the while my fingers explored, learning the hard planes and solid muscles of his body.

Fearless in the arms of the man I loved, I gave myself to him again and again through that blissful night. After the last time, toward dawn, we lay together still joined. He was, I thought, the other half of myself. My smile stretched so wide that my cheeks hurt. I ducked my head, nuzzled the underside of his chin, and began to inscribe tiny letters on his bare chest.

"What are you doing?" he asked in a sleepy, contented voice.

"Writing my initials. You belong to me now."

When he laughed, I felt it across every inch of my body, inside and out.

22

I was back in the maidens' tent before any of the others were stirring. Although Will left early for Woking, I was up and dressed to watch him ride away. I sent a wife's prayer after him for his safety and success.

If the king seemed to be in a mellow mood, Will would confess what we had done right after the council meeting and ask His Grace's blessing on our marriage. There was risk involved. There was always risk. But I had convinced myself that, at worst, Will would be made to pay a fine for marrying without the king's permission. No matter what happened, I no longer feared I would be forced to marry someone else. It was too late for that.

Feeling smug, I turned to find Nan Bassett right behind me. "You are a fool, Bess Brooke."

"I have no notion what you mean." But my palms began to sweat and I could not meet her eyes.

"I mean that I was awake when you returned this morning. Did you lie with him, Bess? Have you so far lost your senses as to risk getting with child by a man who already has a wife?"

"You are mistaken. I went out to visit the privy, nothing more."

Nan sent me a pitying look. "If you are set upon this course, at least learn how to lie convincingly."

Certain I would have no need to deny Will, I walked away from Nan without saying more. We would be together soon, wed in the eyes of man and God. For we *were* married. We'd exchanged vows and I'd given myself to my husband, body and mind and soul. The pleasure he had given me in return had convinced me that we were destined to be together. Just the memory of our joining made me warm all over.

I did not permit myself to consider the possibility that the king would refuse Will's request. To show favor to Will would please the queen. And Will had been most faithful in his service ever since his return from the Scottish border. He deserved a reward.

To pass the time, I sewed, played my lute, and watched the queen's tumbler perform. From time to time I heard hushed whispers and saw concerned looks. Since they were not directed at me, I paid them scant attention until, at just after four of the clock on that Saturday afternoon, the queen herself came to tell us that the ailing Duke of Suffolk had died.

Will returned to Guildford Castle a few hours later, bringing His Grace's condolences to the duchess and the duke's daughter, Frances Grey. Then he retired to his bedchamber, where I waited.

"You should not be here, Bess," Will said in a weary voice. He poured himself a cup of Malmsey and sank into the chair drawn up to the fire.

"Where else should your wife be, Will?" I took the cup away from him, placing it on a nearby table, and plunked myself down in his lap.

For a moment, I thought he would push me away, but he only sighed and laid his head upon my bosom. I stroked his hair, hoping to soothe him, but I was far from calm myself.

"What happened at Woking?" I asked when he did not volunteer any information. "Did you speak to the king?"

I felt him tense and knew before he spoke that he had not. "There was no opening before the council meeting, and after . . . the Privy Council was still in session when the news arrived." Will lifted his head to run shaky fingers over his short-cropped hair. "I have never seen the king so grief stricken. Suffolk was his oldest friend. His Grace took his death hard, and it was as if a dam opened. Of a sudden, every other loss in this evil year flooded over him. Even as he praised the duke's life, he remembered there was famine in the land, and sickness, too. He spoke of the *Mary Rose* and the sailors who went down with her. The king was there in Portsmouth that day, you know, watching from the ramparts of Southsea Castle when that great ship heeled over and abruptly sank. Hundreds of men drowned and there was nothing anyone could do to save them."

"I am sorry for it, but—"

"Did you know the *Mary Rose* was named after the king's sister, the one who was married to the Duke of Suffolk?"

I did not care. I wanted to wail—to howl—in frustration. We had been so close.

Will ran one hand up my arm to pull me into a kiss. I resisted. As much as I wanted to lie in his arms, in his bed, some vestige of common sense remained to me. "I will not have people think I am merely your mistress."

"You are my *wife*, Bess. Never doubt that. It is only that we must bide our time. Just now the king would not react well to being told we've already wed. When Suffolk married His Grace's sister, even he fell into disfavor for not waiting for permission."

"But he was forgiven."

"In time. And after payment of an enormous fine."

I knew the story, but it was ancient history, so long ago that Suffolk's daughter, Frances, had three little girls of her own—Jane, Catherine, and Mary Grey. I extricated myself from Will's arms and stood. "I must go now."

"I love you, Bess." His misery tore at my heart, but it made no difference. I could not stay. The temptation was too great.

He caught my hand before I could escape and slipped a ring on my finger. "You are my wife now, Bess. There is no going back."

The ring was in gimmal, one part set with a ruby and the other with a diamond. I did not have to take it off to know that the words "Let no man put asunder those whom God has joined together" would be inscribed beneath the bezel.

"It will not be long," Will whispered. "I swear it. Soon we will be able to tell the world that we are wed."

"And until then we must pretend nothing has changed." My voice sounded as hollow as I felt.

Will loved me. I did believe that. But not as much as I loved him. Not enough to go straightaway to the king and announce that we were married. I removed the ring from my finger and tucked it into my bodice, close to my heart.

23

In November, Jane Lisle gave birth to another daughter. The child was baptized in London with the widowed Duchess of Suffolk and the Princess Mary as her godmothers. I attended the ceremony and came away from it longing for a child of my own, Will's child.

I had not conceived as a result of our one night together and I was glad of it, but I despaired of ever being able to claim my husband, let alone bear his child. Since the duke's death, His Grace's health had gone into a decline. His good days were few and far between.

In the new year, the king's physical ailments became even more debilitating. He was fifty-four years old, but looked a decade older. He could only climb stairs with the help of a winching device and he was obliged to use what he called his "tram," a chair fitted with wheels, to get about on level ground. That he had to suffer such indignities made King Henry even more short tempered, irritable, and intolerant.

On a cold day in mid-February, Mary Woodhull, Alys Guildford, and I huddled on low stools pulled close to a brazier in the middle of the maids' dormitory, trying to keep warm while we hemmed shirts for the poor.

"Queen Kathryn has ordered more secure coffers and boxes with new locks and they are to be kept in Her Grace's garderobe." Mary spoke in a voice so low that I had to strain to hear her. The only other person in the chamber was one of the tiring maids. She was some distance away, returning laundered shifts to one of the wardrobe trunks, but it was obvious that Mary did not want her to overhear.

"Why?" I asked in an equally soft voice.

"To keep her personal papers and letters safe from prying eyes."

"Who would dare spy on the queen?" Alys asked.

"Any number of people," Mary said, "including her husband."

"Queen Kathryn has enemies," I said, "Bishop Gardiner chief among them."

"Her Grace has sent some of her more controversial books away to her uncle in Northamptonshire, for safekeeping," Mary confided. The queen's uncle, Lord Parr of Horton, was Mary's grandfather.

I wished I could ask Will what he thought of his sister's actions, but he was away from court. By the time he returned and we could steal an hour together, his kisses drove every other thought out of my mind.

We did not couple for fear of creating a child, but Will knew other ways to pleasure me. The first time, I thought he meant only to indulge in a few kisses and touches, but his caresses soon became more intimate and before I knew what was happening, he had driven me to the same height of ecstasy I had experienced in his bed. He held me close as I shuddered and wept in the aftermath of those powerful sensations. Then he showed me how to satisfy him.

In May, with alarming suddenness, the matter of the queen's books took on new importance. The Privy Council summoned Edward Warner, a minor member of Queen Kathryn's household, to answer a charge of "disputing indiscreetly of Scripture." Master Warner knew all too well what reading matter had, until recently, been available in the queen's privy chamber. Several more volumes abruptly vanished into the locked caskets in the garderobe.

Throughout June there was an increase in the number of quiet, intense conversations between members of the queen's inner circle. This elite group was comprised of ladies who shared the queen's evangelical views—Anne Herbert, the queen's sister; Jane Lisle; Anne Hertford; Catherine, Duchess of Suffolk; Elizabeth Tyrwhitt; and Joan Denny. None of the maids of honor was included. We formed an attractive backdrop for the queen, but she did not confide in us. Mary Woodhull, however, served the bedchamber. Little escaped her notice.

"There is trouble over Mistress Anne Askew," Mary reported. "She is a gentlewoman from the north who has been arraigned for heresy. She has been questioned about her ties to the queen's household. Some of the queen's ladies sent her aid, as they are wont to do for many unfortunate prisoners. Because of that, they fear they will be questioned, too. And because they are close to Her Grace, the queen may also be in danger."

"Of accusations of *heresy*?" I whispered, horrified. "But she is the *queen*."

Mary hushed me, glancing over her shoulder to be certain no one was near enough to overhear. We were in the presence chamber, where anyone could enter. "The queen has a copy of Coverdale's English translation of the New Testament."

My expression must have betrayed my bewilderment. I did not understand why that fact should worry me.

"The king has just issued a proclamation ordering that heretical books be searched out and destroyed," Mary explained. "Henceforth, any man or woman, of whatever estate, condition, or degree, is forbidden to receive, have, take, or keep in their possession the text of the New Testament in either Tyndale's or Coverdale's translation. This royal decree goes into effect on the first day of August."

I had no strong feelings about my faith. I did everything that was expected of me when it came to attending church and prayer services, but I only pretended to pay attention when members of the queen's household read aloud from the Bible.

As soon as I could after Mary returned to her duties in the queen's bedchamber, I sought Will out and repeated all that Mary had said. We sat on a stone bench atop a knoll under an arbor in the gardens at Whitehall. It was a fine day in mid-July and we had an excellent view of our surroundings. We were in plain sight, but no one else was near enough to trouble us.

Will's shoulders slumped. "This is worrisome news, Bess. That royal decree means that my sister must either confess to her ownership of heretical books or conceal them and risk having them found by searchers. And if any member of her household is caught with such books he, or she, can be tortured into confessing that they were obtained from the queen."

"Tortured? But surely no one would dare harm one of the queen's ladies."

But the queen was afraid. Why else would she hide some of her books and send others to her uncle? Jane Lisle and the other ladies read the queen's books and held avid, even heated, discussions about them. I'd paid little attention, having far more interest in frivolous things. But I had been present. Was I in danger, too?

"Anne Askew," Will said, "was put upon the rack to make her confess her heresy, and to persuade her to name other people who share her beliefs."

"But she's a gentlewoman." It was unheard of to torture women of gentle or noble birth.

"That did not save her. What was done to Anne Askew broke the law, but no one dared go against Stephen Gardiner, bishop of Winchester." Will swiped a hand over his face, as if he would rub away a horrible image. "You know that Gardiner has hated my sister for a long time, Bess. He believes she influences the king in religious matters, making him more inclined to be lenient toward reformers, and it is true that His Grace often indulges Kathryn, allowing her to debate matters of religion with him. But lately, with His Grace so often ill and out of sorts, he's had little patience with her harping on reform. Gardiner uses that, making His Grace feel ill used and put upon."

"King Henry thinks himself henpecked," I murmured.

My choice of words provoked a brief, rueful smile but did not lighten Will's black mood. "If only His Grace would remonstrate with Kathryn directly, all would be well, but it has always been his way to let his huntsmen shoot for him."

"So he will allow Bishop Gardiner to take aim at the queen?"

"I fear so. It will not be the first time he has used a minister to bring down a queen. Cardinal Wolsey arranged the king's divorce from Catherine of Aragon. Lord Cromwell conspired to destroy Anne Boleyn. Archbishop Cranmer found proof to use against Catherine Howard. Kathryn could well end up in the Tower, just like Anne Boleyn and Catherine Howard. Or worse, just like Anne Askew." His voice broke. "I have never seen anything so terrible as what they did to her."

"You *saw* her?" I reached for his hand, instinctively offering comfort.

His expression bleak, he met my eyes. "Gardiner chose two members of the Privy Council to conduct a further round of questioning—myself and Lord Lisle—but since Gardiner was there with us, we could not speak freely. We both urged her to recant and save herself, but she would have none of it. Then Gardiner tried to persuade her to name the Countess of Hertford and Lady Denny as fellow heretics. He hoped for other names. He wanted her to name the queen, but she stood fast, even on the rack."

I sat so close to him that I felt him shudder. I wanted to fling my arms around him and soothe him, but there were eyes everywhere at court. I dared do no more than keep one hand over his.

"You must warn your sister."

"She is already well aware of the danger." He squeezed my fingers, then stood, tugged me to my feet, and released me. We had spent long enough "alone."

"There must be something I can do to help the queen."

"Look to your own safety first. I do not want to lose both of you."

"I am sworn to serve the queen, Will."

He sent me a sweet, swift smile that melted both my resistance and my heart. "But are you not my wife, too, sworn to obey your husband in all things?"

I dropped into a quick, saucy curtsy, forcing away dark thoughts of heresy, treason, and torture. My fingers sought the gimmal ring pinned to the inside of my bodice. "I do not believe we included the words 'love, honor, and obey' in our vows."

"An oversight we must be sure to correct when we repeat them. My part, I believe, is to promise you love, honor, and protection."

24

Anne Askew was burned at the stake for heresy on the six teenth day of July in 1546. A week passed, then two. No one came to arrest any member of the queen's household. Then we moved to Hampton Court for the month of August.

I was on my way to the stair turret that led to the queen's apartments when I noticed a gentleman in the king's livery loitering in the shadows. His hood kept me from recognizing him, even when he looked directly at me, but I could not help but notice when he dropped an official-looking document, rolled and tied with ribbon. Instead of retrieving it, he left it lying on the cobbles and hurried away.

I did not call out to him. It had been no accident that he'd let that roll of parchment fall directly in my path. The move had been made with deliberate precision, and only after he was sure that I'd seen him. I stopped beside the tightly rolled document, regarding it as if it were a snake coiled to strike. It took all my courage to pick it up. I glanced around to be sure no one else had seen. When I was satisfied that I was alone in the southeast corner of the courtyard, I hastily removed the ribbon, unrolled the parchment, and read its contents.

For a moment I fought to breathe. This was as bad as could be. It was a copy of a warrant for the queen's arrest.

The roll rustled as I hid it in my sleeve. Feeling unsteady on my feet as a newborn foal, I entered the stair turret.

To escape the cooking smells that had invaded the apartments used by Jane Seymour, Anna of Cleves, and Catherine Howard, Queen Kathryn had asked the king for new lodgings. Within a year of her marriage, she had been installed in newly renovated, sweet-smelling chambers. She'd chosen rooms facing south, so that she had a view of the pond gardens with their flower beds surrounded by low walls and flanked by neat rows of striped poles supporting a variety of heraldic beasts.

When I reached the queen's privy chamber, where ceilings had been raised and new partitions and wainscoting installed, creating a spacious, luxurious living space, I did not attempt speak to Her Grace directly. Instead, I sought out Jane Lisle and passed the document to her. "Do not let anyone see you read this," I whispered.

Jane left the chamber, using the excuse of a visit to the privy. When she returned a few minutes later, her face was pale as whey. A determined gleam in her eyes, she moved purposefully among the queen's ladies, speaking briefly to a select few. Less than a quarter of an hour later, I was summoned to the queen's private withdrawing room. Jane Lisle, Anne Hertford, Joan Denny, and Elizabeth Tyrwhitt were there already. The queen entered through another door a moment later, attended by her sister, Anne Herbert.

When Queen Kathryn held out her hand, Jane placed the warrant in it. Disbelief warred with shock in the queen's expression as she read the words. "Lord be merciful! His Grace means to have my head."

The warrant passed from hand to hand to be read and exclaimed over while Queen Kathryn regained her composure. Her Grace was too strong minded to let fear paralyze her, and too intelligent to give up without trying to find a way out of her plight. She began to pace, her fingers toying with the small clock suspended from a gold chain at her waist.

She stopped in front of me. "How did you come by this, Bess?"

"You have a friend, Your Grace," Jane said when I'd told my story. "Someone *wanted* you to be warned of your danger."

"Perhaps it was the king himself," I suggested.

Everyone turned to stare at me. I had been bold to speak without the queen's permission. I swallowed hard, but Jane sent a reassuring smile my way. "Bess may be right. Shortly before Your Grace's marriage, my husband heard that Bishop Gardiner was plotting to bring about Archbishop Cranmer's downfall. The king knew of his plans but made no move to stop him. Instead His Grace played one minister against the other for his own amusement. King Henry gave Cranmer a ring, without explanation, saying only that should he ever need to prove he had His Grace's love, he should produce it. Shortly thereafter, faced with soldiers who had arrived with a warrant for his arrest, the archbishop did just that and so won his freedom. King Henry amused himself at the expense of both prelates."

"A cruel jest," Lady Denny murmured, "but a true story. My husband shared this same tale with me." Her husband, Sir Anthony Denny, was as close as any man to the king and was even authorized to sign documents with His Grace's stamp when King Henry was unavailable to write his own name.

"Is it possible," Jane asked, "that the king intends to toy with Your Grace in a similar way?"

"If you have offended His Grace with plain speaking," Lady Hertford chimed in, "he may wish to punish you. But not, I think, with imprisonment or death."

"I pray you are correct," the queen said, "but this warrant . . ." Her voice trailed off as her hands crept to her throat.

I shivered, remembering that two of King Henry's previous wives had been beheaded on His Grace's orders.

"You have never betrayed the king," Elizabeth Tyrwhitt said. "Not by word or deed." She was a tall, thin woman, and utterly devoted to her royal mistress.

"But I have annoyed him," Queen Kathryn whispered.

"His Grace *encouraged* you to dispute with him on matters of religion," Anne Herbert reminded her. The queen's sister, and Will's, was a quiet little woman, adept at fading into the background, but she was flushed with anger on Queen Kathryn's behalf.

"The truth is of little worth against the king's whim," Her Grace said, and resumed pacing.

"You must convince him that you are contrite," Jane said.

"And give him cause to pity you," Joan Denny added.

"Take to your bed, Your Grace," Lady Tyrwhitt suggested. "Give out that your health is in a dangerous state."

The queen sent a rueful smile her way. "Under the circumstances, that is no lie."

"But the king has an aversion to illness," Lady Denny objected. "Hearing that you are ill will only drive him farther away."

"What if Your Grace's physician tells him that your illness is caused not by some physical ailment but by distress of the mind," I suggested.

The queen stopped pacing, her forehead creased in thought. "That ploy might succeed, especially if His Grace *did* arrange for you to find the warrant. He will delight in imagining me struck down by terror . . . and he will want to see the results of his little game for himself."

It was incomprehensible to me that a man who claimed to love his wife should do such a thing. Perhaps he would not send her to the Tower and the rack, but this was torture, too, deliberate and cruel.

No wonder Will hesitated to ask favors from His Grace. King Henry would as soon give pain as pleasure. Likely he *would* have demanded that I share his bed, had I gone through with my plan to solicit his help. Convinced I'd had a narrow escape, I forced my thoughts back to the present crisis. The queen's ladies were still refining my suggestion.

"By rights Your Grace *should* be out of your mind with fear," the

Countess of Hertford said. "A few hysterical screams would lend credence to that idea."

"And the uproar will bring Dr. Wendy running." Jane smiled faintly. Dr. Thomas Wendy was the fussiest of the royal physicians, always on the lookout for the first sign of some dread disease. He was also a great advocate of bleeding and purging.

"I believe I can persuade Dr. Wendy that only a visit from His Grace can cure me," the queen said.

"But what will you say to the king when he comes?" Lady Herbert asked her sister.

"I will confess to being laid low by the terrible fear that I unintentionally displeased him. I will show myself eager to win his forgiveness. And eager, too, to please him. I will tell him how much I have missed his embraces. And since I will already, conveniently, be in my bed, perhaps he will join me there. But first," the queen added, regarding each of the ladies of her inner circle in turn, "we must take precautions. If any of you still have in your possession any proscribed books, no matter how well hidden, you must destroy them. We cannot risk having them found by searchers."

Nods of agreement all around proved that although these women were zealous in their religious beliefs, none was foolish enough to risk dying for them.

The queen's gaze came to rest on me. "You'd best leave now, Bess, but I thank you for your loyalty."

I was glad to escape. The queen's plan was dangerous to everyone in her confidence. I returned to the presence chamber, found the embroidery I had abandoned hours earlier, and waited.

Within a quarter hour, loud shrieks and lamentations issued from the queen's bedchamber. They would be just as clearly audible in the king's apartments, adjacent to the queen's on the other side. It was not long before Dr. Wendy, his face deeply creased with worry, hurried through the presence chamber on his way to the queen. When he emerged a short time later, he looked even more troubled.

A nerve-racking hour followed before the king appeared. I suspected it had taken that long to hoist His Grace to his feet so that he could hobble from his apartments to the queen's. He might have gone to her with less difficulty by using the connecting room between his secret lodgings and hers, but he seemed to want the entire court to bear witness to his willingness to visit his ailing wife.

His Grace did not stay long, but the next evening Queen Kathryn was admitted to King Henry's bedchamber. I shuddered to think what Her Grace might have to do to win back her husband's affection. Submitting to his views on religion would be the least of it! But I was as relieved as anyone else when they appeared fully reconciled the next morning.

The following day, the king accompanied the queen and her maids of honor into the garden. King Henry found walking difficult, so they sat side by side on chairs, enjoying the view of the river. I had just settled myself next to Alys on a blanket spread on the ground when a contingent of uniformed guards from the Tower of London approached. The lord chancellor led them. He carried the warrant for the queen's arrest in one hand. By his somber expression, he anticipated carrying out an unpleasant but necessary duty. He stopped short, his eyes widening in alarm, when he saw that the king was holding his wife's hand.

Showing a great lack of common sense, he still attempted to make an arrest.

King Henry seized the warrant, read what it said, and turned purple with rage. "Knave! Arrant knave! Beast! Fool!" King Henry bellowed so loudly that his words echoed off the walls of the palace.

Alys and I exchanged a nervous look. This roaring seemed to bode well for the queen, but the king's temper was always uncertain. And he *had* signed the warrant.

"Get out of my sight!" King Henry shouted.

Only after the lord chancellor and the guards had gone did I breathe freely again.

25

Once the king and queen were reconciled, I began to hope that there might soon be an opportunity to ask the king to sanction my marriage to Will. My love for him burned as brightly as ever, but he always seemed to have some good reason to delay.

In the summer the court went on progress again, this time to visit the king's smaller houses. It was September before we settled in for a long stay at Windsor Castle. There His Grace fell ill and kept to his bedchamber for the best part of two weeks to recover from a catarrh.

In mid-November, the court moved to Oatlands. His Grace's health was still uncertain, as was his temper. For no apparent reason, he abruptly left all but a few of his favorite courtiers behind and went to London, spending several days there before he returned.

In the first week of December we were back at Nonsuch. The king seemed cheerful, but the reason for his good mood discouraged Will and I from broaching the subject of our clandestine marriage. The king had ordered the arrests of the Duke of Norfolk and his son, the Earl of Surrey, charging both with treason. They were quickly condemned to death and their estates seized by the Crown. I never did understand what either had done to provoke King Henry's wrath, but the imminent execution of the earl, someone Will had known and considered a friend since their days together in the Duke of Richmond's household, convinced him that this was no time to ask favors of the king.

I agreed with him, until King Henry granted him Norfolk House, in Lambeth. Surely that was a sign that Will had the king's affection. It was the queen herself who stopped me when I would have approached His Grace.

"Have a care, Bess," she warned. "The king takes away as easily as he gives. Remember just *how* he acquired Norfolk House in order to pass it on to Will."

"But His Grace remains devoted to you, Your Grace," I said. Ever since the king had thwarted Gardiner's scheme, he had showered his wife with expensive gifts.

"Does he?" Queen Kathryn's eyes tracked a man chatting with friends on the far side of the presence chamber. I recognized him as Sir Thomas Seymour, Lord Hertford's younger brother, and suddenly remembered all the old stories about Seymour and the queen.

He was a handsome man with a reddish-brown beard and sleepy hazel eyes that instantly put images of darkened bedchambers into a woman's mind. He had been largely absent from court since I'd been a part of it, but he had returned in August, just in time for the celebrations surrounding the signing of a peace treaty with France. He knew who I was. He and Will often played tennis together. That did not stop him from scattering improper suggestions in among a flurry of compliments. Only Will's timely arrival prevented me from telling "Tom," as he insisted I call him, what I thought of his crude innuendos.

"He's a good fellow," Will said as we took our leave of Tom Seymour, "and a master of inventive cursing."

"That can hardly endear him to the king." King Henry's only oath was a mild "By St. George!"

"The king appreciates Tom's skill as a diplomat," Will said.

I supposed he was more subtle in his dealings with other gentlemen than he was with the ladies. Then again, many women seemed to find his swaggering self-confidence appealing. Nothing about Tom Seymour was attractive to me. Compared to Will, he was a crude, self-centered brute.

Without warning, King Henry left Nonsuch for Whitehall. He took with him four gentlemen of the privy chamber and the members of his Privy Council, including Will. Everyone else, even Queen Kathryn, was forbidden to follow them. Queen and court were to go to Greenwich for Yuletide, but His Grace did not intend to join us there.

"What do you think it means that the king is at Whitehall and Her Grace is here?" I asked Mary as we watched the masque performed on Christmas Eve.

"No one knows," Mary said, "but I can tell you that Lady Hertford, Lady Lisle, and Lady Denny are concerned because they have not heard a word from their husbands since they left Nonsuch."

A few days later, Lady Hertford approached me as I sat sewing in a quiet corner of the presence chamber. "Walk with me, Bess." It was an order, not an invitation.

We made our way to the queen's gallery, where we could stroll without going out into the cold. The frigid weather had arrived early this year, making roads even more treacherous than usual.

The only sounds were our footfalls on the rush matting. Pale sunlight filtered through the window glass, full of dust motes. When we reached the end, Anne Hertford laid a surprisingly firm hand on my arm, preventing me from starting back the other way. "Queen Kathryn wishes to know if you have been in communication with her brother."

I shook my head. "Not a word, my lady. Not since Will left here with the king."

"That is unfortunate."

"Is . . . does the queen think . . . I mean . . ." I stammered to a halt, reluctant to put my worst fears into words.

The Countess of Hertford had to look up to meet my eyes, but my greater height did not give me any advantage. She might be small of stature, but she had a forceful personality. "I know what you would ask: Does His Grace mean to cast off yet another wife?" She released me and turned to stare out at the orchard and the great garden beyond. "Shall I tell you what I think? I believe the king is dying and that he knows it. He has left Her Grace behind because he does not want to risk having her meddle in his plans for the succession."

Shocked, I could only stare at her.

Ever since the day I'd found the warrant for the queen's arrest and warned Her Grace of her danger, she and the ladies who knew of it had been friendlier toward me. I was not in their confidence, but they seemed to trust me. Now Anne, Countess of Hertford, notorious for treating underlings with disdain, had taken it upon herself to speak to me of the most forbidden topic in the realm—the king's death. I was honored. I was also very afraid.

"Things are changing at great speed, Bess. Those of us who are forward thinking must look ahead."

"I do not understand what you mean." But I was beginning to have an inkling.

"My husband is Prince Edward's uncle on his mother's side," Lady Hertford said. "Although the queen believes she will be named regent during his minority, it is clear that King Henry has his doubts about her ability to rule for the boy. The lords on the Privy Council have been meeting at my husband's London house rather than at court. I take that as a sign of what is to come."

So, I thought, Lady Hertford *had* been in contact with her husband the earl. I wondered if the other ladies in the queen's inner circle knew.

"I sympathize with your . . . situation with the queen's brother, Bess. There is no question in my mind that his first marriage is invalid and, since it never existed, there is no barrier to a wedding between the two of you."

When I said nothing, Lady Hertford's expression turned grim.

"My husband is prepared to help you, for a price. Everything you desire can be yours, Bess. All you need do is set pen to paper as I dictate."

What she proposed was simple. As Lord Parr and Earl of Essex, Will would throw his support to Edward Seymour, Earl of Hertford, urging the dying king to name Hertford as regent during Edward's minority. Once King Henry was dead and Hertford had control of the government, he would reward Will by elevating him in the peerage, granting him land and houses, and giving him permission to marry me.

"The queen would do the same," I said.

"The king left her behind," Anne Hertford reminded me. "Kathryn Parr will not be made regent."

"And can a mere regent issue a royal decree?" This seemed to me to be a flaw in the plan. Besides, King Henry was the only one who had the right to decide how England should be governed after his death. I found Lady Hertford's scheming distasteful.

"A regent acts in the place of a king." The countess sounded impatient. If she'd been tall enough, she'd have been looking down her nose at me. "Must I sweeten the pot, Bess? Very well. Think on this: when the king dies, the queen will become queen dowager only and must leave the court. You will lose your post and be sent home to your family. If you wish to stay close to your lover, you must join the household of someone certain to remain, such as the regent's wife. If you do as I say now, I will appoint you as one of my waiting gentlewomen until such time as you marry."

I had a sudden vision of Lady Hertford taking over the queen's apartments, even sitting in the chair of estate under its canopy to receive foreign dignitaries. What arrogance! But if the Earl of Hertford's regency came to pass, far better for me to be on his wife's good side than to make an enemy of her.

"Will may not pay any attention to my wishes," I warned her. But I went with her to find pen and paper and wrote the letter she dictated.

26

King Henry died in the early hours of Friday, the twenty-eighth day of January. Change came rapidly. Suddenly we had a king who was not yet ten years old. His coronation took place on the nineteenth day of February, but even before King Henry had been buried at Windsor, next to Queen Jane, Edward Seymour, Earl of Hertford, had been created Duke of Somerset and appointed lord protector, a fancy name for regent. His first act was to dissolve Parliament. Shortly thereafter, Lord Lisle became Earl of Warwick, Sir Thomas Seymour was created Baron Seymour of Sudeley and appointed lord admiral, replacing Lord Lisle. And Sir William Parr, Lord Parr of Kendal and Earl of Essex, was elevated in the peerage to Marquess of Northampton.

As Lady Hertford, now Duchess of Somerset, had predicted, Will's sister, as the queen dowager, had no role in the new government. Queen Kathryn retired to Chelsea Manor, her dower house. Princess Elizabeth was to live with her there. Mary Woodhull and Lady Tyrwhitt accompanied them to Chelsea, but for the most part, the queen's household was dissolved. With some trepidation, I took up my new post as one of the Duchess of Somerset's ladies-in-waiting.

Although the duchess had promised to help Will obtain a royal decree, it was April before he was able to petition the king. Even then, it was not for His Grace's approval of our marriage, but rather to request that King Edward establish a commission to determine whether or not Will would be *allowed* to remarry.

"We are *already* married," I reminded Will.

"But that is not known to anyone but the two of us."

"We could *tell* them."

We were in the tiny room I'd been assigned at court. It was barely big enough to turn around in, but it was private. I had furnished it with pieces Will-had given me—rich tapestries and a soft feather bed. My wardrobe trunk occupied the rest of the space, leaving only a small rectangle of open floor beside the bed. There we stood facing each other, almost touching. I had not intended to spend this precious time alone with Will in arguing.

"Patience, Bess."

I seized a crewelwork pillow off the bed and hit him with it. He tugged it out of my hand and tossed it carelessly atop the trunk, then took me in his arms.

"Talk to the king," I pleaded, avoiding his lips. "Young Edward is a studious, sweet-tempered boy and he is fond of you. As you are his stepmother's brother, he considers you another uncle."

"But it is his real uncle, the Duke of Somerset, who is in charge, and he does not want to set a bad example for the general populace by making it too easy to discard one wife and take another."

"Hypocrite! He did the same." And Lady Hertford, his current spouse and the newly made Duchess of Somerset, had promised me her husband's support.

"His first wife conveniently died *before* his second marriage." Will sat on the edge of the bed and pulled me down beside him.

I sprang right back up again and glared down at him. "There are times when I wonder if you no longer want to be married to me."

"How can you say such a thing?"

His dismay seemed genuine, but I hardened my heart. I was wont to give in too easily, seduced by Will's easy charm and skillful kisses. Too many times to count, we had both forgotten to be careful and had gone beyond pleasuring each other to couple fully. So far I had not caught a child, but I did not think my luck would hold forever.

"You must insist. Remind Somerset of his promise."

"His *wife's* promise, you mean."

"She rules him."

"Then you must plead our case to her."

I blanched.

Will sighed. "The real problem is that Somerset is an evangelical. He intends to continue reforming the church. To do so, he cannot be seen to support divorce. What if *anyone* could cast off a spouse? There would be chaos."

"I am not learned enough for theological debate, but how can I accept this reasoning?"

"We will not have to wait forever. It is true that, for the moment, we cannot live as man and wife, but once the commission the king has sanctioned decides in our favor, no one will ever again be able to question our right to be together." He reached for me. "In the meantime, let us not waste the afternoon."

I swallowed bitter disappointment and schooled myself to be patient. But oh how I resented the necessity.

In the following week, my father returned to England, escorting a French envoy who had been sent to bring King Edward word of the death of King Francis of France. Father sought me out in my lodgings, regarding the furnishings with a jaundiced eye.

"I have a husband in mind for you, Bess," he announced. "It is past time you were married."

"I thank you for your kindness, Father, but I have made my own choice."

He ignored that. "I am your father, Bess. You will marry where I say. You will find him agreeable, I think. Sir Edward Warner. You know him from Queen Kathryn's household."

"You cannot force me into marriage. I am above the age of sixteen, old enough to make my own decision in this matter."

"That is questionable. You will not be of full age until you enter your twenty-first year."

"A matter of a few months only," I reminded him. "And you cannot coerce me into marriage no matter what my age." I took a deep breath. "Not only have I the right to refuse, but Will and I have already exchanged wedding vows *per verba de presenti*." Let him make what he would of that!

A vein in Father's forehead bulged. "So that is what is behind this commission he's asked for."

"As soon as it is formed, the members will declare Will's earlier marriage invalid, thus removing all barriers to ours."

"I would not be so certain of success. The commissioners will no doubt be churchmen and conservative in their thinking, at least in matters such as this. If they forbid remarriage, what will you do then, eh?"

"I will live with Will as his mistress!"

The words burst out of me before I considered how Father would react. I quailed before his fulminating glare. I had never seen him so angry. For a moment I thought he might strike me. Or worse, take me forcibly back to Cowling Castle and lock me in the highest tower. Instead he took several deep breaths as he backed away from me.

"I have raised a fool," he said when he reached the door. "I pray you will come to your senses soon, before a respectable marriage is no longer possible."

"I have a good marriage already, Father," I whispered when he had gone. I wished I dared shout that truth to the world, but Will was right. We needed to be cautious until the commission gave its ruling.

Caution. Patience. I came to hate both those words, especially when the eight men chosen to decide our fate were, as Father had predicted, conservative and mostly churchmen. One was Archbishop Cranmer. It was May before they even took up Will's petition. There seemed little hope of a prompt decision.

"Is there no way to hurry things along?" I asked the Duchess of Somerset, who still claimed to be sympathetic to our plight.

"Patience, Bess," Anne Somerset advised.

That was what everyone said, unless they were telling me how foolish I was to pine for a married man. It did not help that so many of my friends were gone from court.

Jack Dudley was one of the few who remained. With his father's elevation in the peerage to Earl of Warwick, Jack had acquired the courtesy title of Lord Lisle. He had grown into his feet, as they say, and now bore a strong resemblance to both his father and his late brother, Harry Dudley. Jack had retained, however, his admiration for me.

"You could still change your mind and marry me," he said as we stood together to watch the gentlemen pensioners muster in Hyde Park. Will's standard, yellow and black with a maiden's head, his sister's emblem, flew above them.

"I scarce think that would please your father." Jack made the same suggestion every time we met, even though there had been talk for some time of a match for him with the Duke of Somerset's eldest daughter, a girl named Anne, after her mother.

Jack was silent for a time, watching the well-trained, beautifully caparisoned horses go through their paces. Their riders, dressed in yellow velvet, paraded with the levies of other nobles, each dressed in distinctive livery.

"Do you truly love Will Parr, Bess?"

"I do."

"Why?"

"Love has no reason, Jack. Or perhaps it has too many to name. I cannot explain it. I only know what exists between us."

Trumpets sounded. To entertain the crowd, Will's fifty gentlemen pensioners began a carefully staged attack on one of the other bands. The "battle" raged for a quarter of an hour, raising a great cloud of dust and pleasing the spectators, especially the young king, who cheered the combatants on as lustily as any shopkeeper's son.

"Toy soldiers," Jack sneered. "They've never seen a real battle."

"Nor have you." I was quick to take offense at the insult to Will. "You were the lucky one. Instead of going to war like Harry, you entered the young prince's household and remained with him throughout King Henry's reign."

Jack regarded me with mild curiosity. "Did you ever love Harry?"

I hesitated. "I liked him. In time it might have become more."

"Father says love is not important in marriage. Most people marry without it."

A shout went up as the gentlemen pensioners made another mock sally.

"Your parents love each other," I said. "So do mine."

"I wonder if that was always true."

I considered before I answered. "I think so, at least in my parents' case, or so my grandmother told me when I was young." I repressed a sigh. I had not seen Grandmother Jane since her long-ago visit to Cowling Castle. If she hadn't approved of Will as a suitor for her daughter, I doubted that opinion had altered now that it was her granddaughter who was in love with him.

Jack's face was impossible to read. "I wish you well, Bess. Know that. Always."

27

Will and I continued to bide our time through June and into July, waiting for the legal process to work in our favor. Others were not as prudent. A screech of rage from the Duchess of Somerset sent all her ladies scurrying for cover. She prevented my escape by shouting my name just as I reached the door.

Wary, I approached her, braced for a slap. She'd boxed more than one of her ladies' ears in the past. I bobbed a curtsy. "Your Grace?"

"Do you know what that jumped-up country housewife has done?"

"No, madam." Nor did I know who this "housewife" was.

Lady Somerset's nostrils flared. "The queen dowager has secretly married Tom Seymour."

I felt my jaw drop. I took a quick step back, but there was no blow aimed at my head. She was too busy cursing Will's sister. Once the duchess had been Queen Kathryn's devoted friend. Now she looked upon her as a bitter rival.

Her displays of temper went on for days. She had convinced herself that her brother-in-law had married the king's widow in a bid for power.

She suspected Tom Seymour of conspiring to put himself in his brother's place as lord protector. And she accused Will of being hand in glove with the newlyweds. This made me guilty by association.

Any possibility that Anne Somerset would eventually persuade her husband to support Will's right to remarry vanished overnight. I thought of leaving her service, but Will insisted I stay. Since we did not wish to provoke Lady Somerset further, I gritted my teeth and persevered.

The sad truth was that I had nowhere else to go. After our last quarrel, Father had forbidden me to return to Cowling Castle unless I was prepared to forsake Will and marry a man of my family's choosing.

Matters came to a head when Kathryn Parr, the new Lady Seymour, came to court to visit her stepson the king. The queen dowager and the lord protector's wife met in the king's watching chamber. At court, matters of precedence were never trivial. My place was clear. Since no one knew of my clandestine vows to Will, which should have made me Marchioness of Northampton, I was naught but a lady-in-waiting to a duchess. But that duchess was also the wife of the lord protector. No one had held that position before.

Lady Somerset approached her sister-in-law with fire in her eyes. "I will enter first," she announced.

Queen Kathryn glared at her former lady-in-waiting. "My superior rank must be observed. You may have the honor of carrying my train."

"It is unsuitable for me to perform such a menial service for the wife of my husband's younger brother."

The queen dowager refused to give place. Ordering Lady Tyrwhitt to carry her train instead, she advanced toward the king's presence chamber.

The Duchess of Somerset elbowed her aside.

For two such tiny women, each possessed formidable strength. The moment Anne Somerset tried to dart ahead of her, Queen Kathryn gave her a shove and swept through the door in triumph. Furious at the insult, Lady Somerset followed at a run. I trailed after them, heartily wishing I was anywhere else.

The young king greeted his stepmother warmly. He seemed unaware of the tension between the two noblewomen. He was a slender lad with angelic looks—golden hair, pink cheeks, and his mother's pointed chin. Indeed, there seemed to be little of his father in him. Edward had, however, approved Kathryn's marriage to Tom Seymour *before* it became public knowledge. The lord protector and his wife were thus prevented from taking overt action against the newlyweds.

If only, I thought, Will and I could appeal directly to the young king. But that was no longer possible. Tom Seymour's coup had cost all of us private access to His Grace.

Anne Somerset was still fuming when she returned to her own lodgings, formerly the queen's apartments. She vented her feelings by throwing a hairbrush, a wooden box that held trinkets, and her prayer book, ranting all the while.

"Who is she but a nobody?" the duchess demanded. "If her new husband cannot teach her better manners, then I will do so."

Keeping an eye peeled for flying objects, I began to gather up the trinkets. I had just retrieved the hairbrush when the lord protector entered his wife's bedchamber.

"Was it wise to create a scene, my dear?" he asked in a quiet voice.

I froze, trapped on hands and knees on the rush matting, hidden from view by the duchess's bed. Why did this sort of thing keep happening to me?

Lady Somerset flung herself into her husband's arms and burst into tears. "She is a wicked, wicked woman to marry again so soon after her husband's death."

"Impulsive, certainly."

I peeked around the edge of the heavy velvet bed hangings. The duke's hand inscribed soothing circles on his wife's back. He was so tall that her head barely reached the bottom of his long, flowing beard.

"She must not be allowed to profit from her wanton behavior." Lady Somerset's smile was sultry as she gazed up at her husband's angular features.

His well-formed lips curved upward, making the beard twitch. "What did you have in mind, sweeting?"

"Her jewels. I want her jewels. The ones she has been asking be delivered to her."

He frowned. "The jewels were left to her in the king's will." He spoke in a slow, deliberate manner, his words carefully measured. "It was only by chance that they happened to be stored in the King's Jewel House in the Tower at the time of his death."

"If you say they are the property of the Crown, you can refuse to give them to her." She purred the suggestion, putting me in mind of a sleek, pampered kitten—with very sharp claws.

"And I suppose that next you will say that I also have the authority to let you borrow them?" His wry tone suggested that he knew his wife very well.

"Why not?" She pouted and began to toy with the laces at his throat. I winced, remembering the countless times I'd done the same thing to Will's clothing. I knew what came next.

"They are *royal* baubles, my sweet." He kissed the tip of her nose.

"She should not have the keeping of anything royal. Bad enough that the king's sister was sent to live with her. You must forbid her to visit His Grace again."

"I will deny her the jewelry," he temporized.

"You are executor of the late king's estate," Lady Somerset murmured. "That gives you the authority to make decisions about her dower lands."

An avaricious gleam came into the lord protector's eyes. "I do have the right to lease parks and other properties. Still, it is customary to obtain the widow's consent before doing so."

"Customary but hardly *necessary*." The duchess went up on her tiptoes and kissed him on the lips.

While they were both distracted, I scurried around the bed and slipped quietly out of the chamber.

As summer advanced, relations deteriorated further between dowager and duchess. It galled Lady Somerset that her rival continued to have custody of Princess Elizabeth. When she heard that the king's sister had been allowed to go out at night in a barge upon the Thames, unaccompanied by any older ladies of consequence, she used this as an excuse to meddle. She ordered Elizabeth's governess, Mistress Astley, to present herself at Syon, the mansion near Richmond Palace where the Somersets lived when they were not at court.

The duchess ordered me to attend her. Her sense of her own consequence was such that she was never without at least one waiting gentlewoman.

Mistress Astley crept into the room, timid as a mouse. I had expected someone with a commanding presence, accustomed to giving orders in a royal household and being obeyed. Instead, she was short, plump, and so nondescript as to be almost invisible. Her plain, round face was twisted into a mask of anxiety.

"You failed in your duty!" Lady Somerset's words snapped out like a whip, causing the governess to shrink into herself. "To give the princess too much freedom is to put not only her reputation but her very life at risk."

The duchess continued in this vein for some time, heaping abuse on the poor woman's head. When she paused for breath, Mistress Astley tried to defend herself.

"It was little more than a moonlight boat ride, my lady. Her Grace was not alone. Two of her maids of honor accompanied her."

"Girls like herself," the duchess scoffed. "Not proper chaperones. The princess is not yet fourteen and her attendants are only a few years older."

"They are sensible young women," Mistress Astley countered. Meek and mild she might be, but she was brave enough to defend her young charge.

"And you yourself most assuredly are not! If you do not exert greater control over the princess in the future, you will be replaced as Her Grace's governess."

Mistress Astley's face lost every vestige of color at the threat of being separated from the young girl she had nurtured since she was a toddler. Smiling in satisfaction, Lady Somerset unleashed yet another wave of invective.

After that incident, life in Lady Somerset's household became well nigh unbearable. She delighted in making everyone miserable. I was careful not to offend her, but when the end of summer came with no decision yet by the commission, I took matters into my own hands. I begged leave of the duchess, claiming I wished to return to my parents. She granted it with unflattering swiftness. Before she could change her mind, I packed my belongings, hired a boat, and set off downriver.

I had no intention of going to Cowling Castle. My destination was Will's house in Lambeth. Norfolk House stood just west of the archbishop of Canterbury's palace and across the Thames from Westminster. I was done with being patient. Although we would have to keep my presence secret for the nonce, I meant to make Norfolk House my home, living there with Will while we waited for the commissioners to sanction our union.

28

We renewed our vows in the private chapel of Norfolk House, and although there was still no priest to bless our union, this time I kept Will's ring on my finger afterward. We would have to wait until the commission stopped dawdling and made its ruling before we could announce our married state to the world, but in the meantime we would be together, living as man and wife.

We had our own private marriage feast to celebrate, just the two of us. Will ordered his cook to prepare all my favorite foods. His musicians played for us while we ate, and when the meal had been cleared away and the table removed, we danced to the sound of lute and pipe and tabor. Candlelight played across the strong planes of Will's face to show me the look of devotion—and desire—in his eyes.

"Have you naught planned but dancing?" I whispered when the next tune came to an end. Smiling, I fluttered my eyelashes, affecting the shyness of a demure maiden.

He knew my meaning, but he could not resist teasing me in return.

"Would you have a masque to celebrate our wedding, love? Or mayhap a tournament?"

"I would have you, Will, all to myself." I sent a pointed look toward the grinning musicians. They were not the Bassanos this time, but simply trusted members of Will's household.

A gesture sent them away. Then Will swept me into his arms and carried me to his bedchamber. Our bedchamber.

Sweet-scented herbs had been strewn and a low fire made with applewood burned in the hearth. A brace of candles lit our way to the bed, another of the enormous carved and gilded pieces Will favored, richly furnished with feather beds and down-filled coverlets.

I had no need of a tiring maid. Will had me out of my wedding finery in a trice and himself undressed in half that time. We stared at each other, completely naked together for the first time since we'd exchanged vows at Guildford, before the Duke of Suffolk's untimely death had interfered with our plans. I laughed in delight.

"Are you pleased with your bargain, wife?" Will asked.

"Well pleased, husband, except that you are standing too far away from me."

He obligingly closed the distance between us and took me into his arms. Then we consummated our second marriage ceremony even more thoroughly than we had our first.

That set the pattern of our nights. Our days passed just as pleasurably.

No one knew I was living at Norfolk House save Will's two sisters; his recently acquired brother-in-law, Tom Seymour; and the queen dowager's faithful waiting gentlewoman—she had been promoted from chamberer—Mary Woodhull. Mary, who was herself betrothed to Davy Seymour, was happy for me. Tom Seymour thought we should have waited. Fine talk from a man whose own marriage had been scandalously precipitous!

My family continued to think I was still in the service of the Duchess of Somerset. The only others I might have confided in also resided at some distance. My first mistress, Jane Dudley, had remained in the country since becoming Countess of Warwick instead of Lady Lisle, and my friend Alys Guildford, who had returned to her kinswoman's service, was with her.

The months that followed our decision to live together as husband and wife were filled with quiet contentment. I loved Norfolk House from the first moment I saw it. The mansion, adjoined by substantial gardens, several paddocks, and a two-acre close, boasted a great chamber for dining, a gallery for walking, an oratory, several privy closets, and a great many other rooms. We had one just for music—Will played the virginals while I strummed my lute. There was a library in which Will delighted. And the largest bedchamber, with that magnificent bed, continued to please us both.

Will went often to court to attend meetings of the Privy Council, but this required no more than a quick trip on the horse ferry that plied the Thames between Lambeth and Westminster. All the rest of his time, he spent with me.

When the cold weather came, we made one of the smaller chambers our withdrawing room. We placed two Glastonbury chairs close to the hearth, one for each of us. The first time it became so warm in the chamber that beads of sweat formed on our foreheads; we took off each other's clothing, piece by piece, spread it out before the fire as a makeshift bed, and made love. Afterward, we watched the flames and dreamed of the future.

"I have put several of my northern estates in your name," Will said, "to assure you of an income should anything happen to me before you are officially acknowledged as my wife."

I sat up, my mood shattered. "Nothing will happen to you."

"So fierce," he murmured as he drew me back into his arms and made me forget he'd ever mentioned the matter.

When the court traveled to Enfield to celebrate Christmas, and the queen dowager, her husband, and Princess Elizabeth joined King Edward there, we remained in Norfolk House. It was our first Yuletide together.

We enjoyed blissful solitude until my old friend Jack Dudley barged in. He left most of his men, in their bright new Lisle livery, to wait in the courtyard while he boldly strode into our little withdrawing room. Two burly fellows wearing the Duke of Somerset's badges on their sleeves came with him.

"How dare you invade my home?" Will demanded. Fury mottled his face and deepened his voice to a growl.

Jack avoided looking directly at me by keeping his attention on Will. "I have been sent by the Duke of Somerset, lord protector of this realm, and I have here the authority to carry out his orders." He produced a roll of parchment.

Will snatched it out of Jack's hand. As he read, his color changed so rapidly from red to white that I feared he was about to have a seizure. Already on my feet, I tried to go to him, but Jack stepped between us. I shoved at him, but I could not budge him. When I attempted to duck around him, he caught me and tugged me close against his side. I curled my hands into fists and hit him, but it was like striking armor. I stomped on his foot with even less effect, since I wore thin leather shoes and he had on heavy riding boots.

"Behave, Bess," Jack hissed in my ear. "Better to yield to me than some other."

I stilled, but only because Will was ripping the document to pieces. Jack signaled to Somerset's men to seize hold of Will.

"This is an outrage," Will shouted as they hauled him out of the room.

"What did that paper say?" I began to struggle again, with no more success than before. "What is going on?"

"You and Will are commanded to separate," Jack answered. "You are to be placed in the queen dowager's keeping at Chelsea."

"No! I will not leave him."

"You do not have a choice, Bess," Jack said, not unkindly. "Nor do I." Then he gave orders for the servants to pack my belongings.

He would not allow us a proper farewell, or even a few words in private. When I tried to ask questions, he ordered me to be silent.

Tears streaming down my cheeks, I watched from a window as the lord protector's men rode off with Will in custody. My limbs felt like ice, and those frozen appendages refused to support my weight. I sank into my chair, engulfed by a suffocating anguish. Time passed. I had no sense of how much later it was when Jack escorted me out of Norfolk House and onto a waiting barge. We were to be rowed upriver to the queen's dower house—a little more than two miles away.

"I do not understand," I whispered as the oarsmen set us in motion. "Where have they taken Will? What have we done to deserve such treatment?"

"You have been living in sin for months," Jack said. "Surely you cannot be surprised to have been found out."

"I am not Will's mistress. I am his wife."

"Yes, more's the pity. If you had not gone through a form of marriage with him, you'd not be in so much trouble now." At my bewildered expression, his finely arched brows lifted. He took off his bonnet, raked one hand through his dark hair, and shook his head. "You truly did not realize, did you? Or else you ignored anything it did not suit you to know. Aye, that's more likely. You always were one to go your own way."

"That is unfair, Jack. And I've always been good at finding my way *out* of trouble."

"Yes, I remember how we escaped from the maze at Woodstock." He sighed. "Norfolk House is hard by Lambeth Palace. Did you think that your neighbor, the archbishop of Canterbury, would not notice that you were living there?"

"Even so, what have we done that is so wrong?" I asked. "It is only a matter of time before the commission—"

"That was your first mistake. The archbishop is a member of that commission. By his lights, you should have waited for them to make a ruling before you did anything. He reported your presence to the lord protector and Somerset flew into a rage." Jack's lips twisted into a rueful smile. "You can imagine Lady Somerset's reaction."

I shivered, and not because of the icy river water on every side.

"The charge against you, Bess, is adultery."

I felt as if I'd been kicked. For a moment all the breath went out of me. "Must I do penance?" I whispered. I knew the punishment. It was to walk barefoot to church wearing nothing but a shift.

"You will be spared public humiliation, but you are confined to Chelsea until further notice. The queen dowager and her husband, the lord admiral, should return there within the week."

"And Will? What of him? Where has he been taken?"

"To court."

I breathed a sigh of relief. I had been afraid he would tell me Will was bound for the Tower of London, where his old friend the Earl of Surrey had so recently been executed. Surrey's father, the Duke of Norfolk, the last owner of Norfolk House, was still a prisoner behind its impenetrable walls.

"Will is to be deprived of his seat on the Privy Council and reprimanded." A look of pity came into Jack's dark eyes. "And the charge against him is not just adultery, but also bigamy. He is forbidden, on pain of death, to see you or write to you until after the commission has rendered its verdict."

29

The queen dowager and her husband, Tom Seymour, were entirely on her brother Will's side. Kathryn's dislike of her brother-in-law, the lord protector, and his grasping wife had increased tenfold since the day Anne Seymour, Duchess of Somerset, first tried to claim she had precedence over that "jumped-up country housewife," Queen Kathryn. Kathryn was furious on Will's behalf when Tom brought word that Will had not only been deprived of his seat on the Privy Council but had also been banished from court.

"I take heart from the fact that he was not imprisoned," I said.

"Wise of you," Kathryn allowed, but I could see she was fuming.

"Will still has all his titles and properties," Tom said. "He continues to live at Norfolk House."

"Waiting for me," I said, and sighed. "I do not understand why the Duke of Somerset will not see reason. He cast off his own first wife for adultery back when he was still plain Sir Edward Seymour. He should sympathize with Will's dilemma."

"My brother is a hypocrite and a thief," Tom said.

Kathryn stopped pacing long enough to smile at him. "It is fortunate for him that he did not attempt to approach me when we were at Enfield, else I might have done him bodily harm."

"It is forbidden to strike a man at court, Your Grace," Tom teased her.

"I could have *bitten* him. There is no law against that." The queen dowager might have been small of stature, but she was fierce.

She reminded me at that moment of Rig, her spaniel, who had once dared to nip King Henry's ankle. Rig was at Chelsea, too, but he was getting on in years and spent most of his time sleeping in a basket in a corner of the solar. In addition to Kathryn's pets, her household numbered some 120 people, including Mary Woodhull; Lady Tyrwhitt; Will's other sister, Anne Herbert; and Anne's youngest son.

"I do not know which makes me angrier," Kathryn continued, "that the duke has been leasing my dower properties without my permission, or that he still has not returned the jewelry left to me in Henry's will. He will not even release my wedding ring, or the cross of gold my mother gave me. You remember the piece, Bess, the one with diamonds on the cross itself—and three pearls pendant as well."

What I remembered was that the queen's jewel chest had been locked up for safekeeping in the King's Jewel House in the Tower at the time of King Henry's death. No matter what was in it, the Duke of Somerset had possession of it now. I wondered if Lady Somerset had convinced her husband to let her wear the queen's jewels.

"A pity that the duke cannot see what a bad influence his wife is," I said. "Perhaps then he would not let her lead him around by the nose."

"I do not believe it is his *nose*," Tom quipped.

Kathryn made a choking sound. Then she started to laugh. In spite of my troubles, I joined in. For a little while, I felt less sad.

A few days later, Kathryn asked a favor of me. She was concerned about her stepdaughter the princess. Elizabeth Tudor had her own household within the queen dowager's at Chelsea. Her Grace's tutor, a young man named William Grindal, had recently died. Elizabeth was so distraught over his loss that she was refusing to consider any of the suggestions the lord admiral and the queen dowager had made to her for a suitable replacement.

The last time I'd spoken privily with the princess had been just after the death of Jack Dudley's brother Harry. Princess Elizabeth had advised against love, since it always led to loss. She'd been barely eleven years old at the time. I wondered if, at fourteen, she still felt the same way.

I found Her Grace walking in the gallery for exercise. Mistress Astley and several maids of honor were with her, but they faded into the background to allow me to converse in relative privacy with their mistress.

She had grown taller, slimmer, and more graceful since our last encounter and already had a well-developed bosom. Innate or learned, she also possessed the dignified bearing of a member of the royal family.

"How am I to address you?" she asked bluntly, once she'd granted me permission to walk beside her.

"Bess will do, Your Grace."

"Have you come to lecture me on my morals?" she asked.

Surprised into a laugh, I denied it. "I cannot imagine why you should think so," I added.

"It was only a kiss." She sounded defensive.

Since I had no idea what kiss she meant, I said nothing. After a moment, she gestured for me to sit beside her on the padded bench at the end of the gallery. From that height we could just glimpse the spires of London's tallest churches, off to the east.

"Is my stepmother wroth with me?" Elizabeth Tudor asked.

"I do not believe so, Your Grace. The only concern she expressed to me had to do with the selection of a new tutor."

A shadow crossed her face. "They want me to accept some relative of Master Grindal's, as if putting another with the same name in his place will make up for his loss."

"Is there someone you wish to have as your tutor, Your Grace?"

"Roger Ascham," she said at once. "My master Grindal studied under him at Cambridge. I will have no other teach me."

Noting the stubborn tilt of her jaw, I did not argue. Elizabeth stared past me out the window. She betrayed no nervousness. Her long, tapered fingers lay still in her lap. She did not toy with any of the many ornate rings she wore. But I sensed there was something else on her mind, something she debated sharing with me. Perhaps my current troubles, the fact that I had risked so much for love, made her think I would be a sympathetic listener. After a few moments, she unburdened herself.

"There is nothing wrong with a kiss beneath the kissing bough on Twelfth Night."

"It is an old and honored tradition," I agreed.

"Lady Tyrwhitt would make something out of nothing. She is an interfering busybody."

I thought for a moment. "I have never had much to do with her, but she always seemed to me to be the most evangelical of the queen's ladies." A half-forgotten detail popped into my head. "She was writing a book of prayers when I knew her at court."

"*Everyone* thinks the lord admiral is a most toothsome man," Elizabeth said.

I began at last to see where this conversation might lead. Like so many other women, the princess had been charmed by the queen dowager's husband. Still, I could not see the harm in it. Tom Seymour was safely married to Elizabeth's stepmother and Kathryn was here at Chelsea to chaperone her young charge. So were Mistress Astley and all the other members of Elizabeth's entourage.

The princess's cheeks were pink and she could no longer meet my eyes. "He kissed me under the kissing bough at Enfield just as the queen dowager came upon us. It was a *real* kiss, and she did not like it."

My heart went out to her. The casual kisses exchanged on meeting meant nothing, but the kind of kiss that held desire was something quite different, especially the first one a girl received from a man she found attractive. Only eight years separated us, but I suddenly felt decades older.

"There was no reason for the queen dowager to be so upset,"

Elizabeth continued. "Why should she be when she had no objection to anything he did last summer."

"Last summer?" I prompted her, remembering that she had escaped proper chaperones for a moonlit ride on the Thames. Had there been more to the incident than I'd realized? I felt a faint stirring of alarm at the thought.

Elizabeth kept her head down and mumbled, "Naught but tickling games, and a race through the gardens. Her Grace and the lord admiral both." She lifted reddish lashes to reveal dark eyes filled with despair. "And on Twelfth Night I *wanted* him to kiss me," she whispered. "I wanted him to desire me. And all he said, when the queen dowager interrupted us, was 'God's precious blood, Kate, you make a fuss over nothing.' *Nothing!* I am *nothing* to him."

Her ladies, hovering at the far end of the gallery, sent worried glances our way but did not approach.

"He is married, Your Grace," I said in a low voice. "It would not be right for him to desire you."

"Being married does not stop the Marquess of Northampton from desiring you!"

I winced as if she'd struck me.

The princess drew in a steadying breath. "I beg your pardon, Bess. That was uncalled for. I know that the lord admiral and my stepmother have a true marriage and that they care deeply for each other. The matter of Lord Northampton and his estranged wife is entirely different."

I did not contradict her, nor did I tell her how foolish she had been to encourage Tom Seymour, a man well known to be a devil with the ladies. Neither did I repeat my entire conversation with the princess to the queen dowager, only Elizabeth's request that Roger Ascham be appointed as her new tutor.

30

My time at Chelsea Manor passed slowly. I felt cut off from the outside world. The many-turreted redbrick house had been designed as a country retreat and could only be reached by water and by a single narrow road that led to a tiny village of no importance.

I saw little of the princess, who was busy with her studies once Master Ascham arrived to take charge of them. Most of my time was spent with my two sisters-in-law and their ladies, including Mary Woodhull, and with Will's nephew, three-year-old Edward Herbert. I enjoyed being "Aunt Bess" to the boy. Will and I had talked of having a child, but we had taken precautions to prevent conception during our time together, even after we were living as man and wife at Norfolk House. We'd wanted to be sure there was no question of legitimacy when I bore his heir.

In March, Mistress Lavina Teerlinck the paintrix arrived to make a portrait of the little boy. While she was at Chelsea, I commissioned her to paint me in small. When the miniature was finished, I gave it to Tom Seymour to take to Will. No one had thought to forbid him to own my likeness.

At long last spring arrived, making it possible to stroll out of doors along newly mown alleys and enjoy the gardens. I wandered beside hedges of privet and whitethorn and between banks of rosemary and borders of lavender, inhaling their warm scents. If I closed my eyes, I could almost imagine myself back in my own garden at Norfolk House.

I ventured into the orchard as well, where a mixture of trees had been planted less than ten years before—cherries, filbert, and damson. There were also two peach trees, already in flower and giving promise of a bountiful crop. The orchard was surrounded by fields. Sometimes, looking out across all that open space, a vista filled with cowslips, daisies, and gillyflowers, I found it difficult to remember that I was only a few miles from the center of London.

I walked as far as the postern gate that led to the road but I did not pass through. There was nowhere to go. I glanced back at the house that had been my home for more than three months. Surely the commissioners would make their decision soon.

My spirits lifted when I saw that young Edward had come outside with his nurse. There was a little stone basin in the privy garden that had been turned into a fishpond. Edward had his pole at the ready and the queen dowager herself was giving him instructions on how to land a fish.

She smiled when I joined them. "Are you an angler, Bess?"

"My brothers tried to teach me but I lacked the patience for the sport."

"Why does that not surprise me?"

We stood side by side to watch Edward try his luck. Several minutes passed before I noticed that Kathryn kept touching her hand to her abdomen. "Are you unwell, Kathryn?"

A shy smile reassured me even before she answered. "Very well indeed, Bess. I am with child."

I struggled to find words. This was most unexpected. Kathryn had been married three times before without conceiving. For a barren woman of thirty-four to suddenly prove fertile was the next thing to a miracle. "I envy you," I said at last.

"Your turn will come."

I hoped it would arrive before I was as old as she was, but I gave her the smile she expected before we went back to watching our mutual nephew catch fish.

A few days later, my sister Kate arrived at Chelsea. It had been years since I'd last seen her. At nineteen, her resemblance to our mother was striking. That was shock enough, but the news that she was en route to her new home in the company of a husband left me speechless.

Experienced at smoothing over awkwardness, the queen dowager expertly separated the newlyweds, engaging John Jerningham in conversation so that Kate and I could steal away to my chamber. I'd heard not a word from anyone in my family since I'd arrived at Chelsea. The letters I'd sent to Cowling Castle had gone unanswered.

I did not know what to ask Kate first. Before I could decide, she rushed into my arms and embraced me. "I have missed you, Bess! It was very bad of Father to forbid us to write to you, but he was furious when he heard you were Northampton's mistress."

"I am his wife, Kate."

Her eyebrows winged up. "If you say so."

"I do. And I do not need Father trying to arrange my life."

"He means well," Kate said. "And I am well pleased with the husband he picked out for me."

"Then you are fortunate. I doubt I would have been happy with the results of his matchmaking. I have nothing against Sir Edward Warner, but I do not want him as a husband."

Kate's eyes widened. "Sir Edward Warner? Is that why he came to Cowling Castle?" She started to laugh.

"Why is that so funny?" I had the feeling I'd been insulted, but I could not fathom how.

"Because he's to marry Elizabeth Brooke, after all. Just not you."

That took a moment to work out. Then I was the one gaping. "Aunt Elizabeth?"

Kate nodded. "They announced their betrothal last month."

She rambled merrily on, telling me all about my brother William's new wife, and what the younger boys were up to, and how excited she was to be going to her new home. It was the lot of daughters to wed and leave their childhood homes behind. Sometimes they moved so far away from their parents and siblings that they never saw any of them again. Tears welled up in my eyes. I was not so very far away, but because of the lord protector's vengeful wife and her hatred of the queen dowager, I had lost both husband and family. I flung my arms around Kate and hugged her as tightly as she'd earlier embraced me.

"Promise me we will see each other as often as possible," I begged her. "Swear to me that Father's disapproval will no longer keep us apart."

Kate used her own handkerchief to wipe away my tears. "I promise. Oh, Bess, if only you could be as happy with your Will as I am with my John."

After Kate's visit, it was harder to convince myself that everything would come out right in the end. Try as I might to distract myself from longing for Will, he was always in my thoughts. There were even times when I imagined that I heard his voice.

I was walking in the garden, inhaling the soothing scent of the lavender border, when it happened again. Resolutely, I continued on my way, certain my mind was playing tricks on me until I heard the thud of running footsteps and turned to see my own dear Will loping toward me.

He caught me by the waist and swung me around, grinning from ear to ear. "My lady Northampton," he said, "are you ready to come home with me?"

31

We went first to Norfolk House for a private reunion but the next day we were off to court so that Will could formally present me to King Edward as his wife. My marriage to Will had been validated by the commissioners. He was permitted to remarry, they said, because his first wife's adultery had been proven, and proven adultery dissolved a marriage, allowing the aggrieved party to take another wife. The decision was controversial because there was no precedent in canon law, but it had been made. I was not only Will's wife, but also Marchioness of Northampton, one of the highest-ranking ladies in the land.

I found myself strangely awed by the ten-year-old boy king. He was dressed all in white silk, with a white plume in his bonnet and a sword buckled to his belt. In attendance were two boys his own age clad all in black. Following protocol, I curtsied three times as I approached His Grace and sank to my knees when he addressed me.

King Edward had a somber mien for one so young, and a direct gaze that reminded me of his sister Elizabeth. His eyes were less disconcerting, perhaps because they were gray rather than black. He seemed genuinely pleased to accept me as kin—his aunt through my marriage to Will and the fact that Will was Edward's stepmother's brother—and gave his blessing to our union in a clear, high voice. I fancied I could hear the Duchess of Somerset gnashing her teeth in the background. I thanked him, kissed the hand he extended toward me, and then walked backward from the room. I made my final curtsy at the door as it was opened behind me by one of the king's pages.

The king's acceptance of our marriage quieted any remaining rumbles of dissent. The lord protector pretended to be pleased by the commission's verdict, as did his wife, but I knew it galled the duchess that I now came directly after her in precedence. My high position was all the more obvious because none of the women who outranked us both was at court.

Princess Mary stayed away because she wished to practice her own religion and it was best to do so quietly and at a distance from the reformers on the Privy Council. Princess Elizabeth remained at Chelsea with the queen dowager, and neither put in an appearance during April or May. The early months of Kathryn's pregnancy had been difficult. Already ill and irritable, she had no wish to encounter Lady Somerset. The Lady Anna of Cleves, who had become King Henry's "sister" when he'd had their marriage annulled, preferred her own palace at Richmond. King Henry VIII's nieces—Lady Margaret Douglas, Countess of Lennox, and Frances Brandon, Marchioness of Dorset—spent most of their time at their husbands' country estates. The widowed Duchess of Suffolk, Frances's stepmother, likewise preferred to remain far removed from court. There had been one other duchess in the land, the wife of the Duke of Norfolk, but with his attainder for treason, she'd lost her rank.

That left only Frances Brandon's eldest daughter, ten-year-old Lady Jane Grey, granddaughter of the late king's sister Mary by Charles Brandon, Duke of Suffolk. She was in London as the ward of Tom Seymour and made frequent visits to her cousin the king, since they were the same age, but she had importance only as a marriage pawn and was too young to participate in ceremonies at court.

Will and I were assigned lodgings in various royal houses in accordance with Will's place in the peerage and his position as a privy councilor. They were very fine indeed, made more splendid by the addition of our own furnishings. We lived in great comfort and luxury and, as a marchioness, I was entitled to keep a bevy of attendants with me at all times.

There I experienced the first small check in my happiness. I wanted my sister Kate with me, but she was expecting a child and refused to leave hearth and home. I tried to persuade Mary Woodhull to come with me from Chelsea, but she insisted that the queen dowager needed her more than I did, especially during Her Grace's coming confinement. I did not see what good an unmarried gentlewoman would be at a lying-in, but I did not argue. Loyalty was a quality I admired. Alys Guildford likewise turned down my invitation and remained in the service of Jane, Countess of Warwick.

I had hoped Jane would be at court, but John Dudley, her husband the earl, was in poor health. I had to rely on letters to maintain my friendship with her and with Alys, although the three Dudley sons at court—Jack, Ambrose, and Robin—also relayed news. When Jane recommended a Mistress Crane as one of my waiting gentlewomen, I accepted the young woman sight unseen. In all, I had six such females attending me—women of gentle birth and flawless upbringing who gave me consequence but did not become my confidantes.

I went back to Chelsea in mid-May, with Will, as an honored guest of his sister and her husband. I was pleased to see Kathryn and Mary again, but Tom Seymour was another matter. The way he looked at me—at every woman!—made me uncomfortable, but his heated verbal attacks on his older brother alarmed me even more.

"The cursed Lord High Popinjay does favors for everyone but me," Tom complained, prowling his wife's privy chamber while Will took his ease in a comfortable chair. Kathryn and I shared a window seat that overlooked the river and the gardens on the south side of the house. I nibbled at a piece of marchpane and forced myself to smile. Kathryn obviously thought the name amusing.

Tom went on in this same vein for some time, his language colorful and sometimes blasphemous. His vocabulary was eloquent in that area. Will quaffed ale and waited until his friend wound down. "Accept it, Tom," he advised. "Somerset has control and is not likely to relinquish it. We must all make the best of things."

"You have lands in the north and so do I. We could go there and set up house," Tom grumbled. "We might build our own little kingdom there."

"I was not raised in the north and have no affection for the region," Will said. "I much prefer to remain at court and in favor."

"I am not in favor now and doubt I ever will be again so long as my brother lives."

Even Kathryn looked shocked at this statement, and she had no cause to love the Duke of Somerset or his wife. Will tactfully changed the subject. While he and Tom discussed horse breeding, I searched for another neutral topic. Below us, in the garden, I caught sight of Princess Elizabeth walking in company with a tall, slender, red-haired young woman all in black. Her manner of dress told me she was a widow.

"Who is that with Her Grace?" I asked.

"That is Elizabeth, Lady Browne. Her husband, Sir Anthony died not long ago and she is on her way to take up residence in her dower house at West Horsley, in Surrey. She stopped to pay her respects to me and to Elizabeth. A very pleasant young woman."

"There is something familiar about her, but I do not think I have ever met her."

"Are you speaking of fair Geraldine?" Tom asked, coming up beside his wife to peer out the window.

At my puzzled expression, Will explained. "Fair Geraldine was what Surrey called her in the sonnet he wrote to her when she was just a child."

"She was wasted on old Browne," Tom Seymour said. "He was too feeble to appreciate a nubile young bride."

"I am sure they managed as well as most couples," Kathryn chided him. "Still, she was very young when they wed, and he had already seen over sixty winters."

"And now she is a wealthy widow. Not a bad bargain for her, alhough I imagine she thought she'd have her freedom somewhat sooner."

"Perhaps she came to care for her husband," I said, annoyed by Tom's callous attitude.

He had the gall to laugh at my suggestion. I turned my back on him and resumed watching the two young women below, wondering once again where I had seen Lady Browne before. I was still wondering later that evening when I turned a corner and unexpectedly came upon her. She was not alone. Tom Seymour had her backed up against the wainscoted wall, one hand flat against the surface on either side of her shoulders. His face was only inches from hers and about to move closer.

A moment later, the pomander ball Lady Browne wore suspended from her waist by a long chain flew upward to strike Tom on the side of the head with a dull thump. He jumped away from her with a yelp, cursing fluently. The casing was heavily enameled and studded with semiprecious stones.

"Neither your behavior nor your language does you any credit, Lord Seymour," Elizabeth Browne said, "and you do not deserve the fine woman who is your wife."

Tom, still holding his head, paled at her words. "There is no reason to say anything to the queen dowager about this. You know I meant you no harm. You are a beautiful woman. You tempted me."

"That is a pitiful excuse." Contemptuous, she shoved him out of her way. She stopped in midstride when she saw me.

Tom swore under his breath.

Suddenly uncertain, Lady Browne sent a nervous smile in my direction. That expression, combined with the shape of her nose and the color of her hair, triggered my memory. I remembered where I had seen her before.

"You were at the banquet King Henry gave, the one to which he invited only unmarried ladies."

She blinked at me in surprise, then slowly nodded. "That was a long time ago. I was only fourteen."

"It is not surprising that King Henry should have taken an interest in two such charming girls. He always . . ." Tom's words trailed off as we both glared at him.

I thought of several tart responses, including one about making a habit of taking the king's leavings, but I thought better of saying such a thing aloud. Instead I turned back to Lady Browne. "He cannot help being a fool," I said, "but it will serve no purpose to force the queen dowager to see him for what he really is, especially now when she carries his child."

"I will say nothing," Lady Browne promised.

"You are wise as well as charming." Tom seemed unable to stop flirting even when it would have been the better part of valor to remain silent.

Lady Browne toyed with her pomander ball until he went away.

"He should not be allowed around young, impressionable girls," she remarked when we were finally alone.

I agreed with her, but there was nothing either of us could do to change the fact that the Princess Elizabeth was in the queen dowager's keeping, or that Tom held the guardianship of the Marchioness of Dorset's eldest daughter, ten-year-old Lady Jane Grey, who lived in his London house, Seymour Place.

Whit Sunday of that year fell on the twentieth of May. On the twenty-seventh, Mary Woodhull wrote to tell me that Princess Elizabeth and her entourage had left Chelsea to take up residence at Cheshunt, Sir Anthony Denny's manor in Hertfordshire. She gave no reason, making me wonder if Tom's ongoing flirtation with the princess had finally come to light.

In June, the queen dowager and her household, which now included the young Lady Jane Grey, moved to Hanworth, in Middlesex. Tom chafed at not being able to leave London to join her there, but he was both lord admiral and a privy councilor and there were fresh rumors of a new French plot. As soon as he could, however, he left Westminster for Hanworth, and soon after that he and Kathryn retreated to Sudeley Castle in Gloucestershire. Tom was still there on the thirtieth day of August when his daughter was born.

We had only just received a letter announcing the birth when Mary Woodhull arrived at Norfolk House in person. The moment she entered my withdrawing room, she burst into tears. "Oh, Bess," she sobbed. "She's dead. The queen dowager is dead."

The news stole my breath. I felt as if I'd taken a physical blow. It was not just the loss of a former mistress and a former queen that left me stunned and shaken, but the sudden void that can only be created by the death of a kinswoman. I could not have felt more bereft if it had been my own sister Kate who was dead.

"We thought Her Grace was recovering," Mary said when she'd taken a few sips of a reviving posset, "but then her condition began to worsen." She glanced at Will, who had joined us as soon as he heard the news. "The queen grew disturbed in her mind toward the end. She pushed the lord admiral away when he would have lain in the bed with her to offer comfort."

Eyes brimming, I heard Mary tell us how it had taken nearly a week after giving birth for the queen dowager to lose her battle for life. Beside me, Will sat as stiff and still as a statue. I could sense his struggle not to show the depth of his grief and wished he could give way to tears, as a woman would.

"The lord admiral left orders for Her Grace to be buried at Sudeley with the Lady Jane Grey as chief mourner, and he commanded that the queen dowager's household be broken up immediately after."

"She has already been interred?" The furrows in Will's brow deepened. "She was queen of England. She is entitled to lie in state and to be buried with King Henry at Windsor."

I placed a restraining hand on his arm. "Tom was her husband. He had the right to make that decision."

As I dashed away my tears, I remembered the reason Kathryn was dead. "Mary, what of the baby?"

Mary had to blow her nose before she could answer. "We left her at Sudeley. The lord admiral wished to travel in all haste to Syon."

Will and I exchanged startled glances. It was not the custom for a husband to attend his wife's funeral, but it seemed strange that Tom would have gone to his brother's house. Before Tom's departure for Sudeley, they'd been the bitterest of enemies.

32

After Kathryn's death, Tom Seymour was a changed man. He lost weight, giving him a gaunt and haunted appearance that was emphasized by the black garments he wore in mourning. His eyes blazed with a burning intensity.

He was often with us at Norfolk House, once more full of complaints about the lord protector. He had brought suit against his brother touching the queen dowager's servants, jewels, and the other things that were hers. He talked of making his manor of Bewdley in Shropshire his country seat and keeping as great a house there as he had in Kathryn's lifetime.

"I have been considering remarriage," Tom confided just before Christmas. "A number of noble, even royal ladies are well disposed to consider my suit." Catching sight of Will's disapproving expression, he hastily added, "But not, certes, until my year of mourning is past."

Will busied himself refilling our glasses and the awkward moment passed.

Tom sipped the fine, imported Xeres sack, then lowered his voice.

"There are stirrings in the countryside, Will. You know that well. My brother has been trying to force his brand of religion on everyone, and the steps he's taken are not popular with the people. They cannot see how it serves God to strip their churches of all images and melt them down for the gold."

"Nor did the common man understand how dissolving the monasteries did so, but King Henry's reforms moved ahead despite objections and ended by enriching those of us who supported them. Never say you did not gain by the establishment of the Church of England, Tom."

"Some who objected to the closing of abbeys and priories and nunneries rebelled," Tom reminded him. "There are rumblings in the land. More troubles are coming."

"You come perilous close to speaking treason."

"Only if you believe that my brother and not young Edward is king. Because the mighty Edward Seymour, Duke of Somerset and lord protector of England, insisted upon purging so much all at once, those who have always taken comfort in tradition are cut adrift. The average man does not understand why there are no longer any candles on Candlemas or ashes on Ash Wednesday or palms on Palm Sunday. When the new Book of Common Prayer, rendering the entire Latin mass into English, is forced upon every church in the land, there will be riots."

"Perhaps Kathryn's death has unhinged his mind," I suggested after Tom left us. "He must be mad to talk openly of rebellion."

"He's always been a hothead. Even Kathryn found him difficult to manage and I believe he did truly love her."

"Not enough to stop him flirting with every other woman who crossed his path. His words about remarriage to a noble or *royal* bride disturb me."

"Just talk." Will dismissed the idea, but I remembered the confidences Princess Elizabeth had shared with me at Chelsea and worried.

During the next few weeks we heard all manner of rumors. It was said that the lord admiral sought to marry Anna of Cleves, King Henry's fourth wife, whose marriage to the king had been annulled so that he could wed Catherine Howard. Then Princess Mary's name was mentioned as a possible bride. And then it was Princess Elizabeth he was supposed to be courting. By then Her Grace had taken up residence in her own house of Hatfield, only seventeen miles from London. At first I discounted such stories, but more accusations surfaced. I heard that Lady Tyrwhitt, who had been with the queen dowager until the end, now claimed Tom had poisoned Kathryn. And that he'd promised Lady Jane Grey's parents he would arrange a marriage for her with Jane's cousin, King Edward.

I had no love for my lord protector's grace, and I was certain he had already heard the same wild tales, but as the year drew to a close I became more and more uneasy. Tom maintained close ties with Will, and continued to hint that he should exploit his ownership of so many estates in the north and remove there. If Tom was plotting rebellion, it made sense that he would want someone in place to raise those counties against his brother.

I tried to warn Will, but he had a blind spot where Tom Seymour was concerned. In the end, I took matters into my own hands. I went to the Duchess of Somerset and told her everything I suspected about the feckless brother-in-law we shared, including what Princess Elizabeth had confided to me when we were both living with the queen dowager at Chelsea. If Tom had not been attempting to seduce Elizabeth then, he was certainly considering it now.

At first nothing happened. I told myself my warning had been unnecessary. I consoled myself with the thought that I had demonstrated our loyalty to the Crown. That could never be a bad thing.

Then, on a cold morning in mid-January, Will returned to our lodgings at Hampton Court only a short time after leaving them for the daily Privy Council meeting. "Tom's under arrest," he announced, and went straight to the cupboard for a bottle of Rhenish.

My hands flew to my mouth to stifle a gasp.

"The damned fool went armed with a pistol," Will said between deep swallows of wine. "In the hope of speaking to His Grace in private, Tom and two servants broke into the privy garden and reached the king's bedchamber without passing through the watching chamber, presence chamber, or privy chamber." Shaken, Will drained his goblet.

I refilled it in silence.

"Tom had a key to the outer door of the bedchamber, but one of the king's spaniels attacked him before he could reach the inner door. Tom lost his head and shot the dog."

"Worse and worse," I whispered. He'd signed his own death warrant with that bullet.

"The sound of the pistol being fired woke the king's bodyguards and they raised the alarm. They caught Tom standing over the spaniel's corpse, the smoking pistol still in hand. He tried to bluff his way out of trouble. He claimed he was conducting a test to make certain that His Grace was well guarded. No one believed him."

"Is he to go to the Tower?"

"He is likely halfway there already. And the order has been given to search Seymour Place, his house in London, for more proof of treason."

I clutched his arm. "Will they find anything there to implicate you, Will? Do not try to spare me. If we need to prepare—"

His fingers touched my lips, stopping the spate of words and stilling my fears. "I have long been Tom's friend, Bess, but there's not a man who knows him who would trust his judgment."

And women? I wondered. Had they trusted him?

The answer was not long in coming. Princess Elizabeth's governess, Mistress Astley, was arrested five days after Tom's attempt to kidnap the king. She was taken to the Tower and questioned about her part in Tom's plan to marry Elizabeth. In time, she confessed to aiding and abetting the lord admiral's courtship. She claimed she'd seen no harm in it.

My heart went out to the young princess, deprived of her beloved lady governess. Elizabeth Tyrwhitt, who had always despised Tom Seymour, was sent to Hatfield in Mistress Astley's place.

Tom himself was executed for treason on Tower Hill on the nineteenth day of March. Crowds gathered on that day shouted that the Duke of Somerset, who would kill his own brother, was a "bloodsucker" and a "ravenous wolf."

ALTHOUGH I WAS aware of growing unrest throughout the land, I was preoccupied with another matter. In spite of my best efforts since the validation of my marriage to Will, I had not become pregnant. I wanted a child, and the queen dowager's baby daughter had been orphaned by her father's death. The child, christened Mary, was in the keeping of the Duke and Duchess of Somerset, but they did not want her. Tom's wish had been that she be raised by the Duchess of Suffolk, but he had not bothered to ask Catherine Suffolk if she wanted the responsibility. She did not. She agreed with me that I should have little Mary.

"Are you mad?" Will demanded when I broached the subject. "We narrowly avoided being implicated in Tom Seymour's treason and now you want to call attention to my friendship with him by taking his spawn into our house?"

"That *spawn* is your sister's child! Your niece! How can you be so callous?"

"Political necessity, Bess. I thought you understood that. My sister Anne and her husband have not asked for custody of the baby, either. Lord Herbert is a canny fellow. I mean to follow his example."

"An innocent child should not be made to suffer for her father's sins. If Lady Suffolk will not take her, she'll be raised by Anne Somerset. I can think of no worse fate."

Exasperation made Will's voice harsh. "You've never even laid eyes on the girl. She may have inherited all of Tom's worst qualities."

"I long for a child," I whispered. It had been just over a year since our union was validated. By this point in her marriage, my sister Kate had already borne a son.

Will took me in his arms and kissed me tenderly. "It cannot be this one, my love. It is better to be safe than sorry, and I want you to be safe, Bess. I want that more than I want my next breath. The lord protector will take good care of Tom's daughter, if only to keep control of her in-heritance from her mother. And for that same reason he will never yield her to us."

"Then let us try again to make a baby of our own."

He was happy to oblige, but although we made fervent, passionate love that night and each of the ones that followed, I did not conceive.

33

There was rebellion brewing in the land. The first riots were in Cornwall and Devon, protests against the new liturgy everyone was required to follow after Whit Sunday, which that year fell on the ninth of June. It did not seem a matter of such great importance to me whether the Mass was said in English instead of Latin, but to some people it mattered a great deal.

The other great cause of dissension was easier to understand. Noblemen, Will's brother-in-law, Lord Herbert, among them, had enclosed land once used in common by all. This had caused great hardship and much bitter resentment. By early July, rebel encampments had sprung up in dozens of locations. By the middle of the month, the lord protector had declared martial law. He ordered Will to take troops into East Anglia.

My husband came home in September full of anger and resentment. The Duke of Somerset had sent him to Norwich ill equipped and ill prepared. Will had entered the city in an attempt to pacify the rebels and talk them into surrendering. Instead it had been Will who'd suffered an ignominious defeat.

Will drank deeply of his ale, glared at the dregs, and threw his cup into the empty hearth. It bounced off the tiles with a clatter so loud it made me wince. We were in our little withdrawing chamber at Norfolk House, but the sense of security this place had once provided was long gone.

"The more I consider the circumstances, the more likely it seems to me that Somerset orchestrated my humiliation from the start. He painted me as a coward and a fool for abandoning the city."

"You recaptured Norwich." From my chair I watched him pace, reminded of his late sister when Bishop Gardiner had plotted against her. Gardiner, at least, was no longer a threat to anyone. The lord protector had imprisoned him on some charge or other. He was languishing in the Tower along with the Duke of Norfolk, who had been there since King Henry's time.

"Warwick defeated the rebels, not I. At the head of an army twelve thousand strong. I was with him, but no longer in command."

"But why would Somerset wish you to fail?"

"Revenge." Will stopped pacing to fix me with a pleading look. "Don't you see, Bess? I bested him in the matter of our marriage. Ever since the commission reached its decision, he has been seeking a way to punish me for my presumption."

The Duke of Somerset had never seemed that devious to me, but I could easily believe such a thing of his wife. Even back when Anne Seymour had been Countess of Hertford, she'd had an eye out for the main chance.

"Why else would Somerset relieve me of my command? He gave me no opportunity to redeem myself. If he'd had his way, Warwick would have left me behind."

I soothed him as I always did, with praise and kisses, but he did not forget his grievances and I soon discovered that Will was not the only one who regarded the lord protector as his enemy. Most of the Privy Council had turned against King Edward's regent by the time the rebels were put down. On the fifth day of October, they met at Ely Place, the

Earl of Warwick's mansion in Holborn, with the intent of finding a way to remove the Duke of Somerset from power.

I had not seen a great deal of Jane Warwick in the past year and begged Will to take me with him to Ely Place. It was located outside the city gates of London and north of the Strand, the great highway that ran between Ludgate and the city of Westminster.

"Let us walk in the cloister," Jane suggested. "It is peaceful there." In spite of being so near the city, Holborn had many of the advantages of the country, including gardens and orchards. One of Jane's neighbors even boasted a vineyard. I felt a pang of regret for how long it had been since I'd visited Cowling Castle or seen any of my family save Kate. Father still had not forgiven me for marrying Will against his wishes.

The cloister at Ely Place, where once monks had strolled, was far removed from the noise and bustle beyond the gatehouse. I had seen troops massing there when we arrived, but I could barely hear any sounds of men or horses. The galleries that ran around the enclosed garden contained equally quiet rooms, from bedchambers to the countess's solar. The great hall was situated at its northwest corner. Every time we passed those windows, I strained to hear, but all I could make out was the occasional raised voice. I could not tell if it was Will speaking out in anger or some other privy councilor.

"Do you think Somerset knows what is afoot?" I asked Jane.

"He must suspect something," she said.

I envied Jane her calm demeanor. We both understood how very dangerous our husbands' undertaking could be. I was terrified that Will might end his life on the headsman's block, just like Tom Seymour.

"I am certain he has heard rumors," she continued, "and he knows there are many who think he should be removed from office for usurping power and subverting the laws of the realm."

"Who is to replace him?" The king had just passed his twelfth birthday. He was still too young to rule for himself. I'd heard Princess Mary's name suggested, but she was an unlikely candidate. Her Grace clung to the old religion.

"Does it matter?" Jane asked. "The important thing is to stop Somerset before he does any more harm. He has made too many bad judgments. Taken together, they very nearly brought about wholesale rebellion. He pounded the final nail into his own coffin when he ordered all soldiers who'd been mustered to leave London and proceed to their appointed commands without authorizing the rewards he'd promised them. The English troops and foreign mercenaries who put down the riots in East Anglia and elsewhere deserve better. My lord husband is furious on his men's behalf."

A servant in Warwick livery, emblazoned with the emblem of the bear and ragged staff, darted across the garden to whisper in Jane's ear. For just a moment, her composure seemed shaken. "Go inside and tell the earl," she said. "All the councilors must hear this."

"Hear what?" I asked.

Jane sank down onto a stone bench. When I sat beside her, I saw how pale she had gone. She drew in a deep, steadying breath.

"It has begun. There is no going back now. That messenger brought word that the Duke of Somerset has moved the king into his own lodgings at Hampton Court. As if we would hurt His Grace! Somerset plans to take King Edward and move into the Tower for greater safety."

"You have a spy at court."

Jane looked at me as if I were mad to doubt it. "Several. Including three of my sons."

By EVENING IT was the Privy Council, not Somerset, who had control of the Tower of London. That night Somerset fled with the king to Windsor Castle, as it was better fortified and easier to defend than Hampton Court. At once, the Earl of Warwick, with Will at his side, began negotiations for the return of His Grace. No one wanted bloodshed, but we all knew it might come to that. Even if there was no battle for possession of the king's person, there would likely be executions after.

I remained at Ely Place with Jane Warwick while our husbands rode out of London to lay siege to Windsor Castle. We women took comfort from each other's company, and chafed at having to sit and wait while others decided our fate and the fate of those we loved.

"Will the council execute the Duke of Somerset?" I asked Jane. We sat in her solar, pretending to sew. Neither of us had taken more than a few stitches.

Jane shuddered. "I hope not. Our families have been friends for a long time. You know we talked of having Jack marry Anne Seymour, Somerset's oldest girl."

"The lord protector did not hesitate to have his own brother beheaded," I reminded her. "I doubt he'll show any mercy to either of our husbands if he is victorious."

"Executing Tom Seymour is yet another example of his poor judgment. And we will prevail. Somerset cannot. He has too many enemies ranged against him."

I prayed she was right, and as I sat there, a sunbeam playing over my neglected embroidery, I wondered if there might be something we could do to bring an end to the standoff at Windsor. Somerset, Warwick, even Will were hotheaded individuals accustomed to settling matters with violence. Men were trained for warfare, even if they never expected to see a real battle.

"Is Lady Somerset with her husband at Windsor?" I asked.

"She is still at Beddington," Jane said, naming one of the many properties Somerset had claimed for himself since he'd come to power. "When this began, the lord protector had only just returned to Hampton Court after spending a few days hunting with his wife in Hampshire. She went to Beddington, which is nearby, to oversee the progress on renovations to the house." The Duke of Somerset had begun many such projects, and had ordered the destruction of no fewer than three churches to get building stone for Somerset House, the great mansion he was erecting on the Strand.

"Do you think she might be more apt to listen to reason than he is?"

Jane laughed. "You know Anne Somerset as well as I do. More likely she is the reason the lord protector pursued such an unwise course.

Anne's sudden rise to prominence at court went straight to her head. Her husband had not been regent for a month before she began to assume the privileges of royalty. Only remember how badly she treated the queen dowager."

"But if she could be made to understand that now, for the good of the realm, the duke must step down—"

"She would sooner see him dead."

I thought of the way the Duke and Duchess of Somerset were in private, as I had once seen them when they did not know I was there. Had it all been manipulation, or did she truly love her husband, as I loved Will, as Jane loved John Dudley, Earl of Warwick? I sighed. Even if she did, the lord protector's wife was not a likely candidate to act as the voice of reason. And yet, if there was a chance she could help avoid bloodshed, how could we not ask for her cooperation?

A few hours later, accompanied by our ladies and a few armed guards, Jane and I left Holborn and rode posthaste to Beddington.

"This is outrageous!" the Duchess of Somerset shouted when we explained the situation. "My husband is the most powerful man in the realm. Lesser men do not make demands upon him. He gives orders and they obey."

Both Jane and I were physically bigger than the duchess, but she had not lost the knack of looking down her nose while looking up. I started to back away, then remembered that she was no longer my mistress. I held my ground, refusing to be cowed.

"Your husband has kidnapped the king," I said.

"Edward went willingly with his uncle."

"So, you know already that they went to Windsor." Did her arrogance know no bounds? "I am surprised you have not already joined them there. I am sure your venom could be a useful weapon to repel troops sent against the duke."

If she was so determined to retain her place and his power, then she would have to be removed along with her husband. All the wretched things the Duchess of Somerset had said and done to me and to Will came back in a rush. If she had not been so much smaller and weaker, and if she had not suddenly looked stricken, I might have been tempted to do violence to her person.

"Windsor?" Lady Somerset asked. "Not the Tower?"

"A slight change of plans." Jane stepped deftly between us, bringing calm with her. "King Edward only went with your husband the duke because he was intimidated by Somerset's position as lord protector. You know this to be true, Anne. And you know that Somerset's day is over. But with your help, matters can still be settled peaceably."

"What if I do not want peace? What if I'd prefer to see your husbands tried for treason? If they overthrow the duly appointed lord protector, that is no less a crime than what Tom Seymour plotted."

"It is the lord protector who imitates his brother," Jane said, "not the earl or the marquess. And like his brother, he will fail. Let us pray Somerset does not follow Tom to the block. I know your husband is a good man at heart, Anne. Out of fear of harming the king, if for no other reason, he will eventually give in. Then he will be arrested, and with him your two eldest sons, who are with him at Windsor. Will you not try to save your boys, at least?"

Lady Somerset blanched at the threat to her children but would not yield.

"If you could but persuade your husband to surrender the sooner—"

The door to the chamber flew open and banged against the wall, cutting short Jane's plea for sanity. Will stood in the opening, a dozen armed men at his back. His eyes widened when he saw me, but he spoke first to the duchess. "I regret to inform you, Lady Somerset, that your husband is in custody at Windsor Castle. He has been deprived of his office as lord protector and removed from his lodgings next to the king's bedchamber."

A look of cold hatred removed every vestige of beauty from the duchess's face. With a howl of rage and frustration she hurled herself at Will. She clawed at his face, leaving a trio of long, deep scratches in one cheek. She beat on his chest, shouting invective. With surprising gentleness, he caught her wrists to stop her attack and eased her back toward her waiting gentlewomen. When they helped her to a chair, she collapsed, sobbing.

I went to Will's side. Jane tried to comfort Anne Somerset.

"When I left Windsor," Will continued, as if there had been no interruption, "Somerset was under guard in the Beauchamp Tower. He will shortly be removed to the Tower of London. I have orders to escort you there to join him, Lady Somerset."

Her spine stiffened at his words, which had somehow penetrated her wails of despair. She abruptly fell silent and drew herself up as much as a person of her small stature could, especially when seated. She sent a cold and haughty, if somewhat damp, glare in Will's direction. "Am I your prisoner, then?"

"You are, my lady."

"I require time to pack a few necessities, and so do the women who will accompany me."

"You are to bring no one with you." Will's voice equaled hers for coldness. Standing only inches away from him, I shivered, uncomfortably reminded of the day when Jack Dudley had forcibly taken me to Chelsea. "You will be assigned servants when you enter the Tower."

"My women will accompany me as far as London. Go and pack," she ordered one of her ladies. "Now, what of my sons?" It was as if her bout of hysterics had never occurred.

Will unbent a little. "You need not be concerned for them. King Edward will keep them with him. He is very fond of Lord Hertford and his younger brother." As Jack had become Lord Lisle when John Dudley was elevated in the peerage to Earl of Warwick, so the Duke of Somerset's eldest son had been granted his old title.

I breathed a sigh of relief, but Lady Somerset only gave a curt nod of acknowledgment. She folded her arms across her chest and waited in fulminating silence for her women to return with her baggage.

Jane and I returned to London in company with Will and his prisoner, leaving the duchess's ladies behind. My heart came near to bursting with pride when I learned what a crucial role my dear husband had played in Somerset's downfall. By repudiating the lord protector in public, Will had convinced his sister's husband, Lord Herbert, who had just returned from the West Country with an army at his back, to support the new Privy Council instead of the Duke of Somerset.

"Who will be the new lord protector?" I asked as we rode toward the city. It was a perfect, cloudless mid-October day, the kind of day when it felt good to be alive and free. I could almost find it in my heart to feel pity for Anne Somerset. She rode ahead of us inside a well-guarded litter.

"The Privy Council has revoked that office. No one will assume the title."

"Surely you do not mean to let Edward rule for himself?" His Grace was still much too young for such responsibility.

"Warwick is now lord president of the Council. He will help the king make decisions."

"Why Warwick rather than you? You are a marquess. He is only an earl." I did not pretend to understand political machinations, but it seemed to me that greater rank should count for something. Then again, the first thing Somerset had done when King Henry died was make himself a duke. Perhaps Jane's husband would do the same.

"I do not want the responsibility, Bess." Will sent a rueful smile in my direction. "And you'd not care to have me burdened with it. It would leave me with little time for you."

A small, shallow part of me wished that Will would be just a trifle more ambitious. What if Warwick turned out to be another Somerset? But if I was honest with myself, I had to admit that Will was better suited to diplomacy than to the day-to-day administration of the realm. He certainly knew how to flatter and charm. I smiled back at him.

"I will have a great deal to keep me busy as it is," Will continued. "From now on, to keep the king's person secure, he will always be attended by two noblemen and two gentlemen. These will be men selected by the Privy Council to offer guidance as well as protection. I am one of the six noblemen who will guard the king's person in shifts."

"Are you to carry a halberd?" I asked, picturing Will in the crimson livery of the yeomen of the guard.

He laughed. "No need to go that far!" He slanted a teasing look my way. "Have you realized yet that you will also have a new role at court?"

I frowned in puzzlement. "Of what nature?"

But before he could answer, understanding burst upon me and I laughed aloud in delight. With Lady Somerset gone, and if the king's sisters and female cousins and the Lady Anna of Cleves continued to absent themselves from court—as they likely would, since they all seemed to prefer life in the country—I would be the highest-ranking noblewoman at King Edward's court. I would act as his hostess when foreign dignitaries visited. I would be the next thing to royalty myself.

34

*I*t had long troubled me that I remained estranged from my family. The commission's decision that Will and I were legally married had not brought about the reconciliation I'd hoped for. Then again, both my father and my brother William spent much of their time in Calais, where Father was lord deputy. Mother was often with them, although for the most part she remained in Kent. I thought often of visiting her there, in spite of Father's disapproval, but I had much to occupy me at court. I did see Aunt Elizabeth, who had duly married Sir Edward Warner, having met him when he came to Cowling Castle to discuss a possible betrothal to me.

When I heard that Father was to be installed as a knight of the Garter, one of the greatest honors an English king could bestow upon a subject, I was determined to make an opportunity to mend fences. My entire family came to court for the ceremony on the thirteenth of December. At my urging, Jane Warwick invited them to sup with her, then slipped quietly away, leaving Will and myself to host the meal.

"A neat trap." My father's grudging acknowledgment gave no hint of what he would do next. He could walk out, taking the others with him.

Mother placed one hand on his arm and smiled up at him. "Sit down, George. This foolishness has gone on long enough."

Soft music drifted out from behind a screen. Well-trained servants carried in platters and flagons and vanished as soon as they'd placed them on the table. Despite a certain awkwardness, we began to eat.

I studied each of my brothers in turn. It had been years since I'd last seen any of them. I was a mature married lady of twenty-three, while William had grown into a tall, sturdy young man of twenty-two. He sported a fine spade beard. As if he felt my gaze upon him, he glanced my way, hazel eyes intense. "You look well, Bess. Being Marchioness of Northampton must agree with you."

"Are you important?" nine-year-old Edmund piped up.

Father snorted. Mother shushed him.

"We like to think so," Will said. He dealt daily with the young king and was more at ease with a boy of Edmund's age than I was.

"Do you think, my lord, that there will be another invasion of France?" This question came from my brother George, named after our father. He was nearly seventeen and likely to see battle if hostilities did break out again. He had shot up in height and now stood a full head taller than our brother Thomas, who was ten months George's junior.

"As far as I can see," I answered, "we are always at war with France, and with Scotland, too. It matters little whether peace treaties are signed."

"Can you tell us what the king is like?" John asked. At fourteen he bore a strong physical resemblance to Father, having inherited his square face and serious brown eyes.

"King Edward is a very studious, religious youth, weighed down by great responsibilities," Will answered. "But he excels at many sports, too. In time, I think, he will be as great a monarch as his father was."

At eleven, my brother Henry had a particular interest in the twelve-year-old king. "I should like to be one of his schoolmates," he declared. "Can you arrange it?"

Will glanced at Father, who merely shrugged. "I can mention your interest to His Grace, Henry, but I cannot guarantee he will invite you to court. Most of his companions have been with him for many years. He would have to displace someone to make room for you."

"He could dismiss the Duke of Somerset's sons," Henry suggested. "Send them to the Tower where they belong."

Will looked so uncomfortable with the suggestion that I rushed to intervene. "The king is loyal to his friends. Besides, young Lord Hertford and his brother are innocent of their father's crimes."

At last Father spoke. "And what is to be done with the Duke of Somerset himself? Is he to be executed, as he executed his own brother?"

"I do much doubt it," Will said. "Lady Somerset has already been set free."

"And is already scheming," I muttered. She'd lost no time ingratiating herself with Jane Warwick, who was far too softhearted when it came to old friends. The duchess had gone so far as to remind Jane that their children—Jack Dudley and Anne Seymour—had been all but betrothed before Somerset's arrest.

"The Privy Council is not an instrument of vengeance," Will said. "We seek only to do what is best for England."

Father's fulminating gaze would have disconcerted a lesser man, but Will met and returned it. Mother ended the standoff by poking Father in the ribs.

"This is a rare pleasure," Mother said. "A *family* gathering. Have done with talk of war and court alike. My husband and older sons will soon return to Calais and who knows when I will see Bess again."

For the remainder of the evening, she kept control of the conversation.

35

The Duke of Somerset was released from the Tower of London on the sixth of February. On the eighteenth he received a full pardon. At about the same time, Will was made great chamberlain of the king's household. In May my father became a member of the Privy Council, although his duties at Calais kept him from attending most of the meetings. And, on the third of June, Jack Dudley married Somerset's daughter Anne Seymour. King Edward himself attended the wedding.

Following the ceremony the duke provided a wedding feast of great magnificence. For entertainment there was a masque. It was the usual allegorical fare, with young ladies in absurd costumes representing various virtues. At nearly twenty-four, I was no longer asked to participate in such entertainments. I was a "matron," only without the children that term usually implied.

I had begun to suspect that I might be barren. Will and I had been together now, barely apart for more than a night or two, for over two years, and that was without counting the months we'd had at Norfolk House before I'd been exiled to Chelsea. In all that time, I should have conceived. I should have had two plump babies by now, as my sister Kate did. And I'd heard that my old nemesis, Dorothy Bray, in six years of marriage had produced four healthy children.

The wedding, with its constant harping on fertility, put me in a pensive mood. It was time, I decided, to reopen the subject of adoption. I approached Lady Somerset to ask for news of our mutual niece.

At the blank look on her face, I prompted her. "The queen dowager's daughter. Little Mary Seymour."

"Oh, that one." She gave a dismissive wave of one hand. "You will have to ask the Duchess of Suffolk if you wish to know how she fares. We sent the girl to her, and I have had naught to do with the child since." She did not even know where young Mary was lodged, but supposed she lived on one of Lady Suffolk's Lincolnshire estates.

I went in search of Will, but it was time for the tilting. No festivity the young king attended was complete unless it included coursing. I found my husband with King Edward in an antechamber made all of boughs. From this "bower" we were to watch two teams of six young gentlemen each run two courses in the field.

"Will," I whispered, tugging at his arm to draw him to the back of the company. "I wish to visit the Duchess of Suffolk."

He went very still. "You mean you want to see the child." The clatter of lances from the field and the shouts of the crowd drowned out my reply, but he could see the answer in my eyes. "Perhaps in the autumn?" he suggested when it was quiet again. Before I could object to the delay, he added, "A French delegation is due to arrive soon. You know the king relies upon you to act as his hostess."

His Grace shouted encouragement to both challengers and defenders. He was as bloodthirsty as every other boy his age, and many years away from having a wife to charm and flatter foreign envoys, one of the responsibilities of a consort. At present, for want of a queen and lacking a woman of higher rank in residence, the task of entertaining ambassadors and other important visitors continued to fall to me. Most of the time, this pleased me. Just now it seemed a great burden.

"It is to our advantage to keep the French sweet," Will reminded me, seeing my reluctance, "and you, my own dearest Bess, have a unique ability to delight every man you meet."

I did not need to be flattered into doing my duty, but I took pleasure in Will's compliments. Indeed, I took pleasure from everything about my husband, even after so much time together. I knew just how to please him, too, and as the wedding festivities continued, my thoughts drifted often to the night ahead.

I was not so very old. I could still conceive. We would simply have to try harder. I hid my smile as Will and I joined the other couples forming up for a dance.

"Perhaps we should return home soon," I suggested when we made our reverences to each other.

"Are you not feeling well?" His voice was anxious, but the steps of the pavane carried us apart before I could answer.

"I would be glad to go to bed early," I told him when we touched hands and paused for a moment face-to-face. I recalled the first time we had danced together and relished the memory.

"Ah," he said. "I see."

But first there was another tradition to observe, that of escorting bride and groom to their bed. Will and I had skipped this step, and I was glad of it. Jack Dudley's brothers stripped him naked before they shoved him toward his young bride. Her blushes turned her flesh bright pink, all the way down to midbosom, the point at which it disappeared beneath the sheets.

Will caught me staring at Jack's body and made a low, growling sound. I fixed him with a bland look, although I knew my eyes must be full of mischief. "He has a well-formed backside," I observed, trying to sound innocent.

"That is not the part of him you were admiring," Will complained.

"And I suppose you never peek at another woman's bosom?" I teased him.

"I prefer yours."

"And I prefer your . . . parts . . . to Jack's."

The flare of desire in Will's eyes was so powerful that it had me gulping to take in air.

We were at Durham House, another of the Earl of Warwick's properties near court. It was located on the Strand, just where the Thames curved, so that Whitehall Palace was in sight. Norfolk House was only a short distance away by boat or barge, but Will and I could not wait that long. We left the nuptial bedchamber with the other guests, but instead of heading for the water gate, Will seized a lantern in one hand and my arm with the other and hustled me along a corridor and up a flight of stairs until we came to a small room in a tower.

I was out of breath and laughing when he locked the door behind us. It was, by the evidence of desk and papers, some kind of workroom for a clerk. Beyond that, I glimpsed little except the narrow bedstead onto which Will tumbled me.

"We should have had all this," he whispered. "The pomp. The ceremony."

I shook my head, helping him unfasten his points and squirming to get my skirts out of the way. "I would change nothing."

"I need you, Bess. Now."

"And I need you." I was more than ready for him, and as he slipped into my body and began to move, I sent a fleeting prayer winging heavenward that, this time, I would conceive. Then I thought of nothing but Will and of my own pleasure, for it was not only in the hope of children that we loved. We were as attuned to each other's needs and desires as we had been that first night at Guildford. Will completed me, and I, him.

Later, replete, we rose and dressed and crept out of Durham House to return home. There, in our own bed, we made love again, more slowly this time, and I confided in Will my fear that I might be barren.

"I want children, Will," I whispered.

"Children come as God wills."

"What if it is not my fate to bear a child?"

"Then it may be I should say a prayer of thanksgiving."

I sat straight up in bed to stare at him. "What?"

He tugged me back down beside him and tucked me in close against his side. "I mean only that I could not stand to lose you as I lost my sister."

"Many women die in childbed, it is true." My breath caught on a sob, thinking of Kathryn. "But others have large families with no ill effects— my mother; my grandmother, Jane Warwick. Even Anne Somerset." She had seven more children living besides Lord Hertford, the Somerset heir, and the daughter she'd just married to Jack Dudley.

"We must leave it up to fate," Will said in a soothing whisper. He kissed me gently on the cheek, the forehead, the lips. I cuddled close to him, secure in his love for me. I resolved to stop fretting about our lack of children. What we had already was unique and precious.

Out of respect for Will's wishes, I did not mention Mary Seymour again for some time after that blissful night and, when the delegation from France arrived, I did my best to make them feel welcome. I must have succeeded. One wrote a poem to my beauty. Another gave me an enameled chain worth two hundred crowns as a parting gift.

36

By the time Yuletide came around again, celebrated with masques at Greenwich and Westminster, I was too busy to dwell on my continued barrenness. Besides, I believed Will when he insisted he was content to have a wife he loved and who loved him. I knew what a rare gift that was when so many of those around us existed in loveless arranged marriages. Some were happy enough. Other couples came to love each other in time, although not, I thought, with the passion Will and I shared. But far too many, like my brother William and my young uncle, Lord Bray, were shackled for life to women they could not abide.

Will and I were blessed. We certainly wanted for nothing except a child. We had wealth, honors, land, and no fewer than 154 domestic servants to look after us.

We spent Twelfth Night at Cowling Castle, finally reconciled with my father. Once our marriage had been declared legal, he'd been obliged to accept it, but it had taken some time for him to get over his annoyance with me for having defied his wishes.

In the spring, Will left England at the head of a delegation to the

French court that numbered 251 men, including a personal entourage of 62. My brother William went with him. So did Jack Dudley, Lord Lisle, and John, Lord Bray, my mother's brother. Their mission was to bestow the Order of the Garter on King Henri II and to negotiate for a bride for King Edward.

This embassy to France was a most prestigious one. It was a great honor for Will to lead it. But his departure meant we would be separated for months. I dreaded that, even more so when I realized that, with him gone, I would be in an ambiguous position at court. I could continue to live there without my husband, but so long as the young king did not have a wife, such an arrangement would be awkward. Instead, I decided to retire to Esher, a small manor near Hampton Court.

I planned to move there right after Will left for France. Our parting was as painful as I'd feared. We made love with near frantic intensity on the night prior to his departure. Then I went with him to the dock in the morning, demanding one last kiss before he climbed into the waiting rowing boat that would carry him out to his ship. I watched him clamber aboard and continued to stare at it as the fleet caught the tide and sailed away. I stood with my hand shading my eyes, my gaze intent, until Will's flagship was nothing more than a speck in the distance. Only then did I mount my horse and ride hard for Esher. It was more than a day's journey, but I did not stop to rest until I was too exhausted to do anything but fall into a bed at the nearest inn and sleep till sunrise.

My fine, large house overlooked the River Mole, and while Will was away, I redecorated every room to suit my fancy. That passed the time for a week or two, but I was already growing desperate for distraction when, to my delight, I discovered that one of my near neighbors was that same Lady Browne I had met at Chelsea. Her dower house at West Horsley was a mere eight miles distant, an easy ride for an accomplished horsewoman.

"We are both named Elizabeth," she remarked the first time I paid her a visit.

"As are half the women in England," I reminded her. "Those not named Catherine, Mary, or Jane. My friends call me Bess."

Her lips quirked up in a rueful smile. "And I am known as Geraldine, thanks to that wretched sonnet the Earl of Surrey wrote to me when I was but a child. He meant well—he thought to praise my virtues so that I would attract a noble husband—but I would have been far happier to have remained unnoticed."

"You did make an excellent match."

"Sir Anthony was very good to me."

Geraldine had something of Jane Warwick's calm demeanor. I found her company soothing and we exchanged several more visits over the next few weeks, until an outbreak of the sweat put an end to such diversions, as well as to my plans to journey to Cowling Castle to see my family during Will's absence.

The sweating sickness was no respecter of rank. The last time it had ravaged the land, hundreds had died, healthy one hour and ready for the winding sheet the next. As summer advanced, the death toll climbed.

Only England was afflicted, not France, for which I was thankful. But every day brought more letters from family and friends telling me of loved ones lost. A particularly terrible tragedy befell Catherine, dowager Duchess of Suffolk. Her sons, the young Duke of Suffolk and his brother, both King Edward's longtime companions, died within a day of each other. I had barely absorbed the enormity of her loss when Will's sister, Anne Herbert, sent word that the duchess had also lost the third child in her keeping.

Two-year-old Mary Seymour was dead.

I had no close friends among my ladies with whom I could share my grief, or the terrible guilt I felt. If I had insisted upon adopting the queen dowager's child, she might still be alive.

But there were deaths everywhere. Even the Duke of Somerset's household was afflicted, although none of his immediate family died. Then one of my own ladies succumbed, and I realized that no place was safe. If Will and I had taken Mary Seymour in, or if we had been blessed with babies of our own, we could have lost them to this terrible illness. A child could die as easily at Esher as anywhere else.

In the lonely, lonesome days that followed, I grew introspective. I had never had occasion before to look so deeply into my own heart. What I discovered there were unsettling truths. I had concealed my true feelings even from myself.

I had the capacity to love deeply. That was to my credit. But I had long since given all that love, every bit of it, to my husband. I did not have any to spare for a child. That was the real reason I had not pursued the adoption of Will's niece. And it was why, although I was saddened by the fact that I had not given my husband an heir, I now realized that I would not have been a good mother. I'd desired a child only because I'd known I *should* want children. That was expected of women, even though so many of the babies they bore would die young.

Had I truly possessed a maternal instinct, Will would never have been able to talk me out of raising his sister's child. He had not had to work very hard to convince me to leave her with Lady Suffolk, because all I'd truly craved was for the two of us to be together. A child, even one of my own, was not necessary to my happiness.

I did not share this conclusion with anyone. Few would understand. Many would think me unnatural for holding such an opinion. Even Will, who swore he needed only me, might wonder at my sudden change of heart about the state of motherhood.

Hard on the heels of my epiphany, a messenger delivered an official-looking document to Esher. It was addressed to Will, but I did not hesitate to open it. He had empowered me to deal with all matters concerning his estate while he was out of the country. The contents left me speechless. Lady Anne Bourchier, the wife Will had cast off for adultery, had brought suit against him, claiming that since the commission had found that she and Will had never been married, she was therefore her father's legal heir and entitled to the lands that had come to Will when he was created Earl of Essex.

My melancholy mood lifted. I had a purpose again—to fight for my absent husband's rights. I sent for a lawyer and began to muster arguments as to why this faithless woman, who had deceived and betrayed the man I loved, should never be allowed to regain a single acre of Essex land.

37

The clatter of hooves on the cobblestones in the courtyard at Esher had me rushing to the window. My first reaction on hearing so many horses arrive at speed was apprehension, but it took me only a moment to recognize Will. At once, my heart beat faster. He swung off his horse, throwing the reins to a groom, and abandoned the riders who'd accompanied him to race toward the nearest entrance. Tears of joy flowed down my cheeks as I hoisted up my skirts, ignored the restrictiveness of my whalebone corset, and ran for the stairs.

Will met me before I was halfway down, catching me by the waist and lifting me into a smoldering kiss. He smelled of sweat and leather and horses, but I did not mind in the least. He was real. He had come back to me, safe and sound.

"I died a hundred deaths fearing for your safety," he whispered. "You are well? You have not been ill?"

"There was sickness everywhere, but I was spared." I ran my hands over his arms, his chest. "And you, Will?" I could scarcely believe he was really with me again. I'd known he was to return sometime in August, but sailing ships must wait upon wind and weather. And sometimes, they sank.

Will had left for France on the twenty-second of May. It was now mid-August. We had been apart for three long months. We barely stopped kissing long enough for me to direct him to the bedchamber I had chosen for us and furnished in his absence, but he needed no guidance to find the bed.

Hours later, we still could not stop touching. It was as if we both needed proof the other was really there.

"I had not thought the separation would be so difficult," Will said as he tenderly stroked one finger down the side of my face. "We endured time apart before."

I smiled, content just to look at him, now that our lustful longings had temporarily been satisfied. But one question nagged at me. "Have you already been to court?"

He chuckled. "Only because Hampton Court was on the way here. I left the rest of the embassy behind in Dover, all but a few outriders, and rode ahead. I made my report to Warwick in the briefest manner possible. It is as well he is an old friend. He knew how anxious I was to be reunited with you."

Yes, I thought. Beneath the title, Warwick was still the man, John Dudley, who had married Jane Guildford, his childhood sweetheart. Will and I were fortunate in having their friendship.

"We must both return to court soon," Will murmured, his lips close to my ear. His hands were busy elsewhere, making me shiver with longing even though a moment earlier I'd been sated.

"*Must* we?"

He laughed. "Never tell me you did not miss being at the center of things!"

"A little, perhaps. But I missed being with you more."

We had exchanged frequent letters during our separation, but the written word was no substitute for speaking face-to-face. Our reunion was both tender and passionate, and for the best part of the next two days, when we were never apart, we shared our separate experiences. I found the courage to tell him of my new insight into myself and found him accepting. He swore once again that I was all he needed to be complete. I believed him. I believed him, too, when he promised to put a stop to Anne Bourchier's scheme to take her father's estate away from Will. In spite of my best efforts, her lawsuit had not been dismissed.

Once Will and I returned to court, life went on much as it had before—full of entertaining amusements, secret intrigues, alarming rumors, sudden betrayals, and new rewards. John Dudley, Earl of Warwick, was elevated in the peerage to Duke of Northumberland. Henry Grey, Marquess of Dorset, was created Duke of Suffolk, claiming that title in the right of his wife, Frances Brandon, since the deaths of both her half brothers of the sweat had left the title in abeyance. When the Earl of Warwick became Duke of Northumberland, his oldest son—Jack Dudley, Lord Lisle—was created Earl of Warwick in his own right. Will's brother-in-law, Lord Herbert, became Earl of Pembroke. Other honors were granted, too, both titles and knighthoods. Will received no greater title, but he was granted a bishop's palace, formerly the property of Stephen Gardiner, bishop of Winchester, the same prelate who had once tried to have Queen Kathryn arrested for heresy.

Winchester House was located in Southwark, just across London Bridge from the city, and it boasted its own wharf, called the Bishop of Winchester's Stairs. I stepped off our barge, the small one with the striped awning, and stared up at the house in delight.

"It is magnificent," I breathed, impressed by its fine stone walls.

The interior was even more spectacular, containing as it did so many large, well-proportioned rooms, all of them luxuriously furnished. The bishop had been fond of Flemish tapestries, Turkey carpets, and well-cushioned chairs.

We moved from the great hall along a narrow passage and entered the enormous kitchen, where gawking servants did not seem to know what to make of us. Will made a short speech, informing them of the property's change in ownership. Most looked relieved. Having a master in prison had to be unsettling.

We continued our exploration of the house, inspecting bedchambers—also well furnished—and stopping now and again to admire the view from the windows, especially those that looked out over the Thames. Downriver, I could see the houses crowded in cheek by jowl on London Bridge itself. Rising behind were the high, pale walls of the Tower.

"I wonder if Gardiner can see his former residence from his cell?" I mused.

Will laughed. "I hope he can, and drowns in his own bile for thinking about us in possession."

"We've space enough for all manner of improvements," I remarked.

A courtyard graced the land side of the house, together with a privy garden. To the west were a small orchard and a kitchen garden. It was difficult to believe we were in the center of an area as populous as any in London proper. Sounds from beyond the wall that surrounded the entire property were so muffled they were almost nonexistent.

"I am of a mind to add a gallery," Will said, "and we could put a tennis court there." He gestured toward an open space on the eastern side of the property. "And perhaps a bowling green. We can begin renovations at once."

"What of the furnishings?" I felt a strong aversion to sleeping in the bishop of Winchester's bed. "And I would like new wainscoting in the great hall."

Will agreed to everything I suggested and I looked forward to weeks of absorption in the project, but I was soon distracted from such domestic pursuits by the news that Edward Seymour, Duke of Somerset, so recently freed from the Tower and restored to most of his former status—although not to the post of lord protector—had been caught plotting to the kill both John Dudley, Duke of Northumberland, and my own dear Will. It did not seem to matter to Somerset, or his wife, that their daughter was now married to Northumberland's son Jack. They gambled on the chance of regaining control of King Edward's government . . . and lost. The Duke of Somerset was arrested again, along with his duchess. So was his distant kinsman, Davy Seymour. I appealed to Northumberland on behalf of Davy's wife, my old friend Mary Woodhull, and secured Davy's release, but I had no sympathy for Somerset himself. He deserved a traitor's death.

Will was present at his beheading. I thought it bad enough that I had to hear about it. Although men and women alike flocked to public executions, and this one, on Tower Hill, took place in a great square that could accommodate a considerable crowd, I could only feel relieved that noblewomen were not expected to attend such spectacles.

King and courtiers soon put the whole ugly affair out of their minds. The state visit of the regent of Scotland replaced Somerset as a topic of conversation. Marie of Guise, who was also the queen mother, was returning north after a visit to her daughter. When even younger than King Edward, Mary Queen of Scots had been spirited away to the French court a few years earlier to keep her from falling under English control. At the moment, however, France and England, and therefore Scotland and England, were at peace. It was safe for the French-born Scottish regent to visit the English court. Together with Will's sister, Anne, newly Countess of Pembroke, and Geraldine Browne, and some sixty other ladies, I was chosen to greet Marie of Guise at Hampton Court and escort her to Queen Kathryn's old rooms.

Although I enjoyed all these festivities, I could hardly wait for the regent to continue on her way back to Scotland. As soon as she left, Will and I could move into Winchester House.

All that winter I had my husband to myself, day and night, in our beautiful, newly renovated palace. And when Parliament convened, Will dealt handily with the troublesome lawsuit his first wife had brought against him while he was in France. He returned home from that day's session with a light step and a grin so wide I was surprised his jaw didn't crack. He slung an arm around my shoulders and gave me a smacking kiss on the cheek.

"Parliament," he announced, "has just passed a private bill to confirm my right to the Essex inheritance."

"And Lady Anne's claim? Will she get anything?" If her marriage to Will was null and void, then they had never been wed at all. On cooler reflection, I'd had to admit to myself that there was some merit to her claim. If she had no husband, then it followed that she would then be her father's sole heir. She was living, it was said, in great poverty, and we were certainly not in need of more property. We might spare her a crumb.

She betrayed Will, I reminded myself, absently touching my wedding ring. *She forfeited her rights when she was unfaithful to him.*

Will chuckled, well pleased with the outcome. "I've outsmarted her, Bess. The wording of this bill specifies that the nullity allows me to proceed *as if the said Lady Anne had been naturally dead.* Both our marriage and my claim to the Essex lands have been upheld. We have it all, my love. Just as we deserve."

I should have been glad. I *was* glad. But after I'd taken my husband off to bed to celebrate, I surprised myself by feeling a spark of pity for Lady Anne.

38

The remainder of that year passed rapidly. Will was busy at court and I was often there with him. On several occasions I served as the king's hostess when he entertained foreign visitors. We visited Lady Browne at West Horsley in May, and in July King Edward embarked on a royal progress that lasted into September. Will and I went along, although we often detoured to stay at our own houses along the way rather than be crowded in with the rest of the court. When the progress ended at Windsor, Will and I settled in at Esher. Jane Northumberland and her husband were at Chelsea, Queen Kathryn's dower house having been granted to the duke.

In October I attended Lady Browne's wedding. For her second husband, Geraldine had chosen a baron, Lord Clinton. He was also lord admiral of England, having replaced Tom Seymour in that post. This was his third marriage. His first, much older wife had been King Henry's cast-off mistress Bessie Blount. He'd been her second husband. By her first she'd had a daughter, Elizabeth Talboys. Young Elizabeth had become Baroness Talboys in her own right on the death of her brothers and, a week after her stepfather's remarriage, she wed Lord Ambrose Dudley, Jane Northumberland's second-oldest surviving son.

Since many matrimonial connections were similarly complex, they served to strengthen political alliances. Good parents looked for security when they arranged their children's matches. I had remained close to Jane Dudley who, as Duchess of Northumberland, now had precedence over me at court. I knew that her youngest son's wife had been chosen for her fortune. A month after Lord Ambrose's wedding, Lord Henry Dudley married thirteen-year-old Margaret Audley, a great heiress. She was also the niece of Henry Grey, the new Duke of Suffolk, giving the Dudley family a connection to royalty, since Suffolk's wife, Frances Brandon, was one of the daughters of Henry VIII's sister Mary.

Lord Robin Dudley had wed a few days after his brother Jack married Anne Seymour. He'd persuaded his parents to let him choose his own bride. Robin seemed happy with his choice, but I felt sorry for Jack. His wife blamed his father for her father's execution and her mother's imprisonment. I pitied the young woman, but I felt far sorrier for my old friend, who had to live with a woman who hated him.

Mary, the eldest surviving Dudley daughter, was married to Sir Henry Sidney, one of King Edward's boon companions, and had been for some time. The daughter Jane had given birth to when I was in her service, Temperance, had died. Lord Guildford Dudley's nuptials would likely be next. Northumberland had been negotiating for months with the Earl of Cumberland for his daughter Margaret's hand. Margaret was the only child of Frances Brandon's late sister. Once that match was made, only seven-year-old Lady Katherine Dudley's future would remain unsettled.

The court celebrated Yuletide that year in lavish style at Greenwich Palace. There was hawking and hunting and no fewer than six masques to entertain us. I gave Will a ring that cost me £100 but considered every penny well spent when I saw the pleasure on his face. The last thing we had to worry about was money. We reckoned his annual income at above £5,500.

In early February, Princess Mary arrived in London with a retinue of two hundred people to pay a formal visit to her brother the king. She was met by one hundred of the king's men, who escorted her to St. John's Clerkenwell, where she had a house. King Edward was unwell, suffering from a painful cough and a fever. This postponed their reunion for a few days, but in expectation of that meeting all the highest-ranking ladies of England—or at least those within traveling distance of Westminster— had gathered to escort the princess to court. As we had when the regent of Scotland visited, we would provide a glittering backdrop for Princess Mary when she rode up to the gates of Whitehall. I spent the night before the procession at Durham House, Northumberland's great mansion on the Strand.

"The Earl of Cumberland has refused his consent for a marriage between his daughter, Margaret Clifford, and our Gil," Jane confided.

Durham House stood just in the middle of the curve of the Thames, a fact of which I was well aware since Jane and I stood looking out of one of the turret rooms located on either side of the water gate. I had fond memories of the other and had to force myself to concentrate on what my old friend was saying.

"The more fool he," I said to Jane, "but I've no doubt you will find him another, better match."

In a family of dark-haired, muscular men, Lord Guildford Dudley stood out by virtue of being tall, slender, and fair. Privately I thought he was conceited about his looks, but he was only seventeen. In time, he'd mature. The other boys had turned out well. The only fault I could see in any of them was their extreme subservience to their father, and most people would count obedience to a parent a virtue.

"Lady Margaret Clifford is the king's cousin. Her late mother was the Duchess of Suffolk's younger sister," Jane reminded me.

"Then marry Gil to the Lady Jane Grey," I suggested with a laugh. "She has precedence over Lady Margaret, being Frances Brandon's oldest girl. That will put Cumberland's nose out of joint."

Jane chuckled. "How wicked you are, Bess." Then her expression turned thoughtful. "It is not a bad idea. Lady Jane is about the same age as Gil, and she is sound in religion. Well educated. A pretty little thing, as I recall, although somewhat quiet and reserved. At one time, Somerset talked of marrying her to his eldest son, Lord Hertford, but nothing came of it."

"And Tom Seymour," I recalled, "once wanted to have the Lady Jane wed King Edward."

Although she was His Grace's cousin, the match would have been most unequal. Far better the royal betrothal Will had negotiated during his diplomatic mission to France. King Edward was to wed Elisabeth, daughter of King Henri II of France, at present still an infant. Only time would tell if that marriage ever came about. Peace with France never seemed to last long, and royal betrothals could be set aside just as easily as treaties.

"Hertford," Jane mused. "I have always liked that boy. He could benefit from having a wife, as well."

How Lord Hertford felt about his father's execution, his mother's imprisonment, and his sister's unhappy marriage to Jack Dudley, Earl of Warwick, was anyone's guess. He was a cautious young man who did his best not to attract too much attention to himself.

"If you are bent on matchmaking, there are others more likely to welcome an alliance with your family." From our vantage point, even so late in the day, I could see into and over the river and had a clear view of Whitehall Palace. Flares of light dotted the scene as lanterns were lit on boats moving up and down and across the river. Candlelight spilled out of houses and shops on the opposite shore.

"Who did you have in mind?"

"You might consider the Earl of Pembroke's younger son for your Katherine." Edward Herbert, the little boy I'd played with at Chelsea, was old enough for a betrothal, if not yet a marriage. Since his mother, Will's sister Anne, had died the previous year, I did not hesitate to promote his interests.

"Why not the elder boy?" Jane asked.

"Lord Herbert is already promised to Lady Catherine Grey, Lady Jane's younger sister."

"Is he indeed?"

"Perhaps the Duke of Suffolk already has someone in mind for Lady Jane. It would be a pity if Gil lost the prize simply because you did not act quickly enough to secure it."

"Both the Lady Jane and her mother will be escorting Princess Mary to Whitehall on the morrow," Jane said thoughtfully. "I will have to take a closer look at the girl."

She was pleased with what she saw. On the twenty-fifth of May, in the chapel at Durham House, the Lady Jane Grey married Lord Guildford Dudley, Lady Catherine Grey wed Will's nephew, Henry Herbert, and little Katherine Dudley married not Edward Herbert, as I had proposed, nor Somerset's son, Lord Hertford, but rather the Earl of Huntingdon's heir, Lord Hastings. Northumberland wanted to expand his circle of marriage alliances.

If Will and I had been free to marry when first we loved and had had a child, our progeny might have taken vows on that day, too. I could not stop the thought, but I soon pushed aside any regrets. The union of these powerful evangelical families was a triumph for which I had been partly responsible. I set myself to enjoying the spectacle.

Lady Jane, Lady Catherine, and their parents had arrived by barge from Suffolk Place. Delicate as a flower, Lady Jane wore a gown of gold and silver brocade sewn with diamonds and pearls. Her reddish-blond hair was plaited with more pearls, strings of them. Her golden-haired sister, Lady Catherine, was prettier—it was said she resembled their grandmother, King Henry's sister Mary, who had briefly been queen of France before she married Charles Brandon, Duke of Suffolk. It was Lady Jane, however, who had a quality about her that spoke of royalty. Although she was shorter and lacked her cousin's vivid coloring, something in Lady Jane reminded me of Princess Elizabeth.

"The boy's ill," Will whispered to me. "He should not have been taken from his sickbed."

I followed his gaze to young Lord Herbert, Will's nephew. "The doctors said it was nothing to worry about," I whispered back. But the fifteen-year-old looked as if he was about to keel over.

"They say the same about King Edward," Will muttered.

I sent him a questioning look. His Grace had moved to Greenwich because the air there was more salubrious than in London, but I had not heard that he was seriously ill. I shivered, even though it was a mild day.

John Dudley, Duke of Northumberland, had spared no expense to make the triple wedding memorable. He'd hired two teams of masquers to entertain, one male and one female. There were also jousts and games. The festivities lasted two full days. Afterward, the Lady Jane remained at Durham House with Gil and his mother. The Lady Catherine moved into Baynard's Castle with Will's nephew and his father, the Earl of Pembroke. I returned to Winchester House, exhausted but well pleased with the outcome of my first foray into matchmaking.

39

In early June, the king's doctors told the Duke of Northumberland that fifteen-year-old King Edward was dying. They predicted that His Grace would not survive more than a few more months. Northumberland said nothing to anyone at first. He needed time to think, and to learn what the king's wishes were. Only then did he confide in Will. The next day, Will brought the terrible news home to me at Winchester House.

"Under the terms of King Henry's will and the Act of Succession of 1544, confirmed by the Treasons Act of 1547, Edward's sister Mary will succeed him. That will be a disaster, both for England and for us."

"What does Princess Mary have against you?" I asked, looking up from my embroidery to see that he'd begun to pace.

"I was responsible for limiting her right to hear Mass. She had been inviting all manner of people to attend church services with her, knowing full well that the Catholic Mass is illegal in England. It was only by the goodwill of King Edward that Her Grace was permitted to continue to practice her religion in private."

"I suppose, then, that she will not keep you on the Privy Council."

His laugh was short and bitter. "That place is not all I will lose. The first thing she will do as queen is restore Catholicism to England. She will reverse nearly twenty years of reforms."

"Perhaps she will show tolerance." I took another stitch, then set my needlework aside. "I have never heard that she is unkind." Will's sisters had spent time in Her Grace's household and so had Geraldine. None of them had ever had a bad word to say about her. Even the Duchess of Somerset had remained on friendly terms with the princess, and that after the lord protector had instituted the most radical of religious reforms.

"She'll want revenge, mark my words. Or her councilors will. She'll release Stephen Gardiner from the Tower."

I saw at once what that would mean. "He will not tolerate what he deems heresy."

"And heretics who do not recant will burn."

I remembered what Gardiner had done to Anne Askew and repressed a shudder. "Then we'll recant. We'll go back to hearing Mass in Latin. Statues and stained glass will reappear in churches. What difference do such trappings make? Given a choice between returning to the old faith and death, I choose life and so should you. Pretend to convert to Catholicism. Even if you do not continue to serve on the Privy Council, you'll still be Marquess of Northampton. We will continue to have a place at court."

Will raked one hand through his hair in exasperation. "Don't you understand, Bess? There is more at stake here than religion." He captured my face between his hands. "If Mary becomes queen and returns England to the Church of Rome, our marriage will be invalidated. I will still be married to Anne Bourchier."

Stricken, I could do no more than stare at him. He dropped his hands to my shoulders but held my gaze with his serious light brown eyes. "There may yet be a way to preserve what we have, both the Church of England and our marriage."

"Tell me."

He steered me to a long, padded bench with a low back. "It is King Edward's idea, his wish. Months ago, in secret, His Grace composed what he called a device for the succession. He does not want either of his sisters to inherit." Will snorted a laugh, but it had no humor in it. "In truth, he does not want any woman on the throne, but there's no help for that."

"After Mary and Elizabeth come the children and grandchildren of King Henry's two sisters—all females," I said slowly, remembering that Frances Brandon, Duchess of Suffolk, had three daughters and her late sister only one child, another girl. "Why not Princess Elizabeth then? She is sound in religion and she is King Edward's half sister."

"Is she? There has always been some doubt about her legitimacy."

"One has only to look at her to see she's a Tudor."

"But King Henry executed her mother for adultery. The taint lingers. In any case, King Edward's plan is to leave a will, as his father did, setting out the order of succession. He will disinherit both of his sisters because King Henry annulled his marriages to both their mothers, making Jane Seymour, who gave birth to Edward, Henry's first true wife."

I nodded, although I had difficulty following the logic of it all. "Who succeeds, then? The little queen of Scotland is descended from King Henry's eldest sister."

"King Henry passed over that line and King Edward wishes to do the same. His Grace's first version of the device left the crown to 'the Lady Frances's heirs male' and 'for the lack of such issue to the Lady Jane's heirs male.'"

"But Frances Brandon has no sons. And the Lady Jane has only just married."

"I know." Will's voice was sharp, his manner agitated. He moved restlessly from window to table, pouring himself a cup of wine, then leaving it behind as he returned to my side. "The king soon realized that he would not live long enough to see any sons born to either woman, so he has made a change in the wording. The crown now goes 'to the Lady

Frances's heirs male, if she have any such issue before my death' and 'to the Lady Jane and her heirs male' by default."

I stared at Will in shock. "To the Lady Jane *and* her—do you mean to say that His Grace has cut the Duchess of Suffolk out of the succession in favor of her eldest daughter?"

"Say rather in favor of her daughter and her daughter's *husband*. No one really expects a woman to rule England."

"I did not foresee this." I stared down at my hands. They were clasped so tightly in my lap that my rings had left deep impressions in the adjoining fingers.

"Nor did any of us, not even Northumberland."

"Guildford Dudley will be king."

"Yes."

A self-centered seventeen-year-old younger son would rule England. I felt slightly ill. It had been my suggestion that he wed the Lady Jane.

Still, it might all come right. Gil's father would continue to be the power behind the throne. Perhaps very little would change, after all.

"A King Guildford is better than a Queen Mary," I said, but my voice sounded uncertain even to my own ears.

"It is not as if we have a choice, Bess. We must support him or lose everything."

"We will. Others will, too." We were not the only ones who had much to lose. I managed a brave, bracing smile, but I prayed with all my heart that a miracle would occur and young King Edward would recover.

40

The tempest began with a downpour in the early evening of the sixth day of July. Before long, hailstones fell from the sky. They crashed against the windows that overlooked the Thames, peppering them so hard that cracks appeared in the expensive glass. The wind howled. My ladies lent their shrieks to the cacophony until I ordered them to be silent.

"It is only a storm," I said, turning away from the disturbing sight.

My chief waiting gentlewoman, Mistress Crane—known as Birdie both for her sharp blade of a nose and her surname—let out a terrified shriek and pointed at the window behind me. "The hailstones have turned bloodred! It is an evil portent. Soon real blood will be spilled."

Frowning, I looked for myself. It was true that the hail did have a pinkish tinge. "It is only light reflected from the setting sun," I said, still striving for calm.

"But the storm clouds obscure the sun."

A flash of lightning and the nearly simultaneous crack of thunder saved me the trouble of answering. I gave thanks that Winchester House had been built on a sturdy stone foundation. We would remain safe so long as we stayed within its walls, no matter how unnatural the weather. I was not quite ready to believe in omens, but I could feel the odd quality to the air. It made my skin prickle.

Cautiously, not quite certain I wanted to take a closer look, I approached the cracked window. The water in the Thames roiled and churned. It had swamped several wherries, caught halfway across the river when the storm hit. Passengers and boatmen alike clung to the overturned watercraft. Bigger vessels docked at the many wharves along the riverfront were likewise battered by the high winds and driving rain. The hail, at least, had passed, but the strip of ground below my window was littered with gray-white pebbles, some as big as tennis balls.

Lightning flashed again and I gasped as it struck one of the many church steeples in the city. The spire slowly tumbled to the street below. Now that, I thought, *was* a bad sign. My gaze shifted downriver, toward Greenwich. I could not see that far, but my thoughts continued on past London Bridge, past the Tower, straight to my husband and his death-watch.

If nature rebelled at the loss of a king, then Edward was gone.

Superstitious nonsense, I told myself.

But what else could account for the devastation in front of my eyes? As I watched, a house on the opposite shore was swept away by the rising water. "A heavy rain at high tide always causes flash floods," I murmured, but a shudder racked my body from head to toe.

The storm passed as abruptly as it had begun. When night fell, I lit every candle in my privy chamber and waited. I knew something momentous had happened, but it was nearly midnight before Will arrived home.

"He's dead?" I asked.

There were tears in Will's eyes as he confirmed that King Edward had departed this life at the exact hour the storm had struck London. "He suffered terribly at the end, Bess. Poor lad. He's at peace now."

"And we are left behind to carry out his wishes."

"His and the duke's. Northumberland wants to keep the king's death quiet for a day or two, until everything is in readiness to proclaim Jane queen."

"Until he has Princess Mary in custody, you mean."

"He's dispatched his son Robin with a small force to secure her person. And he's sent word to his duchess to inform Queen Jane of her new status."

"And Lady Jane's mother, Lady Suffolk?"

"She met in private with the king a few days before his death and agreed to cede her claim to the throne to her children."

I wondered how Northumberland had coerced her and her husband into giving up the chance to rule England themselves, but I did not ask. All that mattered was that they had, and that the Lady Jane, who would support the religious reforms of her predecessors and with them my marriage to Will, was now queen of England.

Will stayed the night. We made love in silence, finding satisfaction and comfort in each other's arms, but it was not a celebration. He left to return to Greenwich at the crack of dawn.

I boarded our second, smaller barge and was rowed upriver the short distance to Durham House. Although the sun was barely up when I arrived at the water gate, Jane Northumberland was already dressed in court finery.

"How fares our new queen?" I asked.

"Wretched girl. She is not here. She is at Chelsea."

"Be careful, Jane," I said with a weak smile. "That 'wretched girl' is queen of England now."

"I should have locked her in her chamber." Jane's words carried more heat than was her wont. "She's been difficult from the first. And once my lord husband informed her of her new status as King Edward's heir, she grew more unmanageable still."

"It is only natural she should be upset at the news that His Grace was dying. They spent a good deal of time together when they were younger." When Tom Seymour was her guardian he'd seen to that. Tom had meant to marry Lady Jane to King Edward. I wondered if the girl had known of his plans for her.

"She was surprised, I suppose, by her good fortune," Jane Northumberland allowed, "but she seemed willing enough to accept that Mary Tudor should not rule, given Mary's religious leanings. The only thing that seemed to bother my new daughter-in-law was that she had taken her mother's place in the succession. She demanded to speak with Frances, and when I refused permission, pointing out that the king's death was imminent, she left on her own, hiring a wherry to take her to Suffolk Place."

The girl's boldness astonished me. I'd not thought her so enterprising, or so determined to have her own way. "You got her back, I trust."

"She refused to return. I had to send word to Frances that I would keep Gil here until his wife relented. Lady Jane—Your pardon, I mean *Queen* Jane has grown very fond of her husband. Or at least she's learned to like the coupling. Frances obligingly reassured her daughter that she does not want the crown for herself, but the foolish girl still balked at coming back to Durham House. Frances and I compromised by sending both newlyweds to Chelsea."

"Perhaps it is just as well."

For once, I was the one soothing Jane Northumberland. She was more settled in her mind by the time her daughter, Mary Sidney, arrived at Durham House. Mary had a sensible outlook on life. I supported her suggestion that she should be the one to inform Queen Jane of King Edward's death and bring her to Syon, another of Northumberland's houses, this one on the Thames, near Richmond Palace. There those of us most closely involved in the matter would gather to form a water procession that would end at the Tower of London.

"Mary is closer to the new queen's age," I argued. "Queen Jane will be more inclined to trust her than one of us."

"But she is *my* daughter-in-law," Jane Northumberland objected.

"And you will be there to greet her when she arrives at Syon."

A few hours later, after the Duke and Duchess of Suffolk arrived at Durham House, Mary Sidney left to fetch Queen Jane. She was instructed not to tell the new queen that King Edward was dead. That unhappy duty was to be left for the Privy Council. At the same time, the Duchesses of Suffolk and Northumberland and I, as Marchioness of Northampton as well as Lady Northumberland's close friend, embarked for Syon. By the time Queen Jane arrived there, so had the Duke of Northumberland and Will and other councilors. Lord Guildford Dudley was conspicuous by his absence. He had not been at Chelsea when his sister arrived. The new queen's father, Henry Grey, Duke of Suffolk, was hastily dispatched to find him.

Together with the two duchesses and several other ladies who were privy to what had happened, Geraldine Clinton among them, I waited in an anteroom while the councilors informed Queen Jane that she was their new sovereign.

After a considerable time had passed, Mary Sidney hurried in. "The lords are having difficulty explaining the situation to Her Grace. My father requests your assistance, Lady Suffolk."

When Frances followed Mary Sidney into the other room, Jane Northumberland and I were close behind. The Duke of Northumberland had seated Queen Jane on the dais in a chair placed under the canopy of state. While we listened, he told Her Grace that King Edward was dead. He spoke of the legacy His Grace had left and then officially informed Queen Jane that Edward had nominated her to succeed him.

Her Grace promptly burst into tears and was inconsolable for some minutes. When she could finally speak, she blurted out what was in her heart: "The crown is not my right and does not please me. The Lady Mary is the rightful heir."

Shock rippled through the chamber. Jane Northumberland gasped aloud. Frances Suffolk took a step toward her daughter, hand raised as if she would slap sense into her. She stopped short of landing a blow, remembering that it was treason to strike a queen.

"Your Grace wrongs both yourself and your house," Northumberland said. "It was King Edward's command that you succeed him. The Lady Mary and the Lady Elizabeth have no legal claim to the throne. Their mothers were never married to King Henry VIII, while you, Your Grace, are a direct and legitimate descendant of King Henry's father, Henry VII, through *his* daughter Mary, your grace's own grandmother."

"It is your duty to your faith to accept the crown," Frances Brandon, Duchess of Suffolk, told her daughter. "Would you give England back to Rome?"

Neither argument had any effect on Queen Jane. She continued to sob.

At that moment, the Duke of Suffolk arrived with Gil Dudley. That young man did not resemble either Harry or Jack physically, but I searched his face, hoping to find some vestige of his brothers' sense of responsibility. Lord Guildford seemed hesitant to thrust himself forward and remained silent, but his eyes never left Queen Jane. Was that out of genuine concern for her? Or because he was waiting for his father's orders?

I sidled closer. When I was near enough, I caught hold of Gil's sleeve and tugged on it to get his attention. "A gentle wooing would not go amiss," I whispered. "Your bride is frightened by the burden so suddenly thrust upon her. Let her know that she has someone with whom she can share it."

Gil followed my advice, approaching the queen to offer first a handkerchief and then kind words. Light touches followed. She turned her tear-ravaged face to him and listened and in the end accepted the responsibility she owed both God and country. With her tall, handsome husband standing behind her chair of state, Queen Jane allowed those gathered before her to pledge their fealty.

We stayed that night at Syon, celebrating with a great banquet. Queen Jane retired early, with her husband. The next morning, we set out for London, traveling downriver on barges from Syon to Westminster. I felt as if I had never truly seen the city before, with its towering walls of silver-gray stone and redbrick. The houses of the gentry and lesser nobility, simple structures of wood and plaster, were dwarfed by Westminster Abbey and Whitehall Palace. We stopped at the latter so that Queen Jane could be dressed in a green velvet gown trimmed in gold. Gil's garments were a dazzling white, so that the Tudor colors would be on display.

"Her Grace is too short," Northumberland complained, looking Queen Jane up and down. She was a tiny girl and looked even more so standing next to her husband. "The crowds will not be able to see her."

The problem was solved by a high, white, close-fitting headdress heavy with jewels and by attaching three-inch chopines to the bottoms of Queen Jane's shoes.

We moved on to Durham House to dine. While we ate, the Privy Council made final plans. Then we were on our way again, traveling downriver through the city of London to the Tower of London. The royal apartments there had been prepared to receive the new monarch.

It was a heady journey. Huge crowds gathered and cheered, although they must have been puzzled by the display—the king's death had yet to be announced. Queen Jane and Lord Guildford were not the only ones resplendent in luxurious fabrics and glittering jewels. We all wore our best. I had rarely seen so many diamonds and sapphires and emeralds. When the sun struck them, they shone in all their brilliance.

Cannon boomed as we approached the Tower. By the time Northumberland helped Queen Jane onto the wharf, rumors of the king's death had begun to spread. The crowd expected to see Princess Mary and was confused when Queen Jane and her young husband appeared, walking beneath a ceremonial canopy. Having this held over their heads clearly indicated royal birth, but no one recognized the couple.

"They do not know her," I whispered to Will.

"As soon as we are safely within the Tower's walls," he whispered back, "proclamations will be read to announce to the people of London that Jane is their new queen."

We passed through the Lion Gate. Waiting just inside were the lord lieutenant of the Tower, Sir Edward Warner, and his wife. Once Queen

Jane passed by, Aunt Elizabeth enveloped me in a warm hug. I had seen her from time to time since her marriage, but not often. I promised to come and sup with her in the lord lieutenant's lodgings and then hurried after Her Grace.

"This way, Lord Guildford," Sir Edward said when Queen Jane had been shown into the royal apartments. "I will take you to the consort's lodgings."

"You will address me as Your Grace," Lord Guildford said.

"You are not king, Gil," Queen Jane said in a soft voice, laying one hand on her husband's white satin sleeve.

He stiffened and glared at her. "I will be."

"No, Gil, you will not. You are my consort only."

"I was promised—"

"Not by me."

Gil continued to protest in heated terms. The queen remained firm. She had issued her first royal decree and did not intend to change her mind. After a few more minutes of fruitless argument, Lord Guildford stormed off in high dudgeon. His mother went after him.

Queen Jane studied those of us who remained, then told everyone to leave except her own woman, Mistress Tilney, and young Lady Throckmorton, a knight's wife.

I exited the royal apartments and went in search of Will. We were to remain in the Tower for the time being. Officially, I was one of the great ladies of the household to Queen Jane.

When I found him, I recounted the scene between Queen Jane and her husband. "Her Grace may not be as easy to control as Northumberland believed," I warned, "and yet I think she may have the makings of a strong ruler. She certainly put Lord Guildford in his place!"

The Duke of Northumberland, and Will with him, left the Tower after dinner on the thirteenth of July. Mary Tudor had eluded capture by Lord Robin Dudley and was gathering support in the countryside. Northumberland forces, six hundred strong, were mustering at the duke's Durham House and at the royal palace of Whitehall and would march out, passing through London, the next morning. This army included Will and three of Northumberland's sons—Jack, Ambrose, and Robin Dudley—but Gil would remain with Queen Jane in the Tower.

A few privy councilors were also to stay behind, among them my father. We supped together with Aunt Elizabeth that evening in high spirits. We were confident that Mary would be in custody within the week and Queen Jane's hold on the throne secure. I gave a passing thought to Elizabeth Tudor, but everyone said she had no legitimate claim to the Crown and I soon forgot about her again.

On the morning of the nineteenth, Queen Jane announced, after breaking her fast, that she intended to leave the Tower to attend a christening at the church of All Hallows Barking.

"You cannot go," her mother said. "It is neither safe nor seemly for you to leave the Tower before your coronation."

"I promised Master Underhill that I would stand godmother to his six-day-old son." The queen's lower lip crept forward in a pout.

"Send a proxy," Jane Northumberland suggested. "That is what queens do."

"I suppose it is." Her Grace looked thoughtful. "Lady Throckmorton, you will go in my stead. You are to name the boy Guildford, after my husband."

"As you wish, Your Grace," Lady Throckmorton said. "May I ask a boon? I should like to dine at my own house afterward and retrieve one or two things I did not have time to collect before I came here."

Queen Jane graciously granted permission.

Soon after Lady Throckmorton left the precincts, my father sent word for me to meet him in the lord lieutenant's lodgings. I was glad of the excuse to leave the queen's apartments. The day seemed likely to proceed exactly as those preceding it had—uneventful, even dull, with entirely too much praying for my liking. I was counting the days until Will's return, but had no premonition that everything was not going smoothly. By now, I was certain, Mary Tudor had been captured.

"I am about to leave, Bess," Father said. "It would be best if you came with me."

"Leave?" I stared at him blankly.

"The other lords of the council have already fled."

The image of rats leaving a sinking ship sprang immediately to my mind. A sick feeling crept into my belly. "But why?" I whispered.

"The tide has turned. Mary Tudor is marching toward London at the head of an army. The common people flock to her. In their understanding, she is her brother's rightful heir. That matters more to them than their fear of a return to the Church of Rome."

"But . . . but King Edward made his cousin Jane his legal heir. We are only carrying out the late king's dying command."

His pitying look told me that this signified nothing. A terrible coldness encased my limbs. The people had turned against Northumberland, and Will was with the duke's army. He was in danger. My legs suddenly felt too weak to support my weight. I grasped Father's arm for support.

He broke my hold with no more effort than it would have taken to dislodge a clinging toddler. "There is only one course open to us now, Bess, if we want to avoid attainder for treason. Pembroke, Clinton, and some of the others have gone to the Earl of Pembroke's London house, Baynard's Castle. I will join them there and together we will proclaim Mary queen. I pray to God this gesture will be enough to save me from the headsman's ax. If you know what's good for you, daughter, you will make haste to Winchester House, gather up those possessions most dear to you, and abandon the rest."

"But where am I to go? And what of Will?"

"Cowling Castle should be safe. You can take refuge there with your mother."

"What of Will?" I repeated.

Father sent a pitying look my way as he opened the door. "You can do nothing for him. He's too entrenched as Northumberland's second in command."

As shaken by Father's abrupt change of allegiance as by his news and his warning, I turned to Aunt Elizabeth after he'd gone. "I do not know what to do," I wailed. "Will expects me to stay here with Queen Jane, but if I could find him, warn him—we might escape Queen Mary's wrath if he joins the others at Baynard's Castle." What did I care who ruled England, so long as Will was safe?

"If your father is right," Aunt Elizabeth said, "we will all suffer for our support of Queen Jane. I have no advice to give you, Bess. I am worried about my own husband's fate."

"How could things change so fast?"

"Bad luck." Some of my aunt's old bitterness, absent since her remarriage, surfaced when she added, "Did the duke think Mary Tudor would not hear rumors that the king was dying? He should have secured her person weeks ago."

I returned to Queen Jane's apartments in a troubled state of mind and nearly collided with Geraldine, Lady Clinton, hurrying the other way. She hesitated when she saw me.

"Is something amiss?" I kept my voice level but my heart was in my throat.

"I . . . I am unsure how to answer you." She avoided meeting my eyes. "My husband has sent word that I am to join him immediately at Baynard's Castle. He . . . he bade me tell no one that I am leaving."

At this proof of what Father had already told me, I clamped down hard on my growing fear and forced myself to smile. "You must go, then, and at once."

"Come with me, Bess."

But I shook my head. "I cannot go yet."

Inside the queen's apartments, nothing seemed to have changed. But even as that thought crossed my mind, a messenger delivered a note to Queen Jane's father, the Duke of Suffolk. A look of pure horror crossed his face before he blanked out all emotion. Quietly and without fuss, he left the room.

I told Jane Northumberland what my father had said, but I did not mention Geraldine's defection. Her absence would be noticed soon enough.

"Nonsense, Bess," the duchess said, and refused to discuss the matter further. She was as blind as I had been to the possibility of failure.

An hour passed before the Duke of Suffolk returned. Protocol demanded that he bow upon entering the presence of his sovereign, even if she was also his daughter. Instead, he walked straight up to her chair and spoke in a voice loud enough for everyone in the room to hear. "The Lady Mary has been proclaimed queen. Soldiers have arrived to claim the Tower in her name. I have ordered my men to lay down their arms and surrender."

The Lady Jane Grey, queen no more, stared at her father in disbelief. Then her hands clenched into fists on the arms of her chair. Her voice was cold and brittle. "You helped persuade me to accept the crown, and now you would take it from me."

Suffolk did not reply in words, but he took hold of the canopy of state under which his daughter sat and ripped it from its moorings. The Lady Jane fled to an inner room, her ladies and Jane Northumberland trailing after her. The Duchess of Suffolk stayed behind to question her husband in low tones, and after a moment they left together, abandoning their daughter now that she was no longer queen.

I stared at the empty chair. A moment ago, it had been a queen's throne. Now it was just an ordinary piece of furniture again. The torn canopy lay on the floor where Suffolk had thrown it, ruined, as everything we'd hoped for had been ruined by Northumberland's failure to capture Queen Mary.

Once Mary was officially proclaimed queen, I would no longer be at court, no longer be Marchioness of Northampton, and no longer be married to Will. For Will the future might be even more bleak. To Queen Mary, Will was a rebel. If her men captured him, she'd execute him for treason. King Edward's will would be meaningless against the might of a victorious army. Lady Jane Grey's right to be queen. My right to be married to Will. Both would be overturned because the people supported the heiress they knew—a king's daughter—over a royal cousin most of them had probably never heard of.

But I'd wager they all knew that the Duke of Northumberland had married that cousin to his own son. Their leaders, and no doubt Queen Mary herself, imagined a dastardly plot in the triple weddings of last Whitsuntide. No amount of argument was likely now to sway them from that false conclusion. Father was right. It was too late for Will to salvage anything. We had been too closely linked to Northumberland for too long.

I rested my forehead against the cool stone of a window casing. Eyes closed, I fought tears of despair. My thoughts circled round and round, going nowhere, until finally, drawing in a deep breath, I lifted my head and looked out at a view of the Thames and Southwark and my gaze fell upon my own home, Winchester House.

Suddenly I knew what I had to do. I would be no use to Will if I was trapped in the Tower. Escape was still possible.

If Will could elude capture, he would look for me at Winchester House, not here in the Tower of London. Once we were reunited, we could go into exile in France. Will had friends there, people he had met when he'd gone to the French court as an ambassador of the king.

I left the royal apartments in haste and made my way through the Tower precincts and out through the Lion Gate. No one tried to stop me. As I hurried along Thames Street on foot, I caught a glimpse of Lady Throckmorton returning from the christening she'd attended as Queen Jane's representative. I started to call out to her, but thought better of the impulse to warn her. I could not risk drawing attention to myself. She passed into the dark maw of the fortress that was both palace and prison, never suspecting what awaited her within, and the heavy gate closed behind her with an ominous crash.

41

For the next week, no news reached me at Winchester House. In some ways that was worse than hearing every frightening rumor that spread through London and its suburbs.

My servants had worked themselves into a state of panic even before I returned from the Tower of London. They knew Will and I had backed the wrong side and feared being clapped into prison for treason. Many of them ran away that first night and I was afraid to send one of the few who remained to discover what was going on, lest he, or she, not return.

"Drink a little of this posset, my lady," Birdie Crane said, holding out a steaming goblet. "It will give you strength."

I accepted the offering and sipped. The sweet, hot liquid warmed me from within, but I was no less worried when I'd drained the cup to the dregs. I handed it back and paused to consider my waiting gentlewoman. Birdie had joined the household shortly after my sojourn with the queen dowager at Chelsea. She fulfilled her duties and stayed in the background the rest of the time, having mastered the art of remaining so very still that her presence often went unnoticed. I'd never felt particularly close to her, but I was grateful she had elected to stay at Winchester House.

"Do you wish to return to your family?" I asked.

She had come from somewhere in Kent. I could send her back to her kinfolk. I could send all of my household away to safety. I had no illusions about what would happen once Queen Mary reached London. She would take this house, Will's titles, and every source of income available to him. Even the manor he'd put in my name when we married would go, once the new queen's men discovered its existence. They'd claim it for the Crown along with all the rest.

"I will stay with you as long as you need me, my lady," Birdie said. "My parents died of the last epidemic of the sweat and I have no brothers or sisters."

It said something about the events of the last few days that my first thought was to wonder if she'd been sent to our household as a spy. Studying her through narrowed and suspicious eyes I saw a slender woman four or five years younger than myself with blue eyes and light brown hair; a sharply defined nose; and a small, pointed chin. One eye had a slight droop at the corner and both were reddened with weeping.

"Do you cry for the marquess?" I asked.

Her laugh was bitter. "I cry for myself, and for a good gentleman who marched out with the Duke of Northumberland's troops."

"A lover?"

"You are surprised," she said with a tinge of bitterness in her voice. "I know I am no beauty, nor am I an heiress, but I still can love."

I covered her hand with mine. "I know what it is to love and be loved. I pray he will come back safe and sound."

"What good will that do? He'll be a prisoner."

"Queen Mary will not punish everyone who supported the Lady Jane. She will imprison the leaders"—I had to stop and swallow hard—"and free the rest." I hoped that would be the case, although it would do Will no good.

"That will not help me," Birdie lamented. "My lover is married. He will never be mine." Fresh tears sprang into her eyes. "And if I cannot stay with you, my lady, I have nowhere else to go."

"Dry your eyes," I said. "I will not send you away."

But I did send her out into the city, to try to discover the fate of Northumberland's army. Griggs, the groom who had accompanied Will to Cowling Castle so many years before, went with her. He was an old man now, bald as an egg and his broad red beard gone gray. He'd been in service to the Parrs since Will was a boy.

While they were gone, I sent the rest of the household away. It was no good pretending we could stay at Winchester House. One of Queen Mary's first acts would be to release Bishop Gardiner from the Tower, and he would lose no time reclaiming both his bishopric and his house in Southwark. A few of the servants, who had been with Will almost as long as Griggs, did not want to leave but I insisted. The rest made haste to escape.

By the time Birdie and Griggs returned, the house felt as empty as an unused tomb. Their news was as bad as I'd feared. Northumberland had surrendered and declared for Mary. He'd been taken into custody along with his sons and Will and too many others to count. They were prisoners now, and would soon be incarcerated in the Tower of London, for that was where traitors to the Crown were always sent. But Will was alive. I took heart from that. So long as he lived, there might be some way to win his freedom.

On the day the Duke of Northumberland was escorted through London to the Tower, I ventured out for the first time since I'd fled the royal apartments. I disguised myself in plain clothing and a dark cloak and took Birdie with me.

The crowd shouted abuse and threw rotten produce when the duke came in sight, pelting him with cabbages and eggs. Jack and Ambrose, who rode just behind their father, were also targets.

"Death to the traitors!" shouted a man standing next to me.

"Hang, draw, and quarter them," bellowed someone else.

I strained to see the other prisoners, hoping to find Will, and yet praying that somehow he had escaped. When I realized he was not there, a wave of panic hit me so hard and fast that it nearly brought me to my knees. I staggered, caught myself, and fought for control of legs that suddenly seemed weak. Did Will's absence mean he was free . . . or that was he dead?

Light-headed, I clung to my waiting gentlewoman for support, but she scarcely seemed to notice. Her attention was fixed on one of the young gentlemen being marched toward imprisonment in Northumberland's wake. Her lover, I presumed. He looked vaguely familiar, but I could not focus my mind on anyone else's troubles. Not when I had so many of my own.

"There will be more traitors brought in tomorrow," someone in the crowd said.

A spark of optimism flared to life. I looked again at the prisoners and saw that others besides Will were missing. Only two of Northumberland's sons were with him. I knew that Lord Guildford was in the Tower with the two Janes, his mother and his wife, but Lord Robin was unaccounted for and so was the youngest boy, the second Henry Dudley. It seemed a lifetime since the first brother with that name, the Harry Dudley I'd once thought to marry, had died of a fever on one of King Henry's French campaigns. It had, in truth, been not quite nine years, but I was no longer an innocent girl of eighteen. At twenty-seven, five years Will's legal wife, I was surely old enough and seasoned enough to think for myself and to find a way to save Will's life.

I returned to the same spot near the Tower the next day. This time I did not have long to wait before I caught sight of Will's familiar face and form. He was on horseback, clearly visible above the heads of the people lining the street. Determined to close the distance between us, I pushed my way to the front of the crowd.

Sunk in misery, pelted with rotten fruit as the duke and his sons had been the day before, Will kept his head down and looked neither left nor right. He did not know I was there. Robin Dudley, who rode next to him, was in even worse condition. A livid bruise covered one side of his face and his clothing was torn and stained.

As they rode past the place where I stood, I reached out and caught

Will's stirrup, jarring him out of his trancelike state. He looked down, straight into my eyes. For a long, agonizing moment he did not seem to recognize me. Then he gave a start.

"Bess," he said in a hoarse whisper. "Get away. You must not—"

A heavily callused hand clamped down on my arm and jerked me apart from my husband. "Begone, wench," the soldier ordered. "The prisoner has no time for dalliance."

He shoved me back into the crowd. A stranger cursed when I trod upon his foot and gave me a push that sent me sprawling. Two women helped me to unsteady feet. Blinded by tears, I staggered away.

A young girl stepped into my path and spat at me. "Traitor. You should be a prisoner with them." She had no idea who I was, but she'd seen me consorting with the enemy.

By some miracle, Birdie Crane made her way through the surging mass of bodies to take my arm in a surprisingly firm grip and guide me back toward London Bridge. Once we reached it, we made better progress. The single street that ran between the towering houses on either side was nearly empty.

"I have to go to the queen," I murmured. "To Queen Mary. If I can reach her, plead with her . . ."

My voice trailed off as I caught sight of the heads. They were such a permanent part of the Southwark side of London Bridge that no one paid much attention to them. Now I saw them for what they were—the rotting remains of traitors to the Crown. My stomach lurched. I would not allow Will to end up there. Not while there was breath left in my body.

My determination to save him from a traitor's death, my conviction that I could manage it if only I could gain an audience with the queen, carried me the last few steps to the gates of Winchester House, only to find them barred.

In my absence, the palace had been overrun by former servants of the bishop of Winchester. Armed guards now stood in front of the gatehouse, questioning all who tried to enter. They did not know me in my plain attire, and although I would have liked to demand that I be allowed to fetch my personal clothing and jewelry, I did not dare risk revealing my identity. If I ended up in the Tower, too, I would lose any hope of saving Will.

Griggs hissed at us from the shadow of the nearby church of St. Mary Overy. I broke down and cried when I saw that he had managed to spirit three horses out of the Winchester House stables before the others were confiscated, Will's black gelding, a dapple gray mare, and my own bay. I clung to Prancer's neck and sobbed until all my tears were gone.

"What now, my lady?" Birdie asked when I had control of myself again. Her eyes were huge in her pale face.

With an effort, I subdued the last tendrils of panic. "I will seek an audience with Queen Mary. I have never done her any harm and she is known to have a kind heart. Perhaps she will be merciful in victory."

We rode back across London Bridge, through the city, and out again, heading for Newhall in Essex, where the queen was reported to be staying until she made her official entrance into London. We had not gone far before we overtook Jane, Duchess of Northumberland. She had been allowed to leave the Tower when the duke was brought in, and now she, too, was bound for Newhall to plead for her husband's life.

"Everyone fled from the Tower when you did, Bess," Jane told me, "except the Lady Jane and her two women, myself, and poor Lady Throckmorton, who returned from that christening at just the wrong time. When she tried to leave again, she was told she could not go. Sir Edward Warner took it upon himself to make prisoners of all who remained in the royal apartments. I suppose he hoped in that way to retain his post under the new regime."

"And Lady Jane is still there?"

Jane Northumberland nodded. "I had to leave my daughter-in-law behind in the Tower. And now John is there, too, along with all our sons. Not just Gil, but Jack and Ambrose and Robin and Henry."

And Will, I added silently. My husband. The other half of myself.

Together, two desperate wives, we pushed on to Newhall, but we need not have hurried. We were turned away. The queen would not see either of us.

There was no lodging to be found nearby. Every house, every inn, overflowed with Queen Mary's supporters. We began to wend our weary way back toward London, disconsolate and miserable.

"What do we do now?" I asked.

"Survive," Jane said.

"I know the choices. Accept the old religion or flee abroad. I imagine that the most dedicated of the evangelicals are already taking ship for the Continent."

Jane sent me a pitying look. "I would not be so sure of that. Some will be willing to die for their faith, to become martyrs to rally the rest. And others will gladly abandon their religious beliefs in exchange for the opportunity to remain at court. We were betrayed, Bess. By men who swore to support Queen Jane."

She rattled off the familiar names. The Earl of Pembroke, Will's brother-in-law, widower of his sister Anne. Lord Clinton, Geraldine's second husband. Even Lord Cobham, my own father. Although I could not condone their disloyalty, I hoped that Father and Pembroke's sons, my nephews, would be safe from retaliation by Queen Mary. And my friend Geraldine, too.

"And the Duke of Suffolk!" Jane's voice vibrated with contempt. "The Lady Jane's own father. He was always a weakling, but this treachery surpasses understanding."

"Perhaps," I ventured, "if my father is forgiven, he will help us to reach the queen and appeal to her for mercy."

I was struck with a sudden longing to be home at Cowling Castle. It had been years since I'd felt the need of my mother's reassurance, but all at once I ached to be held in her arms. I wished I could be a little girl again, secure in the love of my family, protected and cosseted by everyone around me.

"We would do better to approach Her Grace through her ladies, I think." Jane had a determined look on her pale face. "We must discover what women are closest to Queen Mary and solicit their help. If I cannot speak to them, then I will write letters. I will never give up trying to win a pardon for my lord husband."

"Nor will I."

When we reached London, we separated. Jane went to her own house at Ely Place. I made my way to the Earl of Pembroke's residence, Baynard's Castle. Had Pembroke been there, he'd likely have turned me away, but Henry Herbert, his son and heir, had always been fond of his uncle Will and aunt Bess. He ordered the servants to admit me and my two servants. He even provided much needed food and drink.

As we ate, I questioned him, hoping for news of Will. Young Lord Herbert had inherited Anne Parr's wide-spaced gray eyes and her open nature, but he had been brought up to obey his father. When I asked about his bride, Lady Catherine Grey, his face hardened.

"She is not my wife. The marriage is to be annulled and she'll be sent back to her mother."

I was not surprised. It would be difficult for Pembroke to advance at Queen Mary's court while the Lady Jane's sister was married to his son. "I suppose the Earl of Huntingdon will set aside his boy's marriage to Northumberland's daughter, Katherine Dudley, too," I murmured.

"Oh, no. He's going to keep her," Henry said. "Father thinks Huntingdon's a damned fool."

An hour at Baynard's Castle was sufficient to convince me that I'd get no help from the Earl of Pembroke, even if he was Will's brother-in-law. I did not ask to stay, nor did I rejoin my close friend Jane Northumberland at Ely Place. I doubted the queen would allow her to remain there long. All the possessions of a traitor were forfeit to the Crown.

Griggs helped me to mount Prancer. "Do we ride to Cowling Castle, my lady?"

"No, Griggs. I need to stay close to the Tower and to Will."

And I had remembered something Aunt Elizabeth had told me during one of our shared suppers in the Tower—Sir Edward Warner owned a house in Carter Lane. I would go there.

42

*A*unt Elizabeth and her husband made me welcome. They invited me to stay with them as long as I wished. Unfortunately, Sir Edward was at home because Queen Mary had already removed him from his post as lord lieutenant of the Tower. I had been hoping to make use of his position there to communicate with Will.

"Your husband was well when I last saw him," Sir Edward assured me. "I put him in the Beauchamp Tower and ordered that his own furniture and clothing be brought to him from Winchester House. And I can assure you that he will not want for proper food and drink."

"But he is still a prisoner."

"So are many others. I half-expected to join their number myself."

Aunt Elizabeth, who sat on the arm of her husband's chair, touched one hand lightly to his shoulder. "You did nothing wrong, Edward."

"Nor did any of them," I interjected. "Naught but carry out the king's last wishes."

Sir Edward grimaced, making his mustache and his long, pointed beard twitch. "Queen Mary does not see it in quite that way. But take heart, Bess. Suffolk is free. Others may follow."

"The Lady Jane's father has been released?"

"He has. The Duchess of Suffolk was granted an audience with the queen at Newhall. Well, why not? Frances Brandon and Queen Mary are cousins and have always been on friendly terms, despite their differences over matters of religion. Her Grace pardoned the Duke of Suffolk the very next day. The duke and duchess have already left London for their house at Sheen."

"What of the Lady Jane Grey?"

Sir Edward drooped lower in his chair. "Poor girl. She's been charged with treason."

I, too, felt sorry for Jane Grey, but I could do nothing to help her and I might yet find a way to rescue Will. Between them, Sir Edward and my aunt had a remarkable number of friends, and some of those friends had kin in the new queen's household. Through these channels, Aunt Elizabeth gleaned more news. Thus I learned that Anne, Duchess of Somerset, who had been living quietly at Hanworth since her release from the Tower a few months earlier, had also been able to trade upon her old friendship with the new queen. Two of her daughters were to come to court as maids of honor, and young Anne, the eldest, although married to Jack Dudley, was to join her mother and sisters there.

"A pity that young woman cannot be relied upon to beg for mercy for her husband," I said, "but she has no love for him." Not when Jack's father had been responsible for the execution of her father, the Duke of Somerset

My own father's timely change of allegiance had succeeded in winning him his freedom. He'd prudently retreated to Cowling Castle to await a formal pardon for conspiring to put Lady Jane Grey on the throne in Mary Tudor's place. Father sent word that I was welcome to come home and my mother wrote to second the invitation, but I chose to remain in Carter Lane. The last thing I wanted was to put more distance between myself and the man I loved. I needed to be close to Will, even if I was not able to see or communicate with him.

By early August, less than three weeks after Northumberland and Will surrendered to Queen Mary's troops, most of their followers had been pardoned and released. But not Will and not Northumberland or his sons. All of them were shortly to be arraigned for treason. At that time, Will would officially be stripped of his titles, his Order of the Garter, and very probably his life.

"I could be content as plain Lady Parr as long as I had Will by my side, free and whole," I confided in Aunt Elizabeth as I helped her inventory the plate in the Carter Lane house. With matters so unsettled, Sir Edward intended to sell some of it for ready money.

"But you will not *be* Lady Parr. That title, and Countess of Essex, and Marchioness of Northampton, too, will soon be restored to Anne Bourchier. I heard this morning that Queen Mary has sent for her. Her Grace means to make Lady Anne a lady-in-waiting."

Stunned, I struggled to take in this development. "Will warned me that Queen Mary would undo our marriage, but it never occurred to me that the queen would bring a proven adulteress to court."

"Perhaps Queen Mary does not know why Will divorced her."

"Then someone should tell her." Anger filled me and I snapped out the words. "Have you any connection at court able to whisper in the right ear?"

"If I had, I would not ask them to blacken her name. Think, Bess. Anne Bourchier's presence could help Will. If he is executed for treason, the Crown will claim all he owned, including the Essex inheritance. She will have none of it. And no title. It is to her advantage that he be spared. If I were you, I would pray that she intends to plead most eloquently with the queen for the restoration of his estates, even if it is only because she hopes to claim them for herself."

I took a deep breath. My aunt was right. Anne Bourchier could save Will's life. She could go where I could not.

Dibs and dabs of news continued to filter down to the house in Carter Lane, but all of London knew of it when Will was attainted and sentenced to die. The Duke of Northumberland was condemned at the same time. So was Jack Dudley. And on Tuesday the twenty-second day of August, the duke was executed.

"The Duke of Somerset's sons—the Earl of Hertford and his brother—were present to witness Northumberland's death," Edward Warner told us afterward. They had been two among a crowd of thousands who turned out to see the condemned traitor die. "Northumberland apologized to them for killing their father. An irony, that. Now both men lie buried together, lying between the bodies of Queen Anne Boleyn and Queen Catherine Howard. Or so they say." He chuckled, but his expression was grim when he added, "Northumberland died in the faith of his childhood."

"As a Catholic? When he fought so hard and so long to keep the Church of England alive?"

"His eldest son converted, too. And so did Will Parr." His disapproval of what Will had done was a palpable force in the room.

"I do not see what difference it makes," I said with some asperity. "All our prayers go to the same God. I can kneel at a Catholic Mass with idols in the niches as easily as I can worship in a whitewashed chapel with an English prayer book in my hand."

"We will not have any choice in the matter now." Sir Edward's tone was bitter.

"We did not have any choice before. And if converting to Catholicism saves their lives, then I am heartily glad Will and Jack had the good sense to recant."

Sir Edward glared at me, but he dropped the subject.

Northumberland's widow became plain Lady Dudley again after the duke's attainder and execution. Throughout those troubled days, I kept in touch with her. Neither she nor I were charged with any offense, but while I was left homeless and destitute, she was granted control of her jointure lands and allowed to live at Chelsea Manor. Although devastated by the loss of her husband, Jane continued to petition the queen for her sons' release. She wrote to everyone she knew at court to solicit their help. As a result of her efforts, Ambrose, Robert, and Henry Dudley were allowed visits from their wives.

"To whom should I apply for permission to visit Will?" I asked Sir Edward Warner.

He snorted. "The new lord lieutenant might let Will's wife in but, Bess, *you* are not his wife." He drained his tankard. He'd consumed a great quantity of ale since he'd lost his post at the Tower. "As soon as Parliament convenes, the law confirming your marriage will be struck down."

The reminder stung. In my heart I could not accept that ruling. Defiantly, I continued to wear my wedding ring. And, in imitation of Jane Dudley, I wrote to friends and family to solicit their help on Will's behalf. Some, like the Earl of Pembroke, ignored my pleas entirely. Others, like my father, were in no position to take up Will's cause because their own hold on the new queen's favor was so tenuous. He sent a welcome gift of money but could not do more. Geraldine Clinton promised to speak to her husband on Will's behalf, but Lord Clinton, like my father, lacked influence with the new queen.

From my window in the house in Carter Lane I could see the highest battlements of the White Tower. Half of London lay between my chamber and the walls behind which Will was held prisoner. Carter Lane was nearer London Stone than London Bridge. But each night I stood looking out at the distant lights, imagining Will pacing the confines of his cell, wondering if he was thinking of me.

And then, on the twenty-fourth day of October, I was separated from my husband in yet another way. The act of 1552 that had pronounced Anne Bourchier as good as dead, the act intended to make my marriage to Will finally and irrevocably legal, was rescinded at the order of the queen. By royal decree, I was plain Bess Brooke again.

43

*N*ovember was a bleak and dismal month. It suited my mood. I was not cheered in the least to hear that the Duke of Suffolk—title and estates intact—was back in London. This news, however, seemed to improve Sir Edward Warner's spirits. On the twenty-sixth, he accepted an invitation to dine at Suffolk House and came home again buoyant and smiling.

I paid little attention to his goings and comings, save to note that he was no longer drinking himself into a stupor every night. That pleased me. My aunt deserved better than to be married to a drunkard. Neither did I think anything of it when Aunt Elizabeth's son, my cousin Sir Thomas Wyatt the Younger, who had his own lodgings in London, paid a visit. Aunt Elizabeth had been reconciled with Tom for some time, even though she still disagreed with his decision to be so generous with his late father's mistress. Tom supped with us, and then he and Sir Edward went out together. They were well acquainted, having both been friends of the late Earl of Surrey. They aped the same fashions, too, both sporting long, pointed beards and short-cropped hair. Sir Edward was only some ten years older than his stepson.

I rarely paid any attention to the comings and goings of my host. All my thoughts centered on ways to free Will from the Tower and on memories, sweet but painful. I missed my husband not only as my lover, but as my dearest friend and companion.

As November turned into December, I steeled myself to ask for help from the last person in the world I wanted to be beholden to—Anne Bourchier. The court had been at Whitehall since Queen Mary's coronation in early October. Among the queen's ladies was Mistress Nan Bassett. We had been maids of honor together, and while never fast friends, we had not been rivals, either. I used the money Father had sent me to purchase an enameled brooch and sent it to Nan as a token of my esteem, along with a letter begging her to meet with me. She sent word to come to the fountain in the palace gardens via the public right-of-way that passed through the grounds and suggested a specific day and time.

I waited nearly a quarter of an hour, fretting all the while that she'd changed her mind about talking to me. Then I caught sight of her hurrying toward me along one of the many paths that intersected the gardens. She was older by some six years since the last time I'd seen her, but she did not seem much changed. She greeted me warmly, with a sisterly embrace, and together we made our way to the riverfront, where we could be private.

Low tide permitted us to walk along the shore. Courtiers' houses two and three stories high lined the land side of our route, and behind them rose what remained of the old palace of Westminster, largely destroyed by fire well before I'd first come to court.

"How can I help you, Bess?" Nan asked when we were certain we were far from listening ears.

I studied her face for a long moment before I spoke. There was compassion in her intensely blue eyes, but also a certain wariness. "You know that my marriage has been nullified and that my husband . . . that Will Parr remains in the Tower under sentence of death."

She nodded, but held up one hand, palm out, to stay my next words. "If you wish an audience with the queen, that will not be possible. Her Grace will not undo what she has done. Will Parr did much offend her over the matter of her celebrating Mass during the late king's reign. I was with Her Grace in those days, and I heard the harsh words he used to her. Her Grace is convinced that his evil persuasions were what made her impressionable young brother behave so cruelly toward her."

"I know nothing of that." Will had never told me of the incident, but I had always known he favored religious reform . . . until his life depended upon returning to the old ways. "I would ask Her Grace's forgiveness for him, now that he has recanted."

"He claims he has accepted the true church," Nan said, "but it remains to be seen if he is sincere."

We continued on past Canon Row. I saw the young Earl of Hertford come out of his house. He exited by the water gate but had to cross yards of half-frozen ground on foot before he could hail a wherry. He, too, had embraced the old ways. We all had. I attended Mass every Sunday now with Aunt Elizabeth and Sir Edward.

"We have no choice but to accept the will of the queen," I said, "but I don't want Will to die!" My anguish broke through despite my best efforts to remain calm.

"I will do what I can," Nan promised, "but I do not have much influence. No one does save the Spanish ambassador and a few members of the Privy Council. Her Grace disregards all other advice."

"I want to meet with Will's other wife." I swallowed bile. "Since Queen Mary has brought Anne Bourchier to court, Her Grace must have some fondness for her."

"She may not wish to meet with you, Bess."

"Will you ask her? I beg you, Nan. Intercede for me. She can help Will. Perhaps if I . . . if I assure her that I will not . . . oh, Nan, just find a way for us to meet!" I dashed unwanted tears away, embarrassed and humiliated by them but willing to humble myself further if it won Will's freedom.

Nan sighed and turned back toward the palace. We walked in silence until we reached the water gate. "Come by boat tomorrow afternoon," she said, "and ask for the sergeant porter. His name is Keyes and his private rooms are situated on the upper floors of the gatehouse. If she is willing to meet you, she will be there."

THE NEXT DAY, I met Will's other wife face-to-face for the first time. He had once described her as a bone-thin, whey-faced girl. I'd pictured her as a slovenly whore. She was neither. Anne Bourchier was a tiny, delicate woman with a long narrow face, a slightly pointed chin, and chestnut-colored hair. She was older than I by nearly a decade, but if age, poverty, or disgrace had marked her, it did not show. Her features were as smooth as a child's. She was also in full court dress, resplendent in dark, wine-colored velvet sparkling with jewels. I recognized some of them as baubles I'd left behind in Winchester House.

"So, Mistress Brooke, we meet at last." She had a soft, tinkling voice, like fairy bells. I could not imagine what fault Will had found with her.

"Lady Parr." I choked out the name and pasted a neutral expression on my face.

"I am styled Viscountess Bourchier." She circled me as if I were a horse offered for sale at a fair. "I have been curious about you."

I was well aware of the contrast we made. In plain, unadorned garments, I looked drab and unimportant, but I'd had no finery to wear. That, too, had been left behind when we fled.

When I'd borne her scrutiny as long as I could stand, I blurted out what was on my mind. "I will never trouble you again if you will but promise to plead for my . . . for *your* husband's freedom with the queen."

"Why should I care what happens to Will Parr? He treated me most cruelly."

"*You* betrayed *him*." The words were out before I could stop them. I began again, more diplomatically this time. "I do beg your pardon, my lady. But it does seem to me that there was fault on both sides."

"We are quite alone here." A wry smile twisted her lips. "You may feel free to speak your mind."

"I have no wish to insult you, my lady."

She laughed softly. It was a surprisingly deep sound, considering the timbre of her speaking voice. "Let us begin again, then. What is it you think I can do?"

"Convince the queen to pardon Will."

"So that he can return to you?"

My chest tightened. The next words were physically painful to force out, but I was determined to save the man I loved. "Whatever Will has done, he does not deserve to die for it. It is in your power to help him, my lady. It is also to your advantage to do so."

"Why? I do not want him back."

"If he is executed for treason, all you claim as your inheritance will be lost, along with everything else Will owned." When I'd conceived of the idea of asking her for help, it had seemed logical to me that she would want the security of such a large and prosperous estate.

"The queen can grant those properties to me in any case," Viscountess Bourchier said.

"But will she?"

She walked to the window to look out over the Thames. She had a clear view of Norfolk House from where she stood. Tears blurred my vision, thinking how happy Will and I had been when we lived there.

Without turning, she said, "I am told you have no children."

"We were not blessed." I heard the tremor in my voice but could not control it.

"Be glad of it. They would be a curse upon you now. My children were disinherited, thanks to Will Parr. That ruling has not been reversed."

I bit back a reminder that her children were not her husband's, but rather bastards borne to a lover. Her bitterness alarmed me. If she wanted revenge more than she wanted her inheritance, she would never help Will. I said nothing, too afraid that the words I chose would be the wrong ones.

Lady Anne's hands gripped the sill as she stared out at the late-afternoon sky. A few flakes of snow drifted down, although the sun still shone brightly. In spite of the brazier heating the room, I shivered.

"I am told he weeps continuously," she said.

"Will?"

"Who else have we been speaking of?" She swung around to face me, her hands curled into fists at her sides. "I have made it my business to know everything about him, and about you, as well." She drew in a deep, steadying breath and slowly unclenched her fingers. "However, it *is* to my advantage to do as you ask. I will petition the queen. I have friends and kinswomen here at court who will join me in asking for a pardon." She gave a wry laugh. "But be warned. It will come with conditions. To the queen, I am Will's only wife. She wants us to be reconciled. He will be required to give up his illicit alliance with you if he wants to go free."

She took a step closer to me, forcing me to meet eyes that were cold and calculating, without a shred of softer feelings.

"If you care for him," she said softly, "you must abandon him. The queen will not tolerate any further infidelity."

I held her gaze. "I will do whatever I must in exchange for a full pardon."

44

Will was freed on the last day of December. Griggs stationed himself outside the Lion Gate to bring his master to Edward Warner's house in Carter Lane, where I was waiting for him. I was shocked by Will's appearance. He'd lost so much weight that he seemed but a shadow of himself. His face was haggard. He'd been imprisoned for only five months, but he'd aged five years.

His eyes lit up when he saw me, and he stumbled forward to take me in his arms. I returned the embrace, weeping when I felt the way his bones seemed to protrude from his skin. We clung to each other, kissing, not wanting to let go, but even as we embraced I could not help but think that he did not even smell the same. The miasma of the Tower clung to his clothes, his hair, and his beard.

When we stepped apart, I realized that he was favoring his right leg. I made a small sound of distress.

"It's the damp," he said, trying to make light of it. "Nothing to worry about."

"But you're limping."

He laughed off my concern. "A pity, though, that I don't still have that sturdy staff King Henry gave me."

It had been left behind in Winchester House. I supposed it was in some royal storeroom by this time, unless Bishop Gardiner had claimed it. Our old enemy had risen to the top again and was now Queen Mary's lord chancellor.

In spite of my promise to Anne Bourchier, I had never intended to abandon Will. Since the court had gone to Richmond Palace for Christmas, I did not think anyone would notice if we spent a few days together before I had to leave him again to keep him safe. I said nothing of what I meant to do. I concentrated on restoring my husband to health.

All Mother's training in the stillroom served me well. I made Will drink strengthening possets and evil-tasting herbal brews. By Twelfth Night he was much improved and I could no longer put off telling him about my meeting with Anne Bourchier. I chose my moment carefully, not in private, where he could woo me into changing my mind, but at supper with Aunt Elizabeth and Sir Edward there to support my arguments.

At court the end of Yuletide meant feasts and banquets and a last burst of merriment from the Lord of Misrule. There would be masques and dancing and an abundance of rich food. Aunt Elizabeth, Sir Edward, Will, and I took our meal together in Carter Lane as we always did, but in honor of the day had several more dishes than usual and sweet wafers and a doucet—spiced custard pie—to follow.

I told my tale while we consumed boiled capons, roast chine of beef, pies made with minced meat, and a kid with pudding in its belly. "And so," I said when I'd recounted the entire conversation, "under the law, our marriage never existed and you are still married to her. We risk the queen's wrath if we stay together."

"No power on earth can make me take Anne back," Will vowed.

"It sounds to me as if she does not want you, either," Aunt Elizabeth said.

Will scowled at her.

"I believe we can still be together," I said, "but we must make sure the queen does not find out. I have given this matter much thought and have devised a plan."

"She has always been a resourceful woman," Will said to Sir Edward. The pride in his voice warmed me more than the fire crackling in the hearth.

"In a few days, I will leave London and go to Cowling Castle to ask Father for the use of one of his more remote manor houses. If you wait a few weeks to steal away and meet me there, we should be able to live out the rest of our lives in peace and seclusion, far from those who would keep us apart."

Will looked dubious. "Is that what you truly want?"

"Have you a better suggestion?" I took a bite of capon, but the savory sauce it had been doused in seemed to have lost its flavor.

"We could go into exile in France," Will said. "I have friends among the French nobility who would take us in." He polished off the beef on his plate and reached for his wine goblet. As I'd expected, he was not taking my decision seriously. He did not want to be parted, even for a short time, any more than I did, but I knew we had no choice.

"To live on their charity?" I asked.

"Your father would be supporting us if we lived on one of his estates." He sopped up the last of the gravy with a piece of manchet bread and continued to eat.

Before I could counter this objection, Aunt Elizabeth sent her husband a pointed look. "Tell them, Edward."

"Eliza—"

"Tell them, or I will. You brought my son into it. Why not Will Parr?"

"Will has no tenants left to call to arms."

Sir Edward's blunt assessment confused me, but a gleam of anticipation came into Will's eyes. "You've said too much already not to go on."

"We've been meeting at Suffolk Place," Sir Edward said. "Suffolk and his brothers and others. Tom Wyatt's with us." He named more men, several of whom I recognized as evangelicals, and explained that they planned an uprising on four fronts. One of them would be Kent, where my cousin Tom was to raise the county against the queen.

They were talking about a conspiracy. My stomach clenched in dread. There would be no question about this rebellion being treason. I wanted to clap my hands over my ears so I would hear no more, but it was already too late.

"To what end?" Will asked. "You will not find much support to restore Queen Jane."

Sir Edward shook his head. "Not Jane. The rightful heir—Elizabeth Tudor. Two things happened while you were in the Tower, Will. Queen Mary's first Parliament once again declared King Henry's marriage to Anne Boleyn null and void, thus confirming Princess Elizabeth as a bastard."

"That is hardly surprising," Will said mildly. "And such an act has the force of law. If there had been time for Parliament to ratify King Edward's device for the succession, no one would have questioned Jane's right to succeed."

I held my tongue rather than contradict my husband, but I did not believe that, even with such a law, Queen Mary could have been stopped. Then she'd have ordered the next Parliament to repeal Edward's plan for the succession, as she'd had them revoke the private act Will had secured to free him to marry me.

"A pity, that." Something in the dryness of my aunt's voice made me think she agreed with me.

"You said that two things happened while I was a prisoner, Warner. What was the other?"

"The queen agreed to marry Philip of Spain."

Will came to his feet in a rush. His chair tumbled over backward with a resounding crash.

"It has not yet been announced," Sir Edward continued, "but there is no doubt the proclamation will come soon. You know what that means, Will. A foreigner will be king of England, and this particular foreigner will not hesitate to unleash the Inquisition. Pretending to convert to the Church of Rome will not suffice. Priests will search out every hint of heresy, and if they look, they will find it. None of us will be safe."

I hoped Sir Edward exaggerated the danger, but I could see that both he and Will believed what he was saying. It frightened them. The more I thought about it, the more afraid I became, too.

"Queen Mary already has reason to dislike Will," I said. "She'll send him back to the Tower in a heartbeat if she has any excuse. He must have nothing to do with the uprising."

"All the more reason he should do everything in his power to help us succeed," Sir Edward countered.

"France," I murmured, "begins to look most inviting."

"We must do one or the other." Will righted his chair and resumed his place at table, reaching for his wine goblet. "Flee or fight."

I did not think his choice and mine would be the same. "When is this rebellion to begin?" I asked Sir Edward.

"Palm Sunday."

"But that's months away. Sometime in mid-March and this is only the first week in January. How can you possibly think that your plans will remain secret that long?"

"We are pledged to keep silence."

And yet, I thought, you blithely share every detail with Will who, for all you know, truly has converted to the Catholic faith.

Three days later, when Tom Wyatt paid another visit to Carter Lane, I realized that he was even less adept at secrecy than Sir Edward. He boasted that he'd been in touch with the new French ambassador, and that he expected support from that quarter when he called the men of Kent to arms.

"It is time for me to go to Cowling Castle," I told Will when Tom left.

"What need to be parted now, sweeting? Soon all will be put right."

I had my doubts about that, but short of reporting the rebels to the queen myself, there was nothing I could do to stop the march of events. "I am not supposed to be here with you," I reminded him. "With all this plotting and scheming going on, the last thing we should do is draw official attention to this house."

Reluctantly, Will agreed that it would be best if I left. We spent the night in loving and said a tearful farewell when I set out the next day.

Both Birdie and Griggs had remained with me at Aunt Elizabeth's house and now accompanied me into Kent. Will and I had agreed that I would stay with my parents until after the rebellion had succeeded in deposing Queen Mary. I did not mention it to Will, but I still intended to ask Father for the loan of one of his manor houses. I would make sure it was in readiness to receive us should the rebellion fail.

I reached Cowling Castle the next day. I'd expected my father and mother to be there, and my youngest sibling, Edmund, who was now fourteen, but I was surprised to find all my brothers in residence.

"Have you brought messages?" George demanded. At twenty, he sported a beard just like Father's, but he was taller and thinner than our sire, almost lanky. His eyes were bright with anticipation.

The same fever burned in Thomas and John and Henry and William and made my blood run cold. They were waiting for word from Tom Wyatt. My brothers meant to rise up to prevent the queen's marriage to Philip of Spain.

"I see there is no common sense in this house, either," I said.

They found this sentiment amusing.

"Now you sound like Mother," Henry complained, "always trying to spoil our fun."

I thought it the better part of valor to listen rather than argue. There was no reasoning with men spoiling for a fight. When we joined my parents for supper, Mother and I were the only ones to say aloud that the failure of such an attempt would bring disaster down upon us all.

"You cannot help being afraid," my brother Thomas informed me in a low, condescending voice. He was well equipped to look down his nose at me. That hawklike appendage was the longest in the family. Unlike George and William, he had not grown a beard, most likely because he knew women found the cleft in his clean-shaven chin attractive.

"And why is that?" I asked, well aware that I would not like his answer.

"Women are weak. That is why we must rid ourselves of Queen Mary. Women are always ruled by their husbands. No one was enthusiastic about being ruled by King Guildford, but at least he was an Englishman."

"Gil Dudley would never have been king. Queen Jane refused to grant him the title. She told him he'd have to be content with a dukedom."

"She'd have given in. Women are—"

"Yes, I know—weak. And yet you intend to put another woman on the throne in Mary's place. What if Elizabeth does not marry to suit you?"

Plainly Thomas had not thought that far ahead. I rolled my eyes, amused and appalled at the same time.

"I have no objection to replacing Queen Mary with Queen Elizabeth," I said, "but this rebellion is doomed from the start. The plot is too complex. Even I—a mere woman—can see its obvious flaws."

"What flaws?" Thomas demanded, offended.

"The most blatant of them is the lack of a single leader who can rally all of England to Elizabeth's cause. The Duke of Suffolk is not capable of it. Neither is Cousin Tom."

"Traitor," Henry muttered, meaning me.

Thomas looked me up and down, a speculative expression on his face. "Perhaps we should lock you up until the rebellion is under way."

"I am not about to sneak out of the castle in the dark of night and run off to court to warn the queen. She would not listen to me anyway."

Only from Father did I detect any hint of sympathy, but he made no attempt to defend me from my brothers. Mother, too, remained silent, although the worry lines in her forehead deepened with every harsh word her children spoke to one another.

"Better safe than sorry," my brother John muttered. "We could put you in Aunt Elizabeth's old rooms."

"Truce, Bess," George said, slicing into an apple. He held out a section as a peace offering. When I just glared at him, he ate it himself.

"We have to take up arms," Edmund said with all the seriousness a fourteen-year-old boy can muster. The scattering of freckles across the bridge of his nose made him look even younger. "The Spanish stand ready to invade."

"How do you know that?" I demanded.

"Everyone says so."

Exasperation brought me to my feet. I braced both hands on the table and enunciated each word distinctly. "There is no proof that anything will change with this marriage. Mary Tudor is not weak. You will find out just how strong she is if you go through with this. She will not hesitate to execute every one of you."

George applauded.

Thomas just grinned at me, refusing to take seriously a single word I'd said. "Only if we fail, sister dear," he said. "Only if we fail."

45

Shortly after I arrived at Cowling Castle, my cousin Wyatt sent word from his country seat at Allington Castle to those he had recruited to come to a meeting on the twenty-second of January. It was Master Rudstone who brought the message, the same man who'd come to Cowling Castle years before to inform Aunt Elizabeth that she was a widow at last. He had other news as well. One of the conspirators had been questioned by the queen's men. A second had lost his courage and fled abroad.

Even with the original plot in disarray, Tom Wyatt refused to give in. An insurrection would still take place. It would simply start earlier, before Queen Mary had time to prepare.

My brothers William, George, and Thomas left with Rudstone. Father chose to remain at Cowling Castle and kept the younger boys with him. John and Henry were furious at being prevented from joining what Henry called "the fun." Edmund felt the same but was less vocal about it. All three were big for their ages and eager to prove their manhood in battle.

I shuddered every time I thought of it. I'd chosen the losing side once before. If Mary Tudor crushed her foes again, she would exact a terrible revenge on anyone who had twice turned traitor.

"Is there no way to stop them?" I asked my mother. "If matters fall out in the worst possible way, I could lose not only my husband, but my father and all six of my brothers to the headsman's ax."

"It is worse than that, I fear." Mother's hands shook, but she continued to embroider tiny leaves on a collar. "Only your father is a peer. The others could suffer the full penalty for treason—to be hanged, drawn, and quartered."

I felt myself blanch. "There must be something we can do," I whispered.

Mother patted my hand. "Learn patience, Bess. It is a woman's lot to sit and wait. And pray."

"But which prayer book should the prayers come from?" I snapped at her in my bitterness.

"If you wish to be useful, you can make bandages."

"I would prefer to avoid the need for them." But when she left her fancywork to fetch a length of cloth, I went to work cutting it into long strips.

On Sunday, the twenty-eighth day of January, two messengers arrived at Cowling Castle. One brought word that Tom Wyatt had raised his standard at Rochester, just four miles away, and was now in open rebellion against the queen. The other reported that the Duke of Norfolk and an army of the queen's men were massing at Gravesend to put down the insurrection. Norfolk had been freed from the Tower, where he had been since Old King Henry's time, as soon as Mary become queen. Father rode at once to Gravesend.

He returned with word that the bulk of the royal force consisted of six hundred foot soldiers who had been recruited from the city of London and that among those men were rebels, ready to change sides the moment they encountered Wyatt's forces. "I intercepted a messenger on my way back here," Father added. "A courier en route to France. The

French ambassador sent him to Wyatt's camp first. I relieved him of his dispatches and sent the dispatch bag to Bishop Gardiner in London."

He could not have chosen a more dangerous ally, I thought. Gardiner despised Will for his evangelical views and because he'd been granted Winchester House after Gardiner was deprived of it and imprisoned.

"Whose side are you on?" I asked of father in confusion. "If you expect Queen Mary to emerge victorious, how could you have allowed William, George, and Thomas to join the rebels?"

"I am on the side of the Brookes of Cobham," Father said. "When this is over, either your brothers or I will need a pardon. If Wyatt fails, I've just paid the price to keep my sons out of the Tower."

"But you support a return to King Henry's church, don't you? You cannot *want* England to be Catholic."

"Do not criticize your father, Bess," Mother said. "You would play just as devious a game to keep your husband safe."

The next morning, Father sent a message to the Duke of Norfolk, the late Earl of Surrey's father. Father advised the duke to postpone any confrontation with Wyatt until Norfolk had more men.

By nightfall, Father's scouts brought word that the Duke of Norfolk had not heeded Father's warning. When Norfolk's forces met those of my cousin at Strood, the London men, as expected, turned their coats. To a man, they went over to Cousin Tom, taking with them all the duke's ordnance. The duke had been fortunate not to be captured.

At eleven the next day, just as we were sitting down to dinner, an explosion shattered the peace and quiet of Cowling Castle. The noise was terrifying. Grim faced, father ordered all women and children to stay inside. He and the three of my brothers still at home—John, Henry, and Edmund—went to investigate. Father sent Edmund, the youngest, back to us with the news that we were under siege.

"It's Cousin Tom." Edmund sounded as if he could not believe what he'd seen. "He's brought his army here to attack us. John says the turn-coats must have told him about Father warning the Duke of Norfolk."

In spite of Father's orders, I climbed up onto the battlements to see for myself. The sight before me was daunting. Hundreds of men had spread out before the castle, William, Thomas, and George somewhere among them.

"How can my brothers condone this?" I asked Father. "Would they destroy their own home?"

Another explosion shook the walls, this one from the other side. "He's using two of the guns he captured from the Duke of Norfolk to batter the main gate and the other four to assault the back of the castle," Father said. "Return to your mother, Bess. There is nothing you can do here."

"Can you hold the castle?"

"I will try."

"What if you surrender? Won't that prove you meant Tom Wyatt no harm?" A cold wind eddied over the ramparts, making my skirts whip at my ankles.

"It might, but at the same time it would convince the queen that I'd been conspiring with Tom Wyatt all along. If he fails, we lose everything."

Father's voice was edged with desperation. He faced a terrible dilemma. Three sons were on one side of the walls, three on the other. If the rebellion succeeded, his heir would keep the family fortunes safe. If Queen Mary defeated the rebels, and she believed Father had remained loyal, then all would be well. But to prove his loyalty, he had to hold Cowling Castle as long as he could, even if that meant loss of life. Even if one or more of those lost were his own sons.

"What have you for ordnance?" I did not intend to hide under the bed while a siege was going on. I'd fired a pistol a time or two.

"Besides blackbills we have no weapons beyond four pikes and four or five handguns. We can hold them off for a time, but my servants are not trained soldiers."

"Your sons are." Or at least they'd been trained for the hunt and the tournament. "And I am an excellent shot with a bow."

I had father's full attention at last. "I am surprised you are not more enthusiastic about Tom's plans. With Elizabeth Tudor on the throne, the Church of England will be restored and with it the legality of your marriage."

"I'd not trust Tom Wyatt to organize a masque, let alone take back a country."

Tom had always been a wildhead. I could not help but remember that he'd been one of the Earl of Surrey's companions on the night they'd gone on a rampage in London, breaking windows and vandalizing merchants' property. This was a game to him, albeit a deadly one.

Sir Edward Warner had talked of other rebel leaders in other parts of England. At least two of them had been betrayed to the queen's men, since one was a prisoner and the other had fled the country. A third was Lady Jane Grey's father, the Duke of Suffolk, who had never been known for either intelligence or ability. Their ill-conceived uprising had been doomed before it began, and Tom's haphazard efforts to salvage the rebellion would only succeed in bringing good men down with him.

Cannon fired again. This time one of Father's men was killed by falling masonry. Grimly determined to put a stop to matters before they escalated further, I went to the armory and found the small longbow I'd once used to defeat George in an archery contest. In spite of Father's objections, I rejoined him on the battlements.

"Where is Tom Wyatt?"

"There." Father pointed.

Mounted on a horse of a golden dun color, Tom wore a red velvet cassock and a red velvet hat decorated with broad bonework lace. An easy target. I lifted my bow, took aim, and let the arrow fly.

It struck him full in the chest . . . and bounced off.

"He is wearing chain mail under his cassock," Father said mildly.

Chagrined, I lowered my bow. "He has to be stopped." But my hands began to shake. The enormity of what I'd just tried to do overwhelmed me. I'd attempted to kill Tom Wyatt. I hadn't even questioned the impulse until after my effort failed.

"Not by you." Father took the bow and arrows away from me. "Not by any of us. I don't want bloodshed, and if Tom has any sense, neither does he."

"Then what is the point of this?" We ducked as several arrows sped our way. They clattered harmlessly against stone, never flying high enough to touch us.

"I made him angry," Father said. "I warrant he understands my reasons well enough, and my actions did him little harm." He grimaced as the next volley of arrows flew by, this time passing overhead with at least a foot to spare. "But he's let his temper get the better of his good sense. He wants to punish me for going against him. A pity he couldn't wait to take his revenge, for he'd be halfway to London by now if he had. This ill-advised battle is likely to cost him the war."

"And if it does?"

"Then I will seem wise indeed to have sent intelligence to the queen's men. Think of it as a game of chess, Bess. You must be able to think ahead and understand the consequences of your moves in advance of making them."

I abandoned the battlements, heartsick, confused, and convinced that it was a great pity my arrow had not succeeded in dispatching Cousin Tom. Better to kill one man than let many die. I would gladly have had his death on my conscience if it had meant I'd not have to face losing those I loved.

The siege continued for six interminable hours. Three more of Father's retainers were killed and others wounded. The defenses of the outer court fell, bringing the bombardment to the gates and drawbridge guarding the inner ward. But it was only when our ammunition was gone that Father finally surrendered.

Under a flag of truce, he went out to meet with Cousin Tom. He did not return. On Tom's orders, Father was captured and his hands bound. He was put on a horse and the rebel army moved off, taking him with them.

A few minutes later, a single rider returned. My brother George entered the courtyard. He shot one horrified glance at the inner drawbridge, so battered it looked as if it would collapse at any moment. Then he addressed Mother, who was weeping silently, surrounded by her waiting gentlewomen.

"Father will be taken to Wyatt's camp at Gravesend."

"Will Wyatt attack London now?" John asked. I could tell he was itching to go with the troops.

"How can you support him when he's just destroyed our home?" Mother wailed.

I wrapped my arms around her and glared at John over her head. "The queen won't see the destruction here. She'll only know that Father is with Wyatt now. All his sacrifice will be for nothing."

John had the grace to look ashamed of himself. George couldn't meet my eyes, but he wouldn't stay, either. He rode off after Wyatt without saying another word.

As I watched him go, the glimmer of an idea came to me, a way to help both myself and my family. It was a march of some forty miles by land from Cowling Castle to Southwark. A boat could reach there much more quickly.

"Would you like to go to London, John? If we can get there ahead of the army and find someone who will listen, I may be able to convince the authorities that Father is with the rebels against his will."

If not, then at least I would be in London. If I could find Will, I was certain I could persuade him to stay out of the coming conflict. With luck, we might even slip out of the city again. I was not sure where we would go, but at least we would be together and free.

His admiration of Wyatt shaken by the damage to Cowling Castle, John agreed to my plan. It promised more adventure than staying home with Mother and the younger boys. He and I and Griggs set out at dawn. I left Birdie behind in Mother's keeping.

At first there were no boats to be had. We continued on horseback, hiding more than once to avoid small bands of rough-looking men who might have been part of Wyatt's army or could just as easily have been brigands. I thought it best to avoid being challenged by either. We had reached Deptford before I was able to hire a tilt boat for the rest of the journey. Then there was a further delay while Griggs found a trustworthy lad to take the horses back to Cowling Castle.

Wyatt's army had already reached Southwark by the time I caught my first glimpse of London Bridge. At first I couldn't believe my eyes. The gates had been shut and the drawbridge had been cut down. An entire span had been demolished to prevent the rebels from crossing into London proper. Guns mounted on the broken ends were aimed across the open space toward my cousin's men.

"Looks as if someone's already warned the queen," Griggs observed.

"I wonder if we'll be allowed to land," John said.

But the tilt boat docked without incident on the downriver side of the bridge, and we disembarked.

"What now?" John asked. My tall, strapping brother seemed at a loss.

I did not answer, dumbstruck by yet another unexpected sight—two men marching a third, in restraints, toward the Lion Gate of the Tower. The prisoner was my father.

"He must have escaped from the rebel camp and hired a wherry to cross the river," I murmured.

"But if he reached London and warned the queen, why is he under arrest?" John asked.

"Because Queen Mary's men will arrest anyone the least bit suspicious until this is over." Saying the words aloud gave them added meaning. "Will," I whispered.

I started to run, heading for Carter Lane. They'd arrest Will. I had to warn him, if I wasn't already too late.

John and Griggs followed. We had just passed the Hay Wharf and I was about to turn north along Bush Lane when Griggs swore.

A glance behind us showed me what he had seen. I stopped dead in the middle of Thames Street to stare. The rebels had set fire to one of the buildings on the Southwark side of the river. It was the property of the much-hated Bishop Gardiner now. That was reason enough for them to destroy it. But it gave my heart a painful wrench because it was my former home, Winchester House, that was ablaze.

Turning my back on the dreadful sight, I hurried up Bush Lane, then left into Carter Lane toward the Chequer Inn, the great house known as The Esher, and the much smaller one Sir Edward Warner owned. My steps faltered when it came in sight. I knew even before I reached the door that Will was no longer there.

Aunt Elizabeth did not keep me in suspense. Her voice hoarse with her own despair, she blurted out the news I had been dreading.

"They were arrested a week ago. Will and Edward both. The moment word of Tom's plans reached the queen, she ordered them both confined in the Tower."

46

The city rallied behind Queen Mary. We heard that she gave a stirring speech at the Guildhall, then retreated to the Palace of St. James—the house King Henry had built in the middle of the open fields west of Whitehall. Tom Wyatt and his army dithered on the Southwark side of London Bridge, then marched upriver in search of another way across the Thames.

"Every other bridge will have been broken down as well," I said when Griggs brought the latest news to the house in Carter Lane. My aunt and I huddled there, afraid to venture out. Although she was Lady Warner now, some of her neighbors knew of her connection to the rebel leader. Others had seen her current husband taken away by the queen's men.

Aunt Elizabeth was bitter. "My son's father raised a fool," she lamented.

Wild rumors proliferated until no one knew what to believe. Then the weather conspired to make everyone's life a misery. Shrove Tuesday dawned dark and wet and the downpour soon turned the streets into great water-filled pits. I could only imagine what quagmires the roads outside the city had become.

The next day dawned bright and numbingly cold.

"The Earl of Pembroke and Lord Clinton took Wyatt straight to the Tower after he surrendered," Griggs reported, "and Thomas Brooke with him."

"What of William and George?" I asked.

"Captured but not yet in the Tower."

"Is there any news of Will or my father?"

"Nothing, my lady." Griggs scratched his large, slightly flattened nose and frowned. "But that's good news, isn't it? It would be all over London if they'd been hanged."

I took what comfort I could from that.

Two days later, the bodies began to appear—executed rebels hanging on every city gate, in Paul's Churchyard, and at every crossroads. The remains were left in view for a full day as a warning and then were replaced by more victims of Queen Mary's vengeance.

Lady Jane Grey and Lord Guildford Dudley were executed on the twelfth of February. On the nineteenth, my brother Thomas was sentenced to be hanged, drawn, and quartered at Maidstone. I did not understand why he had been singled out, but I was sick at heart that all his youth, his promise, would be snuffed out even before he attained his majority.

On the twenty-third of February, Lady Jane Grey's father, the Duke of Suffolk, was executed.

Aunt Elizabeth and I supported each other, moving through those terrible days with little to sustain us but prayer. No one came near the house in Carter Lane. Only Griggs went out to dispatch letters and bring back news and supplies. It was early March before any of the frantic messages I sent to Will's wife, Viscountess Bourchier, finally produced a reply.

This time when I went to court, it was to see the queen.

Queen Mary received me in a private room, seated in a chair on a platform under a canopy. She was surrounded by russet-clad ladies, Nan

Bassett among them. Anne Bourchier was present, too, dressed in finery befitting her rank. Music played softly in the background.

The last time I'd seen Her Grace, she'd come to court to visit her brother. She had been a splendid sight then, but she was dressed even more extravagantly now. Her gown was a rich mulberry red embroidered with hundreds of pearls. Rings glittered on every finger. And yet, all the rich trappings in the world could not disguise the air of melancholy that clung to her. If she was relieved to have retained her throne, she did not show it. Instead she looked as if the burden of ruling England had already worn her down.

I had heard she'd been crowned king as well as queen and wondered if that made her responsibilities greater. Once slender, then thin, now she appeared emaciated. The lines in her face were deeper, and her skin was so pale that I could see the veins in her forehead. Had she been anyone but the person who held my husband's life in her hands, I might have felt sorry for her.

"Your Grace," I said as I curtsied.

"Mistress Brooke. You have come to plead for your kinsmen?"

"My father and brothers," I said, "and one other who had naught to do with the late treasons against Your Grace."

"You may state your case."

I told her first of Father's efforts on her behalf, omitting his reason for sending the French dispatches to Bishop Gardiner and warning the Duke of Norfolk and refusing to surrender Cowling Castle until he had no other choice. Then I painted a picture of my brothers as young men deceived by a clever, lying rogue—their own cousin. It was not difficult to blacken Tom Wyatt's reputation. His roistering days with the Earl of Surrey had been notorious. Even as a sheltered, unworldly princess, Mary Tudor had apparently heard the stories.

"I will consider what you have told me." Her Grace's words were a clear dismissal.

"There is one other innocent in this," I said in a rush. "Sir William Parr knew nothing of the conspiracy. He was in prison when the rebels met and plotted. It was only by chance that he was associated with any-one connected to the uprising."

I did not want to say straight out that Sir Edward Warner had been one of the original conspirators. I had no way of knowing if the queen was already aware of that fact and I did not wish to repay Aunt Eliza-beth's many kindnesses by driving another nail into her husband's coffin. On the other hand, I would do anything, sacrifice anyone, to save Will.

"Sir William Parr is not your concern," the queen said.

I bowed my head in acknowledgment, but I could not stop myself from trying one more time to convince Her Grace to spare him. "I have accepted that we had no true marriage. I was not with him when he was arrested. But I know Sir William's heart, Your Grace. He did much re-gret having assisted the Duke of Northumberland. He would never have joined yet another conspiracy against the Crown."

The queen's oddly mannish voice remained stern. "I will consider your request, but if I do release Sir William it will be on the condi-tion that you never see him more. He is another woman's husband. If I should hear that you and he have returned to living in sin, I will be obliged to imprison you both and keep you apart by force."

"I understand, Your Grace." I backed out of her presence before I gave in to the temptation to say anything more.

I left the palace uncertain as to what Queen Mary meant to do with Will. She had made no promises, only threats. And when, on Palm Sun-day—the very day the conspirators had originally planned to stage their uprising—Elizabeth Tudor was incarcerated in the Tower of London, I despaired of ever seeing my Will again. Many disappeared behind those walls. Few were released. Jack Dudley was *still* a prisoner, along with his younger brothers, Ambrose, Robin, and Henry. Their mother, with whom I'd kept in touch by letter, had been unceasing in her efforts on their be-half. She haunted the court and inundated the queen with petitions for her sons' release, but nothing she had done had secured their freedom.

And then a miracle happened. It was on Good Friday, the twenty-third of March, that Queen Mary issued pardons to the men she called "the greater rebels" involved in Tom Wyatt's rebellion. Will was one of them. He was released the following day and came at once to the house in Carter Lane, accompanied by my father and all three of my brothers.

"Have you all been pardoned?" I asked when I'd kissed Will thoroughly and assured myself that he was in good health. In contrast to the last time he'd been a prisoner, he appeared to have been well fed and supplied with adequate heat.

"I was never indicted," Father said, "and do not require a pardon. A letter I wrote to the queen before I escaped from the rebel camp, detailing the siege of Cowling Castle and my efforts on Her Gracious Majesty's behalf, inclined the queen to mercy. And it did not hurt that the Count d'Egmont, an old friend from my time in Calais, interceded for me. He is a good fellow, for all that he is a cousin of the king of Spain."

"We have not received pardons yet," Thomas said, speaking for himself and William and George, although he had been the only one of the three under sentence of death, "but we'd not have been released if she did not intend to grant them."

"She awaits the payment of my fine." Father's good cheer dimmed. "The pardons will be forthcoming as soon as she receives her money." He shook a finger at his sons. "Your lives did not come cheap, lads. The family coffers will be lighter by nearly five hundred pounds before this is over. Perhaps I should reconsider whether you are worth the cost."

Since we all knew that Father would pay far more than that to keep his family intact, this led to a spate of relieved laugher and joking. I did not find as much amusement in this byplay as the others did, but I was relieved to have them all safe. I sat beside Will as he sipped a hot posset, touching him now and again to reassure myself that he was truly there.

"What of you, my love?" I asked. "Did anyone tell you why the queen released you?"

"Other than the fact of my innocence and the lack of any evidence against me?"

I had to smile at his wry tone. "Other than that."

"I'm told that Her Grace no longer believes she has anything to fear from me. The Spanish ambassador wanted my head, but Queen Mary assured him that I will be faithful to her from this day forward."

"How can she be so certain of that?" George asked. Lounging in front of the fire with his feet up on a stool, he had been watching us through half-closed eyes.

"Because I left the Tower with nothing but what I am wearing on my back."

"An odd reasoning," William said. He stood with his back propped against the window frame, as much at ease as George was. "I should think that would make you resent her the more."

"She has left me with my life. For that I am grateful."

Father looked up from the hearty stew Aunt Elizabeth had served all the returning warriors and gave Will a sharp look. "What will you do now, Parr? Where will you go?"

"You cannot stay here." Aunt Elizabeth spoke for the first time. Her husband had not been released. Her son, too, remained in the tower. He had not yet been executed, but it was only a matter of time before he faced a grisly death.

"No," Will agreed. "I cannot, but there are other old friends who will take me in, I think. At least for a little while."

I cleared my throat. "There is a way for you to regain the queen's favor."

Every eye fixed on me.

"She wants you to reconcile with Anne Bourchier."

"Never!"

"You'd only have to pretend. She does not want you any more than you want her."

"I'd rather swim the Thames in the middle of winter."

"That cold, is she?" my brother William quipped.

The tension in the room dissolved in cleansing laughter, but the lighter mood did not last. They soon had the whole story out of me—my earlier meeting with Will's wife, before he was released the first time, and my interview with Queen Mary, arranged by Viscountess Bourchier. I concluded my tale by telling them of the threat against both Will and me if we did not separate.

Although it clearly grieved him, Will agreed that it would be un-wise to offend the queen. "You'll be better off at Cowling Castle for the nonce."

But Father was shaking his head. "We do not need more attention paid to us. There is only one way I could welcome Bess back into the bosom of her family and stay in the queen's good graces. I'd need to ar-range a marriage for her."

"I am already married!"

"No, you are not. You've lost that battle. We've all lost. We have no choice but to accept and rebuild. No more rebellions of any kind. Your only safety, Bess, lies in letting me choose a husband for you."

I knew he meant well, that he wanted only what was best for me, but some small part of me hoped for another miracle, a way to stay with Will. "I cannot marry another. I will not." I turned my beseeching gaze to Will. "Perhaps we can still escape into exile. Or perhaps the queen will die!"

"Devil take it, Bess! Do not say such a thing aloud!" my father said.

"There's no one here but family, Father."

"In these troubled times, a kinsman can be as deadly as a sworn enemy." He sent Aunt Elizabeth a pointed look. She glared back at him, having lost as much as any of us by her son's ill-conceived uprising.

Will said nothing. Like my father, he wanted to keep me safe. As I had been when I'd told the queen I'd give Will up, he was willing to sac-rifice our happiness for our lives. But I had never intended our separation to be permanent. Someday, somehow, we would find a way to be together again. I had to believe that or there was no point in living at all.

My brother George broke the silence. "If you won't come home, where will you go?" he asked.

I drew in a steadying breath. If Cowling Castle was not a choice, then there was only one possibility left. "To Chelsea," I said. "To the Duchess of Northumberland."

47

ane Dudley, who was still popularly known as the Duchess of Northumberland, in spite of her husband's attainder and execution, welcomed me with open arms, glad to have assistance in her quest for pardons for her remaining sons. She was encouraged oby my success in obtaining Will's freedom and hoped that soon Jack, Ambrose, Robin, and Henry would be released from the Tower of London.

Living at Chelsea was not easy. It was full of memories of my time there with the queen dowager and Princess Elizabeth and that other foolish Tom, Tom Seymour. And when Jane was not talking of her plans for the future, she spoke incessantly of her late husband, with whom she'd had a strong bond of love and respect, and of her son Guildford, the boy she'd hoped to see crowned king of England.

I missed my own dear Will more than words could express, but at least he was still alive. I tried *not* to think of him, but to no avail. He was always in my thoughts and in my prayers.

Tom Wyatt was executed on the eleventh day of April.

I accompanied Jane when she returned, again and again, to court.

She was never admitted to the queen's presence, but she pleaded with Her Grace's ladies to petition Queen Mary for pardons for her four sons. After the queen married Philip of Spain, on the twenty-fifth day of July, Jane sought out noble Spaniards at court, hoping some of them might sympathize with her cause. By then Elizabeth Tudor, now known only as the Lady Elizabeth, had been released from the Tower. That might have been an encouraging sign had she not been sent, closely guarded, to the royal manor of Woodstock.

I remembered my first progress and wondered if Elizabeth would be allowed to explore the maze. Perhaps, if she could find her way to the center, she would have some measure of privacy there. With servants who were also her keepers, she was to be closely watched, even though Cousin Tom, to his death, had insisted that she'd never condoned the rebellion or taken any role in it.

By the time autumn rolled around again, Jane's sons were still in the Tower and her health had begun to fail. Her unceasing efforts on their behalf had left her pale and exhausted. The news that Jack was gravely ill sent his mother into further decline. She spent her days staring blindly out her bedchamber window at Chelsea. Only the imminent arrival of her first grandchild finally roused her from her melancholy. In October, accompanied by the entire Chelsea household, she journeyed to Penshurst to await the birth of her daughter's child.

Mary Dudley's husband, Sir Henry Sidney, had been one of the first to be pardoned by Queen Mary. He'd entered her service and been sent to Spain as part of the delegation to escort King Philip to England. As a loyal subject, he'd been allowed to keep Penshurst, an enormous, ancient, and impressive fortified manor house half a day's hard ride from London. Traveling in litters with baggage carts, it took Jane and I nearly three days to reach there, but once we arrived at our destination we settled comfortably into one wing.

It was a largely female household at first, with Lady Sidney's ladies and her mother's women. Bridget Mardlyn and Alys Guildford were still in Jane's service, along with four other waiting gentlewomen. In the years since we'd first met, Alys and I had drifted apart, separated for a long time by the difference in our status. Neither of us had attempted to resurrect our old friendship.

We had been in residence at Penshurst only a few days before Sir Henry Sidney descended upon us. To our surprise and delight, he had all four Dudley brothers in tow. Jack, Ambrose, Robin, and Henry had been freed from the Tower. Even before reuniting with their wives, they'd come to see their mother.

For Jack there had been no other choice. Not only did his wife want nothing to do with him, but he was so ill that he'd had to be carried in a litter instead of traveling on horseback. His sister gave orders to install him in a corner chamber on an upper floor, where the sun would fill the room with light.

As the litter bearers carried him upstairs, Jack caught sight of me. "Bess," he croaked. "There is a God, after all."

"Blasphemer," his brother Robin said on a choked laugh.

Tears sprang into my eyes. That Jack was trying so hard to sound jovial meant he was very ill indeed. He was thin and wasted and his skin had a bluish-purple tinge. The agonized sound of his coughing wrenched my heart.

Jack asked for me as soon as he was settled in a bed. I tried to be strong and cheerful and give him reason to smile through his obvious pain, but in good light the signs of his deterioration were even more obvious. He was feverish and his limbs were swollen, so much so that he could lie comfortably only flat on his back. His fingernails were loose. When I saw that, I lost my composure.

"Were you tortured?" I blurted out.

Jack's wheezing laugh sent him into a violent paroxysm of coughing. He lay there weakly when it was over, staring up at me with wide, agonized eyes. I realized, then, that the loose fingernails were yet another symptom of whatever it was that was killing him.

I knelt by the bed and placed one hand on his forearm. I could hardly see him through my tears, but I could hear his whisper. "You should have married me. We'd both have been happier."

I did not disabuse him of the notion. "You are free now, Jack," I told him. "The queen let you go."

Behind me I heard a derisive snort. Ambrose Dudley and Sir Henry Sidney had remained behind when the other two Dudley boys went to pay their respects to their mother. It was Ambrose who spoke. "We have not yet been pardoned, nor has any of what was taken from us been restored. And the only reason we were let go has naught to do with compassion. King Philip is at war with France. He wants to raise an English army. Where better to find men with training in warfare than among imprisoned rebels?"

"Has everyone been freed?"

"Not all, no," Sir Henry said. "Your aunt's husband, Sir Edward Warner, is still being held. But even in his case there are signs of leniency. Lady Warner has been allowed to visit him, and she continues to receive his revenues."

I was glad for Aunt Elizabeth's sake, but neither the queen's clemency nor King Philip's machinations came soon enough to save Jack Dudley. I felt his arm jerk under my hand and forced myself to look at what remained of the handsome, sturdily built youth I remembered.

"I am lost in the maze again, Bess," he whispered, "and this time I do not think I will find my way out."

"You will." I put every ounce of conviction I could manage into my voice. "We all will. Somehow."

"I am glad you are here." A moment later, he drifted off into slumber. It was not a restful sleep. His breathing was ragged and his ravaged face remained flushed with fever.

Sir Henry took my arm and escorted me from the room. I did not know Mary's husband well, but he had once been in King Edward's service and he'd known Jack from Jack's earliest days at Hampton Court.

"Is there any hope for him? If you send for doctors—"

He shook his head. "I've seen this before. It is the same wasting sickness that claimed King Edward's life. If the cleverest physicians in the realm could not save the king, no one can help Jack, either. He cannot keep food down. He'll grow weaker with every passing day. There is nothing any of us can do but pray for the Lord to have mercy upon him and take his soul when his life ends."

People I'd cared about had died in the past, Jack's brother Harry among them, but I had never had to watch them go. There was something obscene about this lingering, increasingly painful process. Better to have died in battle, I thought, or by a headsman's ax, than to suffer this way.

Jane was with her son when he died. She barely left his side during those last few agonizing days. Then she collapsed.

She recovered sufficiently to attend the christening of her first grandchild when Mary gave birth nearly a month later, but it was a bittersweet occasion. Jane wanted the boy named John, after her late husband the duke and his son Jack. Instead, Sir Henry chose a name that would reinforce his family's loyalty to the Crown. The baby was christened Philip Sidney.

A few days later, Jane and I left Penshurst and returned to Chelsea. In the days that followed, I watched helplessly as Jane's health continued to deteriorate. It was as if she'd lost the will to live when Jack died. By the middle of January, there was no longer any hope she would recover. Then she was gone.

She was buried with all the honor due her. Her daughter was chief mourner, and I bore Mary Sidney's train in the funeral procession, weeping all the while. The other women of the household came after and then the choir in their surplices, followed by poor men and women, two by two, to the number of Jane's years, gentlemen, two by two, yeomen, two by two, and then the coffin, carried by eight yeomen and four assistants.

The funeral sermon was based on the text *beati mortui qui in Domino moriuntur.* I did not understand a word of it, since it was entirely in Latin. The days of prayers in English had died with King Edward.

Jane's three surviving sons and their wives were among the mourners, as were a sprinkling of courtiers, including at least one Spaniard from King Philip's household. Jane had made friends at Queen Mary's court during her ceaseless petitioning for justice.

We laid the Duchess of Northumberland to rest in the church at Chelsea on the first day of February. When the coffin was carried in, I had a place in the world and a roof over my head. When I came out again into the cold, bright daylight, I was once more homeless and destitute.

A crowd had gathered and in the back stood a man in a slouch hat that shadowed his face. My heart skipped a beat and my breath caught in my throat as I recognized Will. Would he dare speak to me? If he tried, I knew I should not allow it. But when he strode boldly toward me, holding my gaze as he closed the distance between us, I did not have the strength to turn away. It had been almost a year since I'd last seen him. My eyes hungrily drank in every detail of his beloved face and form. I wanted to hurl myself into his arms and shower kisses on him. Deep inside, I ached to join with him again.

"I grieve with you, Bess," he said, taking both my hands in his. "She was a good woman."

I felt the jolt of that first contact all the way to my womb. "She was always kind to me," I whispered. Torn between joy at being so close to Will again and sharp regret that we would soon have to part, I felt tears well up and fought to control them. I had cried far too much already.

"What will you do now?" he asked. "Where will you go?"

"I . . . I do not know."

Worry over just that question had kept me awake nights. Every solution I considered had drawbacks. I would be a burden to any of Jane's children, even if they would have me, and I could not return to my father's keeping. Although I had exchanged letters with my family during my time at Chelsea, Father had not changed his mind about his condition for taking me in—he would do so only if I would agree to let him find me a new husband.

With an effort I forced myself to speak of mundane matters, but my body swayed closer to Will's, almost as if it had a mind of its own. "I might go to my brother William," I said. Father's stepmother had finally died, allowing him to make Cobham Hall the family seat. It was William who now lived at Cowling Castle, where he was overseeing repairs to the damages done by Wyatt's siege. I did not think he would turn me away, or betray my presence there to Father, but I could not be certain of it.

"I have an idea," Will said, tightening his grip on my fingers. "Come and live with me. My father's lands in Yorkshire and Lincolnshire have been returned to me and I have a small house in the Blackfriars precinct of London."

"Will, we cannot. The queen—"

"The queen has lost interest in me, Bess. All she thinks of is her husband, King Philip, and all he thinks about is his plan to make war on France with English troops."

His words filled me with hope, but I was still afraid. "What of the queen's threat? If she discovers we are together, she will force us apart and imprison us both." I'd stayed away from Will all this time to protect him. I had no wish to endanger him now, nor did I want to spend the rest of my life locked away in the Tower of London.

"She'll never know. I tell you, she has forgotten all about me." A slow, charming smile curved his mouth. "Besides, what is life without a little risk?"

I felt myself weakening. "Better to ask what is life without love?" I whispered.

"Torment," he declared as he gathered me close. "Be bold, my Bess. For my sake, for I vow I cannot bear to be without you any longer."

I gave in. When Will left Chelsea for Blackfriars that afternoon, I went with him.

48

lackfriars was a walled enclave, nine acres of houses and tenements carved out of what had once been a friary. The precinct was now occupied by physicians, pensioners, and minor noblemen such as my mother's brother, Lord Bray. My father had a house there, too, although he did not live in it. He leased lodgings to tenants, one on each floor.

Will's house was just to the south of Father's property. We had a small garden and stabling for our horses and, as Will had predicted, no one at court or elsewhere paid any attention to us. Those few neighbors who knew who we were were not inclined to cause us trouble. Indeed, some old acquaintances were glad we were together again.

In March, Will and I traveled to Brentford, just outside London, to stand as godparents to Elizabeth Cavendish. Her father and Will had been friends during King Edward's reign and I knew her mother slightly because she—another Bess—had once been a waiting gentlewoman to Frances Brandon, Duchess of Suffolk. Frances's daughter, Lady Catherine Grey, was the child's other godmother.

Remarkably, even after Suffolk tried to rebel and the queen had him executed, along with Frances's eldest daughter, Lady Jane Grey, Queen Mary had invited her cousin Frances to become one of the ladies of her privy chamber. Frances had brought her two remaining daughters with her to court. Lady Catherine, now sixteen, seemed unaffected by the tumultuous events of the past two years.

"What a shallow girl she is," I remarked to Will on our way home from the christening.

He laughed. "She's pretty. She does not need to be clever."

Oh, yes, she does, I thought. If she hopes to survive at court.

I told myself that I was glad we were no longer in royal service. Although we lacked material luxuries in our new life, we were comfortable, and nothing had changed in the way Will and I felt about each other. We were still as passionate in our loving as ever. I thought, sometimes, about children, but when I remained barren, I accepted my fate. I had Will. It would have to be enough to remain as we were, hidden away in Blackfriars, just the two of us.

That first summer after we were reunited was cold, bleak, and sunless. It rained almost every day. If one were inclined to bouts of melanchony, the weather would have been unendurable, but my optimism had been restored. I was further cheered when word reached Blackfriars that King Philip had left England, thwarted in his effort to raise an army to fight the French. England was not prepared to go to war just to please the queen's husband. Soon after that, the Lady Elizabeth was released from confinement at Woodstock and allowed to return to her own house at Hatfield. Apparently, Queen Mary no longer considered her a threat.

I thought that shortsighted of the queen. As long as Elizabeth Tudor lived, there was a possibility that she would one day succeed her sister and restore all we had lost by King Edward's death and our failure to put Queen Jane on the throne.

The only thing that caused me any real concern during our first year in Blackfriars was the queen's war on heresy. In the fires of Smithfield, many of those who'd been called evangelicals under King Henry and

King Edward were burnt at the stake. Their only crime was refusing to recant. Others we had known at Edward's court fled into exile on the Continent, even the dowager Duchess of Suffolk, Frances Brandon's step-mother. Will and I were careful never to miss church services at the little church of St. Anne's in Blackfriars.

Before I knew it, another winter had passed and it was early May again. I had exchanged no visits with kinfolk in all that time. Father and I continued to be estranged. Every time I'd heard from him while Will and I had been separated, he'd tried to convince me to wed some stolid country gentleman he'd picked out for me. My stubborn insistence that I was already married, no matter what the queen or Parliament said, had annoyed him so much that he'd stopped writing to me. I still exchanged letters with Mother, Kate, and William, and knew my brother George was at court, serving in some minor capacity, but I had no warning of what my mother's brother, Lord Bray, was up to until the day Grand-mother Jane suddenly appeared in Blackfriars.

My grandmother was well into her seventh decade, but she looked exactly the same as she had at sixty. She did not like Will one whit better than she had when her daughter, Dorothy Bray, had been his mistress. "Still living in sin, I see," she greeted him.

Will ignored her rudeness. When she was settled in our most com-fortable chair, he offered her Malmsey, her favorite wine.

Grandmother gave a disdainful sniff but took the cup he extended. After a few sips, she ran critical eyes over our furnishings. "You have come down in the world."

I bit back a sharp retort. It was certainly true that we had lived in far more luxurious surroundings, but the hangings were warm and attrac-tive, the chair cushions nicely embroidered and stuffed with fleece, and the rushes on the floor had been changed only a few weeks earlier. The room was redolent with the scent of spring flowers.

Will sat next to me on a cushioned bench, and slung one arm posses-sively around my shoulders. "To what do we owe the honor of this visit, Lady Bray?" Although Grandmother Jane had remarried, her second husband was a mere knight and she continued to be addressed by her title.

"My son, John Bray, is in prison," she announced. "I mean to get him out."

I felt Will go rigid. "On what charge has Lord Bray been arrested?"

"Treason."

My blood ran cold at the word. "No," I said. "We cannot help you. We dare not."

I had seen my uncle once or twice since we'd lived in Blackfriars, since he had a house in the precinct, but although we were the same age, we had never had much in common. He reminded me too much of his sister Dorothy for me to feel entirely comfortable in his presence. I was not willing to risk the quiet, peaceful life Will and I now had for a virtual stranger, even if he was my kinsman.

"Do me the courtesy to hear me out." Grandmother Jane's glower was fierce. "No doubt you have already heard rumors of what Sir Henry Dudley is up to."

I gave a start. "The Duke of Northumberland's son?" The second boy named Henry, married to the wealthy Audley heiress, had been living with his wife at Audley End the last I'd heard of him.

"Not that one. This Sir Henry Dudley is a distant cousin of some sort. One of the Sutton branch of the family. He was dispatched to the French court when that whole debacle over Lady Jane Grey began, sent to recruit help from King Henri. When Northumberland failed, Sir Henry wisely stayed abroad. Less wisely, he began to plot against the Crown and my son is accused of plotting with him."

"I've met the fellow," Will said for my benefit. "Another hothead." He shifted his attention back to my grandmother. "What is it you think we can do to help Lord Bray?"

"You won your freedom. Twice. I want to know how you did it. You were guilty as sin both times. Queen Mary had no reason to spare you, and yet she did."

"Bess won my freedom for me."

Those simple words warmed me to my soul and had my grandmother sending a speculative look my way. "Well, girl, what did you do?"

"I begged. I pleaded. I humbled myself. I swore to do whatever was asked of me." As I spoke, I realized there had been an additional reason for my having been successful in the end. "And," I said slowly, working it out in my head, "I gave Her Grace the means to punish Will in a way mere imprisonment could not. Queen Mary used me to exact revenge. Under King Edward, Will helped deprive her friends of the Catholic Mass. She forced him to give up what he valued most—me."

"And yet, here you are," Grandmother said. "Together. Perhaps Her Grace would reward me with Bray's freedom if I shared this information with her."

Shocked, I sputtered an objection, but she waved it aside.

"I suppose not. You are my own flesh and blood, just as John is."

"And as such will do all she can to help her uncle," Will said smoothly. "Within reason."

"Then tell me how to get in to see the queen," Grandmother demanded. She polished off her wine in one gulp and banged the cup down on a nearby table.

"Your best hope is to apply to the Spaniards. The Duchess of Northumberland did so." I gave her the names of those she had found most compassionate. "But do not approach their wives. They are not received at court. The queen did not want them to come to England and will not receive them." They were also contemptuous of English noblewomen. One had been unforgivably rude to Jane Dudley.

"You must come with me, Bess," Grandmother Jane said.

But I balked at that. "I dare not risk attracting the queen's attention."

As it turned out, the queen would not have noticed had I danced naked in the gardens at Whitehall. According to Nan Bassett, the only courtier with whom I dared communicate, Her Grace had sequestered herself after receiving word that her husband, King Philip, would not return to England as soon as he had promised. He had his own lands to rule, and his enmity with the French to pursue, with or without English help.

Grandmother installed herself in her son's house, along with her ladies and her young second husband. He made himself useful soliciting information in the taverns and alehouses of Westminster, but otherwise was as much a part of the background as any of Grandmother's servants. I felt a little sorry for him until I learned that she was not his first wife and that he had gained a considerable fortune by that earlier marriage.

Grandmother Jane was nothing if not tenacious. She visited us often during the months that followed to keep us apprised of her lack of progress. In contrast to the previous summer, when we'd been inundated with rain, this one was blighted by widespread drought. I found the dry, still air more unnerving than I had the constant damp. So dismal was my outlook that I felt no surprise when my uncle was indicted for treason, even though it had taken the Crown six months to decide to charge him.

Grandmother was frantic. She increased her efforts to find supporters at court. She even ignored my advice and went to the Spanish noblemen's wives. She railed for days about their superior attitude and their refusal to help.

Little changed until March, when King Philip did, at last, return to England. Within days, he granted my grandmother an audience. John, Lord Bray was released in the first week in April, with the promise of a pardon to follow. His Most Catholic Majesty, it seemed, was still intent upon building an English army to fight in France.

When Grandmother Jane went home to Eaton Bray, Will and I breathed a sigh of relief and celebrated by spending an entire day in bed. The servants took that in stride. We had always reveled in the physical side of marriage, although many people regarded it as odd to be so affectionate with one's own spouse. I might have been thirty years old, but Will could always make me feel like a giddy girl again.

"Are you content, my love?" I asked him when we were temporarily sated.

The brief hesitation before he assured me that he was told me more than his words.

"You miss being at the center of power," I murmured. "You enjoyed life at court, even with all the pettiness and backbiting."

He sighed. "I was brought up to it, Bess. I value having you in my life more but, yes, if I had all I desired, I'd be at court again with you at my side."

"Queen Mary will not live forever. Someday—"

He touched a finger to my lips. "Hush, Bess. Speak no treason, not even here." He caught me at the waist and rolled until I was on top of him. "We have better ways to occupy us in our own bed than longing for what cannot be. I would rather enjoy what we have."

As always, our lovemaking both reassured and distracted me. But afterward I found myself brooding. I wanted Will to be happy, to have *everything* he desired. And I had to admit that, occasionally, I, too, missed our old life. Who would not relish being wealthy and influential?

At Easter that year, we talked of paying a long overdue visit to my family in Kent. Mother's letters were no substitute for spending time with her and she wrote that she was sure Father had given up the idea of marrying me off to someone other than Will. Since the queen appeared to have lost interest in us, we deemed it safe to go.

Before we could make any firm plans, however, my brother George came to call.

The last time I'd seen him, he'd just been freed from the Tower. He looked considerably better now, and his clothes, though plain, were finely made and expensive.

"Whatever your duties at court, they seem to agree with you," I commented after I'd provided him with a tankard of ale and a bowl of nuts.

Will stood by the empty hearth, his own tankard in hand, his eyes narrowed suspiciously at my brother. I could hardly blame him. It had taken nearly a full year to rid ourselves of the last family member who'd sought us out. "What is it you do, George?"

"As it happens," George drawled, amused by the wary reception, "I am an undersecretary to the Privy Council."

I exchanged a startled look with Will. The post might be minor and lack influence, but it was one of trust. I was amazed George had been given it, considering that he'd once been condemned for treason for taking part in Wyatt's uprising against Queen Mary.

As if he read my thoughts, George grinned. "Do you doubt my loyalty to England, Bess? I obtained my position by showing proper gratitude for the pardon Her Gracious Majesty granted me, and by reminding certain influential parties that Father was taken prisoner by our wicked cousin Wyatt. I told them of how that showed me the error of my ways, and Father was pleased to confirm that I helped him escape from the rebel camp so that he could make his way into London with crucial information about Wyatt's armament and manpower, thus giving the queen's men an advantage."

Some of that was likely true, but not all. George was too glib in telling the tale. And he had been too passionate a follower of our cousin, Tom Wyatt, before the rebellion failed. "I never thought to see you support Spanish rule in England." If I had not been watching him closely, I would have missed the brief tightening of his jaw and the spark of anger in his eyes. I smiled. "Why are you here, George? The truth, this time, if you please."

He glanced at Will first, then fixed his steady gaze on me. "England needs you, Bess."

I blinked in surprise. "*England* does?"

"It is true that I am employed by Queen Mary's Privy Council," George said, "but I have also been serving my country in another way, as an informant."

Will pushed away from the hearth, no longer the casual observer. He reached George in three long strides and seized him by the collar, jerking him to his feet. "Serving England? How does it serve England to be a spy? Who is your master?"

"He cannot answer you while you are choking him." I circled warily around them, having no desire to get in the way if they began to exchange blows.

Will released my brother. George coughed, then held both hands in front of him in surrender. After a moment, when he could speak normally again, he directed his words to me. "Call me spy if you must, Bess, but what I do, I do for England. I have been trying to prevent the spilling of English blood in this accursed war between France and Spain." As soon as he'd returned to England, King Philip had once again begun to recruit an English army to fight with the Spanish against the French.

"De Noailles," Will said, naming the French ambassador. "You are spying for him?"

George nodded and backed away when Will once again advanced on him with raised fists. "Think before you try to throttle me again. We've been forced to accept Philip as Queen Mary's consort. Open rebellion cannot succeed. But the queen is barren, and in spite of her efforts to eliminate the Lady Elizabeth from the succession, to the common people of England, King Henry's younger daughter remains heir to the throne."

"What does that have to do with the French?" I asked.

"A very great deal, but it should be the ambassador who explains the situation to you, not I. Will you meet with him?"

"He wants to see me?" Will looked thunderstruck.

"No," George said. "He wants to talk to Bess."

49

François de Noailles, bishop of Acqs, French ambassador to England, was a stocky, soft-spoken man in his late forties. Close-cropped, receding, light brown hair, a short fringe of a beard, and a drooping mustache surrounded a plump, pale face with a high forehead and sad eyes. George took me to a nondescript London house in Lawrence Lane to meet with him, a place clearly used only for such assignations. The rooms were nearly bare of furnishings and the rushes on the floors were in dire need of changing. I lifted my skirts clear of the moldering, vermin-infested straw, and was glad I had worn sturdy boots.

De Noailles spoke excellent English and for my benefit conversed in that language. He had with him only one servant, a man he introduced as his secretary. He did not waste time on meaningless pleasantries.

"I will tell you of a grave danger to your princess," he said when we were seated facing each other on hard wooden stools. My brother stood by the window, while the secretary guarded the door. "For some time now, King Philip has hoped to marry the Lady Elizabeth to his kinsman, Emmanuel Philibert, Duke of Savoy, in order to bind England to one of his allies in the event of Queen Mary's death without children. The princess's refusal to consider the suggestion is responsible in large part for the queen's recent treatment of her. The entire household at Hatfield has been reorganized with the intent of leaving Her Grace friendless. A widowed gentlewoman has replaced Her Grace's beloved governess. Sir Thomas Pope, who is in charge of the household, is under direct orders from the queen to allow no frivolity."

Impatient, I interrupted. "What has this to do with me?"

"The king and queen hope the Lady Elizabeth, made melancholy by such a tiresome existence, will come to court, there to be wooed and wed." The ambassador gave an expressive shrug. "And if they cannot convince her by pleasant means, they will use threats."

The picture he painted alarmed me, but I did not see what I could do to help the princess. "I cannot prevent this," I objected. "I have no influence at court."

The ambassador had a charming smile. In spite of my determination to avoid taking risks, I found myself hoping that there *was* some way I could come to Elizabeth's aid.

"The princess has, through various convoluted means, sent to me to explore the possibility of flight into France. There are those, even some with Her Grace's best interests at heart, who encourage this idea, but it would be folly for her to leave England, most especially now. The queen is not well." He looked to George for confirmation and received a curt nod.

"I have seen Queen Mary in council meetings," George said. "She is not on her deathbed, but I doubt she will last another year. That is why King Philip is so anxious to push his wife's heiress presumptive into a marriage with someone who owes him fealty."

"The Lady Elizabeth must be in England when her sister dies." The ambassador went on at some length to explain why, but the only fact that mattered to me was that if she were elsewhere, married or not, England would be thrown into chaos upon Queen Mary's death.

"What do you want of me?" I asked, resigned to the inevitable.

"Someone the princess trusts must deliver my message, advising her to resist all efforts to spirit her out of England, whether they be made by friend or foe. She must also continue to refuse to marry any man chosen for her by the king or the queen."

"And how am I to accomplish this?"

I expected the ambassador to have an answer for this question ready, but de Noailles surprised me. "I leave that to you, my lady. I believe you possess the skills you need to succeed. And the friends to help you."

I gave George a hard look, wondering what stories he had been telling.

"I have no friends at Hatfield," I said. "As far as I know, I am not acquainted with any members of the princess's household. Not since the queen sent Mistress Astley and the princess's ladies-in-waiting away." I frowned. "You said someone there sent word to you, my lord. Who was it? Will they help?"

But he shook his head. "There will be less chance of compromising us all if you find your own way in. And there can be no repetition of this meeting," he added, "although you may send word to me through your brother if needs must."

He had little more information to offer, other than that a garrison of soldiers guarded Elizabeth at Hatfield. She was not a prisoner the way she had been at Woodstock, but the comings and goings of visitors were noted and no doubt reported to some higher authority at court.

I would be walking into danger. I could easily end up in the Tower, charged with treason.

"You would be doing nothing more rebellious than visiting an old friend," George pointed out after de Noailles left with his secretary and I'd voiced this fear to him.

The little house seemed more dilapidated than ever with just the two of us there. "Visiting the princess would call attention to me," I argued, "and from me to Will. We cannot bear close scrutiny from the Crown."

"If you go as plain Bess Brooke, there is nothing to tie you to Will. Not anymore."

I prowled restlessly while we debated the issue, circling the small upper room. "What if someone questions where I have been living since the duchess died?"

"Father will swear you've been at Cobham Hall." George sat on the stool I'd vacated and propped one foot on the other.

"Will he?"

"He will if I ask him to."

"He knows what you've been doing?"

George grinned at me. "Whose idea do you think it was in the first place?"

"I had hoped to avoid intrigue. Will and I have been safe in our obscurity."

"You think none of the queen's men know where you are?"

His question chilled me. "Who? Who knows?"

"Any number of courtiers and councilors. For God's sake, Bess, stand still. You're making me dizzy watching you."

Hands on my hips, I glared at him. "You are attempting to frighten me into doing as you wish."

"I am trying to help us all survive longer than the queen."

Looking into his eyes, I could not doubt his sincerity, but what de Noailles had asked of me had me quaking in my boots. "I have hidden away in Blackfriars for so long that I no longer know how to do anything else."

George's voice gentled. "You helped Grandmother Jane."

"Only with advice. I did not have to venture out where I might be recognized." I began to pace again.

George stood and crossed the small, dusty room to put his hands on my upper arms. "Bess, think. If we do nothing, others may convince the princess to leave England."

"Perhaps she should go. Perhaps we should all go into exile." I could hear the rising hysteria in my voice and clamped my lips together.

"Running away is no answer."

I closed my eyes. I felt uncertain and afraid. I had learned from sad experience how easily plans could go awry. "Take me home, George. I need to talk to Will about all of this."

"Do you need his permission, Bess?" Gentleness abandoned, now my brother taunted me. "Can you not act without his approval? You never used to be afraid of a challenge."

"We are not children any longer, wagering on the outcome of an archery contest."

"But it *is* a game, Bess. And a game of chance, too. Wager on the winning side and you profit."

"A careless wager can cost you your life," I shot back.

George gave me a shake before he released his grip on my arms. "I suggested you to the ambassador for a reason, Bess. Your aim is true. The same clearness of mind that allowed you to hit Tom Wyatt with your arrow from the battlements of Cowling Castle is just what you need to reach Elizabeth and warn her."

"My arrow bounced off Tom's chain mail and did nothing but make him angrier with Father."

"But you hit your mark," he insisted, as if that was all that mattered.

"Why is it that men think comparisons to sports are so compelling?" I muttered.

Turning my back on him, I went to stand at the window that overlooked Lawrence Lane. It was a busy street, crowded with horsemen, pedestrians, and carts—noisy, smelly, alive. The upper floors of the houses on both sides jutted out over the ones below and were only a few feet apart at this level. I found myself staring into the solar across the way. A merchant's wife and her maidservant sat together sewing while three small children played at their feet. I envied her the simplicity of her life.

My hands clenched into fists on the windowsill. Part of me wanted that sort of security and contentment, but there was another part that would never be satisfied until everything the queen had taken from my husband was restored to him. Elizabeth would one day have the power to right the wrongs of her sister. If I did as the ambassador asked, I would be performing a service for the future queen. She would be in my debt.

"If I am to reach the princess," I said to my brother, "I will need your help."

"You have it," George promised.

I thought for a moment. "Find out what houses are near Hatfield and who owns them and what persons are in residence."

I EXPECTED OBJECTIONS from Will when he heard what the ambassador wanted me to do. I was not disappointed. He warned that I was meddling in a matter of the succession.

"This is nothing like Northumberland's effort to carry out King Edward's wishes," I insisted. "No one questions that Elizabeth is Queen Mary's heir. Even Mary herself accepts that now. All I agreed to do is help keep the princess safe so that she *can* inherit one day. There is no treason in that."

"The Lady Elizabeth will not be so foolish as to leave England. She does not need you to advise her."

"The thought of finding asylum in France, safe from forced marriage, safe from being imprisoned in the Tower again, has to tempt her. Her Grace needs to hear the ambassador's reasoning, to understand the disadvantages of that plan, especially if some of her own people have been encouraging her to flee."

"Why must *you* go?" Will demanded.

I knew his agitation was for my sake. He feared for my safety. So did I, but I would not change my mind. "I have been chosen because the princess will know I have not been sent by her enemies. I have no reason to cooperate with Queen Mary because the queen will never grant the one thing that matters most to me—the legality of our marriage. Think, Will. If Elizabeth is grateful to me for bringing her this warning, then she will reward us both when she becomes queen. She will give back all that her sister took away from us."

Will did not try to argue with my reasoning, but neither did he stop worrying. What I had agreed to undertake weighed heavily on my mind, too. The enterprise had an aura of danger about it, and the secrecy necessary to carry out the mission increased my concern that I was risking everything Will and I had managed to salvage. And yet, how could I not try?

It did not take long for George to locate a small manor less than an hour's ride from Hatfield that was currently occupied by an old friend. I took this as a sign that the fates smiled on my endeavor, but Will was appalled.

"Lady Clinton?" he yelped when George told him her name. "You want to send Bess to a woman whose husband betrayed Northumberland and led the queen's forces against Wyatt?"

George helped himself to a goblet of wine and left it to me to answer.

"Geraldine Clinton remained my friend while you were in the Tower," I reminded my husband. She'd written to me, promising to do all she could on Will's behalf. True, nothing had come of her efforts, but at least she had not shunned me. "She is well known to the Lady Elizabeth," I continued. "It will not arouse suspicion if she pays a visit to her neighbor at Hatfield."

"But why should she? And if her husband hears of it, he'll stop you."

"*Lord* Clinton does not have to know anything about the matter."

George lounged in my chair, looking as if he had not a thought in his head beyond the next tennis match or horse race. "You've nothing to fear from Clinton even if he does find out," he drawled. "It will serve him well to turn a blind eye. Queen Mary may not have imprisoned him for his early support of Lady Jane Grey, but neither has she advanced him, and she took away his lucrative post as lord admiral."

I went to Will and rested my head against his chest, comforted by the steady thump of his heart. "I must go, Will," I whispered. "Elizabeth is our best hope to regain what we have lost."

"So long as I have you, Bess, I can live without the rest."

"You'll live easier with it," George said, sotto voce.

Will's sentiment warmed my heart, but I wanted more for him. More for us. "We can go on as we have been, Will, but think how much better our life together *could* be if I earn the gratitude of our future queen."

50

The next morning I left London, taking only the elderly Griggs for protection on the road. He was hardier than he looked and we reached the pretty little Hertfordshire manor house that was our destination without incident. Such country estates customarily offered hospitality to travelers, even strangers, and soon after we arrived I was shown into a comfortably furnished chamber hung with tapestries depicting scenes from a tournament. A few minutes later, Geraldine Clinton swept into the room.

Her second marriage agreed with her. Although black mourning dress had shown off the pale skin and bright green eyes that went with her red hair, she looked far healthier in bright colors. Her face lit up with pleasure when she recognized me. "Bess! What a lovely surprise. I have thought of you so often, but no one seemed to know where you were living."

"Quietly," I said before I was engulfed in a lavender-scented embrace.

In no time we were nibbling marchpane, sipping barley water, and telling each other some of what had happened to each of us since we'd parted in Queen Jane's apartments in the Tower. I was careful not to mention Will, since I had agreed not to give all my trust to the woman who was Lord Clinton's wife, but by the time she refilled our goblets I had come to the point of my visit.

"I cannot give you details, for your own protection, but I have a message to deliver to the princess, one that is of vital importance to Her Grace's future. Is it possible for you to visit Hatfield and take me with you?"

Although my request clearly surprised her, she did not hesitate to agree. "I have been there before. When Sir Thomas Pope was first made Her Grace's guardian, before Queen Mary put a stop to such things, he arranged several masques and pageants for the Lady Elizabeth's entertainment and invited the local gentry to attend. Pope is a witty and intelligent man, and his wife is pleasant, too."

"But he will look askance at me."

"Perhaps." She toyed with a long lock of red-gold hair that had come loose from her coif while she considered the situation. "You could accompany me as my waiting gentlewoman. No one would question that." Her grin was infectious. "Now, let me see—what shall we call you?"

"Birdie Crane?" I suggested.

She laughed. "You do not look a thing like Mistress Crane, but the name will do nicely. Is she still with you?"

I shook my head. Sometimes I missed Birdie, but so long as I had Will, I did not crave other companionship. "Birdie is with my mother and has been for some time."

"And you are with Will," Geraldine guessed. When I said nothing, she rolled her eyes. "You worry too much. You and I and Elizabeth Tudor, too, are young and healthy. We will survive the present regime and go on to be part of something new and glorious."

"I pray you are right, but for the present I prefer to be cautious."

I stayed the night at Geraldine's house and the next morning we set out early for Hatfield. Sir Thomas Pope did not question my disguise, but the Lady Elizabeth recognized me at once, even though it had been years since she'd last seen me.

One pale red eyebrow shot up when Geraldine presented me under Birdie's name, but all the princess said was "Do you like flowers, Mistress Crane? My gardener has grown an unusual one called a tulip. It is native to a faraway place called Armenia."

The redbrick palace of Hatfield had beautifully laid out flower beds, and since it was the end of April, they were especially fragrant and colorful. Roses vied for attention with more common blooms—cowslip, stock, gillyflowers, and white violets. In the orchard beyond, apple trees were just bursting into sweet-scented pink and white blossoms.

Geraldine pretended great interest in the tulips to distract the waiting gentlewomen the queen had sent to watch Elizabeth's every move. While they were occupied, the princess whisked me into the concealing shelter of a grape arbor. I rushed into speech as soon as I was certain we could not be overheard.

"Your Grace, the French ambassador sends his warmest greetings and trusts you are well." I summarized quickly, apprising her of King Philip's intention to coerce her into marriage. "The ambassador was most particular in stressing that Your Grace must not yield to such persuasion."

"I would rather die than bend to Philip's will." Elizabeth's composure never wavered and her voice was firm and resolute. This was no longer a solemn, somewhat naive young girl, but a woman of twenty-three, well aware of the danger of trusting anyone.

"The ambassador wished me to relay one other warning. He advises that Your Grace remain in England. Flight into France at this time would not serve Your Grace's best interests."

"Not even if I am at risk of being sent back to the Tower at the queen's whim?" One long-fingered hand momentarily crept up to touch her throat.

I searched my mind for some way to convince her that de Noailles was right and remembered one of the arguments the ambassador had used to persuade me. "Did you know, Your Grace, that your sister the queen once contemplated flight to Flanders? It was during King Edward's reign. At the last minute Her Grace decided to remain in England. Had she not, she would have lost her chance to rule."

There was a new rigidity in Elizabeth's spine when she straightened from pretending to inspect the grapevine. "That would have suited you well, would it not, if Mary had not been in place to raise an army against our cousin Jane?" Her piercing black eyes bored into mine.

Since I could not deny that I had supported making Lady Jane Grey queen, and by doing so had conspired not only against Queen Mary, but also against Elizabeth, as Mary's heir, I remained silent.

"I am told," the princess continued, "that it was your suggestion that the Lady Jane Grey marry the Duke of Northumberland's son." Her tone implied more.

I had heard the rumors, too. "Despite what his enemies have claimed since, Your Grace, Northumberland did not plan all along for his son to be king, nor did he poison King Edward. Nor did *Lady* Northumberland. These are no more than attempts to discredit a good man and his wife. At the time of the wedding, there was as yet no thought of the Lady Jane as King Edward's successor. No one even knew how ill your brother really was."

I was not sure she believed me, but her ladies were rapidly drawing near. Our conversation came to an abrupt end. The remainder of my visit to Hatfield passed without further opportunity to speak in private with the princess.

When I left Hatfield later that day, I thought that I'd succeeded in convincing Her Grace to heed the French ambassador's warning, but I was less certain that I had done myself any good. Although the princess had been gracious throughout the remainder of our visit, she had directed her conversation to Geraldine, not me. Had she been acting for the benefit of those who watched her? Or had this been a sign that Her Grace bore a grudge against me and mine?

I had supported Lady Jane Grey's claim to the throne. I had also betrayed Elizabeth's girlhood confidences by telling the lord protector's wife about Tom Seymour's attempt to seduce the princess. Did Elizabeth know that? If she did, her succession might not mean that Will and I could return to court after all. Not unless the warning I'd just brought her from de Noailles balanced the scales. Elizabeth was a Tudor. Once she was queen, she would reward those who'd served her well, but she would also punish those who she believed had acted against her. I returned to Blackfriars hoping for the best.

When I resumed my quiet life there, I was no longer quite so content. Once again I had to school myself to patience. To wait. I chafed at the inactivity, and Will's restlessness grew worse.

In June, England declared war on France. De Noailles left the country. On the sixth of July, King Philip embarked with his contingent of English troops. Will's former brother-in-law, the Earl of Pembroke, was in command of the English forces, seconded by Geraldine's husband, Lord Clinton. My uncle, Lord Bray, went with them. So did Ambrose, Robin, and Henry Dudley and hundreds of other gentlemen trained in warfare.

The incessant clanging of every church bell in the city brought me out of my chair on a sunny afternoon in August. Hands over my ears and heart racing, I rushed to the nearest window. My embroidery fell to the floor, forgotten.

"What is it?" I asked in confusion as Will joined me. Distantly, I heard shouting and—more bewildering still—singing. "What has happened?"

Griggs burst into the room. "Victory!" he shouted. "Saint-Quentin has fallen and Cambray, too. The way to Paris lies open before the king's troops."

Will and I exchanged a startled glance. The normally taciturn Griggs was all but dancing a jig.

We went out into the streets. How could we not? I was reminded of the annual fairs held in the countryside, where everyone was in buoyant spirits. I did not think I had ever seen so many smiling people.

Bonfires blazed from dusk to dawn. The church bells continued to ring. *Te Deums*—hymns in praise of God—were sung not only as part of the liturgy but in the streets, where every conduit ran with free wine. I found myself smiling, too.

But the joy did not last. We soon received word that Henry Dudley—

Northumberland's second son with that name, not the rebel leader—died in the battle. My uncle, Lord Bray, was wounded. Although he returned to England, his injuries were mortal. My father served as chief mourner at Bray's funeral. It was his duty as the husband of Bray's oldest sister.

"He was also the only one of Bray's brothers-in-law to attend the service," Will told me when he returned home to Blackfriars, where I had remained lest old enemies see that we were still together. We did not dare become complacent. The queen still had the power to imprison us both.

I was not surprised by this news. John Bray had been a traitor before he'd been a soldier and he had not had the good fortune to die a hero.

Will appeared to be brooding. I went to him and wrapped my arms around him. "What is it, my love?"

"Your father has aged since I last saw him."

"Has he been ill?"

"He admitted to having been laid low by a quartan ague but insisted it was nothing to worry about. He reminded me that half the troops coming back from France have been ill of fever."

Concerned, I went to visit my family in Kent. The reunion with Father did not go well. If he'd ever been reconciled to my decision to live with Will after our marriage was invalidated, he'd reconsidered. He'd made a new list of "suitable" gentlemen for me to wed. I stayed two days before I returned to Blackfriars, vowing never to go back to Cobham Hall.

ON THE TWENTIETH day of January, news of the surrender of Calais reached London. Guisnes fell ten days later. King Philip's war had cost England the Pale, the last English outpost on the Continent. After that, nothing seemed to go right. It was a year of heavy thunderstorms and hail, of floods, and of new outbreaks of fever. The cold, wet weather in summer and autumn produced food shortages.

At the end of September, some ten months after we'd parted with harsh words, my father died.

I returned to Kent for his funeral.

"He wanted only the best for you," Mother said, a note of reproach in her voice.

"I know." We clung to each other and sobbed, but shared grief could not change what was.

We'd barely buried Father when word came from Bedfordshire that Grandmother Jane was deathly ill. Mother and I reached her bedside only just in time to say farewell. She died on the twenty-fourth day of October. Devastated by the dual loss of husband and mother, my mother seemed to lose her will to live. The sickness that had taken my father and grandmother seized upon her weakened state and carried her off eight days later. It was left to me to take her body back to Kent.

My brother George arrived from London the next day. What I read in his face robbed me of my last vestige of strength. "Will?" I whispered.

"Ill of a fever." He made a rueful grimace. "As who is not? I was sick myself shortly after Father died." His flushed skin and persistent cough gave the lie to his claim that he had recovered.

I remained healthy, but I felt numb with grief and guilt and fragile in a way that I'd never been before. I could barely remember any longer what it felt like to be optimistic about the future. "I must return to Blackfriars," I told George.

"I'll take you," he offered. "There is little either of us can do here."

Our eldest brother, William, who had become Lord Cobham upon Father's death, had matters well in hand for Mother's funeral, just as he'd made arrangements for Father's.

George and I left at first light the next day, taking Birdie Crane with us. With Mother's death, Birdie had nowhere else to go.

We traveled by water and reached Blackfriars Stairs before nightfall. Griggs met me at the door of our little house, his face so grave I knew at once that he had more bad news to deliver.

"Is he dead?" I asked bluntly.

"Not yet, but he has taken a turn for the worse. I called a physician in. He says it is some new variety of ague that is raging throughout England. Our soldiers brought it back with them from France." He spat to express his opinion of anything French.

I did not care where the disease had come from, only that it was killing my family. That Will might follow Father, Grandmother, and Mother to the grave was more than I could bear.

"The queen has been stricken, too," Griggs said. "Some think the fever may carry her off."

"The queen is about to die? Again?" I did not believe it. It seemed to me that all those I loved would be gone before Her Grace had the decency to succumb.

I nursed Will day and night, bathing him with cold cloths to bring down the fever, forcing him to drink strengthening broths. I tried every remedy Mother had taught me in the stillroom, but nothing seemed to help. Birdie Crane nagged at me to rest. She warned me that I risked my own health, but what point was there in living if Will did not?

When the bells began to ring on the seventeenth day of November, signaling the death of Queen Mary, I barely lifted my head from Will's chest. I had fallen asleep sitting beside his bed.

Stiff and sore, I considered rising and going to the window. That required too much effort. Even when Birdie came in to confirm the news that the clanging meant the queen was dead and that her sister, Elizabeth, was queen, I felt no elation, no surge of hope. It was a struggle merely to overcome my sense of despair.

"Elizabeth?"

I gasped and turned to stare at Will. His eyes were open and clear for the first time in days.

I touched my hand to his forehead. The fever was gone.

"I'm here, Will," I whispered.

"Not you, Bess." His voice was hoarse from disuse. "Elizabeth. Elizabeth is queen?"

He'd heard the bells, heard Birdie's announcement. "So it seems."

He tried to throw off his blankets. "I must get up. I must ride to

Hatfield. Everyone will flock to her now, seeking advancement. To stay away would—"

"You cannot go!" I pressed with both hands on his shoulders, forcing him back. When he lay still again, I glared at him. "You will kill yourself if you try to get out of bed too soon. You almost died, Will."

"Then send word to her. Let her know we are her loyal subjects." His agonized plea tore at my heart. "We must remind her, Bess. She must remember what we've suffered all these years at her sister's hands. You must tell her."

"I will write to her."

"No. No, you must go in person." With agitated fingers, Will plucked at his covers.

"I will not leave your side, not even to assure our future. If you die, Will, I *have* no future."

He was too exhausted to argue for long. When he fell asleep, I wrote to Her Grace. The new queen was under no obligation to restore Will's title or estates or marriage. And if she was as skilled at holding a grudge as others in her family had been, we had no hope of advancement. But I put my heart into my words and hoped for the best.

That done, I concentrated on helping Will recover. I made strengthening broths with my own hands, and gave him infusions of herbs to restore him to full health. In the days that followed, he continued to improve. I counted my blessings, resigned to accept whatever fate awaited us. We would continue the life we'd lived these last few years. What did it matter if we had titles or wealth? We had each other.

But one thing worried me. If the queen refused to restore the legality of our marriage, the Church of England could step in to separate us, as they had once before through the machinations of the lord protector. I'd been exiled to Chelsea. Will had been forbidden to see me again on pain of death.

Never again, I vowed. We would go into exile in France if we had to. After all, the former ambassador owed me a favor. A bubble of hysterical laughter escaped me at the irony of that!

Queen Elizabeth left Hatfield on the twenty-third of November, accompanied by over a thousand people. Over a thousand supplicants, I thought when I heard of it. With all of them vying for favor, what hope of preferment did Will and I have?

Her Grace moved into one of her own houses, the Charterhouse in Smithfield, outside the city gates, postponing her return to the Tower. I could understand why she was in no hurry to be installed there to await her coronation. She would remember all too well the months she had spent there as a prisoner.

The morning of the twenty-eighth of November dawned crisp and clear. Will was out of bed. He was still frail, but the Blackfriars precinct extended north to Ludgate and the houses along that wall overlooked the new queen's route as she made her formal entry into the city. Will and I could sit in a window and watch the royal procession pass by.

When Queen Elizabeth came in sight, glittering with jewels and mounted on a brightly caparisoned palfrey, Will staggered to his feet and pushed the shutters open wider. He leaned out so far that I feared he would fall. I clasped both arms around his waist to keep him in. Only when I was sure he had his balance did I release him and glance away from his face.

Elizabeth Tudor's piercing black gaze met mine. She had reined in her horse directly beneath our window.

Awkwardly, Will bowed while I made a deep court curtsy.

"We are glad to see you so well, my lord marquess," the queen called out, using the title her sister had taken from him. "When you have fully recovered your health, you must come to court." Her gaze shifted to me and she smiled. "And you must bring Bess—*your wife the marchioness*—with you."

AUTHOR'S NOTE

On Christmas Day in 1558, William Parr resumed his seat on the Privy Council. On the thirteenth of January in 1559, he was restored as Marquess of Northampton and his divorce from Anne Bourchier was reinstated. His marriage to Elizabeth Brooke was legal once more.

By Royal Decree is the fictionalized story of Elizabeth Brooke's life from 1542 to 1558, crucial years in English history. She was at the center of events and often a key player in them. I've tried to stay as close to the facts as possible, while at the same time fleshing out the personalities of the people involved and making their actions comprehensible to readers living in a far different world.

Among the things that seem strange today is the rarity of female friendships. Noble households were predominately male and often a nobleman's wife was the only woman in residence aside from a few servants. Even cooks were usually men. Although I would have liked to give Bess Brooke another woman to confide in throughout the period of the novel, such a thing would have been very unlikely in real life. It is possible that Will Parr was her best friend as well as her husband and her lover. I'd like to think so. But that, too, would have been unusual for the times.

Most of the characters who populate this novel were real people. I found several biographies particularly helpful in researching their lives, among them Leanda de Lisle's *The Sisters Who Would Be Queen* (2008), Eric Ives's *Lady Jane Grey: A Tudor Mystery* (2009), Susan E. James's *Kateryn Parr: The Making of a Queen* (1999), and David Loades's *John Dudley, Duke of Northumberland* (1996). The "Who's Who" section at the end of this note will tell you more about the principal characters who were based on real people. You will find additional information on Tudor women at my website, www.KateEmersonHistoricals.com.

The only characters who are entirely fictional are Matthew Rowlett, Birdie Crane, Griggs, and Alys Guildford, although there was a Guildford among Queen Kathryn's maids of honor and also in the Duchess of Northumberland's household in 1555. I have, of course, invented dialogue, guessed at motivations, and extrapolated from the facts when there were gaps in history. I have not attempted to write in accurate sixteenth-century language. It would end up sounding like a third-rate Shakespeare imitation. I hope you will think of Bess's story, told in her own words, as a translation into modern English and enjoy your trip into the past.

A WHO'S WHO
OF THE TUDOR COURT
1542–1558

Bassano, Jasper (d. 1577)
A musician, he came to England from Italy with four of his brothers under the sponsorship of William Parr. When Parr's sister Kathryn became queen, they joined her household. By 1552, they were living in the Italian quarter of London (St. Mark's Lane) where they made as well as played a variety of instruments.

Bassett, Anne (1521?–1557?)
A maid of honor to Jane Seymour, Anna of Cleves, Catherine Howard, and Kathryn Parr, and later a member of Queen Mary's household, Anne (here called Nan) Bassett is also the protagonist of the previous volume in the *Secrets of the Tudor Court* series, *Between Two Queens*.

Bourchier, Anne (1517–1571)
Daughter of the Earl of Essex, first wife and child bride of William Parr (later Marquess of Northampton), she took a lover and had children by him. This allowed Parr to divorce her for adultery, but he was not permitted, by church or civil law, to remarry while she still lived. Anne came to court as one of Queen Mary's ladies while Parr was in the Tower for conspiring

to put Lady Jane Grey on the throne in Mary's stead. Known as Viscountess Bourchier, she was instrumental in securing his release, since to have him executed as a traitor would have cost her both income and position. After Queen Mary's death, Anne retired to rural Hertfordshire.

Brandon, Frances (1517–1559)

Daughter of Henry VIII's younger sister, Mary Tudor, by Mary's marriage to Charles Brandon, Duke of Suffolk (both of whom appear in *Secrets of the Tudor Court: The Pleasure Palace*), Frances became Marchioness of Dorset through her marriage to Henry Grey, and Duchess of Suffolk after the deaths of her two half brothers in 1551. Frances Brandon is best known to history as the mother of Lady Jane Grey. After the executions of her daughter and husband, Frances married a commoner, Adrian Stokes.

Bray, Anne (1500–1558)

Lady Cobham and therefore Bess Brooke's mother, she was one of those women who stayed in the background, but her tomb in Cobham Church assures us that she was "blest with her children's love." She died in the influenza epidemic of 1558.

Bray, Dorothy (c. 1524–1605)

Lady Cobham's sister and Bess's aunt, Dorothy was a maid of honor to Catherine Howard and Kathryn Parr. She had a brief, scandalous love affair with William Parr while Catherine was queen (see also *Secrets of the Tudor Court: Between Two Queens*) and later married Edmund Brydges. He succeeded to the title Baron Chandos. After his death, when Dorothy was married to a much younger man, she was known as "old Lady Chandos."

Bray, John (c. 1527–1557)

Lord Bray was the brother of Anne and Dorothy Bray and Bess Brooke's uncle. He conspired with rebels in 1555–6, but fought for King Philip at Saint-Quentin in 1557. He was wounded during the siege of that city and died of his injuries several months later.

Brooke, Elizabeth (c. 1505–1560)

Lord Cobham's sister and Bess's aunt, she was the cast-off wife of Sir Thomas Wyatt the poet and the mother of Sir Thomas Wyatt the rebel. After her first husband's death, she married Sir Edward Warner, lord lieutenant of the Tower of London under Edward VI and Elizabeth I.

Brooke, Elizabeth (1526–1565)

Bess Brooke was Lord Cobham's daughter. In 1542, the Spanish ambassador thought that King Henry VIII was considering her as a prospective bride. Bess was, on and off, depending upon who sat on the throne of England, the legal wife of William Parr, Marquess of Northampton. She never wavered in her devotion to him. Bess is credited with suggesting that Lord Guildford Dudley marry Lady Jane Grey. She was asked by the French ambassador to take a message to Princess Elizabeth at Hatfield in 1557, warning Elizabeth not to leave England. When Elizabeth became queen, Bess was high in favor at her court. She never had any children and died of breast cancer seven years after the last events in *By Royal Decree*.

Brooke, George (c. 1497–1558)

Lord Cobham and Bess's father, he was lord deputy of Calais and later a member of the Privy Council under Edward VI. He backed Lady Jane Grey but changed sides when he realized Mary Tudor was going to prevail.

He held Cowling Castle against Wyatt's rebels even though three of his sons were with Wyatt's army. He died in the influenza epidemic of 1558.

Brooke, George (1533–1578)
Lord Cobham's second son and Bess's brother, he was one of Wyatt's rebels and was condemned to death for treason. After he was pardoned, he became an undersecretary to Queen Mary's Privy Council and one of the French ambassador's informants.

Brooke, William (1527–1597)
Lord Cobham's eldest son and heir and Bess's brother, he was sent to Italy for his education. He sided with his cousin, Tom Wyatt, against Queen Mary and ended up in the Tower of London. He succeeded his father as Lord Cobham in 1558 and spent the rest of his life in service to Queen Elizabeth. When Bess fell ill in 1564, William and his second wife went with her to the Low Countries in search of a cure.

Dudley, Henry (1526–1544)
Oldest of the Dudley sons, called Harry in *By Royal Decree*, he died in France after the campaign against Boulogne. Very little is known about him except that he was at court from an early age.

Dudley, John (1504–1553)
Viscount Lisle, then Earl of Warwick, then Duke of Northumberland, Dudley ruled England for King Edward VI after the Duke of Somerset's fall from power. He attempted to place Lady Jane Grey on the throne when Edward VI died, and his failure led to his execution. He was not popular with the common people of England, but he was known to be a devoted family man.

Dudley, John (c. 1528–1554)

The second Dudley son, called Jack in *By Royal Decree*, he became Earl of Warwick when his father was elevated in the peerage to Duke of Northumberland. He was married to the Duke of Somerset's eldest daughter in an attempt to make peace between their fathers. He was condemned to death as a traitor after the attempt to place Lady Jane Grey on the throne failed but he was not executed. He died of natural causes at his sister's house at Penshurst, Kent, shortly after his release from the Tower.

Dudley, Mary (1531–1586)

The eldest of the Duke of Northumberland's daughters, Mary married Sir Henry Sidney in 1551. She was with Lady Jane Grey in the Tower but was allowed to return home to Penshurst when Mary Tudor was declared queen. A few weeks after Mary's brother John died at Penshurst, she gave birth to her first child, a boy who was named Philip after Queen Mary's husband. He grew up to be Sir Philip Sidney, the courtier and poet. When Elizabeth Tudor became queen, Mary Sidney was one of her closest friends. She caught smallpox while nursing the queen in 1562, which destroyed her looks.

Edward VI (1537–1553)

Edward succeeded his father in 1547, but he never ruled England. The government was first in the hands of Edward Seymour, Duke of Somerset and lord protector, and then of John Dudley, Duke of Northumberland. The idea of Lady Jane Grey as his successor, however, seems to have been Edward's own. He was deeply committed to the Church of England and did not want his Catholic sister, Mary, to become queen.

Elizabeth (1533–1603)

Elizabeth was third in line to succeed to the throne by the terms of her father's will, but there were many who felt the irregularity of her parents' marriage disinherited her. She was not even considered in her brother's device for the succession. Under Queen Mary, Elizabeth pretended to accept the Catholic religion but refused to marry the man King Philip picked out for her, his kinsman the Duke of Savoy. She contemplated fleeing England and taking refuge in France but was warned against that action by the French ambassador, who sent Bess Brooke to Hatfield with that message early in 1557, shortly before war between England and France broke out. Elizabeth succeeded her sister Mary the following year.

Fitzgerald, Elizabeth (1527–1589)

Dubbed "Fair Geraldine" because of a sonnet written about her when she was still a child, she married first Sir Anthony Browne, a much older man, and later Edward Fiennes de Clinton, Lord Clinton. As Lady Browne she is recorded as having been with Princess Elizabeth at Chelsea and later at Hatfield, but it is not clear if she was sent there to be part of the princess's household, or to spy on her, or if she was merely visiting. As Lady Clinton, she was with the princess during a meeting with the Spanish Count of Feria shortly before Queen Mary's death, but again it is not clear if she was part of Elizabeth's household at that time or merely hosted the dinner at which they met. She was at court during Elizabeth's reign and was considered one of the queen's close friends.

Gardiner, Stephen (1490–1555)

As Bishop of Winchester, Gardiner opposed the evangelicals who advocated further changes in the church. He plotted against Queen Kathryn Parr, but his schemes failed when King Henry was reconciled with his wife. Under King Edward, Gardiner was imprisoned and his estates seized. Winchester House in Southwark was given to William Parr, Marquess of Northampton. Gardiner took the property back as soon as Mary Tudor became queen and restored him to his seat.

Grey, Lady Jane (1537–1554)

Lady Jane Grey was King Edward's choice to succeed him. She was the great-granddaughter of King Henry VII. Accounts vary as to whether she was willing or not, just as they vary as to whether she had voluntarily married Lord Guildford Dudley a few months earlier. What is certain is that she was a scholar of some renown and that she was a devout Protestant. She was executed following Wyatt's Rebellion.

Guildford, Jane (1509–1555)

Married to John Dudley, her father's ward, Jane was the mother of Henry, John, Mary, Robert, Ambrose, another Henry, Guildford, Temperance, and Katherine Dudley, among others who died young. She was Viscountess Lisle, then Countess of Warwick, and finally Duchess of Northumberland and was at court as part of the queen's household during the reign of Henry VIII. She was one of Kathryn Parr's inner circle. Exactly what part she played in the plan to make Lady Jane Grey queen is not known. It is often said that Lady Jane's husband, Guildford, was Lady Northumberland's favorite son, but there is no hard evidence of this. She certainly found her new daughter-in-law infuriating, but that may have been as much Lady Jane's fault as Lady Northumberland's. After the arrest of her husband and sons for treason, the duchess haunted the court of Mary Tudor seeking pardons for them. She was granted the manor at Chelsea by the queen. Although her husband and son Guildford were executed, her remaining sons were eventually released, in large part due to their mother's ceaseless efforts on their behalf.

Hallighwell, Jane (1480–1558)

As the dowager Lady Bray, Bess's "Grandmother Jane" married a much younger man when she was in her sixties. She campaigned to win her son's freedom after Lord Bray was arrested for treason in 1556. She died during the influenza epidemic of 1558.

Henry VIII (1491–1547)

By 1542, King Henry had gone to seed. He was fat, ill, and crotchety. In a scene that also appears in *Secrets of the Tudor Court: Between Two Queens* (in that version from the point of view of Nan Bassett), he gathered together a great number of eligible young ladies at a banquet in the hope of finding a sixth wife. Bess Brooke was one of those who caught his eye, but soon after that he met Kathryn Parr and married her instead. In 1546, rumor had him considering a divorce from Kathryn so he could take a seventh wife, Catherine Willoughby, widow of his old friend Charles Brandon, Duke of Suffolk.

Mary (1516–1558)

Upon the death of her brother in 1553, Mary became both king and queen of England and promptly restored Catholicism as the state religion. One of the first acts of her first Parliament was to rescind the bill permitting William Parr, Marquess of Northampton, to remarry while his first wife still lived. Mary invited that first wife, Anne Bourchier, to court.

Parr, Kathryn (1514–1548)

As Henry VIII's sixth wife, she supported evangelicals—those who wanted even more reforms in the church. Henry was her third husband, but contrary to popular belief, the first two were not old men. One was a sickly boy, the second a gentleman in his prime who did not suffer ill health until about a year before his death. After the king died, Kathryn married Thomas Seymour, who had courted her before King Henry singled her out as a prospective bride. Kathryn had custody of Princess Elizabeth until she sent the princess away, some say out of jealousy, in mid-1548. After Kathryn died in childbirth and Thomas Seymour was executed, their baby daughter was placed in the care of Catherine Willoughby, dowager Duchess of Suffolk. Mary Seymour disappears from the historical record about two years later.

Parr, William (1513–1571)

Queen Kathryn's brother, he was married as a teenager and later divorced his first wife in order to marry Bess Brooke. The legality of this second marriage varied from reign to reign. He was an excellent diplomat but not a very good soldier. After Bess died, he fell in love with a young woman who was said to much resemble her, but this time Queen Elizabeth forbade remarriage until his first wife, Anne Bourchier, died. This did not occur until 1571. Parr himself died shortly after the wedding.

Seymour, Edward (1505–1552)

Earl of Hertford, then Duke of Somerset, he was the brother of King Henry VIII's third wife and the uncle of Edward VI. He ruled England for the young king as lord protector until his unpopular policies led to his removal from power and his imprisonment. He was eventually executed.

Seymour, Thomas (1507–1549)

The lord protector's younger brother, he courted Kathryn Parr before she married Henry VIII. For the next few years, the king kept him busy on diplomatic missions in other countries. After the king's death, Thomas married Kathryn in secret and without a proper period of mourning. After her death, he schemed to marry Princess Elizabeth, but his fatal mistake was invading King Edward's private apartments while armed. He was executed for treason.

Stanhope, Anne (1497–1587)

As Lady Seymour, Countess of Hertford, Duchess of Somerset, and the lord protector's wife, Anne Stanhope was one of the most unpopular women in England. She was blamed for many of her husband's bad decisions. Before that, she had been at court as a lady-in-waiting. When Kathryn Parr was queen, she had been one of Kathryn's inner circle, but after Henry VIII's death and Kathryn's remarriage to Anne's brother-in-law, the two women became bitter enemies. Following her husband's execution, Anne married Francis Newdigate, a commoner. Later her son, Lord Hertford, provoked Queen Elizabeth's wrath by eloping with Lady Catherine Grey, sister of the executed Lady Jane.

Warner, Edward (1511–1565)

As a member of Queen Kathryn Parr's household and an evangelical, he was questioned about certain heretical books in the queen's lodgings at court. Later, as lord lieutenant of the Tower, he welcomed Queen Jane and her entourage to the royal apartments there. By then he was the second husband of Bess's aunt, Elizabeth Brooke, Lady Wyatt. He was a conspirator in what became known as Wyatt's Rebellion and was arrested in his house in London even before his stepson launched his uprising in Kent. After being held nearly a year, he was released. He was restored to his post at the Tower of London when Elizabeth Tudor became queen.

Willoughby, Catherine (1519–1580)

The other Duchess of Suffolk (see Frances Brandon, page 344), she married Charles Brandon after the death of his previous wife, Mary Tudor

(Henry VIII's sister). She was one of Kathryn Parr's inner circle and an evangelical. She went into exile during the reign of Mary Tudor (Henry VIII's daughter). By that time she had married Richard Bertie, a commoner.

Woodhull, Mary (1528–1548+)

A kinswoman of and chamberer to Queen Kathryn Parr, she was with the queen dowager when she died. She married Davy Seymour, a distant kinsman of the Duke of Somerset.

Wyatt, Thomas the Younger (1521–1554)

The son of Sir Thomas Wyatt the Elder, the poet, and his estranged wife, Elizabeth Brooke (later Lady Warner), he was the only one of the conspirators of 1554 to actually raise troops against Queen Mary. His delay to lay siege to Cowling Castle, for which history has no logical explanation, cost him dearly. By the time he reached Southwark, London Bridge had been dismantled to keep him from entering London. He was captured a few days later and was executed for treason.

G

GALLERY READERS GROUP GUIDE

Introduction

In the third book of Kate Emerson's Secrets of the Tudor Court series, young lady-in-waiting Elizabeth (Bess) Brooke takes center stage amid the tumultuous times of Tudor-era England. As a young gentlewoman, Bess enters court life a naïve and inexperienced maid. But history, fortune, and love change all of that, as young Bess climbs the noble ranks and witnesses the volatile nature of England's royal, political, and religious climate. Holding tight to her one true love, Will Parr, Bess learns just how dramatically a life can be affected by royal decree—and how precious each moment truly is.

Questions for Discussion

1. Under whose rule did Bess and Will's love for each other flourish most? Consider Henry and Kathryn, King Edward, Queen Mary, and Elizabeth Tudor.

2. Would Bess have had a happier, easier life if she had married Harry or Jack?

3. As indicated in the author's note, all but a few characters in *By Royal Decree* were actual historical figures. Which ones did you find most appealing? Which came to life off the page?

4. Were you surprised at Bess's arrow shot during Thomas Wyatt's siege on Cobham Castle?

5. Considering the time, was it right for Bess to marry Will, even with Anne Bourchier entitled to the Parr estate? Do you ever feel sympathetic to Anne? And should true love prevail over royal decree?

6. Discuss the various uprisings and religious controversies that occur over the course of the story. When was the threat of imprisonment/execution most palpable? Were you surprised at how quickly some courtiers changed their religious affiliations? (Consider especially Northumberland and Parr's conversion to Catholicism while imprisoned.) Would you switch your beliefs under duress? How tightly should one grasp to what she thinks is right?

7. What did you make of Tom Seymour's character? Was he nothing more than a lecher? How did you react to his ill-advised breaking and entering at King Edward's palace?

8. Bess's desire for a child remains unfulfilled by the story's end. Should she and Will have fostered Mary Seymour? Do you think Bess is being honest with herself when she says that Will's love is all she needs?

9. Which gentlewoman (besides Bess, of course) did you enjoy most? Can you trace the progress of her initial court mates through the story?

Enhance Your Book Club

1. Partake in Tudor-era sports like archery and tennis while dressed in your finest imitation of livery!

2. If you haven't already, read the first two books in Kate Emerson's Secrets of the Tudor Court series, *The Pleasure Palace* and *Between Two Queens*. How do they compare? Who is your favorite protagonist (Bess Brooke, Jane Popyncourt, or Nan Bassett)?

3. Emerson goes to great lengths to paint a very distinct picture of the era. Discuss the facets of the court that come to life the most. For those with artistic inclination, try to paint or draw one of your favorite scenes!

4. If you get the opportunity, visit the Tower of London and imagine what it must have been like for poor Will Parr!

5. Research and watch any number of movies depicting the Tudor era. How do they compare to each other in terms of bringing the time period to life? Does the visual rendering match the image that Emerson creates in words?

A Conversation with Kate Emerson

1. **Why did you choose Bess Brooke as the focal point for your third book in the series? What about her (compared to Jane and Nan) made you want to tell a story from her vantage point?**

   The first thing that caught my attention was the report that the Marchioness of Northampton had been the one to suggest Lady Jane Grey as a bride for Lord Guildford Dudley. Since this match turned out to be so significant to history, I wondered why she'd suggested it and if she had any idea of the possible consequences at the time. I cannot, however, draw any comparisons between my interest in Bess Brooke and my interest in Jane Popyncourt and Nan Bassett. I have a long-standing fascination with the lives of many relatively unknown Tudor women.

2. **In the opening scene, as King Henry flirts with the gathering of single women, he briefly singles Bess out. She escapes his gazes, but do you think she would have made a good queen?**

   I doubt it. She was still very young at that point—still a teenager. The other teenager King Henry married, Catherine Howard, was not a notable success in the role of queen.

3. **Did Bess and Will ever have children?**

   No.

4. **What is your research process like for writing these books? You obviously have an amazing grasp of the era and its events. Does it ever get confusing, especially with how volatile the regime and title changes appear to be?**

I've been collecting information on the Tudor era for more than forty years, so much of my research is simply a matter of finding the right books on my shelves or notes in my file cabinets. For specific details, I rely heavily on inter-library loans and make frequent visits to the online Oxford Dictionary of National Biography. There are many opportunities for confusion, and it can be a challenge to get the facts straight. It doesn't help that modern screenwriters have taken such tremendous liberties with real people's lives to create dramas for television series and movies. Little-known Tudor women are even more likely to be misrepresented, even by some highly regarded scholars, because there has been and still is less research being done into their lives than on the lives of more prominent women, such as the six wives of Henry VIII. My hobby (my husband calls it my obsession) is A Who's Who of Tudor Women, which can be found at my website www.KateEmersonHistoricals .com. I'm constantly adding to this, and making corrections and additions to the existing mini-biographies. The number of entries will surpass the one thousand mark by the end of 2010.

5. **Your books have done quite well, and the Tudor era has been popular in a variety of other mediums. What about the era keeps readers and viewers coming back for more?**

I suspect it is because the times (and King Henry himself) seem bigger than life, not only in spectacle and pageantry, but also in grandiose schemes. Real treason plots and spy stories abound, fruitful ground for the novelist. And, of course, there was always plenty of court intrigue for the ladies to indulge in.

6 **Did Bess actually take aim at Tom Wyatt with a bow and arrow? What was it like writing that scene? It's a brief moment, but one that I think readers will be shocked by, as Bess would have become a murderer if not for Tom's chain mail.**

This incident is entirely fictitious. We don't know where Bess was when Wyatt attacked the castle. But since we don't, I felt free to have her join her family during the siege. If she was there, frustrated by events, distraught over her situation with Will, fearing she was about to see her father and his men slain by her cousin the rebel, why wouldn't she be driven to help defend the castle? Since her ability with a bow had already been set up in an early scene in the novel, shooting at Wyatt didn't seem to me to be at all out of character. Of course, she is shocked by her own action afterward, but I'm not sure she would have regretted it if she had succeeded in killing Tom. As it was, several of Bess's father's men were killed during the siege.

7. **Who is your favorite queen?**

I don't have one. I'm not particularly taken with any of King Henry's six wives, or with his niece, Lady Jane Grey, or with his daughters, Mary and Elizabeth. Many sixteenth-century Englishwomen are far more interesting to me—but I don't have a favorite among them either.

8. **How do you choose where to embellish/alter history and where not to?**

I try very hard never to change historical facts. If there are two interpretations of what happened, however, I feel free to pick the one that works best for my plot. I do embellish what is known, if my characters are involved, in order to offer a rationale for the behavior recorded by history.

9. **Do you create characters with a single purpose in mind?**

I create very few purely fictional characters, but when I do, they are usually servants—a maidservant to act as a sounding board for my protagonist or a go-between to discover information she could not obtain on her own.

10. **Is it difficult writing an established character who has a pre-determined personality and a well-known history of decisions? Are you still able to find artistic freedom within the confines of historical accuracy?**

I find it a challenge to write about real people. There may be certain facts known about a real person, but his or her background and relationships to others are usually unrecorded by history. This gives me the freedom to extrapolate from what is known. I just keep asking myself *why* someone would have done what s/he did and look at the other people around him or her and the events both earlier and later in his or her life to find answers.

11. **Are you working on another book in the series? If so, who are you going to focus on next?**

The next book in the series, *At the King's Pleasure*, is the story of Lady Anne Stafford, who was at the center of a scandal at the court of Henry VIII in May 1510.